Who Will Die?

"Who has courage enough to attack them?" Devlyn asked, studying the dark-cloaked figures below. "What if it's true that they can't be killed? That any weapon loosed on them returns to kill the one who let it fly?"

"I have courage enough." Kley strung his bow. "And so do you, my lord Celwalda."

Devlyn laughed without humor. "Sometimes bravery and foolhardiness are hard to distinguish."

"Perhaps," Kley said, selecting an arrow. "We'll see, won't we?"

Devlyn rose swiftly to his feet. He nocked his arrow and drew back, aiming at the Somber Rider nearest the fire.

"If we die now," he murmured, "we die for the Summer Run. Now, Kley!"

"Delightful . . . both lyrical and certain. . . . Sparks of all sorts fly, including magical ones."
—*Magazine of Fantasy and Science Fiction*

BOOKS BY ANN MARSTON

The Rune Blade Trilogy

Kingmaker's Sword
Western King
Broken Blade

The Sword in Exile Trilogy

Cloudbearer's Shadow
King of Shadows

Published by HarperPrism

Second book in the Sword in Exile Trilogy

KING OF
SHADOWS

Ann Marston

HarperPrism
A Division of HarperCollinsPublishers

HarperPrism
A Division of HarperCollinsPublishers
10 East 53rd Street, New York, NY 10022-5299

This is a work of fiction. The characters, incidents, and dialogues
are products of the author's imagination and are not to
be construed as real. Any resemblance to actual events or
persons, living or dead, is entirely coincidental.

ISBN 0-06-102041-9

HarperCollins®, ♟®, and HarperPrism® are trademarks of
HarperCollins Publishers Inc.

Cover illustration © 1999, Yvonne Gilbert.

First printing: December 1999

Printed in the United States of America

Visit HarperPrism on the World Wide Web at
http://www.harpercollins.com

❖10 9 8 7 6 5 4 3 2 1

For Marilyn, Sandi, Shirley, Radecka, Kathy and Val, and all the volunteers who work so hard, with unstinting dedication, to kindle the light of literacy in the world.

The Royal Houses of Celi, Skai and Tyra

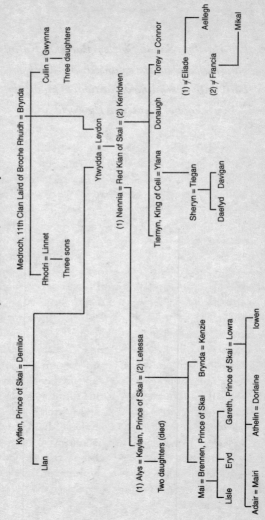

Prologue

Hakkar of Maedun stepped out onto the graceful terrace adjacent to the guest quarters in what had once been the Ephir's palace in Honandun. The Ephir, of course, was long gone, his place taken by Weigar of Maedun, who was now the Lord Protector of Isgard. Honandun, capital of Isgard, was a prosperous city, with diversions and entertainments enough to satisfy even the most jaded taste. But Hakkar wished himself to be back in his own city of Clendonan on the Isle of Celi, where he in turn was Lord Protector of that island kingdom.

The Conference of Lord Protectors was held once a year to keep Hakkar's kinsman, King-Emperor Vrokinnir of Maedun, informed of the situation in his far-flung empire. This year, Weigar was host, and making the most of it with his elegant receptions and sumptuous feasts.

Hakkar had been happy to leave the running of his Protectorate to his son Horbad and to the cadre of warlocks entrusted to maintaining the spell across Celi. He had thoroughly enjoyed last evening's entertainment. But something had wakened him when the sun was still low on the eastern horizon, far too early in the day to leave a luxurious bed after a late and strenuous night.

An uncomfortable uneasiness knotted in his belly—a vague sense of something, somewhere, being unaccountably and horribly wrong. The discomfort brought him out onto the terrace to stare northwest across the Cold Sea to where Celi lay hidden beyond the horizon. A frown drew his thick, black eyebrows together above eyes that were as dark as his brows.

Something was definitely wrong—

Then, even across a hundred leagues of sea, the sudden knowledge that his son was dead hit Hakkar like a physical blow from a sword. In the space between one heartbeat and the next, a third part of his power evaporated into the air.

His son was gone. Horbad was dead.

And because Hakkar was not nearby to reabsorb the power that rose from Horbad's body like black steam from a dark kettle, that portion of his power that had passed to his son upon their bonding was gone forever, lost to him as surely as his son was lost to him.

The devastating blow nearly knocked him to his knees, but a scalding combination of rage and pride stiffened his back, brought his head up straight. The knuckles of his hands were deathly white as he gripped the smoothly carved white marble of the balustrade around the terrace.

Under no circumstances could he let any of the sorcerers attending the conference know that his power had been weakened. If they had so much as a glimmer of suspicion, they would tear him down as a pack of wolves tears down an injured deer. Of all of them, he was the strongest, the most powerful sorcerer. He alone owned the secret of stealing another's magic, a secret handed down from father to son beginning with his great-great-grandfather, who had been in his time one of the most brilliant generals of the Maedun Empire.

Slowly, he turned away from the panorama of sea and rocky shore and strode back into his apartment. He closed the door firmly behind him and drew the drapes tightly across the windows. Only then, when he was certain he was alone and unobserved, did he give vent to his rage.

All that power—gone! Wasted!

He slammed his fists down onto the polished wood of the massive desk beside the window. But what had happened to Horbad? How could he have been so stupid, so clumsy, so inept, as to get himself killed? And who had killed him? Who *could* have done it? Who on that accursed island was capable of raising a weapon against Horbad?

Hakkar had left the spell securely over Celi when he left to come to Isgard. Surely the warlocks had kept it strong. Without his presence, the spell would eventually dissipate, but certainly not this soon. And with the spell in place, no Celae should have been able to lift a weapon to *any* Maedun, let alone the son of the Lord Protector. The spell should have struck down an attacker and tangled him in debilitating, killing pain. What had happened to Horbad?

All that power ... Gone. Gone like mist in the sun. And all but irreplaceable.

Hakkar turned from the desk and stared unseeingly at the richly embroidered tapestry wall hangings. He took several deep breaths to calm himself, and tried to marshal his thoughts rationally.

He might be able to replace some of the power by using the secret ritual. The bloody ritual allowed him to take the power of any hedge wizard, mage—or sorcerer, too. The loss of even one Lord Protector would, of course, be noticed, but that couldn't be helped. He was certain he could arrange things so the disappearance would seem to be part of a plot of insurrection. But without a son, without Horbad, he was not sure he could make the acquired sorcery work properly for him.

There was no help for it. He must have a son. That was imperative. He would have to return to his ancestral fortress in Maedun and find a strong woman to bear him another son. Sorcerers' children did not come easily into the world. Too many times the women died in childbed delivering a stillborn infant. Women carrying boy-children seemed to die more often than women who gave birth to all but useless girls. But there were strong women in Maedun he might bring into his bed and who could certainly present him with a son.

Until he could find one, though, he could allow no one to suspect that he had lost such a large portion of his power. He must carry on with the conference as if nothing were wrong.

No one must know.

He returned to Celi with no unseemly haste as soon as the conference finished. Within hours of his arrival, he knew what had happened to Horbad.

Celae treachery, the commander of the fortress known as Rock Greghrach told him. Horbad had been struck down by a Tyadda man bearing a Rune Blade—the blade that belonged to the man who styled himself the exiled Prince of Skai.

"A Tyadda man?" Hakkar repeated.

The commander would not meet his eyes. "Yes, my lord. The Tyadda are immune—"

"To my spell, yes," Hakkar interrupted. "But that does not explain how this Tyadda man managed to kill my son."

"The Celae man had magic, my lord," the commander said. "He used it somehow to nullify Lord Horbad's own sorcery . . ."

". . . Allowing the Tyadda man to kill my son," Hakkar said.

The commander raised his gaze, but still did not meet Hakkar's eyes. He stared resolutely at a spot somewhere beyond Hakkar's right shoulder. "Yes, my lord," he said.

"Have you exacted justice upon these treacherous murderers?" Hakkar's voice was soft and silky, but did not conceal his quiet, seething rage.

The commander shuddered. "No, my lord," he said hoarsely, his voice almost too faint to be heard. "They have vanished. My patrols have searched, but they have been unable to find them."

"Then I can only assume that you are inadequately suited to the requirements of your position." Hakkar's tone flowed like boiling oil over the commander. If the commander had been in any doubt as to his mortal danger, all question was now gone.

The commander shut his teeth on his protest and bent his head in resignation. Hakkar gestured sharply with his right hand. Two of the guards stepped forward.

"Take him away," he said. "Execute him immediately." He watched coldly as the guards escorted the commander from the throne room. He noted with detachment that the commander marched stiffly erect, his head held proudly high. Clumsy and inept as a garrison commander the man might be, but he would die like a Maedun. Hakkar allowed a small smile to curl one corner of his mouth.

When the guards and the commander were gone, he summoned his chief aide. "A dispatch," he said. "I want a copy to go to every commander west of those accursed mountains. Hunt down and destroy every Celae, every Tyadda, running free in the mountains. I will personally reward the man who can prove to me that he has destroyed any enclaves of the rebellious vermin. And I will pay two silvers for every Tyadda corpse delivered to a garrison commander."

The aide wrote quickly on his slate. "Is that all, my lord?" he asked.

"No," Hakkar said. He looked out the tall, arched windows facing westward. From here, the tall peaks of the Spine of Celi were invisible below the horizon. But he could feel them looming there, tall, implacable, impenetrable to his spell. "Tell them I will pay ten golds for the body of the man who killed my son, and another ten golds for the body of the impostor Prince of Skai."

Within a fortnight, as early spring turned to late spring, Hakkar took ship for the Continent. He took up residence in the fortress manse at Lake Vayle and began his search for a woman.

He found five women. Sorcerers' children came hard into the world and there was a lack of women willing to bear them. His father had waited through fifteen years and six wives who bore seven stillborn sons before Hakkar himself was born. Hakkar did not have fifteen years to spare. He needed a son immediately.

Finding the right women to bear his son took longer than he had planned. The season had turned for the second time at midsummer before he returned to Celi and to his throne in the palace at Clendonan. He left behind two of the women growing great with child.

Word came to him not long after the Autumnal Equinox that one of the women died giving birth to a stillborn child, and the other had been brought to bed with a son. The woman, like the first, was dead, but the child thrived at the breast of a wet nurse.

The infant, of course, was called Horbad. And as he grew to boyhood in Maedun, protected and sheltered in the heart of the Maedun Empire, Hakkar paid out small fortunes to his troops in bounties. But the two bodies he most wanted to see never turned up among the trophies.

Rumors came to him that the renegade Prince of Skai had taken refuge in Tyra, where Hakkar's troops could not reach him. Other rumors placed the impostor prince in the north of Celi, but no one could tell exactly where. Hakkar sent patrols of Somber Riders searching through the northern mountains, but they found nothing worth a second glance. As always in the west and the north, the mountains blocked his sorcery. He could not send his spell into the high country. What lay beyond those forbidding crags in the north, no one could say.

Horbad was fifteen when Hakkar finally brought the boy to Celi. He was well grown, Hakkar decided, measuring the boy as he stood before him in the throne room. He looked strong enough. Still only a boy, though, without a man's shape to match the gangly height. But that would change with time.

"Are you ready?" Hakkar asked.

The boy met his gaze calmly. "I am," he said.

"Then come."

Hakkar led the way out of the palace, out into the courtyard to the blacksmith's hut.

The blacksmith's arm gleamed with sweat as he brought his hammer down for the last time on the glowing blade. He wrapped a scrap of leather around the long, hiltless tang and lifted the sword from the surface of the battered anvil, turning to Hakkar.

"It's ready now for final quenching," he said.

Hakkar took the half-finished sword, still glowing dull orange from the forge, and beckoned to the two Somber Riders who stood just outside the door of the smithy. They stooped and, between them, dragged a bound man from the ground at their feet.

The prisoner slumped between the soldiers, his legs unable to support his weight. His head lolled against his shoulder, his dirty and matted dark gold hair falling into his eyes. As Hakkar stepped forward, the man opened golden brown eyes and stared in horror at the blazing metal in Hakkar's hand.

"Horbad," Hakkar said quietly, "come here."

Horbad, straight and slim as a sword himself, stepped from the shadows behind the Somber Riders. "Yes, Father?" he asked.

"Stand beside me. We forge our bond now. Are you ready?"

"Oh yes, Father." Horbad leaned forward avidly, watching the Celae prisoner, his black eyes dancing with anticipation.

"Lay him on the anvil," Hakkar said to the two Somber Riders.

One of the soldiers gripped the Celae's hair and yanked his head back as the two of them pulled him back across the silvery gleam of the top of the anvil. The man's body arched painfully as the two guards stretched him to his full length. The prisoner moaned as Hakkar stepped forward, then screamed in agony as the tip of the orange-hot blade touched his groin.

Grunting with effort, Hakkar forced the blade upward, through the skin and muscle of the Celae's abdomen, up through his chest, into his heart. The sizzle and crackle of scorching blood filled the forge, and steam rose from the ruptured body.

The Celae prisoner spasmed in the soldiers' hands. His head snapped back, his neck rigid. He tried to curl his body, but the impaling blade held him straight. His eyes bulged, and his throat distended as his scream trailed off into death. Then his head fell limply back as if the neck itself had been broken.

Slowly, Hakkar withdrew the sword. The blade now appeared to be made of black glass or obsidian, gleaming wetly in the hot light of the smithy. Holding the sword in his right hand, Hakkar turned and placed his left hand on Horbad's head.

The bonding was instantaneous. The power stored in Hakkar since the death of his first son burst forth, flashing and flaring around him in a black mist laced with twisting ropes of red-and-orange fire. The force of it knocked him to the beaten-earth floor, writhing in agony and ecstasy together as it aligned itself to his will. He cried out as his body convulsed and shook. His hair stood on end. He clutched Horbad to him, both of them rolling on the packed dirt of the floor of the smithy, as the magic tied them irreversibly together.

Triumph and elation surged through Hakkar's body. He *felt* the presence of his son, felt the young man's own ecstasy, as the power flared around them. Brilliant flashes of light seared his eyes behind his closed lids, sparking red and orange. The tide of his blood flowed powerfully, then ebbed in a strong current. Chills and fever alternated in his belly, and he held Horbad more tightly against him.

When finally it was over, Hakkar climbed shakily to his feet. Horbad lay in a heap, curled in a puddle of blood near the door of the shed. Hakkar bent and picked up his son, set him on his feet, brushed back the sodden black hair from the pale forehead.

"Horbad?" he asked, a tremor quivering in his voice.

The boy opened his eyes. Hakkar saw the reflection of his own power there. The boy smiled tremulously, but his fear eased visibly as he looked up at his father. "Is it over?" he asked.

"Yes. We are one now. You are my true son."

Horbad shivered, his pleasure gleaming from his eyes.

The sword no longer glowed, quenched by the Celae's blood, but it was still too hot to touch. "This will be your sword, Horbad." Hakkar laid it gently on the rim of the forge.

"Will it be finished soon?"

"It will, my lord Horbad," the blacksmith said.

Hakkar looked up at the blacksmith. He had forgotten the man was there.

"Finish it now," he told the blacksmith. "I want the hilt engraved with silver in the pattern I showed you."

The blacksmith bowed, his face impassive. "Yes, Lord Hakkar," he said. "It will be finished within the fortnight."

Hakkar nodded. Together, he and Horbad left the smithy. He was already stronger, he thought, his hand firmly on the boy's shoulder.

The part of his magic that had gone to Horbad would return to him threefold. His power, blended with that of the boy, would soon be as strong as it had been before the death of his first son.

Part 1

The King Iowen

1

I shivered in the cold morning air. My breath plumed out from my nose and mouth in long, white streamers that shredded instantly in the mild breeze and drifted away in tatters. I drew my cloak more closely around my shoulders as I waded through the new snow toward the practice pavilion. Snow lay in deep drifts along the contours of the glen. The wind that constantly swept down the mountain flanks from the northeast left a pattern of strange, curving ripples on the glittering surface, like wave ripples left in the sand at ebb tide. A curious phenomenon. The winds on Skerry in the far north of Celi didn't leave the snowfields looking like that. But Tyra always had more wind than Skerry, and Skerrykeep was more sheltered than the Clanhold of Broche Rhuidh in Glenborden.

A few sets of footprints broke the soft expanse of wind-driven white. Not many. Mayhaps four or five people. I hoped the Swordmaster had made one set of tracks. That would at least mean I didn't have to wait for him, freezing my fingers and toes, a situation guaranteed not to improve my mood.

I wondered if Brynda, my father's aunt, had encountered the same unwillingness to respect her considerable ability as a swordswoman. Brynda had been bheancoran — soul's companion and personal guard — to the man who would have been High King of Celi had he not perished when the Maedun invaded Celi nearly fifty years ago. Her ability to wield the Rune Blade she carried was nearly legendary on Skerry. After all, had not she and my grandfather Brennen, her brother, managed to spirit the dead prince's pregnant wife right out from under the noses of the Maedun—and the black sorcerer Hakkar himself—and seen her safely to her people in the high mountains of Skai in Celi? When the task was done, Brynda managed to overcome the shattering pain of the breaking of her bond with her prince, and came to Tyra with her husband. Surely she had not merely laid down her sword and never practiced again. How seriously had the Swordmaster in those days taken her? And how often had she had to lay the man out flat in practice battles before he *did* take her seriously?

Not that I'd managed to knock the Swordmaster flat, mind you. He was a formidable opponent, deft and strong and highly skilled. But on two occasions, I'd fought him to a draw. When I'd lost to him, I'd made him work harder than he'd liked to take the victory. Then, panting with the effort, he told me I was lucky.

Lucky! All those years of practice, and he dismissed it as luck.

The brilliant blue of the sky and the dazzling bright sunshine turned the glen into a glittering landscape frosted with crystal. After nearly a fortnight of heavy, dreary overcast and bitter, driving pellets of snow, the light acted as a tonic to my mood. But the sunshine, welcome as it was, hardly marked the coming of warmer weather. Not yet. Vernal Equinox was still a fortnight away when the season turned from late winter to early spring. But winters in Tyra seemed to be harsher than the winters on Skerry. The snow would yet pile deeper in the crevices and hollows of the glen before the warmth of spring came to melt it.

I huddled further into my cloak, pulling the heavy folds of woolen fabric up around my ears to protect them from the biting wind that came howling straight out of the north, pouring over the high peaks with the bitter chill of the northern latitudes in it. I glanced up at the soaring crags that bounded the glen on three sides. The pristine white against the intense blue of the sky nearly hurt my eyes. Tyra, unlike Celi, was still free of the blight of the Maedun Somber Riders. And if an exile from the Celi province of Skai spent in Skerry was any different from that same exile spent in Tyra, it was only that Tyra was colder.

I had been born on Skerry. I'd never seen Skai, the spiritual home of the exiled yrSkai, and there was a good chance I never would see it. I had only the ballads and stories of homesick yrSkai to tell me what Skai was like. But it didn't seem to make the exile any easier to bear.

Behind me, the looming bulk of the Clanhold of Broche Rhuidh soared skyward, and blended with the granite cliff that formed its back wall. In the early-morning sunlight, the stone glowed a deceptively warm gold. Ahead, the huge pavilion sat squatly at the edge of what in summer was the practice field. The pavilion consisted of only a broad, steeply pitched roof, supported by short, heavy wooden pillars all around at regular intervals, open to the air on all sides. Naturally, it provided no protection whatsoever from either the wind or the biting cold. Its only purpose was to keep the snow off the frozen grass, which supposedly gave better footing to those braving the inhospitable cold to practice with the sword.

Supposedly was the right word. My experience had usually proved otherwise as the soles of my boots slipped and slid on the icy, beaten grass. But I presumed it was still better than trying to plunge about through knee-deep snow. I was skeptical about it, at best.

Tyran clansmen pride themselves on their hardiness. It took someone hardier than I to come out every day for hours at a time. I'd contented myself with far less practice than I would have taken at home in Skerry.

The glare of the sun vanished as I ducked under the

low thatched roof, gone as quickly as a snuffed candle. I blinked. Without the dazzle of the sun, sight vanished for an instant. Deep, indigo shadows filled the pavilion. My eyes adjusted quickly enough, and I glanced around. The bulky form of the Swordmaster was not evident among the shadowy figures moving about under the roof.

Irritably, I looked around again. If he was still warm and snug in his bed, recovering from the half butt of good Falian red wine he'd consumed the night before . . . I paused thoughtfully for a moment, aware that my smile was anything but pleasant as I contemplated the galvanizing effect of a bucket of snow tucked under the bedcovers with him.

Oh yes. That would work quite satisfactorily.

"My lady Iowen, you are well come here."

The voice, male and laden with amusement, came out of the gloom behind a pillar to my right, startling me. I spun around. He stepped out of the deep shadow and offered me a small bow. For a moment, I didn't know him. Then I recognized him. Govan dav Malcolm, younger brother to Taggert, the new Clan Laird. My kinsman. Married to my father's cousin and foster sister. He had only yesterday returned to take up his position of Master of Sword, or Captain of the Army, for the Clanhold. Since early summer, he had been on the Tyran–Isgardian border with his company of soldiers, guarding Tyra against invasion by the Maedun army that occupied Isgard. He was very much a Tyran clansman, right down to the wry smile.

"The Swordmaster sends his regrets," he said. "He asked me to stand in his stead to practice with you."

I returned his bow, complete with the sardonic little half smile. "I'm honored you would give up your leisure on your first morning back from the border to dance with me, my lord Govan."

"I assure you, the honor is mine."

The shadows lay thick beneath the thatched roof, but I saw him clearly enough. He stood as tall and broad as most of the clansmen of Broche Rhuidh I had met over the last three seasons. But I didn't have to look up that far to meet his eyes. The top of my head came to within a handbreadth of his. I wasn't as broad, of course, but my muscles were well trained and held the wiry strength to swing a hand-and-a-half sword with enough power to give him a good workout.

Even in the bitter cold, he wore a kilt and plaid in the tartan of Clan Broche Rhuidh. His plaid wrapped his shoulders and hung nearly to his heels behind him. A narrow gold stripe ran though the greens, grays, and blues of the tartan, marking him as a younger son of the House of the Clan Laird. A golden topaz dangled from his left ear on a short length of delicate gold chain. Faint traces of silver streaked the copper-gold of his hair and beard. A thick braid at his left temple hung nearly to his shoulder. And an obviously amused, indulgent smile curved back the corners of his mouth.

I sighed inwardly. I had met that same smile before on the faces of too many men here in Tyra.

By the seven gods and goddesses, I was heartily sick of men who thought to humor me. But becoming angry never helped the quest for perfection in the dance. I swallowed my annoyance and inclined my head graciously enough. I hoped. But there might have been just a touch of a biting edge to my voice when I replied.

"Shall we begin then, my lord Govan? A fifth-level dance, mayhaps, might suit you?"

A fifth-level dance was complex and intricate. Not something to be undertaken by a novice or a dilettante merely toying with swordwork. One of his eyebrows rose fractionally in surprise. A small satisfaction.

"Aye, well," he said. "A fifth-level dance is sprightly enough to warm the blood on a chilly morning." He dropped his plaid to the ground beside the pillar and made a graceful gesture, ushering me to the center of the pavilion where we would have room to swing our swords unimpeded by the pillars. The amused grin stayed firmly in place on his face as I dropped my cloak beside his plaid and stepped past him into the middle of the pavilion.

I drew my sword, heard the whispering susurration of his blade coming out of the scabbard on his back. As I turned toward him, the all-too-familiar exasperation stiffened my lips. The tightening sensation gripped my chest, and a tiny ripple of irritated bitterness curled through my belly. I beat it back resolutely and reached for calm acceptance. But it was happening again. He was going to treat me as if I were a precious and precocious child and he a fatuously doting and tolerant father.

Aye, well. We'd soon see about changing that, we would. I took a firmer grip on my sword and positioned myself for the opening movements of the dance.

His gleaming blade whistled as it cut a glittering arc through the cold winter air, the keen edge coming straight at my belly. I leaned back and lifted my sword to deflect it, then in a lightning-quick movement, cut a flat slice at his bare knees. He leapt back, brought his sword around to deflect the blow, and found my sword stopped in midair, waiting for his response.

It shouldn't have surprised him. It was, after all, the next movement of the dance. I stepped back and grounded the point of my sword.

"Mayhaps, my lord Govan, the hour is too early for a man of your advanced years?" I suggested politely.

"Impudent whelp," he said, but laughter danced in his eyes and softened the sharpness of his words. "I suppose I deserved that. But I will confess, my lady Iowen, I had not expected so gracious and lovely a lady as yourself to be quite so adept in dancing the sword." He sketched a mocking little bow, then raised his sword again. "Shall we continue? I assure you, I shall not make that mistake again."

I smiled. I don't think I betrayed my lack of faith in the statement. "As you wish." I took my position again.

His sword looped through the air, making a lazy arc again aimed for my belly. Exasperation fluttered in my chest, but I pushed it aside. If I were to prove to him that I was truly a Celae bheancoran and not someone to take lightly while I carried a sword in my hands, I could not afford to let anger or annoyance slow me down. I raised my sword, deflected his easily enough, and turned into the next movement. He swung his sword. The blade moved slowly, as if through water, but none the less deadly for all its apparent languidity. I met it, then pressed subtly, gradually increasing the speed of the dance until both of us moved at close to top speed.

The expression on his face changed from benign indulgence to shocked surprise, then finally settled into wary and cautious respect. If I hadn't been so busy fending off the sizzling blows of his blade, I might have found his disconcerted discomfort amusing. But that would probably be uncharitable, and therefore unworthy of me.

Satisfying, though. No denying it was gratifying.

A little over halfway through the exercise, he slipped in the frozen grass as he leapt back. He stumbled and went to one knee. I surged forward, taking full advantage of his mishap, and brought the flat of my blade down onto his shoulder with enough force to bruise. A reminder.

"Killing blow," I announced, very carefully keeping my voice neutral, free of triumph.

He scrambled to his feet with alacrity, but too late. He had brought it on himself, though. To be fair, had he treated me as an equal opponent, I would never have had the chance to bruise his shoulder. I would never, in fact, have been able to get close enough. I was deft and agile and strong for a woman, but he was still a man, a Tyran clansman, and far heavier and stronger than I. Given two opponents of relatively equal skill, victory inevitably went to the stronger and more experienced. And I was certainly not arrogant enough to believe my skill equal to his. His reputation as one of the best swordsmen in Tyra preceded him. He would never underestimate me again.

I smiled as I stepped back to give him a moment to regain his composure. "You should know better, my lord Govan," I said mildly enough. "Surely you've sparred with a Celae bheancoran before."

He rubbed the bruised point of his shoulder, shrewd speculation in his eyes. Then he gave me a broad, rueful grin, unembarrassed and full of laughter. A most unusual man, this. No wonder Brynda was so fond of him.

"You have truly humbled me, my lady Iowen," he said. He made a low, courtly bow. "One tends to forget, even when the bheancoran in question is mother to my lady wife. Who, incidentally, has humbled me more than once herself."

His laughter was infectious, and I found myself genuinely liking him. I grinned at him. "My aunt Brynda has had that effect on several men, I'm told," I said. "She might be upset if she thought you would forget her skills so easily."

"Aye, she might at that," he said, still smiling. "We should ask her just how many times she's reminded me of those skills." He nodded toward the other end of the pavilion.

I turned. I had not seen Brynda enter the pavilion. I barely remembered my grandfather Brennen, but even I saw how much Brynda resembled her brother. The red-gold hair she inherited from her half-Tyran father had faded to a silvery copper color with her age. She sparred with a man, both of them moving slowly and gracefully through a seventh-level dance. As they circled each other, I realized the man was my father.

Gareth ap Brennen was Prince of Skai. It pained me to realize that my father, although no older than Govan, looked at least as old as Brynda. I had never known my father as a young man. Warring magics—gentle Celae magic and murderous Maedun sorcery—had robbed him of his youth even before any of his children were born. He was still a strong man, despite the unnatural aging of his body, and I had never heard him complain. His spirit remained young, and his magic remained strong.

He and Brynda progressed through the exercise as gracefully as Laringorn bhak dancers, who always seemed to be moving underwater. I knew from painful experience how difficult it was to keep the smooth flow of the drill at that slow speed. Muscles complained, wanting to cramp and disrupt the rhythm of the dance. It didn't take much to let the exercise deteriorate into stiff, jerky, uncoordinated movements.

"You favor her," Govan said quietly at my elbow. I jumped, startled. I had almost forgotten he was there. "And I'm told she favors the lady Kerridwen."

I glanced at him. The lady Kerridwen, Brynda's almost legendary grandmother, had been a formidable woman. The comparison pleased me immensely, but I tried not to show it. But I smiled.

"Aye, well, neither of us is what anyone could call delicate and dainty women," I said. "Not like my mother."

Only my eldest brother Adair resembled our father, with his glossy black hair that threw back blue highlights into the sunlight, his dark blue eyes, and his slender build. Both my brother Athelin and I were tall and big-boned, showing our Tyran heritage in our size even if our hair was dark gold like our mother's rather than red-gold like our grandfather's.

A clansman came to Govan's side and murmured something I couldn't hear into his ear. Govan glanced at him, eyebrows raised in what might have been alarm. The expression slid into bland neutrality; I wasn't sure if I'd really seen it. He replied quietly and calmly to the clansman, then turned to me.

"Please excuse me for a moment," he said. "There's something I must attend to. I'll return shortly so that we can resume our match."

He obviously wasn't about to tell me what business took him away so abruptly. I nodded and slid my sword into its sheath on my back. "I'll use the time to catch my breath," I said.

He laughed, but the laughter didn't reach his eyes this time. Preoccupied, he nodded. "You are too kind," he murmured. He and the clansman left the pavilion, walking swiftly, but not running. I stepped out into the sunlight and watched them hurry toward the Clanhold. Their backs were to me, but their stiff, rigid posture spoke eloquently enough of worry.

Brynda came to my side, thoughtfully watching the two men as they strode across the broad expanse of snow toward the Clanhold. "Is something wrong?" she asked. "Govan seems to be in a tearing hurry. Quite unlike him."

I glanced at her. Brynda was well over seventy, but she still carried herself as erect and straight as the sword she wore on her back. Her silver hair lay across her shoulder in a heavy plait, and deep wrinkles furrowed the skin around her eyes and mouth. Still watching Govan, she sheathed the sword. The runes etched deeply into the blade flashed as they caught the sun, then vanished as the blade sank into the leather scabbard.

I still couldn't reconcile myself to the casual, almost indifferent way Brynda handled the celebrated Rune Blade. As if it were merely an ordinary sword, not a wonder crafted by Wyfydd Smith himself for the defense of Skai. The songs and stories called Wyfydd "armorer to gods and kings," the fabled Smith who was nearly a god himself. No one knows when Whisperer was crafted, but the sword has been handed down, generation to generation, for longer than living memory. Brynda inherited it from her grandmother, the lady Kerridwen al Jorddyn, wife and bheancoran to Red Kian of Skai, and Kerridwen inherited it from her father, who had received it from the hands of his mother. Brynda had carried Whisperer for more than fifty years, ever since Kerridwen had placed it into her hand. Mayhaps even a miracle became commonplace after fifty years.

Brynda showed no signs of giving up the sword. By rights, it would eventually go to another bheancoran. That probably meant my brother Adair's bheancoran Liesa, or my brother Athelin's wife and bheancoran Dorlaine. I stood far down on the list with no hope of receiving the sword. I could almost let myself envy Liesa or Dorlaine a little. But living up to a legend was a responsibility I wasn't sure I'd want. And the sword should be carried by a bheancoran. I shared a bond with no one. Born to be bheancoran, I had yet to find the prince I was born to serve.

"Bad news?" Brynda asked, still watching Govan and the clansman.

"I think so," I said. "Or something that certainly displeased him. He didn't say anything to me."

My father joined us, his sword sheathed on his back. He was nearly twenty-five years younger than Brynda but looked far older. He still wore his hair—pure silver now with no trace of the glossy blue-black of his youth in it—in the braid of a clansman, and a blue topaz dangled from his left earlobe on a short length of gold chain.

"I hope it's not trouble," he said.

"I don't know," Brynda replied. "Strange, though."

He crossed the pavilion to where he'd left his cloak. I started toward him to help him pin it, then glanced outside as an odd movement caught my eye.

Two men, wrapped to the eyes in their plaids against the cold, strode purposefully through the snow toward the pavilion. They carried their naked swords in their hands rather than sheathed across their backs, and they came from the track that led only to the shrine on the flank of the mountain above the Clanhold. Today wasn't a holy day or a festival day. Strange that they might be at the shrine so early.

Something about the pair wasn't quite right. In the bright sunlight neither sword flashed with reflected light. One of the men glanced over his shoulder at the Clanhold, a curiously furtive movement. A frisson of chill rippled down my spine, and I reached for the hilt of my sword even before I realized what was wrong.

Both men had tar black hair and black eyes. Not the bright red-gold hair and green or gray eyes of Tyra.

Maedun! They were Maedun.

Assassins!

Before I could clear my sword from its scabbard, one of the men sprang across the pavilion toward my father, sword lifted. My father reacted swiftly. Reaching for his sword, he threw himself between two pillars, out of the way of the lethal blade, tumbling into the deep snow outside the pavilion. The attacker followed him, sword raised for another blow.

The other man turned viciously on Brynda and me. Brynda had just reached for Whisperer's hilt when the assassin swung his arm around and caught her across the lower belly at hip level. She stumbled back and fell. I cried out her name, but she didn't move.

My heart made a determined effort to leap right out of my chest. My mouth dry, my breath rasping, I spun out of the way, ducking the polished black blade as the assassin brought it around. I don't remember drawing my sword, but the silver-wire filigree of the hilt bit into the palms of my hands as I twisted around to meet him.

His lip curled in a sneer as he realized I was a woman. Cold fury burst through me, steadying my wildly beating heart. I used his contempt to my own advantage. He wouldn't be the first Maedun to die because he fatally underestimated a Celae bheancoran and dismissed her as a negligible obstacle. I leapt to one side and swung my sword as the momentum of the assassin's swing brought him stumbling past me. The blade bit deeply into the small of his back. Blood sprayed, and he went down like a felled pine.

I had no time to make sure he was dead. I turned quickly, in time to see my father collapse under the blade of the second assassin. He crumpled to the ground and lay facedown, motionless in the snow.

My heart nearly stopped in fear and horror. "Father," I screamed. I hurled myself across the pavilion, lips skinned back over my teeth, sobbing with effort.

The last assassin was on me like a weasel on a rabbit. I dodged, but too late. His black sword shrieked as he swung it, his face contorted with the effort. I managed to bring my sword up to meet the blow. His blade caught it a handbreadth below the hilt. The shock of it blasted up my arms and right into my spine. My hands went numb. The sword flew from my nerveless fingers. The assassin turned for the killing blow. I scrambled desperately to one side, scrabbling on hands and knees, and only just managed to duck under the deadly arc of his blade.

"Iowen!" Brynda's shrill whisper rang out clearly like a chime. "Here!"

She raised Whisperer, holding it high. I sprang to one side as the assassin lunged for me, the black blade of his sword spilling darkness all around itself. Brynda gathered herself with a supreme effort and tossed Whisperer. Light glittered and flashed on the runes etched deeply into the blade as it spun through the air. Brynda fell back, her face gray with exhaustion and pain as soon as the sword left her hand, as if all her strength had gone with Whisperer. She crumpled to the ground. Around her hips, the snow quickly turned bright crimson.

I had a brief flash of the fittingness of Brynda's gesture as the runes on Whisperer's blade glittered fiercely in the sun. Like the lyrics of a ballad, words ran across the surface of my mind. *From Kerridwen to Brynda to Iowen.* A right and proper progression.

As if guided, the sword dropped neatly and precisely into my outstretched hand, the hilt fitting my palm and fingers as if it had been crafted for me and me alone. A wild tingling sensation shot from my hand, up my arm, and into my chest. It thrummed in my body along my nerves and muscles and sinews the way music vibrates a harp string. My heart thudded violently in my chest, then settled into a quick, light, pounding rhythm. I cried out, half in elation, half in rage, and my voice blended with the savage song of the sword itself. I launched myself at the assassin.

My voice in my own ears shrieked as fiercely and as

shrilly as the sword's own enraged howl. The last assassin stumbled back, probably trying to escape my intense rage as much as the glittering Rune Blade. He was fast, but Whisperer and I were faster. My feet hardly seemed to touch the ground as I leapt at him. Propelled by my frenzied fury, drawn by the sword, I flew over the snow, Whisperer's blade making a low, rising arc as I swung it with all my strength at the retreating assassin. It caught him in the soft tissues of his side, just below the ribs, and nearly split him in two.

I didn't wait to see him fall. I dropped Whisperer unceremoniously into the trampled snow and ran stumbling to my father. He lay sprawled in the shadow of the pavilion, his face nearly as pale as the snow beneath his cheek. A bright, spreading pool of brilliant crimson blood beneath his body steamed gently in the cold air as it cooled and congealed. He lay unmoving, and I couldn't tell if he breathed or not.

2

I threw myself to my knees beside the prostrate body of my father.
My hand shook with fear as I reached out to him. Terrified
that I would meet only the final, utter stillness of death, I
hesitated. I couldn't bring myself to touch him.

"Don't let him be dead," I whispered in agony, pleading with all the seven gods and goddesses and the Duality.
"Please don't let him be dead." If he died, my mother would
die, too, killed by the pain of the breaking of their bond just
as surely as if the assassin had plunged his sword into her
body as well as my father's. I couldn't bear to lose them
both like this. Not like this. Oh, gods, not like this.

I glanced over my shoulder at Brynda. Pain twisted my
heart, snatched the breath from my chest. She lay in the
snow, eyes half open, her face frozen in a grimace of effort.
I hunched my shoulders and looked away, too numb with
grief and pain to even sob.

My mother flew across the snow. I don't think she even
saw me as she flung herself down beside my father, her face
nearly as pale as his. It hardly surprised me that my mother
knew instantly that something had happened to my father.
They were bound not only by the unbreakable bond of
bheancoran and prince, but by nearly thirty years of loving
marriage. They were two bodies sharing a single spirit.
Nothing happened to one without the other being aware of
it. The same bond vibrated between Adair and Liesa, and
between Athelin and Dorlaine.

My mother didn't make a sound as she collapsed across
my father's body. She flung her arms around him and
pressed her face against his back.

A pair of strong hands closed about my arms. I cried out and struggled to free myself, too lost in grief to recognize the man who held me. He pulled me to my feet, turned me to face him, away from the too-still forms of my parents.

"Come away, child," he said gently. "There's nothing you can do for them now."

I tried to tear myself from his grasp, but had no strength left. Tears blurring my vision, I looked up. It might have been Taggert, the Clan Laird, who held me. I stared blankly at him, unable to draw enough breath into my body. Beyond his shoulder, Brynda's husband Kenzie knelt in the snow and gathered her body into his arms. He looked as shattered and bereft as I felt. He didn't look back as he stood up, still carrying Brynda, and made his way slowly and painfully toward the Clanhold.

Father . . . Mother . . . and Brynda, too . . . It was too much. Sobs nearly choked me, and I let my head fall forward until it rested on Taggert's chest. He put his arms around me, holding me protectively, and I let him lead me away.

Frost etched a delicate tracery of crystal across the small panes of glass in the window of my chamber. I looked out across the glen but couldn't see the dark smudge of the thatched roof of the practice pavilion. I shuddered and looked away, up at the soaring crags to the north.

The ice-locked River Borden flowing through the glen gleamed blue-white in the glare of the late-afternoon sun. Light reflected in bright rainbow spears from the great, tumbled blocks of ice, some as big as hay carts, heaved up by the pressure of the ice upstream. Dense stands of winter-stripped oak, ash, and silver-leaf maple stood bare and stark against the snow like spidery black scrawls of ink on a sheet of parchment. Here and there the thick, dark green of fir and spruce and the brighter green of holly made spots of color in the bleak black-and-white landscape.

It was so very beautiful, and my parents would never see it again . . .

Nor would Brynda . . .

I closed my eyes and drew the collar of my houserobe closer around my throat. Cold air radiated from the frosted glass and eddied about my ankles like ice water from the river. The hearth and brazier shedding blessed heat were on the other side of the room, too far away to dispel the chill. I shivered and turned away.

Slowly, carefully, I dressed in a dark gown and drew a cloak about me. I reached up and braided a narrow sheaf of my hair into a slender braid and tied it with a length of white cord. I had just finished when someone knocked softly at my chamber door. Before I could cross the room to open it, Kenzie stepped into the chamber.

He wore his grief for his wife like a mantle shrouding his shoulders. For the first time, I saw that he was very old. Bereavement carved deep lines into his face, dulled the brilliant green of his eyes to sea-haze gray. I knew then that it wouldn't be long before another grief came to tear at my heart. I feared that Kenzie would not live long without Brynda at his side.

"Are ye ready, lass?" he asked. Mourning furred his voice so that he sounded hoarse and ill.

I nodded and crossed the room to take the arm he offered. He covered my hand with his free hand as I slipped it through his elbow. He looked down at me, his eyes bright with tears.

"I canna say how sorry I am, lass," he said softly. "It's nearly a mortal blow, to lose both parents at the same time."

I blinked rapidly in an attempt to banish my tears. "As hard as to lose a wife," I said. "Oh, Kenzie, I'm so sorry. So very sorry. I couldn't help her . . ." My voice broke, and I could speak no more.

He touched my cheek gently in a tender gesture. "There was little you could do, Iowen," he said. "And you did all you could."

I looked at him, my misery a scalding flow across my spirit. "I did all I could, but they're all still dead. My best wasn't good enough . . ."

"Hush, lass," he said. "It's time to go."

Clinging to his arm, I went with him out into the corridor, then down the long, sweeping staircase to the Great Hall. The clan had gathered in the vast room. Taggert dav Malcolm dav Cynan, sixteenth Clan Laird of Broche Rhuidh, stood on the dais at one end of the Hall. Before him, the bodies of my parents and Brynda lay on biers resting on planken tables. My mother and father lay together, bodies touching. The High Priest and High Priestess from the shrine on the hillside stood just below Taggert, bound together at chest, hip, and thigh to represent the twinned aspect of the Duality, neither male nor female, but both. They wore one voluminous robe that left their heads free and the High Priest's right arm, and the High Priestess's left arm. Both looked up as Kenzie and I approached. Neither of them smiled, but their faces contained a wealth of sympathy and warmth.

I let go of Kenzie's arm and went to them. Wordlessly, the High Priest held out a hoop woven of cedar, holly, and sumac, laced through with white and gold ribbons. The High Priestess offered a knife, smaller than the palm of my hand.

The haft of the knife was cold against my skin as I took it. Trying not to look at my parents, I reached up and cut the slender braid from my head, then wove it into the greenery of the hoop that represented the Unbroken Circle of birth, life, death, and rebirth. The dark gold glinted among the leaves and cedar needles. I took the hoop, turned carefully, and drew in a deep breath before approaching the bier that held my parents. Slowly, hardly able to breathe, I placed the hoop so that it lay half on my mother's right shoulder, half on my father's left. Oddly enough, their pale, bloodless lips seemed to be smiling slightly, as if all the fear and pain and horror had left them and gentle contentment taken their place.

I stepped back and stole a glance at Brynda as Kenzie laid a hoop decorated with a narrow braid from his own hair over her folded hands. Even she looked calm and at peace.

Fourteen clansmen came forward, marching in unison to the head of the room, their faces austere and solemn. Six of them took up Brynda's bier, and eight of them lifted my parents.

Somewhere in the Great Hall, a piper began to play, a muted, slow melody in a minor key, so softly at first it was little more than a whisper of sound through the Great Hall. I looked up to see that Govan was the piper. He wheeled slowly and led the pallbearers out of the Great Hall, the eerily melancholy wail of the pipes becoming sweet and poignant in the chill, fading light of late afternoon.

Each phrase Govan played had meaning. As a weaver gathers the threads of a tapestry to weave an image, so Govan plaited the musical phrases together to tell those who knew how to speak the language of the music the story of the three lives ended this day. I was in the music he played for my parents, as were my brothers Adair and Athelin. Even my half brother Caennedd, my father's Beltane child, was there. The lives of Gareth ap Brennen and Lowra al Drywn formed a haunting melody, both powerful and sweet.

Kenzie and I fell into place behind the pallbearers. We

held each other up, I think, as we made our way up the hill-side, past the shrine, to the small stone circle high on the flank of the mountain. Seven tall, roughly carved stones, each representing one of the seven gods and goddesses, stood widely spaced around a plinth in the center. Beyond the circle lay the crypts, carved deep into the living heart of the mountain itself. Someone had already unsealed the entrance. Within lay untold generations of the men and women of Broche Rhuidh. Red Kian of Skai lay in a niche together with his wife and bheancoran Kerridwen al Jorddyn. Brynda's grandparents. My father's great-grandparents. Our roots with the past.

Kenzie and I stood together between the circle and the mouth of the crypts, but we didn't enter the cave with the pallbearers. We had said our final good-byes, and tonight, I would stand vigil for my mother and for Brynda, while Kenzie stood vigil for my father.

A small sound escaped Kenzie's throat as the pallbearers disappeared inside the crypts. A catch in his breathing, no more. But the tiny sound spoke volumes, torn from him by grief and pain. I reached out and took his hand. His fingers closed about mine strongly, and I thought his grip might crush my fingers. But I didn't try to remove my hand. The pain helped to control the grief that tore at my heart.

The sun stood poised on the lip of the horizon to the west, painting the sky and the sea in brilliant tones of red and orange and gold and pink. Dressed now in trews, shirt, and tunic, my cloak pinned about me and an empty scabbard on my back, I made my way to the practice pavilion. I had left Brynda's sword, the Rune Blade Whisperer, lying unheeded in the snow. A terrible thing to do to any good sword, much less a Rune Blade. It deserved so much better than such treatment.

The bodies of the two assassins were gone. Govan had sent a troop of men down to fetch them to the Clanhold for burial in unhallowed ground on the other side of the river. Nothing remained of the blood Brynda and my father had shed. Someone had gathered the bloody snow and disposed of it carefully. But the assassins' blood still lay bright and garish on the snow. I stared at it for a moment. I had killed them. I had killed both of them, one of them with Whisperer. But I hadn't been able to save my father or Brynda. And because my father died, my mother died.

I should have been quicker. I should have been stronger. I closed my eyes. Adair and Athelin, even Caennedd, could never forgive me. I could never forgive myself.

I started to turn away, but something bright, half buried in the bloody snow where the body of the second assassin had lain, caught my eye. I bent and picked up a smooth, oval stone, polished to a satiny sheen and threaded on a narrow leather lace. Broken now, but obviously the second assassin had been wearing it. In the last of the sunshine, the stone glowed a bright, unpleasant, actinic green. Faint lines carved into the surface made sinuous patterns. It made me dizzy trying to follow the curves with my eye.

"What have you there?"

Kenzie's voice startled me badly. I whirled around, heart pounding, to find him behind me. I had not realized he had followed me from the Clanhold.

He reached out to grasp my wrist. "What have you there?" he repeated sharply.

I opened my hand so he could see what I held. "Just an amulet," I said. "But an odd one." I nodded toward the bloody depression where the body of the assassin had lain. "I found it over there. His, I think."

Kenzie pulled his hand back from my arm, and I

offered him the curiously carved stone. He recoiled as if I had tried to give him a pit adder. He shuddered visibly.

"Oh, dear gods and goddesses," he said softly.

"What is it?" I asked. The stone felt strangely warm against my palm. Warm and unpleasantly oily.

"It's a Tell-Tale," he said, his voice harsh.

"A Tell-Tale? I've never heard of one."

He reached out one finger and touched the stone. He shivered again. "I've only seen one before, and that was back in Celi, before Brynda and I came to Tyra after the invasion. It tracks magic. And it can track a person who uses magic."

"It tracks magic?" I looked down at the thin, flat ovoid in my hand. The green glow had faded with the setting sun, turning the edges of the amulet the dark green of a harmless, ordinary river stone.

"Aye, child. It's a black sorcerer's work. And if I've the right of it, a sorcerer can key it to a certain man and track him down." He took the amulet from me, handling it by the broken leather thong, not letting his fingers touch the stone itself. For a moment, he looked down at it, frowning thoughtfully in distaste, then slipped it into his pocket.

"I don't understand." My hand felt cold and prickly where the stone had touched the skin. I wiped my palm on the thigh of my breeks and closed it into a fist. "How can it be keyed?"

"We're not certain," Kenzie said. "I have no magic myself, ye ken, and know little of these things. We believe it has something to do with bringing the stone into contact with something that belongs to the person they want to key it to. Or perhaps with recognizing the patterns of the way the person uses magic. Everyone uses the magic a little differently, ye ken. But we don't know for sure how it's keyed. There would be a blood sorcery spell to go with the keying, too, of course. The stones are extremely rare. We'd heard that Hakkar had finally obtained another one. We knew he'd been searching these last fifty years for one, ever since the other one was lost. And he'd been searching for Gareth, too."

I shivered. "For my father? Whatever for?"

Kenzie gave a humorless snort of laughter. "Gareth was there when Horbad was slain," he said. "Do you think Hakkar would let that go by without the overwhelming need for revenge? He wanted your father dead. He'd posted a rich reward on his head—several Maedun golds, I believe. And now he has a Tell-Tale."

"No, he doesn't." I smiled grimly. "We have the Tell-Tale now. And we're going to destroy it."

"Mayhaps," Kenzie said wearily. "But it's done its work. We can only hope he has no more."

"More?" A cold fist clenched itself around my heart. Adair had magic. Not a lot. Not like the magic our father had held in his hands and spirit, but magic nonetheless. So did Athelin. Again, not much. Even I held a small spark of it. "To search for the rest of us?"

"Mayhaps. But I hope not." He touched the pocket where the stone lay and shuddered again, his face pale. "Fetch Whisperer, Iowen. You mustn't leave her lying in the snow like that. She served you well today and deserves better than that."

I went to pick up the fallen sword. The sun gleamed on the runes. They made no sense to me, but then no one could read the runes on a sword not one's own. It was part of the mystique of a Rune Blade. Mild magic, but certainly magic nonetheless.

But then, something very strange happened.

The runes glittered like the facets of a gem, even without the direct light of the sun. The dazzle flashed into my eyes, and the lines of the runes seemed to flow and run together, like ink in water. They shimmered, then formed themselves into words—words I could read. Dazed and unable to speak, I stared at the bright blade. Stunned, I held the sword out to Kenzie, my breathing ragged and shallow.

Kenzie hesitated, his eyes narrowing speculatively. "What do the runes say, Iowen?" he asked softly, an odd expression on his face.

I didn't have to look. The words burned brightly before my eyes. *"I am the Voice of Celi,"* I whispered.

"And so they do," he said very softly. "Aye, and so they do, child."

I held out the sword again. He smiled and refused to take it. "No," he said quietly. "She always knew this would happen someday. I'm glad it's happening now. She hoped it would be you the sword claimed. You take it."

"Me?" My voice squeaked alarmingly, like a rusty hinge. I cleared my throat and tried again. "But—"

He smiled. "It's time to pass it along, just as Brynda's grandmother passed it to her all those years ago. It belongs to you now. The sword is yours."

I looked down at it in wonder. The Runes blazed before my eyes. *I am the Voice of Celi.* Truly, it was. And I had heard its fierce song ringing in my head. I remembered the expression on Brynda's face as she threw me the sword even as she lay dying. Acceptance. And mayhaps even muted joy.

The sword was mine, commended to my hand from hers. I sheathed it on my back, and went with Kenzie to the stone circle to stand vigil for Brynda, and for my mother, while he stood vigil for my father.

Some time in the stillness of the winter night, they came for all three of them, a line of their people stretching back to the time when Broche Rhuidh was but a rough pile of stones, and the clans were still wild tribes.

When morning came, Kenzie and I walked together back to the Clanhold. We were cold and inexpressibly tired, but we were content. Whatever happened now, we knew my parents and Brynda were safe in Annwn, their days counted and totaled by the Counter at the Scroll.

3

I lay awake listening to the quiet sounds of a sleeping Clanhold.
Not enough light filtered into the room to allow me to see
the sword that lay on the chest against the far wall. The
Rune Blade lay quiescent, waiting, and I thought I heard its
soft voice murmuring gently. On the terrace outside, the
wind picked up the loose, powdery snow and swirled it past
my window. I watched the dancing white mist and shivered.

Cold or excitement? I couldn't answer my own question. It might be both. Or neither. I didn't want to admit
even to myself that it might be apprehension. Or plain and
simple fear. It could be that I simply didn't want the responsibility of carrying a Rune Blade, and especially Whisperer.

The question rose unbidden, and I couldn't banish it.
What if the sword refused to serve me?

Bleakly, I wondered how in the name of all piety I
could hope to measure up to the two women who had held
the sword before me. Brynda al Keylan, granddaughter of
the legendary Red Kian of Skai, had been bheancoran to
Prince Tiegan, heir to the throne of the High King of all
Celi. When he died on the battlefield of Camm Run during
the Maedun invasion, the pain of the broken bond nearly
destroyed Brynda. But she had sworn Tiegan a vow to see
his pregnant wife safe to the Tyadda steading and her people deep in the mountains of Skai. This she had done,
accompanied by her husband Kenzie and her brother,
Brennen, who was my grandfather. Brynda had more than
proved herself worthy to carry Whisperer.

The sword came to her from her grandmother,

Kerridwen al Jorddyn, wife and bheancoran to Red Kian. I had heard enough tales and ballads telling the tale of the adventures of Red Kian and Kerri to fill a library. Whisperer sang fiercely in her hands, as it had sung for Brynda, too.

The two of us, Brynda and I, had looked straight into each other's eyes as we stood facing each other. Neither of us was a small, dainty woman. My mother, Lowra, was Tyadda, one of the strange, fey race that had inhabited the Isle of Celi before the Celae arrived to make it theirs. Like all of her people, she was small, delicately built, and an unlikely choice for a bheancoran, some thought. But I had seen how deadly accurate my mother was with the little recurved bow she carried. A bheancoran didn't have to swing a great sword to be effective. Arrows were just as lethal when launched at an enemy with a sure and certain hand.

"All the way from Kerridwen to me," I said aloud into the empty room. Passed from grandmother to granddaughter, and now from a dying great-aunt to great-niece. An heirloom more priceless than gold or precious stones. "But what shall I do with it? Whom shall I defend?"

The princes of Skai had always been served by a bheancoran, a warrior-maid who acted as comrade, guard, confidante, and soul's companion. King Tiernyn, a son of Red Kian, had had Ylana. Their son Tiegan had had Brynda; my father Gareth, my mother Lowra. My brother Adair had Liesa, and my brother Athelin had Dorlaine.

As far as I knew, there had never been a Prince of Skai without a bheancoran. Had there ever been a bheancoran who had no prince?

Again, the question rose like a specter to haunt me. What if I were not born to be bheancoran after all? Kerridwen had received the sword from her father. Certainly he was no bheancoran. What if I was not either?

Now there was a truly sobering thought.

"What if— What if— What if—" I muttered, disgusted by my jumpy nerves. "What if you fell off a bloody cliff and drowned in the sea?"

Eaten by fishes. Now there was a truly morose thought.

But pity the poor fish who tried to swallow anything as sour as I felt. Surely my brother Athelin would roar with laughter if he could see me. Even Adair would smile.

But Athelin could not see me now. He was still safely across the Cold Sea, snugly ensconced in the north of lost Celi in Skerrykeep with Dorlaine and their two sons. Mayhaps a good thing. My favorite brother was not the most sympathetic soul when it came to tolerating anyone wallowing in a sea of self-pity. As was only right, I supposed.

I sighed, then smiled ruefully. It was hard to hold on to the smothering cloak of self-pity in the imagined face of Athelin's mirth. He had more than once accused me of taking myself far too seriously, and he was probably right. He usually was. But he had always been able to tease me gently out of my blue funks when we were children, and make me laugh at myself. That facility hadn't diminished with time as we grew.

But growing up knowing I was to be bheancoran had never seemed strange to me until I turned eighteen, the age a bheancoran usually bonded with her prince. But there was no prince for me.

I first rode at Athelin's side acting as his bheancoran while Dorlaine was heavy with their first child. After Gabhain was born, Dorlaine didn't exactly step aside, but she did nothing to dispel the fiction that I might be bheancoran to Athelin. Brynda had been bheancoran to Prince Tiegan, who was her first cousin. A prince's sister might conceivably be his bheancoran.

I raised both hands and used my fingers to rake my unbound hair back from my forehead and temples. It still felt a little damp from my bath.

Lying around feeling sorry for myself wasn't helping. Chasing my worries in circles wasn't helping, either. But the tangled threads of fear, grief, and guilt made it too difficult to sleep.

Oh, gods, Father. Mother. I need you. And I need you, Brynda . . .

I rose from my bed and went to the door that opened onto the terrace outside my chamber. Moonlight streamed down onto the flagstones, and a mild breeze stirred the leaves of the ornamental trees planted in pots along the edge of the parapet. Someone stood framed in the embrasure between two merlons, looking out at the play of light and shadow on the sea where the moonpath glittered softly. I didn't bother with my houserobe as I walked out onto the terrace. She turned, smiling, to meet me as I approached, and I realized it was Brynda.

But a different Brynda from the one I had known. She was young and strong and beautiful. She smiled again as I joined her and reached up to cup my cheek with her hand. Her fingers were warm against my skin.

"Don't look so worried, dear heart," she said. "There's nothing to be frightened about."

Her shade didn't frighten me. I had loved her while she lived; how could I not love her still?

"I'm not frightened," I replied.

She laughed. "Not of me," she said. "But I can tell that carrying Whisperer gives you pause."

I hesitated. She was right, but I didn't want her to know that. I tried to put on a brave front. "What makes you think that frightens me?"

She laughed again. "Because I was scared to death when my grandmother gave me Whisperer. I was sure I'd disgrace the sword, and her, and all of Skai and Celi, too."

"You? You were frightened?"

"Absolutely petrified, I assure you."

"But—"

She sat down on the sill of the embrasure, her back toward the sea and the moonpath, and took my hand. She might have worked some of her Healing magic on me—just a little—because the uncomfortable twist in my belly eased, and I felt calmer, more relaxed. It was a lot easier to take a deep breath, too.

"Whisperer will fight for you, Iowen," Brynda said. "Remember how she fought for you at the pavilion."

"But my father died. You died."

Brynda touched my face again. "It was our time," she said. "The sword fought well for you. She'll fight for you again."

I looked out across the shimmer of the sea. "I think I understand," I said. "But Brynda . . ." I let my voice trail off, uncertain how to say what I had to say. Brynda said nothing. She merely waited calmly and patiently. Finally, I raised my eyes and looked at her. "When you received Whisperer, you knew you were to be bheancoran to Tiegan. But I have no prince. I'm nearly twenty-three and still have no prince. How can a Rune Blade—how can Whisperer— serve me when I myself have no one to serve?"

"I don't think you'll ever have a prince, child," Brynda said quietly. I jumped, startled, and my breath caught uncomfortably in my throat.

She must surely hear the terrified, hollow thudding of my heart in my chest. But she merely smiled again. Before I could say anything, she went on. "No, I don't think you'll ever have a prince. But Iowen . . ." She paused and looked out across the parapet for a long moment, her face remote and thoughtful, almost bemused. "Yes, I think, dear heart, that you might one day have a king."

My heart made a concentrated effort to leap out from between my ribs. I stared at her blankly in shock.

"A king?"

"Of course. There is a king out there in Celi, you know. Tiegan's wife had twin sons, and one of them still lives."

"But we've heard nothing of him for nearly thirty years. Not since before my mother and father were married."

"That doesn't mean he's not there. It merely means that communication between Skai and Skerry is difficult and dangerous." She stepped away from the embrasure. *"Remember that, child."* Her outline shimmered in the moonlight, then was gone.

The tapping at my chamber door woke me. I sat up in bed, breathlessly wide-awake, and stared at the snow on the terrace outside my window. I had dreamed. Dreamed of warmth and comfort and spring.

And of Brynda . . .

The knocking came again, and Kenzie's voice. "Iowen? Are you awake?"

I scrambled out of bed and into my houserobe. "I'm coming," I called.

He came in as I opened the door, striding easily and gracefully into the room. A tall man, my kin-uncle, and imposing even yet. He carried himself like a man half his age, as if refusing to relinquish anything to an aging body. Grief and loss etched deep lines into his face, but he stood straight and erect as the greatsword he carried.

"There's to be a conference in Taggert's solar," he said. "Will you come?"

Flustered, I glanced down at the houserobe I wore over my bedgown. "Yes, of course," I said. "But not like this."

He smiled. "Dress yourself then, lass," he said. "I'll wait in the corridor."

"I'll be but a moment."

"They'll wait for us."

It took me only a moment or two to dress. I emerged

from my chamber, still braiding my hair, but otherwise decent. "A conference?" I asked. "Why?"

"I'm sure Taggert will be able to tell you," he said mildly enough. He could be maidenly uncommunicative when he chose to be. I knew from experience that I would be able to pry no further information out of him. "Shall we go?"

We walked the passageway together. He led me past the solar into a small conference room overlooking the sea. The room was sparsely furnished with only a long, polished wooden table with several chairs spaced evenly around it. On the wall behind it hung a huge map of the continent, the countries all color-washed in different hues — Tyra, a tapering green arrowhead running east from the coast, the bleak, gray expanse of Saesnes above it to the north; the blocky yellow shape of Isgard and the sprawl of landlocked Maedun, blood red in the pale winter light streaming through the window. And far to the west, the pale tan of lost Celi, surrounded by the blue of the sea, the small islands of Skerry and Marddyn hardly noticeable beyond the northern shore. I had never seen a more finely detailed map, except perhaps for the one my father had owned, which hung in his study in Skerrykeep. The one could have been a copy of the other.

The room was cold. Two braziers, one at each end of the table, did their best to banish the chill of late winter from the room, but were making little headway. Frost made feathery patterns on the windows. A cold draft flowed from the glass in spite of the thick draperies. I folded my arms across my chest, painfully conscious of the weight of the sword on my back, and hugged myself for warmth. I was sure everyone was staring at the sword, and heat rose in my face.

Taggert dav Malcolm dav Cynan, Sixteenth Clan

Laird of Broche Rhuidh, sat at the head of the table, his plaid with its broad gold stripe through the grays, blues, and greens wrapped around his shoulders. Govan sat to his right, then Kenzie's son Comyn to his left. Taggert rose as Kenzie and I entered and directed us to take seats.

"Thank you for coming," Taggert said. He looked toward Comyn. "Comyn has something that must be discussed."

Comyn cleared his throat. He looked across the table at me, a slight, thoughtful frown drawing the red-gold eyebrows together above his vividly green eyes. "The weather will be good for the next few days," he said. "Clear skies and fair winds."

I couldn't guess what he was leading up to, so I simply nodded. "Better than the blizzards we've been having since Imbolc."

He laughed. "Oh, aye, much better. Much better, indeed. And they tell me I know weather."

Kenzie and Brynda's son Comyn possessed the gift of being able to read the sea in all of its myriad moods. People said Adriel of the Waters herself guided him to the safe path through its shoals and currents, squalls and tempests. He was commander of the fleet of little six-man courier ships that braved even the worst weather plying back and forth between Tyra and Skerry with messages.

"Someone will have to carry the news of your father's death to your brothers back on Skerry," Taggert said gently. "Adair is now Prince of Skai."

My throat went suddenly dry. "Of course," I said hoarsely. "Adair and Athelin must be told." I hadn't forgotten. It was just something I had no wish to think about.

Comyn smiled. "The weather will be perfect to take a courier ship back to Skerry with the morning tide," he said.

My parents and I had left Skerry in late autumn to

attend Taggert's investiture as Clan Laird of Broche
Rhuidh, First Laird of the Council of Clans, and all the
myriad other titles he laid claim to. We had planned to stay
less than a fortnight, but winter with its gales closed in
early, trapping us in Tyra. No sane ship's master would risk
taking a ship into the Cold Sea while the gales raged. And
while being forced to stay in Broche Rhuidh among kins-
men and friends was a far from unpleasant confinement, I
found I wanted nothing more than to go home again. Here
there was no comfort for me. In Skerry, Adair and Athelin
could help me.

"I believe I can safely take a courier ship from here to
Skerry and back," Comyn said.

Home . . . A chill rippled down my back. All the solid,
well-ordered, intricately fitted pieces of my life had come
apart, raining down around my head like broken stones.
Home in Skerry would never again be the same. Or mean
the same thing. Not without my parents.

Taggert had been sitting, one hand on the table, fingers
drumming a soft rhythm on the polished wood. "We've discussed this," he said quietly. "We want to offer you, your
brothers, and all your people sanctuary here in Tyra. We
can certainly use your talents and experience. And in
return, we can offer them all the protection of the Tyran
army."

"Bring all the yrSkai here?" I said, genuinely puzzled.
"But why? They wouldn't come before. What's different
now to persuade them to come? At least Skerry is Celae
soil, even if it's not Skai."

Kenzie pulled something from his pocket and set it on
the table. I recognized the amulet I had picked up in the
pavilion where one of the dead assassins had lain. It had
lost the last of its acid green glow and now looked a dull,
lifeless gray-green. Even the whorls and swirls carved into

it were gone. It looked like little more than a flat, roundish river rock with a hole in it. Any sorcery it had once contained was long gone.

"This," Kenzie said. "The Tell-Tale. We'd heard rumors that Hakkar had found at least one." His network of information gatherers was second to none on the Continent. I couldn't count the number of times I'd heard my father say Kenzie had a definite talent for taking bits and snippets of seemingly unrelated information and coming to surprisingly accurate conclusions. But he had trained under Red Kian — little wonder he succeeded so well. "Disturbing information it was, too. With luck, there's only one, and that's it." But he looked dubious. "You know there was a price of ten Maedun gold on your father's head ever since Hakkar's son was killed. The only reason nobody's managed to collect that reward is that they couldn't find Gareth."

"They found him yesterday," Taggert said quietly. "And we all know the outcome. We can't afford losses like that."

Kenzie flicked the dull green stone with a fingernail. "This was keyed to Gareth's magic. It would have led the Maedun to him wherever he was. It just so happened he was here in Tyra rather than on Skerry when the Tell-Tale led those two assassins to him."

"And you can't take the chance of Hakkar having another Tell-Tale," Kenzie said. "There simply aren't enough warriors on Skerry to defend the island properly. Here, we can offer you all the protection Taggert's army can give you."

"And given gladly, too," Taggert said grimly.

I turned to Kenzie, clutching at a straw of hope. "Can't you do something about that accursed stone? Is there some way to unkey it?"

He shook his head. "We don't know enough about it,"

he said. "We're not sure even now if it's stopped working."

I could think of nothing to say.

"We have no way of knowing if there's not another stone somewhere, perhaps keyed to Adair, or Athelin," he said. "Or you. That's a chance we can't afford to take—for the sake of the yrSkai on Skerry as well as for your sake and your brothers' sakes."

"You'd find out if there was another only when the next set of assassins showed up," Taggert said with grim humor. "Or a shipload of invading Somber Riders arrived in Skerryharbor. Not something any of us would like to see."

"What do you want of me?" I asked.

Taggert and Kenzie exchanged glances. "Go back to Skerry. Speak with your brothers. Tell them sanctuary is available here if they wish it."

I looked down at my hands, clasped together on the table before me. The knuckles were white. I made a conscious effort to loosen them. "I think I can answer for my brothers as well as myself," I said. "I'll put the question to them, but I think they'll both say they'd rather stay in Skerry." I glanced up, met Taggert's concerned eyes. "It's home."

He nodded. "I understand," he said quietly. "But please know you're most welcome here at any time. The offer is always open."

4

We had fair winds and good sailing all the way across the Cold Sea.
The storms that had torn at the coasts a fortnight earlier
had spent their fury and moved on. Comyn guided the little
courier ship across the hundred leagues of sea separating
Tyra from Skerry as easily and smoothly as a swan glided
across a still pond. I could do nothing but sit back and
admire him for a skill I'd never have.

Late on the morning of the third day, we sighted
Skerryharbor directly before the prow. Behind the harbor,
the towering peaks of Ben Warden, Ben Aislin, and Ben
Roth rose vivid white against the blue of the sky. The slant of
the sun across the shoulder of rugged Ben Roth made some
of the houses in the village seem curiously foreshortened.

Comyn brought the little ship smartly into the harbor
and gently up to the stone jetty just as the last of its momentum died away. It nudged against the short wooden pier
angling out from the jetty as softly as a woman caressing a
child's cheek. One of the sailors stepped onto the pier. He
carried a thick hawser slung across his shoulder and made
it fast to the stone bollard.

Snow still lay thick in the fields behind the houses set out
along the gentle curve of the harbor. Man-high drifts sat piled
against the stone fences separating the fields that climbed the
gradual slopes of Ben Warden. The tall turrets and crenellated battlements of Skerrykeep shone silvery gray in the
late-morning sun. Standing on an outthrusting shoulder of
the mountain and built of the living rock of the mountain
itself, Skerrykeep commanded an all-encompassing view of
the village, the harbor mouth, and the sea beyond. The stout,

ironbound oaken gates, usually flung wide to the bright sunshine, were closed tight, and men patrolled the crenellated
parapets.

Three riders left the courtyard and sped down the
track leading from the Keep to the harbor. Even from
where I stood on the narrow deck, I had no difficulty recognizing the tall, commanding figure of Athelin leading
them.

Nearly oblivious to the bustle around me as the sailors
secured the ship and made it fast to the pier, I stood watching Athelin, painfully aware of the ghastly news I bore, and
far too conscious of the weight of the parchment containing
Taggert's invitation to the people of Skerry, which I'd
tucked into the pouch at my belt. Comyn stepped past me
to the pier to speak with the Harbormaster. Unheeding, I
stood frozen in place for a moment. I put my hand again to
the pouch at my belt. The letter seemed to burn my fingers
through the tough leather of the pouch. But that was going
to be the easiest of my tasks.

Gods in the circle, how do I tell my brothers both our
parents are dead? Dead at the hands of Maedun assassins?
And that I could do nothing to prevent it?

The horsemen pulled their horses to a halt at the root of
the jetty. Athelin walked alone down the broad stone quay.
I took a deep breath and clambered ashore. Before I realized it, I was running toward him, calling his name.

He stopped and waited for me to reach him. I threw
myself at him, felt his arms close around me. Still saying his
name over and over, I pressed my cheek against the thick
wool of his cloak where it hung across his shoulder. He said
nothing, but he held me tightly enough to hinder my
breathing.

Something was wrong. The rhythm of his breathing
against my cheek was harsh, too quick. Alarmed, I drew

back and looked up at him. The skin of his face seemed too sharply and tightly drawn across his cheekbones, and he was too pale.

"What's wrong?" I asked. "Athelin? What's wrong?"

He stepped back and peered over my shoulder, then frowned. "Where are Mother and Father?"

I thought my tongue stuck to the roof of my mouth. I couldn't speak for a moment. All I could say was, "In Tyra." My voice sounded like a rusty hinge to my own ears.

He glanced at me quickly, startled. "Until spring?" he asked.

I shook my head, unable to reply.

Sudden understanding widened his eyes. What little color he had drained from his face. He cleared his throat. "What happened to them?"

"Assassins," I said, my voice breaking. "Assassins. They killed Father and Brynda, and Mother died when Father did. The bond breaking . . ."

He closed his eyes and swayed for a moment, then took a deep, resolute breath and steadied himself. "When?"

"Two days ago."

"Two days ago," he repeated flatly, more to himself than to me, shocked but not surprised. He closed his eyes again and nodded. "Aye, I feared it."

Then I knew. I had thought the fall of the light made the village houses look different. But it wasn't the light that changed them. They looked foreshortened because some of the thatched roofs were gone. Burned. And the closed and guarded gates to the Keep.

Raiders. Assassins.

"Here, too?" I asked, my heart twisting painfully in my chest.

"Aye. Here, too." Something moved in his eyes—pain, grief, anger. All three mayhaps.

I had no strength to ask the question. He answered anyway, and confirmed my fears.

"We lost over twenty men. Iowen, Huw is dead."

I bowed my head, eyes closed. Huw and I had grown up together. Mayhaps in time, we might have married. Losing his good humor and strength was another arrow in my heart.

"And Adair?" I asked through dry lips. "Mairi? And Liesa?" Mairi, Adair's new bride, was expecting their first child.

"Safe," he said. "Adair took a sword cut to his left shoulder, but it's just a minor wound."

"Dorlaine?" I asked, hardly daring to hope. But Athelin was alive. Dorlaine, his bheancoran as well as his wife, must surely live. Surely . . .

He nodded. "Well," he said. "And the children."

"Caennedd?"

"Safe. He was on Marddyn when the raiders came."

Relief left me limp and breathless. Caennedd was only twelve, our father's Beltane son by a Marddyn woman. He had come to live with us in the Keep two years ago when his mother died. "Oh, dear gods, Athelin . . ." I had to stop and wet my lips with a tongue that was almost as dry. "Does this mean that Hakkar and his Somber Riders have found us?"

He looked up, beyond me to the open reaches of the sea. "I hope not," he said. "None of the raiders left here alive. But we'll be more vigilant from now on. We've become complacent. They won't catch us napping again."

There is a tale told of Sheryn, wife to Prince Tiegan, who was spirited away from the Maedun by Brynda and Brennen all those years ago. When a man congratulated her on surviving, she looked at him calmly, and said, "I am Tyadda. We endure."

Adair, Athelin, and I inherited Tyadda blood from our mother. And like Sheryn, we endured. We buried our dead, we redoubled the watch on the shores of both Skerry and Marddyn, and we found places for our people to hide in the mountains at the first sign of another raid. Then we carried on with the business of living. Sadly, still in mourning, but we carried on. The men went out into the fields to plant, guarded by Skerry's best soldiers in their watchtowers. Shepherds brought the sheep heavy with their new lambs out of the pastures hidden in the tangle of burns and vales along the flanks of the mountains to ready them for lambing and shearing. Later the women would card and spin the wool. Adair decided that after a suitable period of mourning, he would take up the torc and coronet of the Prince of Skai. Sometime after Beltane, mayhaps.

It seemed I had little chance to dwell on my losses. Within a fortnight of my return, Adair sent me across the narrow strait to the island of Marddyn. We were a small community, the exiled yrSkai of Skerry and Marddyn, and each man and woman had several responsibilities. One of mine was teaching children to speak Tyadda, the first language of the Isle of Celi, and Saesnesi, the language of the men of the Summer Run. Since I had been in Tyra most of the winter, the children of Marddyn had been without a tutor since late autumn. They had a lot of catching up to do. But teaching children was something I enjoyed, and it kept my mind occupied well enough to give my spirit and my heart a chance to begin healing.

A busy season passed. Winter gradually segued into spring, and I hardly noticed it until one day I looked up and saw new leaves bursting out on the trees and green flooding the glens where sheep grazed, the new lambs looking like little dancing clouds on the hillside. Already, the catkins on the willows were yellow with pollen. Birdsong sounded sweetly from the willow thatch along the burn. The sun warmed the soil of gardens planted with herbs, flowers, and vegetables, and neat, precise rows of young plants sprouted almost overnight. In the orchards, the apple, plum, pear, and cherry trees burst into a riotous profusion of pink and white blossoms, filling the air with their heady scent, as the falling petals drifted like fragrant snow on the gentle breeze.

Our lookouts reported no sign of Maedun. We remained safe in our northern aerie.

The turning of the season brought with it an odd, shapeless sense of anticipation I couldn't identify. I felt charged with uneasy, unsettled energy, but had no clear outlet for it. Almost as if I were expecting something, but I had no idea what it might be. I practiced daily with Whisperer, but the strenuous exercise hardly took the biting edge off my restlessness.

By night, vague, fitful nightmares disturbed my sleep — dreams I could not remember upon waking. By day, a nervous agitation seized me so that I had difficulty concentrating. My thoughts kept turning to the south, to the high mountains of the Spine of Celi, and the lost lands of Skai and Wenydd that lay within their western shadows. It was a place I had never seen but something there called, and the demand was clear, imperative, unmistakable. Nearly irresistible.

Then, as suddenly as they had come, the troublesome symptoms vanished. The nightmares faded, the restless energy subsided. Whatever had called me from Skai stopped its urgent whispering. A serene calm settled over me, unlike anything I had experienced before, bathing me in quiet contentment.

Two days before Beltane Eve, I returned to Skerrykeep, still wrapped in that eerie but peaceful calm. The crossing was not a smooth one, and the little fishing boat leapt and twisted like a gaffed salmon the whole way. Sea and sky tried several times to change places. Only strenuous effort on the part of the ship's young master kept the little vessel right side up and more or less pointed in the right direction.

It was not the best crossing I'd ever had. I arrived back at Skerrykeep with a headache and an unsettled belly that threatened imminent rebellion, and the restless, undirected energy was back, as strong as ever, as if it had not abated at all with time.

I had planned to spend the evening quietly in my chambers with a cup of chalery leaf tea for my headache. The short crossing between Marddyn and Skerry had never before affected me this way. The new weakness irritated me and made me inclined to be short-tempered. Best, I thought sourly, not to inflict myself on the people gathered in the Great Hall until I recovered some of my good humor.

The sound of music and laughter came faintly to the upper corridor, invading my chambers in spite of my closed door. Pipes, flute, and bodhran skirled out a reel, then a gavotte to the accompaniment of cheers and shouts of laughter. The lively dance music faded to silence, and after a moment of expectant quiet, something else began. I sat up and listened carefully.

A harp. Surely I heard the sweet, clear strumming of a harp. There hadn't been a harp in the Great Hall since Malchai died two years ago. As surely as the Nail Star draws lodestone, the music drew me out of my chamber and into the corridor overlooking the Great Hall.

Below me, both hearths were lit to ward off the chill of the early-spring evening. It seemed as if half the village of Skerryharbor had gathered in the Great Hall. Adair and Mairi sat side by side on richly carved and cushioned chairs on a low dais near the north hearth, both of them smiling.

Mairi's belly was just beginning to swell with their child. Ever-vigilant, Liesa stood behind Adair's seat. Athelin and Dorlaine sat to their right. Dorlaine held three-year-old Danal on her lap. Five-year-old Gabhain sat on the floor, his head resting against Athelin's knee.

On the other side of the hearth, Rhan sat, red-faced and sweating, his great pipes held quiescent in his lap. Gaetan stood leaning against the stone of the fireplace, his flute tucked carefully against his chest, and Nemedd sat cross-legged on the floor at Rhan's feet, holding his bodhran loosely in his left hand. He held the doeskin padded beater in his right hand and moved it gently across the skin surface, tapping out a soft, slurring accompaniment to the man who sat on a stool directly before the hearth, a harp perched on his knee.

The harper was Tyadda, tall and slender, his dark gold hair falling to his shoulders, glinting with copper sparks from the firelight. I was too far away to see his eyes, but knew they would be golden brown. Fingers, long and tapered, plucked gently at the harp strings. A glittering shower of clear, precise notes sparkled through the Hall. He bent his head over the harp, the dancing notes defining first one snippet of tune, then another, while the people who had been dancing found seats and grew attentively quiet.

I watched him, fascinated. I thought for a moment the air around him fizzed gently, and sparks of light danced above him. My hand went out, reaching toward him of its own accord. I could almost feel the bright energy flaring around him, as if I had immersed my fingers into a bubbling mineral spring.

Finally, he looked up and smiled. Except for the chiming notes he drew from the silvery strings and the pop and crackle of the flames in the hearth, the Great Hall was stilled and silent, waiting.

He struck the harp and sent a swirling glissando of sound sweeping through the Hall. "I have a tale for you." His voice came as strong and clear as the notes from the harp, trained and powerful. He waited for a moment as a murmur of expectation fluttered through the Hall. When it was quiet again, he continued.

"This is the tale of Red Kian of Skai, and how he brought the fabled sword Kingmaker back to the land of Celi."

His voice held his audience mesmerized as he told of the ancient Maedun prophecy that an enchanter would arise from the house of Skai—an enchanter who would destroy the Maedun. I knew the story, of course. My family was entangled deeply within the threads and skeins of it. I had heard it uncounted times, but never grew tired of the telling. This bard told the tale better than any other I'd heard. His voice was by turns soft and light with humor, dramatic and bold with danger, and heavy with sorrow. He made the harp laugh and shout and cry along with his voice. He told how Kian had foiled the Maedun general, ancestor to Hakkar of Maedun who even now sat on his usurped throne in Celi as Lord Protector, and led him a merry chase all around the Continent. The general could not capture Kian, nor could he seize the great sword Kingmaker. I was not sure how many of the adventures and exploits the bard spun out were true, and how many were pure legend, but the story was a good one. The Tyadda harper finally brought the tale to a close with Kian placing the sword carefully on the altar stone at the Dance of Nemeara, there to await the hand of his son Tiernyn, who would be first High King of all Celi. With a slow, final arpeggio, he dropped his hand from the harp strings.

His audience paid him the nearly unprecedented compliment of absolute and stunned silence for nearly a minute after the music stilled. Then they erupted in cheers and clapping.

"Another," someone cried. Instantly a chorus arose, demanding more. The harper smiled, and gave them a lighthearted little ballad of a man who falls in love with a swan. It was as well received, but when he finished, someone called for the "Song of the Swords."

Another song I knew well. It held out the hope that Celi would once again be free of the accursed Maedun invaders—that a king and enchanter would arise to fulfill the Maedun's own prophecy and drive them back to the Continent, and destroy them utterly.

The harper struck a chord from his harp. "Then listen, and I will tell you," he said.

> *"Armorer to gods and kings,*
> *Wyfydd's magic hammer sings.*
> *Music in its ringing tone,*
> *Weaponry for kings alone.*
> *He who forged the sword of Brand,*
> *Myrddin blessed it to his hand.*
> *By iron, fire, wind, and word,*
> *Wyfydd crafts the mystic sword.*
> *Blades to fill a kingly need.*
> *Royal blood and royal breed.*
> *Wyfydd made and Myrddin blessed,*
> *Hilt and blade wrought for the best.*
> *He alone its mettle test.*
> *In but one hand each sword shall rest.*
>
> *Twin the swords that Wyfydd wrought.*
> *Cold iron fired to searing hot.*
> *Two swords both alike he made.*
> *Two split from a single blade.*

> *Made them for the king's own seed.*
> *Royal blood and royal breed . . ."*

I found myself sitting on the top step, elbows on knees, chin in hands, listening raptly as he sang the song. I knew it well enough to whisper the words along with him as he sang. His voice, clear and true and compelling, seemed to fill the Hall.

He sang the song as if he had been there to watch the events as they took place. His grief at the death of the king was as real as if he had held Tiernyn's dying body in his arms and raged at the loss of Celi's hope. His voice soared with the notes from the harp, painting a vivid picture of the swords, the forge from whose heart they had been wrought, and the men who were to carry them.

Dorlaine startled me as she stepped around me, carrying the sleeping Danal to the chamber where the boys' nurse waited. I hadn't seen her get up and make her way across the Hall to the stairway. I moved over quickly to let her pass, my attention still fully on the harper and his song. A moment later, Dorlaine came silently back down the corridor and sat beside me. The harper finished the song with a dramatic flourish.

> *"Where the seed that scattered far,*
> *Blown upon the winds of war?*
> *Hidden long by Myrddin's spell,*
> *Enchanted now 'til blood will tell.*
> *Royal spirit, royal need.*
> *Royal blood and royal seed*
> *Seeks to meet a kingly test.*
> *Rise it will to take the quest . . ."*

The final notes died away to silence. I shivered. Something clutched at my heart, making it difficult to breathe properly. I'd always loved music, but the "Song of the Swords" had never affected me like this before. I felt quivery, even excited, as if I were a child again awaiting a Winter Solstice gift.

The harper tucked his harp into its carry case and rose gracefully from his place by the hearth. He bowed and made his way to the outside door amid protests and shouts for more. He carried himself with an air of quiet assurance and command. He turned as he reached the door and laughed.

"There will be more after Beltane Eve," he said. "I promise. As long as Prince Adair does not tire of me and send me away."

Adair laughed. "Little chance of that, my lord Harper," he said. "You will join us for the Beltane celebration tomorrow evening, I hope?"

The harper bowed deeply. "I should be more than honored, my lord Prince."

He glanced up then. My breath caught painfully in my chest, startling me. It was as if he looked straight at me. Meeting his brown-gold eyes sent a jolt through me like an arrow point. Something flashed in those eyes, something I could not interpret but recognized as surely as I recognized the extraordinary talent with the harp he held in his hands. The expression was there for only a fraction of a moment, then it was gone. An instant later, so was he.

Still half stunned by the overwhelming impact of the meeting of gazes, I leaned toward Dorlaine. "Who is he?" I asked. "Where did he come from?"

"He came from Skai, he says," Dorlaine replied. "He walked most of the way. Bryant of Wenydd gave him shelter for a fortnight or two in Laurelwater while the worst of the storms blew. Then he brought a small boat from the

Veniani shore. He's been here less than a fortnight."

"That's an arduous journey."

"He seems none the worse for it. But Tyadda are stronger than they appear. He asked for Gareth and Lowra."

The painful hook of grief and pain snagged my breathing for a second. "Adair told him they were dead?"

"Yes." Her face reflected my own sorrow. "He seemed greatly saddened. I thought he might weep when he heard about their deaths. Athelin thought he might have met Gareth and Lowra when they were in Skai."

"He might have. He doesn't guest in the Keep?"

Dorlaine shook her head. "No. He has a room in the tavern in the village. I imagine Trenn is happy enough to have him and lets him earn his keep." She glanced at me, then grinned. "And he'll be at the Fire tomorrow night. I'm sure you can become better acquainted with him then."

I looked at her, aware I was blushing, but unable to do much about it. "He is rather intriguing," I said.

"Oh yes," Dorlaine said. She stood up and brushed off the back of her skirts. "Intriguing is definitely one word to describe him." She gave me a decidedly bawdy wink and fled lightly down the stairs to take her place again at Athelin's side.

I knew what Dorlaine was thinking, but I didn't think I was interested in the harper only as a partner for the Beltane celebrations. True, he was certainly handsome and mysterious — almost regal — enough to attract any woman's attention. But there was something about him. Something I couldn't quite define. Even watching him from the top of the staircase, I had sensed an aura of sorrow and loss and grief about him. Nothing definite. Mayhaps just in the slant of his head over his harp, or the curve of his shoulder. Nebulous and vague, like sea mist on a rainy morning. But there. I needed to know more about him.

5

I dreamed, knowing I was dreaming, conscious that I wore a body that was not my own, but in the dream was as familiar and known as the body I wore awake. It was dark—a chill, damp darkness that penetrated clear to the bone. I sensed rather than saw the damp rock walls crowding close around me. From beneath my feet, the scent of moist soil rose like heat from a brazier.

A cave. I was in a cave deep beneath a mountain. The full weight of the mountain above me pressed down ominously, but I did not know which way to turn to find my way out, back into the sunlight and warmth.

A chilling breeze, faint as a whisper, came from ahead. Either the exit lay that way, or the cave was open to the sky again farther into the long corridor. The faint, musical sound of water dripping into water came from somewhere nearby, but the multitude of echoes made it impossible to tell from which direction the sounds came. They were all around and everywhere.

The quiet, hissing scratch of a striking flint came from behind me. A soft light glowed as the torch flared. I saw a figure ahead, dressed in white, a brilliant red cloak thrown over his shoulder, clasped by a round, gold brooch emblazoned with the white falcon of Skai. He stood, motionless and waiting, in the narrow confines of the cave passageway. For a moment, I thought it was my brother Athelin. But then he moved, and I saw it was not he. Whoever it was, he was far too young. Someone else, then. But Tyadda, I thought vaguely. Definitely Tyadda.

He walked deeper into the cave. His shadow leapt and twisted ahead of him, flowing over the uneven floor of the cave, growing and shrinking, advancing and dwindling, with the movement of the torch behind me. I was between him and the torch, and I realized without surprise that I cast no shadow. The young man who reminded me so sharply of Athelin was alone in the cave with the blurred, indistinct figure carrying the torch.

The narrow passageway opened suddenly. I had a sense of the vastness of the cavern, but could see none of it. He stepped into the cavern and paused, waiting for the torchbearer.

The torchbearer did not move in front of him, but stopped at the mouth of the chamber and held the torch higher. The light from the torch illuminated tall, white, limestone pillars where water dripping over centuries had built them up from the ground to meet the stone icicles descending from the ceiling.

The torch flashed and flared brightly. As if each pillar were made of crystal gems, the light streaked from one to the other, glittering, leaping, growing, running like liquid fire from pillar to pillar, striking sparks of green and red and blue and violet. One pillar after the other caught and erupted into evanescent light until I thought we surely were trapped within a crystal that caught the sun and sent it sparking in shimmering rainbows of color and light to all corners of the immense gallery.

A table—almost an altar—carved of crystal or ice, stood alone beside a massive pillar, its shadow looming tall and dark against the glistening white of the limestone. Two tall, slender golden goblets stood on the altar, supporting between them a sword. The steel of the sword blade shone brightly in the scintillating light, and the translucent material of the hilt pulsed with living fire in amber, gold, and warm brown.

"Take up the sword," a voice commanded.

The young man walked confidently toward the altar, his shadow leaping to advance before him, climbing the pristine white of the limestone pillar with the shadow of the altar and the sword. He reached out, closed his hand about the hilt of the sword, and lifted it. On the gleaming pillar behind the altar, his shadow, so sharply defined it looked three-dimensional, raised the sword as he did, and I felt the perfect fit of the hilt in my own hand.

•   •   •

In the morning, the strange dream was little more than dis-
sipating wisps and fragments that I could hardly call back
to mind. All I could clearly remember was the young man
in the dream, and then only because he reminded me of
Athelin by the Tyadda coloring both of us had inherited
from our mother.

But the young man could have also been the harper. A
much younger harper. Again, though, only because of his
coloring. It was certainly untrue that all Tyadda looked
alike, but then, it *was* true that most of them had very similar coloring—the dark gold hair and the brown-gold eyes,
with the same golden tones in their skin. The coloration
tended to be inherited by Celae who have Tyadda blood.
But not always. Both of Athelin's sons, Gabhain and Danal,
had Dorlaine's black hair and deep, dark blue eyes. They
might have inherited them from her, or they might even
have taken them from my father. According to our mother,
in his youth his hair had been as black and glossy as
Dorlaine's, sending back iridescent blue glints into the sunlight like a raven's wing.

I wandered to the window of my small chamber. It
faced southwest, directly at the flank of Ben Warden
behind the Keep. But if I bent forward and looked sharply
to the right, I could just barely pick out the roof of the tavern where the harper guested. Why the impact of meeting
his eyes was so unnerving, I could not say. But it had been
more than strong enough, perhaps, to let him invade my
dreams. Except I could not understand why I would dream
of him as a much younger man. It was an odd twist in the
dream.

He had promised more music after Beltane. And he
had told Adair he would be honored to attend the Beltane
Fire.

I shivered and wrapped my arms around myself for warmth, even though the brazier behind me glowed red with its carefully stacked coals.

"Tonight, then," I murmured. "Tonight, my lord Harper, we shall see what happens." Then I had to smile. "If anything."

I stood quietly in my chamber and let Dorlaine adjust the folds of the traditional plain, white tunic around me. Mine was identical to the tunic Dorlaine wore, identical to those worn by every man and woman old enough to take part in the Celebration of Beltane.

Beltane Eve. The festival eve marking the turning of the season from early spring to late spring. A night filled with great power. The only night of the year when the Duality split into its male and female components to couple as man and woman and ensure a plentiful bounty from field and forest, sea and river. Children born of Beltane night were considered lucky and blessed, able to claim a goddess as mother and a god as father.

Tonight, all over Celi, great fires should have been lighted in oak groves on the flanks of mountains in the west, or on hillsides in the east, in tribute to the Duality. Tonight, all across the length and breadth of the isle, the air should have been full of the music of pipe and flute, harp and chime as the men and women of the island danced around the fires in the celebration of new life.

But no fires would be lighted in Celi this night. None except the ones lighted by the exiled yrSkai on Skerry and Marddyn, and one in Laurelwater, where the exiled yrWenydd had found refuge. Even in exile, we forgot neither the Duality nor the circle of the seven gods and goddesses, nor did we neglect the celebrations marking the hinges of the year. Of the four Fire Feasts of Imbolc,

Beltane, Lammas, and Samhain, Beltane was the most joy-fully celebrated, although Lammas came a riotous second.

I clasped my hands behind my back as Dorlaine fussed with the drape of the light woolen fabric. I wondered if an incarnation of the goddess on this night was supposed to feel as hollowed-out and trembling as I did.

A wispy fragment of my dream fluttered through my mind again. I could remember little of it. Only the cave and a sword. And a man who might have been Athelin but wasn't. Pensively, I wondered what it could mean. I tried to remember what the man in the dream had looked like. The mysterious harper of last night in the Great Hall? Perhaps, but again, much younger. The man in the dream had been not much more than a boy. Younger than I by a few years.

Impatiently, I stepped away from Dorlaine and her meticulous fussing. "Have done," I said more sharply than I intended. "It is enough!" Then, quickly, "I'm sorry, Dorlaine. You're only trying to help, and I'm acting like a maiden at her first Beltane."

Dorlaine let her hands fall to her sides and regarded me gravely. Her blue-black hair fell in an unbound tumble of waves and curls halfway down her back. In the torch-light, her eyes were blue as mountain lakes beneath an autumn sky. Childbearing had not thickened her waist. Although she didn't practice with the sword as often now as she had before the boys were born, she still moved as gracefully as a born swordswoman, or a dancer. Athelin adored her. She was more than just his bheancoran, his soul's companion. She held his heart and spirit in her hands, and in return, she gave him custody of hers. And because my brother loved Dorlaine so deeply, I loved her as if she were the sister I'd never had.

"You're definitely as jumpy as a maiden getting ready for her first Beltane. And I believe I know the reason for it."

She smiled at me, the corners of her mouth curving up in mischievous amusement. "Might it be the harper?"

I blushed again. My face felt hot as the iron of the brazier in the corner. Then I laughed. "I don't know," I admitted. "He's certainly handsome enough, isn't he?"

"Indeed. And a talent with his voice and harp to enslave all the seven gods and goddesses, let alone the daughter of a prince." She reached out and twitched one final fold into place on my tunic. "I have to get back to Athelin. I wish you the joy of the celebration with the harper, my dear kin-sister. May you spill no mead tonight." She kissed my cheek, then turned, still smiling, and hurried out.

I went to stand by the window. Twilight had deepened, and the deep blue of dusk crept over the eastern sky. On the slopes of Ben Warden, the last logs would now be laid on the firebed. The young priest and priestess chosen to lead the procession from the shrine would by now be readying themselves to start. Snatches of music drifted across the meadows as the pipers painstakingly tuned their instruments.

Not since my first Beltane had I felt like this. My stomach fluttered, and my heart refused to lie quietly in my breast. An odd and disturbing combination of apprehension, eager anticipation, and nervousness set my whole body to quivering. And over it lay an overwhelming sense of something important about to happen. Something momentous.

I turned away from the window and took a deep breath. Enough of this nonsense. I was a grown woman and—I glanced at the wall above my bed, where Whisperer hung in its scabbard—I carried a Rune Blade. Flitters and vapors were not something I entertained. If I told myself that often enough, I was bound to believe it. I took a deep breath and left the room.

Adair and Mairi, Liesa with them, had already left for the shrine. Athelin and Dorlaine waited for me at the head of the stairs. I thought Dorlaine might have told him about my silly jitters, and the cause for them, because he smiled at me with silent laughter glinting in his eyes—a teasing expression I knew only too well. But he said nothing. He merely held out his left arm to me, elbow crooked. I slipped my arm through his, glanced at Dorlaine, who held his right arm, and smiled as calmly as I could.

"Are we ready, then?" he asked mildly enough.

"I think so," I said, mustering all the dignity I could, which was pitifully little. From the twitch at the corner of Athelin's mouth, it wasn't enough to make a difference. I made a face at him, then laughed. He made it difficult to maintain an unpleasant mood.

He nodded. "Then we should go. They'll be waiting for us. It will be dark in a few minutes."

Even though I watched for the harper, I didn't see him in the throng of people making their way to the shrine. Nor did I catch sight of him in the thickly clustered mass of people by the shrine. But it would be easy to miss him in the press of the jostling, excited crowd of joyful celebrants.

Darkness closed around Skerry, and the first glimmer of stars appeared in the sky. A crescent of moon, only days past new, gleamed above Ben Warden's massive flanks. Relentlessly pursuing the moon as always, the Huntress Star flared brightly in its wake.

The air all but fizzed with the sense of anticipation, tangible as mist under the oaks. Even the curtains of ivy trailing from the twelve oak trees seemed to quiver with it. The eleven pipers had already taken their places at the foot of the path leading to the clearing higher up the mountain, waiting for the procession to begin. Adair and Mairi stood near the pipers, Liesa close behind him, surrounded by the

people of Skerry. Athelin and Dorlaine stood next to them.
On this night, there was no difference in rank among the
exiled yrSkai. At the Beltane Fire, a princess could offer
mead to a stableboy, or a kitchen girl to a prince.

Four people, two men and two women, came down the
steps from the door of the shrine. Each carried a decorated
and carved pole supporting one corner of a fluttering green
silk canopy. They stood waiting with barely contained glee
at the foot of the wide steps, laughing together as the pipers
made ready. Moments later, the young man and woman
chosen to represent the god and goddess ran lightly down
the steps, arm in arm, and took their place beneath the
embroidered green silk. The first skirl of the pipes sounded,
echoing off the flank of the mountain in the gloaming.
Torchbearers hurried to take their places to guide the god
and goddess to the glade in the oak grove. Rippling flags of
flame streamed back from the torches as the people of Skai
fell in behind the pipers. An excited murmur of laughter
shimmered and fizzed through the crowd as the procession
began to move. Still, I saw no sign of the harper. I joined
with the procession.

At the fire, I stood a little apart from the rest of the
women, watching the men on the other side of the firebed
and holding my goblet of mead carefully to prevent the
excited crowd from spilling it. Spilling mead on Beltane
Eve brought bad luck for the rest of the year, and I didn't
want that.

I searched carefully, trying to study each face in the
crowd of men across the firebed. Although there were
many men with the dark gold hair of the Tyadda, including
my brother Athelin, none of them was the harper as far as I
could tell. Frustrated, I turned away to watch the beginning of the celebration.

The god and goddess incarnate for this night threw

their torches into the pyre to begin the joyous rites of Beltane. A quick murmur of relief and approval rippled through the throng like the soft sound of water as the fire caught immediately and flared brightly into the night. It was an auspicious beginning when the wood took eagerly to the flame. I watched the cloud of sparks rise like a lost constellation of new stars into the sky, then looked around again. I found Adair, tall and straight among the men, the firelight glinting in his glossy, black hair. I caught the quick, flowing arrow of movement that marked where Athelin stood. But I saw nothing of the harper. Sharp disappointment curdled in my belly, and I shivered. Mayhaps he had not come after all, although not many choose to miss the celebrations.

The first drone of the pipes began, like the distant murmur of the sea. Overhead, the stars blazed like beacons in the dark vault of the sky. The crowd fell silent as the god and goddess came together by the fire in the first graceful, stylized steps of their dance.

The skirl of the pipes grew louder in the flickering dark. The god and goddess stepped lightly around each other, miming the chase. Darting first right, then left, first one pursuing, then the other, they whirled and leapt through light and shadow. Then, suddenly, both turned at the same time, caught the other in eager arms, and swirled together like fallen petals caught in an eddy of rippling water. Their bodies twisted and gyrated with the quickened beat of the music as the chase ended and the offering of each to the other began. Then, seizing each other by the hand, they fled lightly out of the firelit circle into the shelter of the oak grove. As they ran, the music cut off as abruptly as if it had been sliced with a sword blade.

As the young god and goddess disappeared, hand in hand, into the deep shadows beneath the oaks, the pipes began again, a soft, haunting, seductive refrain. Men and women swirled like leaves into the circle of flickering light cast by the flames. I stepped out with the rest of the women.

All around me, men and women danced, caught up in the exhilaration of the celebration. Shadows swayed and leapt as the flare and flash of the fire soared high into the clearing. Laughter rose to accompany the lilt of the music.

One of the young men of Adair's small army swirled up out of the crowd in front of me. He danced before me, his face bright with the excitement and elation of the night. I couldn't help responding with a smile.

I lifted my goblet to him. "A sip of mead, my lord?" I asked, still smiling.

If he was disappointed to be offered only a sip, he hid it well enough. He took the goblet from my hands. "Your gift brings me great pleasure, my lady," he said. He took a sip, then handed me the goblet. I was nearly as tall as he, and he didn't have to bend far to claim his kiss. He laughed and let himself be swept off into the swirl of the dance.

Then I saw him—the harper—tall and slender and graceful, dancing on the other side of the fire. He turned and looked at me. If I were ever to take a spear in the chest, I didn't think it would feel any more shocking or stupefying than the impact of meeting his gaze. The blood drained from my head, and I felt a little dizzy. For only an instant, I thought my knees would refuse to hold me up. He froze for a moment, still watching me, his eyes wide in the fire-shot darkness, and I thought he was as stricken as I was myself. Something changed in his face. In the flickering dark, I couldn't tell if it was fear, or expectation, or even relief.

Holding my goblet, I let the music take me, swaying and stepping in the rhythms that were as old as the Isle of Celi itself. The flow of the dancers around the fire swept me with it, just as it caught him up in its tide. I had no need to hurry. He knew just as surely as I that we were to be together on this night. The certainty vibrated in my chest, singing like a plucked harp string. With no conscious volition, or even any effort, we drifted inevitably, inexorably toward each other across the clearing.

The Swordmaster turned and nearly bumped into me. I laughed and stepped back, then offered my goblet.

"A sip of mead, my lord?" I asked.

He chuckled and took the goblet. "Your gift gives me great pleasure, my lady." He took only a small sip, then bent to claim the kiss that was his entitlement. He gave me back my goblet, still laughing, and an instant later, he was gone, whisked away by the ebb and flow of the dancers.

I bowed my head and danced in place, completely and utterly certain that the harper would let himself be swept along to where I waited. When I looked up, he stood there before me, one corner of his mouth lifted in a gentle, bemused half smile. I had not been able to tell his age in the Great Hall the night before. Tonight, in the leaping shadows and flicker and flash of the firelight, he was older than I had first thought. Not as old as my father was, but certainly not a youth anymore.

He was more slender than my brothers, without Adair's blocky strength or Athelin's powerfully muscled toughness. He did not look like a man accustomed to swordwork. But he had the slender, willowy strength that proclaimed stamina and durability. And more, he was nearly overwhelmingly attractive, with his enigmatic smile and his deeply shadowed eyes, laughter glimmering in the corners of his mouth.

He said nothing. He simply danced before me, looking down at me with that odd little lopsided smile on his face. A man couldn't ask for a woman's mead on this night, but he could certainly indicate his willingness to accept should she offer it. He left me no doubts as to his willingness. It was more than evident.

Suddenly breathless, I raised my goblet to offer it to him. "Mead, my lord?" My voice came out sounding rusty, as if I had not used it in far too long.

"Your gift gives me great pleasure, my lady." The timbre of his voice held all the promise of his music, even now. He took the cup from my hands, which I suddenly discovered were trembling. In one long draught, he drained the goblet, then threw it high into the air, neither of us heeding where it fell.

Silently, I held out my hands. He took them and bent— *How tall he is*, I thought, startled—and his mouth claimed mine. It still tasted sweetly of the honey-mead. Then, moving with the music, lost in it, we led each other through the stylized steps of seduction.

We ran hand in hand from the fire to the shelter of the oak grove, both of us laughing for no other reason than sheer excitement and joy and the wonder of being with each other. We nearly tripped over a couple twined together at the foot of an oak. He found a sheltered spot and turned to me.

I discovered that he was as skilled in his handling of a woman's body as he was with his harp. I opened to him like the unfolding petals of a dawn flower.

Never before had I been with a man the way that the harper and I came together that night. I lost track of where I ended and he began. I found I knew how he felt as easily as I knew how I felt. We were no longer two separate people, but a glorious and joyous merging of both bodies, both souls, both spirits. It startled and delighted both of us, and I lost myself in the wonder of the celebration.

When our hearts and breathing gradually returned to normal, he raised himself and looked down at me. His face was hidden by the shadow, but a stray reflection from the fire danced in his dark gold hair.

"I don't even know your name," he said. He drew me down, cradled my head in the hollow of his shoulder. His soft laugh rumbled in his chest beneath my ear.

"Iowen, my lord Harper," I said lightly.

He raised himself again, put his hand to my face and traced the line from my temple, down my cheek to my jaw. Then he said the words that he had no need to say, not on Beltane Eve when god lay with goddess in the oak grove. He said the words that would bind us together forever, and his voice was ragged and hoarse with need.

"Iowen, my soul lies cupped within the palm of your hand."

I closed my eyes for a moment, then drew in a great, shuddering breath, and gave him the only reply I could. "Your soul is sheltered safe within my heart and within my hands—" I broke off with a nervous laugh and stared up at him, wide-eyed. "Oh! I don't know your name, either."

He looked down at me gravely, his face half hidden in the shadows. He was no longer smiling. "My name is Davigan," he said softly. "Davigan ap Tiegan ap Tiernyn."

For a moment, I was certain that my heart would stop. I stared up at him, unable to move, hardly able to muster a coherent thought. When I tried to speak, my voice caught in my throat, nearly choking me. I tried again.

"My lord King," I whispered.

6

I lay under the oaks in the Beltane grove, staring up at the harper in disbelief and wonder. Davigan ap Tiegan ap Tiernyn, he styled himself. Grandson of the first and only crowned High King of all Celi. Now he himself was the uncrowned king.

I knew then what had happened to both of us when our eyes met across Adair's Great Hall the night before, what had happened when we found each other across the fire, and what had happened when we came together in the welcoming shadows of the oaks. A love bond, certainly. And just as certainly, not the first to happen this way, for hadn't Red Kian's parents met and come together in just this manner at a Beltane Fire? Lifetime love bonds blossomed at Beltane Fires—perhaps not all the time—but often enough so that they were idealized in bards' songs.

But what we felt, Davigan ap Tiegan ap Tiernyn and I, was more than just the spinning of bonds of the heart and body. We had felt the full impact of the abiding binding together of spirit and soul, the bond of prince and bheancoran. And I remembered in awe what Brynda had told me in a dream. No prince for me. But perhaps a king . . .

I had no words. A king . . . Brynda was right. And now here was Davigan—my king—with me. I was his soul's companion and guardian, and he was my soul's partner and the man whose life I was soul-sworn to protect.

He leaned over me, firelight and moonlight both glinting faintly in his dark gold hair. Deep pools of shadow hid his eyes, and I could not read the expression in them. But I had no need to see. I felt what he felt. It trembled along the newly formed and unbreakable bond between us, vibrating in my chest like music plucked on a lute string. Fear and triumph. Disbelief and joy. A sense of *completion*. After so long, after an interminable wait, just as both of us were about to give up hope, we had found each other.

An incredible miracle.

Tears I couldn't hold back welled up in my eyes and spilled over my lashes. I reached up to touch his face with tips of my fingers, to assure myself that he was real, that he was there, and I was not dreaming.

"My King," I whispered, using the Tyadda form that meant *my own*, belonging to me, as a woman might say *my husband* or *my lover*.

Slowly, he drew back and shook his head. "No," he said hoarsely. "No. Please, not your king. I'm not a king. I'm but a bard, a poor harper—"

"But you are King of all Celi—"

He put his hand gently over my mouth. "Hush," he said. "Don't let anyone hear you speak that word."

I lay quiet, still cradled against his chest. I could see nothing of his face but the edge of a cheekbone, limned in silver by the moon and the faint glimmer of his hair. I raised my hand again and drew my fingers down his temple, traced the line of his cheek and jaw. He really was here with me. I still could not believe it.

A cold chill of doubt ripped through my belly. How could he be Davigan ap Tiegan ap Tiernyn, who was only four years younger than Gareth, when he looked not more than ten years older than Athelin? Confusion held me frozen. I could not doubt our bond. No, the bond filled me as a sparkling wine filled a goblet, effervescent and scintillating, and a true and joyous wonder. Nor could I doubt the love bond that glowed warmly in my heart. But how could he be who he claimed to be? How could it be that he looked as if he had been plucked out of the world into a time apart for thirty years, into a place where age could not touch him?

Both bonds we shared dictated—demanded—that I trust him without reservation. And I did. On my soul, I did. But I began to shiver, half frightened, half bewildered, and disconcerted. He sensed it, of course, and I knew the moment he knew. It probably quivered along the bond between us, unmistakable and distinct as a note plucked by his fingers from a harp string. He got to his knees and handed me my discarded tunic.

"Is there somewhere we might talk without being overheard? he asked softly. "This"—he made a sardonic, sweeping gesture that included the whole of the oak grove—"is hardly private."

I had to smile. "Hardly, indeed," I agreed. There might be a dozen other couples within a dozen feet of where we lay. It was unlikely they would be interested in what Davigan and I said or did, being thoroughly preoccupied with their own celebrations, but I understood his not liking to take the chance. I pulled on my tunic and scrambled to my feet. "We can go to my chambers."

He stiffened for an instant. "It's hardly seemly—"

"For a betrothed couple to be together in the woman's chambers?" I laughed softly. "I don't know how things are in Skai these days, but it's not only seemly here on Skerry, it's almost expected."

"Betrothed," he said, bemused. "Aye, I suppose we are." He held out his hand, and I took it. "Then let us waste no further time, my lady love."

Hand in hand, we left the shelter of the deep shadows, mindful of other couples still twined together, murmuring and laughing softly. A hushed silence had descended on the

glade amid the oaks. Music no longer filled the air in counterpoint to the roar and crackle of the flames from the
Beltane Fire. The pipes were stilled, and the flute, and even
the bodhran. The fire had settled to a comfortable and comforting glow of bright embers, where only here and there
small tongues of flame danced across nearly consumed
birch logs.

By the time we reached the Keep, we were chilled
almost to the bone. Beltane Eve in Skerry could be a night
borrowed from either midsummer or midwinter, and
tonight was closer to the midwinter night than summer.

Not everyone at Skerrykeep attended the Beltane Fire.
As Davigan and I slipped into my room, a tall, spare figure
straightened from the hearth where a new fire crackled
cheerfully, and turned to greet us. Riada had been my
father's nurse when he was a child, and also been nurse to
all three of his children. She was thin as birch twigs, her
hair whiter than the ashes in the grove, but still carried herself straight and erect. She moved much slower, though,
her only concession to advanced age. Her knowing glance
flicked from me to Davigan and back again. A hint of a
smile twitched at the corners of her mouth.

She dropped a scant curtsy. "The braziers are lit in the
bedchamber, my lady," she said, her voice without inflec-
tion. "And this fire should be providing enough warmth in
only a few minutes. You and your betrothed should be
quite comfortable."

"Thank you, Riada," I said somewhat breathlessly,
holding tightly to Davigan's hand. There was no use asking
how she knew Davigan was my betrothed. She had been
known to read the flames as easily as I read a book or a letter.

Riada inclined her head and, with one swift, curious
glance at Davigan, left the room. The door closed softly

behind her. I turned to him. My curiosity and confusion must have shown plainly on my face, because he stepped forward, put his hands to my arms, and walked me backward to one of the chairs in front of the fire. I fell into the chair as if he had cut my hamstrings. He smiled wryly and took the chair opposite me, stretching his legs out toward the hearth.

"I came here looking for your father," he said. "And your mother. She was my foster sister, you know. My mother married her father when Daefyd and I were ten and Lowra was twelve."

"Yes," I said. "I know."

He gave me that crooked little smile again. "Yes, of course you would know. How very strange this is. I can't think of you as my niece."

"Well, I'm not really," I said carefully. "Not by blood, at any rate. Nor by growing up calling you as uncle, either."

"No," he agreed. He paused, watching the fire for a moment. "Did your father or mother ever tell you about how he saved my life? Not once, but three times?"

"Not really," I said. "He and my mother spoke very little of that time in Skai when they were burned by the black sorcerer's magic. They said very little about either you or Daefyd."

He put his hand to his own cheek, tracing the same line of temple, cheek, and jaw that I had traced in the oak grove. "And you wonder why I look so much younger than I should."

I nodded.

So he told me how he had been wounded and captured by Horbad son of Hakkar, and overwhelmed by the black sorcery. I hadn't known the whole of the story. Neither my father nor my mother spoke much about that episode except to recall how they had met when my father went to

Skai to bring back Brennen's sword, and a Healer because Brennen had been seriously wounded. He had, in the end, brought back both. The sword was Bane, which my brother Adair carried now. And as for the Healer my father set out to bring home, by the time he came back to Skerry, he himself was the Healer. But nowhere in the story did he mention that he had saved the life of Davigan ap Tiegan. He spoke of the tragic death of Davigan's older twin brother Daefyd, who died giving my parents a chance to escape from Horbad and his Somber Riders. He spoke of taking Davigan back to the Tyadda steading where his mother Sheryn took him to make him well again. But except for saying that he and my mother had fetched Davigan from Horbad's grasp, no mention was made of saving his life.

"Three times," Davigan said, staring into the fire and not at me. His thoughts were hundreds of leagues and nearly thirty years away. "Once when he carried me physically out of the posting station where Horbad was holding me prisoner, once when he Healed my wound and drove out the black enchantment that threatened to drown me . . ."

His voice trailed off, and he was quiet for a long moment. I sat quietly, not wanting to interrupt. Presently, he shook his head and continued.

"It was then, when he drove the black sorcery out of me, that he and your mother were burned by the two warring magics." He looked up at me, the expression in his eyes contemplative and far off, as if he watched something long ago. "I didn't know," he said. "I didn't know until much later. My mother finally told me."

"What was the third time?" I asked, almost afraid to speak and break the mood.

"The third time . . ." Again, he paused. He tented his fingers beneath his chin and stared into the fire. "The sorcery had driven me far back into my own mind," he said. "I had gone away. Do you understand what I'm talking about?"

I nodded. I'd seen it twice. Both times after soul-wounds just too heavy to bear, two people I had known had simply curled up as if they were still infants in the womb, and left their bodies while their spirits wandered free somewhere else—somewhere that pain was not even a memory. They never came back, and eventually, the bodies died because there was no spark in them to keep them alive.

"Your father followed me into the far place I'd gone to," he said, still watching the fire. "Followed me and retrieved the little bit of me still remaining." His tone lowered almost to a whisper. "My first memory is of seeing my mother standing over me, something cupped in her hands. It looked like an opal, but it was as big as a plover's egg. Light and color swirled in it. I remember thinking how beautiful it was. She put it down on my chest, and it just vaporized. Smoke and mist came from it, and it sank right down into my chest. Most of the mist went with it. Some of it I breathed back into myself."

"Your stolen spirit?" I asked softly.

He nodded. "What was left of it," he said. "The part Gareth had brought back. When I breathed it back into myself, I awoke. And from then on, my mother and the other Healers from the shrine worked with me to put me back together again into the man I'd been before Horbad nearly smothered me with the sorcery." He smiled wryly. "They pieced me back together the same way you'd repair a broken bowl. If you do it very well indeed, the cracks hardly show."

"I see no cracks when I look at you," I said gravely. "Your spirit is whole and complete."

"Perhaps it is now," he said. "My mother and the

Healers worked very hard. It took a long time. More than twenty-five years. The first thing to come back was my music." He glanced at me and smiled. "I wonder sometimes if the youth that was stolen from Gareth came to me. Or perhaps when the soul's wandering and only comes back one small piece at a time, the years cannot touch the body. At any rate, my mother judged me completely cured just after Winter Solstice. And the first thing I needed to do was to come here and thank your father." He reached across the space that separated us and took my hand. "But, I discovered him gone." His eyes clouded momentarily, then cleared. "And found you, my soul's companion, instead."

I took a deep, unsteady breath. "Then you've come to Skerry to raise an army to free Skai?"

He looked at me, something I couldn't quite read stirring in his eyes. The bond between us quivered with an emotion I didn't recognize. It might have been sorrow; it might even have been shame. But he had nothing to be ashamed of. Nothing!

"Iowen," he said carefully, "I told you the truth back there in the oak grove. I am no king."

"But you are! You're Tiernyn's grandson. His only heir!"

He spread his hands. Even by the fire's soft glow, the calluses on the ends of his fingers were plainly evident, worn there by constant pressure of the harp strings.

"I'm a bard," he said. "All I ever wanted to be was a bard. I was raised amid music, and it runs in my soul and in my spirit and in my body." He laughed softly, sardonically. "I'm not even half the swordsman that Daefyd was. I was raised by Tyadda, Iowen. We're a peaceful people. We have no swordmasters, no weaponsmasters. My brother Daefyd, who was raised to be a king, learned all he knew of swordsmanship from some Celae soldiers who had sheltered with us when the Maedun invaded. Most of them died when Daefyd attempted to lead them against the Somber Riders. I learned very little swordwork. Hardly any before I met your father, and not much as my mother and her Healers were trying to put me back together." Again that sardonic, self-deprecating smile. "What soldier is going to follow a man who's just as likely to slice his own foot off as damage an enemy every time he draws his sword?"

"But you *are* king, Davigan," I said. "And we've bonded. I'm your bheancoran, and because of that, you needn't be a spectacular swordsman. That's why I'll be at your left shoulder." I took a deep, unsteady breath. "We'll have to tell Adair and Athelin. They'll help you gather an army—"

He got to his feet and drew me up with him. "No, Iowen," he said quietly. "I acknowledge the bond between us. Both as bheancoran and prince, and the love bond. But we'll not tell your brothers who I am. There aren't enough men here on Skerry to oppose Hakkar in Skai. I'll not lead men to their deaths or worse, as Daefyd did."

"But—"

"Remember the 'Song of the Swords'?" he asked.

I nodded.

"The king to come will need an enchanter with him. Daefyd was my twin, but he wasn't a warrior king, nor was I ever even close to being an enchanter. I'm not king. Perhaps one day I may sire a king, but I'm not king."

I had no words. I thought I understood why he wished to remain anonymous. It was no shame to be a bard rather than a warrior. But he was right when he said that there were not enough men on Skerry or Marddyn to form an army strong enough to wrest Skai from Hakkar, especially without an enchanter to battle the black sorcery.

He touched my cheek. "Will you be content to be wife

to a simple bard?" he asked.

"A bard, perhaps," I said. "But certainly not a simple one." I put my hand over his. "If that's what you wish, Davigan."

"I do wish it."

"My mother and father would have known who you are."

"They would certainly have kept my secret had I asked them."

"I truly believe, though, that we owe it to Adair as Prince of Skai to tell him who you are."

"Adair first, then your brother Athelin, then all of Skerry and Marddyn?" he said. "No, Iowen. My way is better. When there's need, they'll know. But not until then."

7

I dreamed again of the cave. The damp, spicy scent of earth and rock
and water rose and swirled around me like mist as I followed the
young man in the scarlet cloak through the fire-shot darkness. His
shape wavered in the dim flicker of the torchlight. He looked first like
Athelin, then like Davigan, then changed to someone I did not know.
Watching his blurring and changing figure made me dizzy.

Instead of making his way deeper into the cave toward the
chamber where the sword lay waiting for him, the young man
stopped and turned to me. He made a beckoning gesture with one
hand, and his lips moved as if he spoke. But I heard nothing. An
expression of frustration and pain crossed his face, then his outline
shimmered and faded. In moments, it had vanished, and I stood
alone in the chill, damp darkness of the cave.

I sat up in the bed, my breath coming too fast, my heart pounding in the silence. Moonlight streamed through the open casement
window, falling across the bed in a stream of liquid silver. Davigan
lay beside me in the feather bed, his head at the very edge of his pillow. The light flowing across his face limned his features in silver,
making him appear as if he were carved out of precious metal.

I threw back the eiderdown coverlet and got out of bed, careful
not to waken him. The moonlight drew me to the window. I knelt on
the window seat and rested my elbows on the sill, chin on my hands,
as I looked out over the harbor. Silver and black shimmered on the
water of the harbor, bisected by the hard line of the jetty. The light
turned the ship that lay made fast to the short pier thrusting out
from the jetty into the ethereal idea of a ship rather than solid wood
and rope and canvas sail.

Davigan made a soft sound in his sleep, and I turned, a smile
starting on my lips. He lay as I had left him, but my side of the bed

was not empty as it should have been. Someone lay there, the eider-down pulled up over her shoulders to her ears.

I staggered to my feet, a cry of alarm caught in my throat. I took an unsteady step toward the bed, then froze in shock.

The woman who lay next to Davigan was me.

My hand went to my mouth, and I fell back against the window seat. How could this be? I took a deep breath to steady my wildly beating heart. Dreaming. Of course. I had to be dreaming. Still. Or again.

Something moved in the shadows beside the bed. Carefully, I got to my feet and crept toward the bed. The moonlight flared like a torch, the sudden light illuminating an ornately carved cradle. Startled, I dropped to my knees beside the cradle and hesitated for a long time before peering into it.

An infant—a boy—with a fuzz of hair that looked silver-white in the moonlight gazed up at me solemnly, his eyes shadowed and dark. I stared at him in awe for a moment, then looked back to the bed. The woman was definitely me. And Davigan had not changed.

Dreaming. Of course I was dreaming. I looked again at the cradle. Beside it, the shadows gave a nebulous definition to a second cradle, and within it, another child slept quietly, as if waiting.

Two children? I smiled and hesitantly reached out to the first child.

Davigan rose from the bed to stand beside me where I knelt between the two cradles. I raised my head to watch him. He looked down at first one child, then the other. Slowly, he went to his knees and put out a hand to the first child. The infant seized one of his fingers and held on with the incredible strength of the newborn. I watched Davigan's face as awe and delight lit his features from within as brightly as the moonlight streaming through the window.

When I looked back at the cradles, they were gone.

I awoke in the dark, moonlight still streaming across the bed. Beside me, Davigan slept on, undisturbed. Slowly, carefully, I put my hand to my belly. I could feel nothing there but flat, hard muscle and smooth skin. But his seed had taken root. At Imbolc, I would present him with a son—two sons. Children of Beltane, blessed and lucky throughout their lives.

The young man in the dream of the cave ... I nearly laughed aloud as the solution to the puzzle of his identity came to me. Of course. How simple. He resembled both Athelin and Davigan because he was blood of both. Nephew to the one and son to the other. I had dreamed of my son, my son and Davigan's.

Still smiling, I lay back against the pillow, my hand against my belly. In the morning, I would tell him.

But he was awake. I turned my head to see him smiling at me. He drew me into his arms.

"Tell me now," he said.

Davigan stood by the window, his back to the room and to me, as if something outside held his rapt attention. I came forward to stand beside his shoulder. Cold rain slanted down from the heavy overcast. The water of the harbor reflected the pewter tones of the sky, shimmering in shades of white and silver and gray-green as cold streamers of nearly horizontal rain moved across it. On the far side of the harbor, little fishing boats lay snugged against the line of short, wooden piers, bobbing and dipping in the wind like dancers bowing to each other. The fishers found occupation indoors on days like this, mending nets or repairing small articles of gear out of the damp chill of the wind and rain. Beyond the breakwater at the mouth of the harbor, foam-capped break-ers dashed themselves against the rocks, sending geysers of spume-laden water high into the air.

In the wan light filtering through the uneven, pebbly glass, he looked older than he had while he slept. Pensive deliberation carved deep lines into his face, lines that ran from the sides of his nose down to bracket his mouth. He appeared mayhaps closer to his actual age in the pallid wash of gray light.

Sensing the turmoil churning through his chest, I merely stood quietly and waited. I could not doubt him, or his reaction to my news. Not with the bond so vividly present between us. But even the bond could not tell me his thoughts as he gazed reflectively across the stormy harbor.

Finally, as if he had come to a decision, Davigan smiled without looking at me. The smile lifted the corners of his mouth and turned him back into the young harper I had first seen in Adair's Great Hall.

"A son," he said quietly. "My son."

I put my hand to my belly and nodded.

"You're certain?"

Again I nodded. "I saw a son in a cradle beside the bed." I laughed. "Mayhaps even two of them."

"I had not thought —" He broke off, still smiling and shook his head. "My son?"

I laughed. "Who else's son would I dream of?"

"And mayhaps two of them . . ."

"Mayhaps. One was little more than a shadow, though — in the dream, that is."

"Aye, well, I was born a twin, as was my grandfather," he said. "It might well be that we would have twin sons." He turned to me, an odd, listening expression on his face. "I had given up all hope of ever finding a bheancoran before I came here," he said. "And I had almost given up the hope of ever having children of my own. I thought Tiernyn's line might end with me." He reached out to take my hand. "And then I came here and found you, and you tell me that we're to have a son. Truly, the Duality and all the seven gods and goddesses have smiled on me this Beltane."

"He'll be born close to Imbolc," I said. "A Beltane child, Davigan. Lucky and blessed all his life."

He laughed. "Aye," he said. "Able to claim a goddess as a mother and a god as a father. Fitting for a child formed by the mixing of our bloods, I think." That odd, abstracted expression came over his face again, and he looked out the window, lost in thought.

"Davigan?" I asked.

After a long moment, he turned to me. He took both of my hands in his and held them against his chest, trapped there against the fabric of his tunic like two small birds. "This is the opportunity I've been praying for," he said, his voice quiet but firm. "Finally, I can do something for Celi." He laughed almost breathlessly. "Our son will be a fitting king, Iowen. He'll be trained here among the yrSkai as Tiernyn was. Trained by Adair's weaponsmasters, taught by the best tutors available. He'll learn history and tactics and strategy—all the things I didn't learn because there was no one to teach them to me. He'll be raised to be king as I never was. As even Daefyd never was. And I know what I must do for him."

"You're his father," I said, smiling. Beneath my hands, his heart beat strongly, a light, fast rhythm against my palms. In excitement, I thought. Or eager anticipation. "What more does the child need from you?"

A woman's scream shattered the early-morning stillness of the Keep, harsh and tearing, as if it rasped her throat raw and bloody, ripping itself from her. It died so suddenly, so abruptly, it left an echoing, ringing silence behind.

I don't remember snatching up Whisperer, but I held it clutched in both hands as I burst out of my chamber into the corridor. Davigan was right behind me, his Tyadda long dagger in his hand. Adair went past us as swiftly as an arrow from a war bow, Liesa as close beside him as his shadow. I had only a glimpse of his face as he swept past me—pale, furious, intense.

Athelin appeared in the doorway of his chambers, Dorlaine behind him, the boys crowded up against her skirts, eyes wide. He frantically motioned them back into the room.

"That was Mairi," Dorlaine said breathlessly. She had recognized the voice when I had thought the scream hardly human.

"Get back in there," he cried. "Get back, and don't come out until I come for you."

She started to protest, but subsided quickly as Danal, the youngest, tried to dart past her into the corridor. She seized him around the middle, swung him back, then shooed Gabhain ahead of her back into the room.

"Bard, stay with them," Athelin said, his tone brooking no argument. "Iowen, come with me."

Davigan glanced quickly at me. I hesitated less than a heartbeat. If Athelin could trust Davigan to guard his wife and children, I could trust his bheancoran to guard my husband. Davigan took Gabhain's hand and led the child into the chamber, closing the door firmly behind him.

The Great Hall seemed full of a seething, churning mass of men as Athelin and I hurtled down the staircase. For a moment, I thought the soldiers of the Keep were fighting among themselves. Then I saw the tar black hair of some of them.

Cold fear clutched at my heart. This was Broche Rhuidh all over again. Maedun assassins dressed as Celae had come like wraiths out of the early-spring mist to fall upon us like weasels on a clutch of eggs. But there was no time to wonder why they had come to the island, or how they had made their way across the Skerryrace from the mainland.

"They're Maedun," I shouted. "Assassins—"

Athelin threw me one incredulous glance, then waded into the middle of the fighting, sword swinging.

Across the room, Adair staggered away from a Maedun, blood pouring from a gaping wound in his throat. Liesa surged forward, screaming incoherently, her sword slicing a deadly arc through the air. It caught the assassin just above the hip and nearly clove his body in two.

"Iowen! Your back!" Athelin's voice rose clear and sharp above the tumult and confusion.

I spun about, ducked quickly under an assassin's sweeping black blade. A moment later, I was back-to-back with Athelin in the middle of the Great Hall. I was only subliminally aware of his presence as he swept his sword into the mass of disguised Maedun surrounding us. I felt the blade of my own sword bite into flesh and bone, then dodged to one side as another Maedun leapt at me from my left. The blade of the black sword in his hand whistled as he swung it, gleaming dully in the dim light. I swept my sword backhand. The blade caught on the shoulder of the black sword, just below the crosspiece of the hilt. The shock of the impact shivered all the way up my arm to my shoulder. The black sword spun out of the assassin's hand. He staggered sideways, and Athelin ran him through.

Two of the assassins broke away, heading for the stairs. Dorlaine appeared at the head of the stairway, her sword in her hands. One of the Maedun paused momentarily and the glittering flash of a thrown blade sliced the air. Dorlaine staggered, then fell, her sword clattering on the stone as it fell from her hand and she slid bonelessly down the stairs. The assassins leapt over her without breaking stride.

Instinctively, I flew toward the stairs. The children were up there. And Davigan.

I took the stairs two and three at a time, Whisperer clutched tight in my hands. My foot slipped in a puddle of Dorlaine's blood, and I nearly fell. I scrabbled for purchase on the slick tread of the stair, losing precious time. I could spare no more than a swift glance and a brief pang of remorse and grief for Dorlaine. The assassins had already gained too much distance on me.

I gained the top of the stairway to see one of the Maedun kick open the door to Athelin's chambers. The door opened. Davigan burst out, his Tyadda long dagger flashing as he ducked away from the black Maedun blade and thrust the dagger deep into the assassin's belly. His momentum carried him past the crumpling body, out into the corridor, off-balance. The second assassin raised his sword.

I flung myself forward, using Whisperer like a lance. The point sliced into the Maedun's back just below his ribs. I wrenched it sideways, tearing out his spine. He fell in a heap at Davigan's feet.

A stone amulet on a leather thong spilled out of the man's shirt. Bright, stinging, actinic green, glowing with a monstrous and malevolent sheen. Even as I watched, it sparked as Davigan's foot brushed against it.

A Tell-Tale. Kenzie's nightmare come true.

Keyed to Davigan's bard magic? His music magic?

Whisperer's voice shrieked in my head, harsh and discordant. Howling in savage fury. The blade glowed searing blue-white as I lifted it and brought it down on the loathsome amulet.

A blinding, silent explosion of light smothered the corridor. It felt as if a storm had broken in the corridor. Wind howled, stinging pellets of hail or stone lashed my face. For a moment, I couldn't see, couldn't breathe, couldn't hear, couldn't move. Gradually, slowly, my vision cleared, and the fury of the storm abated.

I looked down. The amulet had broken in two. Even as I watched, the green glare subsided, the dizzily carved swirls faded. It became just another ordinary-looking gray-green river stone.

Whisperer quivered in my stinging hands, its voice in my head sharp and painful. A warning.

8

I knelt by the window in my bedchamber and looked out over the broad curve of the harbor. Too numb to think, I let my mind drift and watched the bleak play of light and shadow on the windswept sea as patterns of drifting rain dappled the pewter-colored water under the low-hanging clouds. It almost seemed that the sky wept with us, sharing our loss. If the sky still had tears, I had not. My eyes were dry and burning as I watched the rain.

Skerrykeep would be in mourning for seasons yet to come for those whose days had been counted and totaled by the Counter at the Scroll. Half of my family were dead. First my father and mother in Tyra. Now my brother Adair. His wife Mairi and their unborn child. Liesa, Adair's bheancoran, who had died still huddled protectively over his body.

But Dorlaine lived. We had been spared that grief, at least. The dagger thrown by the assassin had turned awkwardly in the air, and the heavy brass hilt had struck her forehead, stunning her and opening her scalp so that she bled heavily. But it had not killed her. So while Athelin mourned the loss of our brother and our kin-sister, he did not have to grieve for his wife and bheancoran.

Would Athelin and Dorlaine be next?

Or would it be Davigan, the man I was sworn to protect with my life? The father of my child?

On the cushioned bench of the window seat beside me Whisperer lay wrapped in a silken shawl. Its song still growled and buzzed in my head. It hurt. And somehow, it kept turning my thoughts back to that Tell-Tale. A nasty

piece of goods, that. And thoroughly shocking. If it had
sparked savagely when it touched Davigan's boot, touching Whisperer's blade had caused it to explode literally into
a blinding bright mist of fragments. Almost as if the stone
and the sword had some sort of affinity.

Odd. Whisperer was in Tyra when the assassins came
there after my father. And it was here when the assassins
came. What if it were the sword itself—

A piercing lance of pain shot through my head again,
fragmenting my thoughts as efficiently as Whisperer had
fragmented the Tell-Tale. I closed my eyes and massaged
my temples with my fingers.

Whisperer wasn't here when the assassins came the first
time. It couldn't be Whisperer the stones were keyed to.

The headache had almost faded away when Davigan
came into the chamber, waking slowly and stiffly. He
closed the door gently behind himself and stood there for a
moment, watching me. Grief and sorrow lined his face. No
illusion of youth was left there. Every one of his years
weighed heavily on him.

I turned away from the window, sat on the cushioned
bench, watching him. Something stirred in his troubled
golden brown eyes, but I couldn't quite interpret it.

"Where were you?" I asked.

He paused before answering. "Helping with the
wounded," he said. "So many of them . . . "

I said nothing. Merely waited.

"We know where the assassins came ashore. They
killed a fisherman and his family in a small cove where the
lookouts in the towers couldn't see them. The rain helped.
Then it seems they came straight here."

"Guided by the Tell-Tale," I said.

"Yes. Guided by the Tell-Tale that was keyed to me."
Pain twisted his mouth. "Because of me, so many died."

"We don't know the Tell-Tale was keyed to you," I said quickly—almost desperately. "It could have been keyed to anyone here."

The corners of his mouth quirked in black, sardonic amusement. "Of course," he said heavily. "Which is why it sparked when my foot touched it but lay inert until then."

"Davigan—"

He crossed the room and sat on the bench beside me. He picked up my hand and held it gently in both of his, as if he cradled a small bird. "I shall have to leave here," he said softly. He raised one hand and put a finger to my lips as I started to protest. "No, listen to me first."

I made an effort to quell my response and just nodded instead.

"I can't stay here," he said. "How can I stay and endanger every man, woman, and child on this island? I must go back to Skai. At least I'll be able to lose myself in the mountains there."

"And mayhaps the magic won't penetrate the magic hiding the Tyadda steading?"

"I don't know. I don't think I can afford to take that chance."

"Of course," I said. "How soon would we leave?"

"As soon as possible. Today."

My breath caught in my throat, and my heart made a startled leap in my chest. "Today? But—" Then I nodded. "I'll see about packing the things we'll need."

He shook his head. "No," he said.

A cold hook of apprehension caught at my heart. "What do you mean, no?" I demanded.

"I meant you can't come with me," he said. "I'm leaving here alone."

I tore my hand out of his grip and leapt to my feet, shock, surprise, and fear combining into a blaze of fury.

"You're *what*?"

He got to his feet. He tried to put his hands on my shoulders, but I twisted away. When he lifted his hand to reach out to me again, I slapped it away.

"You're not leaving me here alone," I cried fiercely. "You will *not* leave here without me."

He stepped forward, seized my wrists in his hands. He was stronger than he looked. I could not wrest my hands away from his.

"Listen to me, beloved," he said quietly. "I can't take you with me. I can't. How can I take you from here where you'll be safe and put you into mortal danger? What if Hakkar has another Tell-Tale keyed to me?"

"What if he has a hundred?" I shouted. Trying to pull away from his iron grip resulted only in making my wrists sore. "I won't stay here without you."

"I can't risk you, Iowen," he said. Anguish twisted his face. "I can't risk you or my unborn child. What if Hakkar finds me? He'd try to kill me, and you, too." He shook me gently. I looked up, deep into the troubled depths of his eyes, saw the pain there, the anguish, the misery that leaving would cause him. "Try to understand. All those years, I had nothing. I thought Tiernyn's line would end with me. Now I have you, and we have a child. I can't put you in danger. I can't take a chance with the child's life. He's our future . . ."

I took a deep breath to calm myself. "You don't understand, Davigan," I said gently. "I'm your bheancoran."

He said nothing. But his eyes narrowed, and he frowned, then let go of my wrists.

I closed my eyes briefly, marshaling my thoughts. I had to make him understand. "My mother—Lowra was bheancoran to my father. She died when he did with no wound on her. And Liesa, Adair's bheancoran. She took two minor

wounds, but she's dead, too. Again, she died when he did."
Again, something stirred in his eyes. Alarm, mayhaps, as he
began to understand what I was trying to explain.

"I'm your bheancoran, Davigan. How long do you
think I'd survive if something happened to you? And do
you honestly believe that it would make any difference if
you were in Skai, and I was here in Skerry?"

He started to say something, changed his mind, and
closed his mouth. He tried again. "But Brynda survived
Tiegan's death."

I nodded. "Yes, she did. But only because he had made
her swear a vow to take your mother safely back to her people at the steading. And after, she went with Kenzie
because she loved him. But the pain of the broken bond
tore at her heart every day of her life."

"She told you?"

"She didn't have to. I'm bheancoran. I saw it in her."

"But I can't stay here."

I thought of Tell-Tales, then of swords—Rune Blades.
A sudden, blinding stab of pain went through my head. It
was gone almost as quickly as it came, but it left me breathless for a moment. And it left me with the conviction that
Davigan was right. He couldn't stay here. And neither
could I.

"We'll go," I said. "I'm going with you."

"No, Iowen. You certainly can't go haring around
across seas and through mountains in your condition."

"My condition? What in the name of all piety is wrong
with my *condition*?"

"You're going to have a child—"

I stepped away from him and glared. "Yes," I said. "I'm
going to have a child. I'm not ill. I'm not wounded. I'm not
incapacitated in any way." My eyes narrowed. "Are you
going to say I can't accompany you?" My voice hardened.

"I'm your bheancoran, Davigan ap Tiegan. I go where you go, and that's flat."

"But the child—"

A curl of anger flickered in my belly. He must have felt it as strongly as I along the bond, because he took a step back from me, his eyes widening. "The child will be well," I said. "I'll make sure of that."

"But you can't—"

"I can't what? Ride? Walk?" I put my fists on my hips and glared at him. "Nonsense. May I remind you that your own mother went running all across the length of Celi while carrying you and your brother," I said. "Up mountains and down, and even falling into a river or two. You look quite healthy to me, Davigan ap Tiegan, and your mother is still as strong and active as ever."

"Iowen, no. I can't let you—"

I stiffened. "You can't *what*? *Let* me?" I made no effort to suppress the fury that sparked in my voice. "No man tells a bheancoran of Skai what she may or may not do. Not even the prince with whom she's bonded. I go with you, or you don't go. It's as simple as that, Davigan."

He glared back at me, his own anger flaring in his eye. "You are as stubborn as a rock," he cried.

"No doubt, and so was my whole family back to Red Kian and the lady Kerridwen," I snapped. "I come by it honestly. But you're just as stubborn."

"Aye, well, I can trace my own stubbornness back to Red Kian and the lady Kerridwen, too, so what else would you expect?" One corner of his mouth twitched. He tried to stop it but failed. "I see," he said. "You also have Gareth's stubbornness and Brennen's, too, in your blood. I might as well try to win an argument with an oak tree."

"I come with you, then?"

"Aye. Of course you do."

"We must tell Athelin who you are before we go. So he'll know why we're going."

He hesitated. "I'd rather not," he said quietly.

"But—"

"We can tell them when we get back."

I took a deep breath, then nodded. "Very well."

"There's something I can do in Skai," he said. "I won't just be running away from here. You asked me what more a child could ask of me, besides that I be a father to him."

I looked up at him. His eyes were focused beyond me somewhere. A faint smile curved up the corners of his mouth.

"What is that?" I asked. "What more would a child need from you?"

"A sword," he said softly. "I have no sword to pass on to him. But I think I know how to obtain his sword for him."

I looked up at him in surprise. "His sword?"

"Aye," he said. "His sword. Your father went to Skai looking for his father's lost sword. I shall go to Skai to remove the danger from Skerry, and also to seek my son's sword. The lost sword of Donaugh the Enchanter. Heartfire."

Heartfire. Soulshadow. More Rune Blades. My mouth went suddenly dry.

"The 'Song of the Swords' says he will need the sword," he said. "We shall go to Skai and find it for him."

Athelin gripped the arms of his chair, then came to his feet in a swift, angry surge. His face pale, his mouth stretched into a grim and level line, he stared at Davigan, hostility sparking in his eyes. Davigan stood calmly and quietly before him, me at his left shoulder. I wanted to run to my brother and calm him but didn't move. My place was beside Davigan. And Davigan was perfectly capable of handling Athelin's anger.

"No," Athelin cried. "Are you mad? Go to Skai? No!"

"I must go," Davigan said.

Athelin shot a glance at me, then looked back at Davigan. "Go if you must, Harper," he said grimly. "But you won't take my sister with you. I won't let you endanger her like that."

"Athelin, no," I said, stepping forward. "You don't understand. I have to go with him."

"Are you mad, too?" Athelin demanded. "No. I forbid it."

Dorlaine's voice interrupted him. "Have done, Athelin," she said quietly. She had come into the solar without anyone noticing her, a heavy strip of bandage across her forehead, brilliant white in contrast to her raven-wing hair. She crossed the room and took a chair beside Athelin. She studied Davigan carefully, her eyes glinting beneath her raised eyebrows, an enigmatic smile on her lips. "I think," she said, still looking at Davigan and not Athelin, "that you're in no position to forbid this man to do anything. Not this man . . ."

I stared at her in astonishment. She knew. She knew perfectly well who Davigan was. Her next words confirmed my suspicions.

"They say you favor your lady mother, Harper," she said. "Once my kin-father knew her well."

Davigan smiled in acknowledgment. A touch of resigned acceptance glimmered at the corner of his mouth. "She always spoke well of him, my lady," he said. "She wished to send him her regards."

Athelin began to protest again that going to Skai was far too dangerous. Dorlaine put her hand on his arm and shook her head.

"Enough, Athelin," she said softly. "You might be able

to advise this man as a kin-brother, but you should not seek to give him orders."

Surprised, Athelin stared at her. She smiled and gestured toward me. "Look at your sister," she said. "Don't you recognize it? They've bonded, Athelin. Just as surely as you and I have bonded. And not just the love bond. Iowen has declared. She's his bheancoran."

I glanced sharply at Davigan. An expression of bleak resignation flashed across his face, but was gone so quickly, I wasn't sure I had actually seen it. He straightened and smiled, an almost rueful expression.

Athelin leaned back in his chair thoughtfully. "I see," he said softly. "And there is only one man to whom she might bond as bheancoran, I believe." He rose and went to one knee. "My lord King . . ."

9

The ship carried only enough canvas to maintain headway and hold her steady in the enveloping mist. Unable to contain the quivering sense of excitement and anticipation that bubbled in my chest, I left the small cabin and stood with my hands braced against the deck rail. Stillness lay blanketing the world, broken only by the soft groan of wood as the ship breathed and the gentle murmur of water lapping against the planks of the hull. I took a deep breath, held it in for as long as I could before exhaling slowly.

A fortnight had passed since Beltane—a fortnight during which we had buried Adair, Mairi, and Liesa. Davigan and I solemnized our marriage vows in a quiet, simple ceremony in the shrine. Without fanfare, with minimal fuss, Athelin took up the torc and coronet of the Prince of Skai. And now, two days after boarding the ship, Davigan and I were home.

Skai lay invisible just below the horizon, hidden in the swirl of fog, but I fancied I could smell the spicy, pungent tang of cedar, wet leaves, silver maple buds, and bearberry blossoms. The perfume hung in the air, heavy and thick as the mist—a different scent from the fragrance of either Skerry or Tyra. Unique and evocative, raising visions in my mind of towering mountains and verdant glens I knew only from tales and songs. The fragrance of home. It eased the intensity of my headache and brought to life memories that weren't mine but stories I'd been told over and over until they were a part of me as if they had been mine.

Skai . . .

I shivered. I had grown up with the legend of Skai. My

mother's birthplace. The land where my father had come to find his own magic and reclaim his father's sword. Even those born on Skerry thought of themselves as yrSkai in exile. Skerry was only a temporary home—a refuge until we could return to Skai, where we belonged.

I could hardly believe that the fabled land itself lay just beyond my vision, hidden by the mist and the blurred horizon. Enough had happened since Equinox to leave me breathless. I had been given Whisperer, one of the fabled Celae Rune Blades, I had found my love, and I had at last found my prince—my *king*—and had bonded with him to become his bheancoran for life. And most astonishing of all, I carried the king's child. His son.

So much . . . And now, I stood with Skai itself within my grasp. Shortly after nightfall, I would set my foot on the land of my ancestors.

I shivered again and raised one hand to my forehead to ease the nagging ache behind my eyes. Waiting filled me with an odd, restless, impatient urgency, almost as if something out there wished to snatch me right out of my shoes to bring me close. I wanted to go *now*! I had not felt this keyed up, this anxious since leaving Marddyn for the short voyage back to Skerry, just before Beltane. Nervous energy flooded my body, making it nearly impossible to sit still for more than a moment at a time. The restless agitation made breathing painful. I was unable to take in enough air to fill my lungs.

Athelin had wanted to send a company of men with us on the journey. Davigan could, I thought with amusement, become quite royal and imperious when he wanted to. He had expressly forbidden Athelin to tell anyone about the journey, let alone send any soldiers with us. Athelin, who had been born with the same requisite measure of stubbornness of any of Red Kian's descendants, had bristled

with outrage and frustration, but in the end he had obeyed
his king. He stiffly bid us good journey as we boarded the
ship. The last sight I had of him was as he turned abruptly
on the ball of his foot, mounted his horse, and made his way
at a gallop back to the open gates of Skerrykeep. I had
turned away myself then. It was bad luck to watch someone
as they moved out of sight.

A small sound behind me broke into my jumbled
thoughts. Before I could turn to look, Davigan put his arms
around my waist from behind and set his chin on my shoulder. A strand of his hair brushed across my nose. I pushed
it aside with one finger and leaned back against him, trying
to calm the quivering urgency in my body.

"Skai is just over there," he said quietly in my ear.
"When I left there last autumn, I never dreamed I'd return
so soon. And I'd hardly thought to come back with a
bheancoran or a wife."

"Or both?" I asked, smiling.

He laughed. "Or both," he agreed.

We were quiet for a moment, watching the streamers
of fog interlace above the water. The clouds hid the sun, but
the light had already dimmed perceptibly as twilight
approached.

"Not long now," he said. "The ship's master will take
her within rowing distance of shore as soon as twilight is
deep enough to hide any movement."

I looked up at the shreds of mist swirling around the
tall masts with their burden of furled canvas. "Can he do
that safely in the fog?"

Davigan laughed softly. "I shouldn't think he'd offer to
do it if he didn't think he could get away with it," he said.
"He'd gladly leave us to get our feet wet as long as it left his
ship unscathed."

I smiled, then closed my eyes as a brief stab of pain

lanced through my temples. He caught my swiftly stilled flinch and tightened his arms around me.

"Are you all right?" he asked, anxiety thick in his voice.

"Just a little bit of a headache," I said. "I'm excited and can't wait to get ashore. I'm fine."

I gave up trying to pierce the mist. I wondered if somewhere out there, too, there was a Tell-Tale stone keyed to Davigan. Or to Whisperer. Had it tracked us from Skerry to the far west coast of Skai? Were Hakkar's Somber Riders already aware we were here?

Behind us, a sudden flurry of activity broke the stillness. Men swarmed up the rigging to unfurl the sails. The ship's master, calling half-whispered orders, joined Davigan and me at the rail.

"We're starting in now," he said. "I can't guarantee exactly where we'll be setting you ashore, but it's a bit south of Llewen Flow and north of the Ceg. Without the stars to judge our position, I can't be sure. But the coast should be deserted. We'll make sure, though, before we launch the curragh."

"Thank you," Davigan said gravely.

"Don't thank me," the master said. "I'd not be in your shoes this night for all the gold on the Continent. But if you're sure this is what you want to do—"

"We're sure," Davigan said.

The master nodded. "Then I'll obey my lord Athelin's orders and see you safe ashore. And of my own will, I'll wish you all the luck of your traveling." He sketched us a quick bow, then hesitated. "Both Prince Brennen and Prince Gareth always sent us out to Skai every dark of the moon," he said. "Prince Athelin follows their lead. Should you wish to come back, be down on the shore then, and we'll pick you up."

"That's very kind of you," Davigan said. "But I think we'll be staying here."

"Aye, well," the master said. "But ye'll not forget the time?"

Davigan smiled. "We won't forget. Thank you."

The master nodded, then left us.

Even with more canvas set out, I found it difficult to judge the progress of the ship across the dark and mist-wreathed sea. The ripple of water against the hull seemed scarcely louder than when the ship lay nearly motionless.

Presently one of the sailors came to fetch us back to the mid-deck, where two more sailors worked at unlimbering a curragh from its moorings against the deck rail. The sailors carefully lowered the curragh over the side. It settled gently into the water with barely a splash. One of the sailors held the forward painter to prevent the little boat from floating away while the other unfurled a rope ladder and dropped it over the side.

The master stepped out of the shadows. "Hurry now," he said. "I can't keep the ship here long. Down the ladder and row straight ahead. You should hear the waves breaking onshore before you're a bowshot away from the ship. The tide's nearly at flood. Hide the wee boat above the tide line, or you'll never see it again."

Davigan went down the ladder first, then stood in the curragh and reached up to give me a hand. The ladder swung dizzily as I clung to it, and my belly clenched in momentary nausea. Then I was down to the curragh, and Davigan had my hand firmly in his. I sat quickly on the middle thwart. One of the sailors tossed the painter down. I snatched up the rope and coiled it neatly into the bottom of the little boat as Davigan took up the sculling oar.

In moments, the ship had disappeared into the mist, pulling away with not much more than a faint, ghostly flap of canvas and creaking of wood to mark her passage. The

darkness and mist closed around our tiny boat. I lost all
sense of direction as another wave of dizziness washed over
me. But Davigan stood in the stern, a small frown drawing
the golden eyebrows together over his eyes, plying the
sculling oar as skillfully as if he had spent his life doing it.

Presently, I heard the hushed murmur of water lapping
at a sandy beach somewhere in the distance. A moment or
two later, the shallow bottom of the curragh scraped sand.
I jumped over the wale into water nearly to mid-thigh. The
water was cold enough to force a quickly indrawn breath
with the shock. I grasped the wale of the boat to keep my
balance. The last thing I wanted was salt water drenching
the sword I wore across my back. But it was in no danger.
In relief, I reached out for the painter and pulled as
Davigan shipped the oar. He jumped into the water, and
together we splashed through the chill water, pulling the
little boat up onto the narrow strip of sand.

Around us loomed the rugged shapes of tumbled boulders and broken rock. We stumbled over the ridge of
crisped seaweed that marked the high-tide line. I swore
softly as I went to one knee and lost my hold on the painter.

"Are you all right?" Davigan whispered.

"Yes." I got up, brushed the wet sand from the knee of
my trews, and took hold of the rope again. "Can we hide the
boat in those rocks? Just in case we need it again?"

"I think so. In the morning, we can move it to a better
place. We'll need light to see where we are and plan from
there." He reached into the boat and pulled out one of the
carry-packs that had been tucked securely beneath the
thwart and handed it to me. As I slung it over my shoulder
and adjusted it against my hip, he brought out the second
and flung it across his own back. He looked around,
arranging the carry-pack to accommodate the long dagger
he wore on his belt, his only weapon.

"I think that's everything," he said softly. "Let's see if we can find a dry place to hide until morning, and see if we can get a little sleep."

I climbed the rocks, scrambling up to the overhanging bank. The scent of cedar and pine mingled with the fresh, clean perfume of new grass and leaves drifted on the breeze blowing gently from the land, heady as wine. Somewhere above me, the rugged crests of the mountains, still capped thickly with snow, loomed against the sky, hidden yet by the thick swirls of mist and the darkness. And somewhere nearby, the symmetrical, cone-shaped bulk of Cloudbearer, the highest peak in Celi, stood guard over the triple concentric rings of standing stones called the Dance of Nemeara. I hugged myself and shivered, but not from the chill of the late-spring air.

Home . . . I was in Skai. I was home.

We found a dry hollow among the shattered rock and curled down in its shelter, wrapped warmly in blankets and our cloaks. I listened as Davigan's breathing gradually became slow and even as he fell asleep. But I felt as charged with nervous energy as a thundercloud is with lightning. Sleep would not come, and I lay watching the wisps of floating mists outside our snug little hollow.

I thought of Tell-Tales and swords and Kenzie's fears. He said that Hakkar had been searching a long time for Tell-Tales. He'd found one. Not just one Tell-Tale. Two of them.

How were they made? What combination of sorcery and magic allowed them to reach out to someone who used Celae magic? The two—the blood sorcery of Maedun and the gentle, Tyadda-based magic of Celi that drew its power from the land itself—were incompatible. So much so that the violent reaction of bringing the two together had stolen my parents' youth from them. How could it be that they combined to form a Tell-Tale?

I worried that my restlessness might disturb Davigan. I eased myself out of the nest of blankets and went out. The tide had turned, leaving the sand glimmering wetly in the night. Already the sky to the east was lighter, and if I turned my back on the sea and looked up, I thought I could see the silhouettes of the towering crags of the Spine of Celi even through the mist.

Somewhere in those mountains to the south lay Dun Eidon, where the princes who ruled Skai had lived. And where the twin swords of the "Song of the Swords" had been forged and one of them given over to Donaugh the Enchanter so he might overcome the sorcerer who led the first invading army of Maedun. But the sword Heartfire and its twin Soulshadow had vanished once Donaugh's need of them was gone, and not even legend could provide an answer as to where they now lay.

I raised my hand to touch the hilt of the sword that rose above my left shoulder. Whisperer was a Rune Blade. And Heartfire and Soulshadow were Rune Blades. Might there be an affinity between them that would help me as Davigan and I searched for the lost swords? Legend told of Red Kian using that affinity to help him find Kerridwen, his bheancoran, when Kerridwen had been captured by the enemy.

Legend . . .

How much truth was there in legend?

I whispered a soft prayer to the seven gods and goddesses for help, then went back to the little hollow in the rocks and lay down beside Davigan again. Sleep rolled over me in deep waves, drawing me down into the depths where dreams waited.

Rune Blades.

And Tell-Tales.

10

Dawn came, pearled with mist, thick with the scent of seaweed and salt sea. I woke with a start. Davigan's blanket lay neatly folded against the slab of rock that formed the back of the hollow, but he was gone. I rubbed the morning grit from my eyes and went out onto the sand. During the night, my headache had abated until it was little more than a mild uneasiness behind my temples.

Mist still wreathed the trees edging the shore above the rocks, but the breeze dancing along the sand shredded it to transparent wisps and tatters. I glanced up. Faintly through the layers of mist, the sky showed a pale, milky blue, giving me hope the mist would rise and disappear as soon as the sun climbed above the jagged peaks of the Spine.

Almost hidden in a cleft in the rock, a small fire of dry, bleached driftwood burned. No smoke rose to blend with the mist. The only sign the fire gave of its presence was a shimmer of heat waves above the rock and the piquant scent of the salt-laden wood as it burned.

Davigan dropped lightly from the crest of the rocks to the sand beside me. He held a small kettle of fresh water in one hand and a handful of greens wrapped in a square of cloth in the other. He grinned at me.

"Good morning," he said.

"Good morning," I said. "Where are we?"

He looked around. "I'm not quite sure yet. I'll be able to tell once some of this mist has burned off." He set the kettle on fire. He dropped a handful of mint and chalery leaves into the water from the square of cloth, then sat on his heels to watch that it didn't boil over. "Wherever we are, it's deserted around here. I didn't see any signs of habitation when I went to fetch the water and the mint. There's a deserted farmhouse by the stream, but it's nearly falling apart. Probably no one has lived there for over twenty years."

"No signs of Maedun?" I asked.

"Nothing. I think there's a path on the other side of the stream, but I didn't look to see if there were any tracks. We can check later. But we'll want to keep off the tracks and paths, just in case."

"Have you any idea at all where we need to start looking for the swords?"

He laughed ruefully. "I thought I'd go to the steading—"

"The steading? Where is it?"

"Up there somewhere." He waved at the mountains beyond the stream. "Where I was born. Where my mother still lives. If there's any bard lore to say where the swords are, old Anarawd should know. He taught me all I know about music, but he couldn't teach me all he knows. That would take a lifetime." His mouth twisted. "And if there's any lore about Tell-Tales and where they come from or how to quench them, he'll surely know that, too."

My head pounded with the rhythm of my heartbeat. We had to find where the Tell-Tales came from. If we couldn't, no man, woman, or child on Skerry could ever feel safe again. Nor could any person with even a glimmering of Celae magic. The Tyadda steading was probably as good a place to start looking as any. If there were any stories about Tell-Tales, we would find them there.

The fragrant scent of the morning tea began rising encouragingly from the kettle. It smelled delicious. Just the aroma was enough to make me feel better. I tried not to think about my headache and busied myself getting bread and cheese from our packs to break our fast.

By the time we finished the small meal and extinguished the fire, the mist had risen and rode low above the trees as translucent and fragile shreds of cloud. We climbed from the shore to the edge of the forest, settling our packs comfortably for travel. Davigan pointed to the northeast.

"There," he said. "See that mountain?"

I followed his pointing finger. A soaring, cone-shaped mountain rose on the horizon. Cloud wreathed its shoulders, which were still shrouded deep in winter snow. I could not see the peak, lost as it was in the cloud. But I knew instinctively the mountain was taller than all those around it.

"Cloudbearer," I said softly.

"Aye. Cloudbearer." He turned and pointed east. "And up there, the steading. Mayhaps two days' travel on foot."

I reached up to touch the sword hilt rising above my left shoulder. I thought I felt it quiver eagerly beneath my fingers. Whisperer knew it was home.

"If it will take us two days to get there," I said, "we should start now."

I stopped at the top of the steep ridge and looked back over my shoulder. The headache that had plagued me all day had eased as the afternoon wore on toward evening, and the unsettled uneasiness had faded until it was little more than a vague, undirected sense of anticipation. I raised a hand to massage my temples as I caught my breath after the precipitous climb.

The whole of Cloudbearer stood revealed beneath the deep blue of the sky. Shades of pink, gold, purple, and orange blazed from the snow-covered cone in the westering sun. The beauty and splendor of the mountain caught at my heart.

Cloudbearer . . . The highest mountain on the Isle of

Celi, and home to all the seven gods and goddesses. Somewhere down there in its shadow lay the Dance of Nemeara, the triple-ringed Dance of standing stones the bards called the heart of Celi.

And all of it surrounded by the Somber Riders of Maedun. I shivered.

But even the Somber Riders could not rid the island of its gods and goddesses. They could destroy every shrine, every Dance of stones on the island, but the gods and goddesses would remain as long as the mountains sent their peaks soaring up into the sky, and as long as Cloudbearer stood guard over the whole of the island from this western shore.

"It's beautiful, isn't it?" Davigan asked.

"Yes," I said. "And so peacefully serene, even now." I shifted the strap of my carry-pack on my shoulder. "How much farther now?"

He looked around. "We should be there by shortly after midday tomorrow," he said. "Down there is one of the Maedun fortresses." He pointed to the southwest. "Rock Greghrach. We won't be going anywhere near it, but we'll have to cross one of the main tracks leading to it in the morning. We'll need to be extra careful. There's usually a fair amount of traffic on the track."

"Rock Greghrach," I repeated. "I think I've heard Father speak of it."

"Quite likely," he said. "We should find a sheltered place to camp for the night soon now, I think. I'd like to be settled before it becomes too dark to see."

The track paralleling the small stream was little more than a game trail. Perhaps at one time, it had been a well-traveled road, but the years of neglect had all but given it back to the forest. New growth crowded close to the grassy trail, which was barely wide enough for two to walk abreast. The sun had not yet lifted above the crest of the mountains, and the morning air was cool and damp. Trees thick with new leaves overhung the trail, dimming the early-morning light to a soft twilight. The forest was silent except for the faraway calling of a thrush.

I walked to Davigan's left, scanning the trees around us. My headache throbbed behind my eyes, and the uneasiness curled in my belly like nausea. I felt about ready to leap out of my skin. I reached up to massage my temples, frowning as I peered through the thronged trees, searching anything hidden there that might be the cause of my jitters.

"You've been doing that for the last two days," Davigan said. "Are you ill?"

I looked at him in surprise. "Doing what?" I asked. "No, I'm not ill. Why do you ask?"

"You're rubbing your temples again. I knew you shouldn't have come with me—"

"Don't be silly," I said irritably, and instantly regretted my tone. "It's just a headache. I'm fine. It'll go away by midday. It did yesterday. No, really. I'm fine, Davigan. Don't worry about me." I tried a smile, and found it almost worked. "I'm the one who's supposed to worry about you, you know."

He raised one eyebrow skeptically, but said nothing more. I shifted the strap of the carry-pack to a more comfortable position on my shoulder, then made sure of Whisperer on my back and set out again, my steps brisk and swinging. He caught up to me in three strides. He said no more, but I knew he watched me when he thought I wasn't looking. I fought down a flicker of annoyance, then smiled to myself. He had not been raised to expect a bheancoran to serve him, so had no way of knowing how he should react. I could make allowances for him; there was time enough later to ease him into his role, to teach him how a prince and bheancoran worked together.

Midmorning approached, and the sun lifted suddenly above the mountains. Davigan and I strode briskly down the track. The branches of the trees met above the trail, allowing only small coins of sunlight to splash onto the ground like bright sprinkles of gold. The track twisted and turned, following the contour of the land above the tumbling burn. The noise of the rushing water masked any sound our feet made against the earth.

I held my body tensely, every sense alert for the first sign of trouble. I was aware of the accelerated beat of my heart, the shallowness of my breathing. When I paused to analyze my feelings, it shocked and startled me to discover that it was almost eager anticipation that flooded through me. As if I *wanted* to meet an enemy and prove to Davigan how well I could protect him.

Since I had received Whisperer from Brynda's hand, I had scarcely used the sword. Would it sing for me while we fought together against an enemy? I'd had an intimation of the sword's voice in Tyra against the assassins sent to kill my father and again on Skerry. I'd heard the shrieking, keening wail of fury as the blade shattered the Tell-Tale, and the low, rumbling murmur of the warning. But if I could believe what Brynda said about it, what I had heard had been only a hint of the full-throated song of the sword. I wanted to hear that voice for myself, singing in my mind, fierce and wild and free. Whisperer needed an enemy as much as I. I believed I had bonded with the sword, but we still had to prove ourselves together in a real battle.

Disturbed by the idea, I consciously slowed the pace of my breathing, tried to quiet my wildly beating heart. I forced myself into awareness of danger ahead and the need for great care. A battle between the two of us and even a

small company of Maedun could have disastrous consequences—consequences neither we nor Skai could afford.
But I was still disquietingly cognizant of the need to find
an enemy and a use for the Rune Blade I carried on my
back.

Davigan put out a cautious hand, catching my arm.
"Slowly now," he said just above a whisper. "The main
track is just ahead." He pointed. "Through there."

The little trail followed a wide bend of the stream into
an open area where the trees thinned. Sunlight poured
through the interlacing boughs overhead, turning the new
bracken between the pale trunks to a brilliant golden green.
The murmur and chuckle of water rushing over stones
echoed from the steep, rocky bank opposite the trail.

Unconsciously, I raised my hand to touch Whisperer's
hilt. The sword seemed to quiver gently beneath the pads of
my fingers. For an instant, I thought I heard a soft, metallic
clinking sound. I stopped on the track and held my breath,
listening carefully.

"What is it?" Davigan asked, his voice barely carrying
above the chatter of the stream.

"I don't know," I said. "I thought I heard something."

He frowned, listening. "I don't hear anything."

Whisperer still shivered in my hand. "No, neither do I.
Not now. Just the water." I dropped my hand and wiped it
on the thigh of my trews.

Cautiously, we crept forward, keeping to the edge of
the track, where we were a little more than half hidden by
the bushes and shrubs crowding thickly between the trees
bordering the narrow trail. I stepped quietly to his left side,
my hand going again to the Whisperer's hilt above my
shoulder. Ahead, a horse whickered. I stopped so suddenly,
Davigan nearly trod on my heel.

A troop of men stood where the little trail forded the

stream. I counted eight men, all of them intent on watering
their horses. They wore dark cloaks—brown and deep blue
and dark green—over trews and tunics of brown or green
or dark, rusty red and carried swords on wide belts buckled around their hips. Most of them wore their black hair
cut short enough that it didn't touch their shoulders.

"Celae . . ." Davigan whispered.

My prickly unease intensified, stabbing like needles
into a small, cold area just beneath my right shoulder blade.
I hesitated. Something about these men was wrong. But
what was it?

Before I could puzzle out the answer, one of the men
looked over his shoulder and saw us standing in the trail.
For a stunned moment, he simply stared at us blankly.
Then he turned quickly, and shouted.

"Ho!"

His companions spun around to look. As they did so, I
realized what was wrong with the picture they presented.
All of them wore their swords on their hips. No Celae
would do that, riding though forests where branches and
undergrowth could reach out to tangle a sword worn on
the hip. Celae swordsmen, almost without exception, wore
their swords conveniently across their backs Tyran-
fashion.

These men were Maedun.

Was the whole of Celi inundated with assassins and
murderers?

Davigan and I had walked into a trap.

If I stopped to think about it at all, I would have realized we had no chance to outrun a company of mounted
men, nor could we hope to defeat them all. Our only hope
was a wild gamble—a gamble so outrageous that the stunning impertinence of it might give us the advantage for just
long enough. Then my sword was in my hand, and I leapt

forward, my voice raised in the high, yodeling war cry of
the yrSkai.

I hurled myself into the center of the surprised
Maedun, my sword weaving a deadly arc around my head
and shoulders. At the same moment, Davigan sprang into
the small clearing, his long dagger in his hand. I spun
around, leapt to my right, and positioned myself to guard
Davigan's left side. Even as I swung Whisperer, I was
pleased to see that he managed more than competently with
the long dagger.

I laughed wildly as my sword flashed first right, then
left. I felt the solid connection with bone and flesh and
drew back the blade red with Maedun blood. Then I heard
Whisperer's voice, high, wild, and clear. *I Am the Voice of Celi*
the runes along its blade read, and it sang fiercely in
defense of the island.

The sword sang for me, and I lost myself in the intrica-
cies of the dance.

In the back of my mind, I was fully aware that the
Maedun outnumbered us at least four to one, but Davigan
and I had the momentary advantage of surprise. We might
be able to grab two of the horses and make our escape
before the Maedun recovered from their shock. Beneath
our feet, the dirt of the track turned to sodden mud, slick
with blood.

The Maedun crowded in around us. Davigan cried out
in dismay, and went to one knee. I screamed his name, my
heart suddenly in my mouth, and spun around, still shouting incoherently, to guard him. My sword sliced into the
chest of one of the Maedun. The man fell, eyes wide and
staring in final astonishment. I parried the swing of
another, whirled to meet a third. My foot skidded in the
mud, which was slimy and slippery with blood, and I nearly
went down.

Davigan cursed, clambered unsteadily to his feet. His long dagger flashed in the sunlight as he lunged at an enemy. The blade went deep into the Maedun's belly. The man staggered in the slick mud, and I swept Whisperer backhand, cutting his leg from beneath him.

"The horses, Davigan," I cried. "I'll hold them here. Get to the horses."

He hesitated only an instant, then ducked and scrambled through the opening I cut for him. I could not waste the moment it would take to watch him.

Five Maedun closed in around me. I fought desperately to watch all of them at the same time. No one guarded my exposed, vulnerable back. I couldn't tell if Davigan had reached the horses or not. I was out of breath, the air rasping painfully in my throat. Despairingly, I knew I could not last much longer. The sword in my hand felt as if it were made of lead, and I wondered bleakly how much longer I could lift Whisperer to swing it.

But if I didn't continue to fight, both of us would be dead. And with us the child I carried.

Interlude

Hakkar of Maedun

11

Hakkar of Maedun swept into the empty throne room of the palace in the city of Clendonan and glanced around in distaste. The Celae were a decadent and wasteful lot, he decided again. Had the time, effort, and money expended on the needless luxury of this palace been spent instead on the military, the war might have been less easily decided, despite the weapon of sorcery he wielded.

He walked to the throne, which was comfortably padded in rich purple velvet. The ornately carved back and arms glowed in warm oaken tones, beautifully contrasting with the velvet and complementing it perfectly. But the thing looked unused, and he remembered one of his captains telling him that the long-dead Celae High King had seldom used this palace, preferring instead his own estate some leagues up the river. He needed neither palace now.

Dead leaves left over from last autumn swirled across the unswept paving stones and crunched under his feet as he walked out onto the balcony. He moved to the far side and leaned his hands on the low parapet as he looked westward at the sunset. From there, he could not see the towering peaks of the Spine of Celi, the soaring range of mountains that sheltered the western provinces of Skai and Wenydd. Troublesome places, full of irritating, vexatious people.

The too-familiar flash of frustrated anger swept through him as he thought of those doubly damned mountains. Maedun was flatland, a place of gently rolling steppes, broad rivers, salt marshes, and wide, pine forests. There were none of those exasperating pinnacles of rock thrusting up insolently and arrogantly from the earth to thwart Maedun sorcery. Hakkar had all but exhausted himself trying to extend into that high country the spell that destroyed men's will to resist and sapped their strength. Several of his best warlocks who had been linked with him had died in the attempt—all of them good men he could ill afford to lose.

He did not believe the Celae prisoners who smugly told him the high places were sacred to the old Tyadda gods and goddesses, and their magic was what inhibited his spells. He had destroyed most of the shrines; what gods had once dwelt in them should have been dispossessed and gone. But something prevented his spell from working in the high country, and whatever it was, it enraged him every time he thought about it.

"Father?"

Hakkar turned to greet his son as Horbad came out onto the balcony.

"I have the latest reports here for you," Horbad said, holding up a sheaf of paper. "Do you want to read them now?"

Hakkar looked back at the fading glory of the sunset and silently cursed the mountains again. "No," he said. "Just tell me what they say. I'll study them in detail in the morning."

"The commander of Rock Greghrach sends to tell you his troopers have wiped out a nest of rebels in the mountains south of the Ceg," Horbad said. "There are still some rebels in the high country to the west and north, but he expects to take care of them soon."

"All their petty leaders are now dead?" Hakkar asked.

"We believe so."

"And the man who calls himself the Prince of Skai?"

"We don't know. None of the men we sent out with

Tell-Tale stones returned. Not from Tyra, nor from the north." Horbad shrugged. "We're not even sure the stones found the man who claims to be prince. They seek those accursed enchanted Celae swords more than they seek a specific man, I think."

"Not very accurate."

"No. But better than nothing."

"I suppose so. And the commander of Rock Greghrach?"

"He hasn't been able to identify the prince yet."

"What he means is that he has no idea where he might be."

"Yes. But he says he's not given up."

"They've been looking for thirty years," Hakkar said dryly. "That's more than your lifetime."

"I know. But we'll find him, Father."

"You're sure?" Hakkar slanted a glance toward his son. Horbad was young yet, and sometimes let his enthusiasm run away with his cold, common sense. But he knew the prophecy as well as any Maedun noble. *From the line of the Prince of Skai will arise an enchanter who will destroy Maedun.* The prophecy was generations old now, but an ever-present threat. "Your own life will depend on whether or not they are all dead," he said mildly. "Remember the prophecy . . . "

Horbad smiled coldly. "I never forget it, Father. It's the reason I keep returning to the west."

Hakkar's jaw tightened until the muscles at the hinges bulged. "Those accursed mountains. I *will* extend the spell into those mountains . . . " he muttered.

"Father, you cannot," Horbad said in a reasonable voice. "You tried, and you failed. If you continue to try, it might kill you. I have no desire to become Hakkar of Maedun in your stead at this point in time. There are too few Celae there to worry about. Those who are left will make good sport for our soldiers' hunting. Leave it at that.

As for the Veniani in the north, they're the next best thing to barbarians. They have no leadership. They're fishermen and shepherds only. They didn't fight; they simply ran. Leave them. There's no point in exhausting yourself to try to subdue them. They're no threat."

"We can't afford to let any Celae run free," Hakkar said. "They're not like the Falians or the Isgardians. They're all stubborn as rocks, and nearly as stupid. They simply won't accept the fact they've been conquered. And the prophecy is clear. Unless we destroy every vestige of magic here, an enchanter will come who will destroy all of Maedun."

"Father, they're a beaten people. Those few left are too preoccupied with mere survival to mount any counterattack. And if they do, then they'll have to meet us on our own ground, and your spell will take them before they can do any harm."

"I mislike it, Horbad," Hakkar said.

Horbad shrugged. "I know," he said. "But I have an idea."

Hakkar smiled. He was fond of his son, and proud of him. Even disregarding the fact that a good part of his power came from the link forged between them when the boy was barely a half grown fifteen, and without a son, he was only a little more powerful than a warlock himself, he was pleased with Horbad. When his time came and he had to pass both his name and his power on to this son, he could at least be secure in the knowledge that Horbad would bring only more honor to the name.

"What's your idea?" he asked.

"Send more warlocks to the west. You must make sure a warlock goes with each patrol. Some of the rebels have stopped fearing the spell that turns weapons back on them."

"We haven't enough warlocks for that," Hakkar said. "And I need them here."

"It won't take long," Horbad said. "Once the legend of invincibility has been sown again, it won't be necessary to leave all of them in the west. You can bring most of them back here again."

"Do you think that will be sufficient?"

"I'm sure of it."

Hakkar smiled. "You've set out everything exactly as I had been thinking," he said. "You do well, Horbad."

Horbad colored with pleasure. "I am, of course," he said quietly, "your son, my lord."

On the night the Celae called Beltane and the Maedun called Winter's Death, something woke Hakkar. He had heard something, or he had felt something. He was unsure which. But *something* had happened.

He rose from the side of the woman he had chosen for the night and went to the window, looking north and west. His narrowly handsome face drawn into planes of thoughtfulness, he gripped the marble sill of the window for a long time, then sent for his son.

Horbad arrived quickly, dressed in black. "You called me, Father?" he murmured. He left the door open as he hurried into the room.

Hakkar turned back to the window. "Did you feel it?" he asked.

"I felt nothing. What was it?"

"Something . . . I don't know."

Horbad came to the window and looked out at the shuttered, sleeping city. "Important?" he asked.

"I believe so. Something happened. Some magic in the northwest."

"The Celae?"

"Yes. Can you not see the glow there?"

Horbad raised his eyes, looked northwest. "I see something. I don't know what it is."

"Magic," Hakkar said. "More magic."

"I thought we had eliminated it all."

"We need another stone," Hakkar said, still looking out the window. "Can you find another?"

Horbad hesitated. "There may be more where I found the first two. But it might take me a while to find them."

Hakkar turned to study him. "We have time. It's important to eliminate all their magic, and the people who can use it. But we have time."

"Then I'll leave tomorrow."

Part 2
The Courier
Cynric

12

One of the hostlers came running out to meet me as I galloped into the posting station. Even before the horse had slowed, I swung my right leg across its back, my weight held only by my left foot in the remaining stirrup, ready to jump to the ground. Couriers carrying dispatches for the Lord Protector of Celi were not encouraged to waste any time.

The hostler leapt for the reins I threw him as I stepped down to the hard-packed earth, and reached around stiffly to unbuckle the saddle pack containing the dispatches. I had left Clendonan nearly two days ago, and had slept only four or five hours since. My aching muscles would get little rest in the next three days through the mountains until I delivered the documents to the commander of Rock Greghrach on the coast of the Western Sea.

"You're early," the hostler cried in annoyance. I had never yet met a hostler at a posting station who appreciated any upset to his strictly scheduled routine. This one was no exception. He glanced over his shoulder at the paddock. Another hostler had just slipped a bridle over the head of my remount. "We're not quite ready for you, as you can see."

I laughed and slapped the sweating horse affectionately on the haunch. "This one loves to run," I said. "You'd think he was bred for it. I wish they were all like him."

The hostler shrugged and made a sour face. "A horse is only a horse," he said. "One horse is just like any other."

And one man should be like any other man. For a moment, I thought I'd said the words aloud, but the hostler didn't pause as he unbuckled the bridle, didn't even glance at me.

I busied myself with the saddle pack, turning my face from him so he wouldn't see my expression. A horse is only a horse. Mayhaps. Just as a man should be only a man. But in spite of the hostler's cynical opinion, breeding counted in a horse, and it certainly counted far more seriously in a man. And who should know that better than I?

Breeding had certainly counted to the commanders and officers of the Somber Riders occupying this forsaken Isle of Celi. The fleeting, caustic thought surprised me. I had allowed myself to believe that I had let go of the bitterness. Obviously, I had not. That the matter of proper breeding still had the power to curdle my mood and darken my day was unexpected. And completely unwelcome.

I pulled the dispatch pouch from the sweating horse and made sure my expression was carefully neutral as I turned back to the hostler. I didn't think he had made the remark deliberately. It was highly unlikely he knew the secret I kept close inside myself. The circumstances of my birth could not be known, or I would never receive anything but hostility and uncooperative obstruction from the hostler. From him, and the whole of the posting station as well, here and elsewhere. Just the fact that he spoke to me, and the horses were ready when I rode up, confirmed that my secret was still my own.

The hostler was already leading the tired horse to the stable to care for it. The other stableman had finished saddling my replacement mount and brought it forward. The horse was well trained. From long practice, it placed itself in exactly the right position so that all I had to do was turn, swing the saddle pack up, and let it fall across the horse's back behind the saddle. The thongs were positioned so I could simply lift them and secure the leather pouches without fuss, with minimum effort. Efficiency in action.

The stable man made doubly sure of the saddle girth,

then tossed me the reins. I gave him a curt nod of thanks, then vaulted into the saddle and set my heels to the horse's flanks. The horse gathered itself beneath me and leapt forward as I eased myself more comfortably into the saddle. By the time we reached the end of the paddock, the horse had settled into an easy hand gallop, a pace it could keep up for most of the several leagues we had to cover together.

Ten minutes later, the Dead Lands closed about us. The track no longer ran ahead, straight as the flight of an arrow. The foothills rose around me and the track rose with them, curving to follow the contour of the land. I hunched myself closer into my black cloak, ducking my chin down onto my chest.

I hated this stretch of my route. I understood the reason Hakkar had blighted this wide strip of land bordering the western mountains. It prevented the wild Celae of the mountains from raiding the tamed lands to the east, and it acted as a barrier to any Celae who might wish to try to escape from Maedun domination. It might have been only a thickening and intensifying of the spell Hakkar kept over the whole of the land to keep the Celae tractable and tame, but no Celae could penetrate this bespelled area and maintain his sanity. Even the vegetation felt the sorcery, turning withered and brown and shriveled.

The last of the winter's snow hid the sere, burned vegetation that climbed the slopes of the foothills, but I thought the snow had a different texture in the Dead Lands. Grainy and gray, as lifeless as the ground beneath it. It made me think that if I tried to taste it, the snow would be bitter and burning as lye on my tongue.

I let the horse slow to an effortless canter on the uphill slope and rolled my shoulders to ease the tight muscles. Even though I wore a talisman prepared especially for me by a warlock to enhance my inborn resistance to the spell, the Dead Lands never failed to send unsettling curls of uneasiness akin to nausea through my belly. The very air itself made my skin itch, as if I were infested by a colony of vermin.

The horse didn't like the Dead Lands, either. Horses were supposed to be immune to the spell, but I sensed the horse's nervousness. It might be that it was only reacting to my own agitation. Its ears twitched, and it wanted to shy at its own shadow. I kept it firmly under control and, at the same time, tried to take my own restive disquietude into hand. I couldn't quell it completely, but over the years I'd learned to ignore it most of the time.

A little less than a quarter of an hour later, we came out on the western side of the Dead Lands. The faint, underlying stench of old burned vegetation disappeared. My muscles relaxed as the malevolent atmosphere dropped behind, and I felt infinitely better. Ahead lay the steeper, more rugged peaks and crags of the mountains themselves. I looked up at the unmistakable gap in the peaks that marked the first pass. Snow lay thicker in the high country, and the air became perceptibly colder as the track climbed. And it smelled fresher. I drew in a deep breath of the chill, sweet air, and smiled to myself.

Mayhaps it was my breeding, but I liked the mountains. They were clean and nearly untouched. It hardly bothered me at all that the sorcery wielded by the warlocks, or even the black sorcerer Hakkar himself, could not reach into the high country. I had never felt uncomfortable or ill at ease amid the soaring crags and cliffs.

But then, I hardly minded being a courier, either, reviled as couriers might be by the troops of Somber Riders occupying the island. I had more freedom than many a trooper. Nearly as much as an officer. I seldom made the journey back and forth across the island more than once in a fortnight. As long as I kept myself inconspicuous in Clendonan, I had more than enough time to pursue my own interests. I made sure those interests remained inconspicuous, too. I had no illusions about what might happen to me should anyone gain any inkling of how I spent my time when not kiting madly back and forth across the expanse of this green island.

The horse was beginning to tire, but the next posting station lay only half a league away, hidden in the tortuous folds of the mountain. I leaned forward in my saddle and patted the side of the horse's neck. The hide was hot and damp beneath my hand.

"Rest soon, my friend," I murmured. "Just a little farther now." I looked up at the towering peaks in the distance, then patted the horse again. "Be thankful you don't have to run all the way up the side of this mountain and down the other."

The horse's pace changed suddenly. Instead of the smooth canter, it began noticeably to favor its off forefoot, becoming lamer with each step. I swore softly, pulled the horse to a halt, and dismounted. Ruining a good horse was foolish. I'd not get to the next posting station any more quickly if I rode the horse until it was completely lame.

"Easy there, lad," I said. It stood quietly and let me pick up the forefoot to examine it. I swore, more vehemently this time. A sharp rock had wedged itself between the shoe and the hoof, burying itself in the tender frog of the foot.

I got my hoof pick from the pouch on my belt and picked up the hoof again. But as I tried to slip the end of the instrument beneath the stone to pry it out, the pick snapped in two. I stood for a moment staring at the splintered wooden handle, and cursed it straight into perdition, then added a few virulent Saesnesi oaths. For all the good it did,

I might as well have saved my breath. I hurled the broken pieces into the dirty snow at the edge of the track. I had no spare, and if the stone remained in the hoof, the horse would be dead lame within fifty paces. It was still a little less than half a league to the next posting station. If I tried to ride the horse, it would be no good for anything for too long, and I would get there no sooner than if I walked, leading the horse.

To my left, far off the track, a thin column of smoke rose above the winter-bare trees. Nothing lived in the Dead Lands, but there were still a few farms on the western side. Most of the yrSkai had fled to the high country, but a few still lived on the farms in the low valleys and worked the land. They were held by Hakkar's spell. Enslaved, I supposed, from their point of view. Tame Celae they were called. They could offer me no harm, and for the most part, I ignored them. But in any event, a farmer certainly would have the means to remove the stone from the horse's hoof.

I gathered the reins and clucked encouragingly at the horse. It followed me, the limp more pronounced now, as I led it down the narrow little path branching off the main track.

The farmstead lay tucked into a cup-shaped little vale, and consisted of a small mud-and-wattle house and a stone-and-timber byre, both freshly whitewashed, both roofs neatly thatched with straw and bracken. Nets hung across the roofs, weighted down with stones hanging from braided sisal ropes, to keep the thatch in place when the wind blew up a gale. As I walked into the farmyard with the horse, the farmer came out of the byre and stood watching me, a sour, suspicious expression on his face. Even from a distance, I read the anger and cold hatred in his face. If he could, this farmer would happily kill me. Even after fifty years of subjugation, these Celae were fierce and hostile.

Only the threat of the spell kept the anger and hatred in check. The spell seldom killed. But let any man or woman raise a hand against a Somber Rider, and the spell brought them swiftly to their knees, agony like fire coursing through their guts and limbs. I'd never felt it, but I'd watched both Celae and Saesnesi suffer. Just watching was enough to twist my belly into knots.

"Good day," I said. My Celae was careful and heavily accented. Not an easy language to get one's tongue around unless one was born to it. "I need some assistance here, if you would please." I took a grim satisfaction from the flash of startled surprise on his face. Courtesy was not something the tame Celae had come to expect from an one wearing the black uniform. And very few Maedun botered to learn the Celae tongue. I knew only a little, but my Saesnesi was excellent. As well it should be. But I shied away from that thought and led the horse toward the splitrail fence of the paddock.

"Do you have a—" I broke off. I couldn't remember the word for *hoof pick*.

The farmer had been watching the horse. He grunted something and went into a small shed beside the byre. For a moment, I wondered if I was expected to follow, but before I could decide, the farmer came out again carrying a small pouch of tools. Without a word, he slid himself between me and the horse and put his hand to the horse's neck, speaking to it in a low, soothing voice. The horse's ears twitched nervously, but it made no objection when the farmer picked up its hoof.

"A sharp stone," I said. "Not long ago. I didn't ride him after he picked it up."

The farmer muttered something and shot a quick, appraising glance over his shoulder at me. He plucked a hoof pick from the pouch and went to work with it quickly and expertly. I stepped back and let him work. He obviously needed no help or guidance.

A movement near the byre caught my eye. I turned just in time to see a child come out of the byre. The child, a small boy with tar black hair and eyes only a shade or two lighter—like mine, might have been five, or perhaps a little younger. He carried a pail of milk, the handle clutched in both small hands, an expression of fierce concentration on the young face. Milk sloshed with each step, but he wasn't about to admit he might need help.

A woman rushed out of the byre and caught the boy's arm. He protested as she tried to pull him back into the byre, then caught sight of me by the paddock. He dropped the pail. Milk spilled into the churned mud around his feet as the woman pulled him back and hugged him tightly against her. The boy ducked behind the woman's legs, clinging to her skirts and peering out, wide-eyed, at me.

The child was obviously not Celae. The mother's hair was black, too, but it was the glossy blue-black I had come to recognize as typical of the Celae. The boy's hair was Maedun black, so black it seemed to absorb the light rather than reflect it in the blue glints that shone in his mother's hair. There could be no doubt that the boy's father was a Somber Rider.

The farmer straightened and let the horse's hoof drop back to the ground. He glanced at the woman and made a quick, shooing motion with his hands, frowning. The woman gathered up the child and ran quickly to the cottage. The door slammed firmly behind them.

"Your daughter?" I asked.

Fear flickered in the man's eyes. The woman was still young and pretty. Still in danger from another passing Somber Rider. "Aye," he said thickly. "And my grandson."

I nodded. "I see," I said.

The farmer put his hand to the horse's neck. "The stone is gone now, sir. He'll be fine now."

"I shall let him rest for a while, though, before I ride him hard again," I said. "Thank you."

Again, the farmer's eyes widened in surprise. "You're welcome, sir," he said. An automatic reply.

I gathered the reins to lead the horse back to the main track. "Do not call me 'sir,'" I said. "I have no rank. See?" I indicated the sleeve of my tunic beneath my heavy cloak, bare of any insignia save Hakkar's raven badge and the lightning flash marking me as a courier. "I am only a messenger." I turned toward the main track, leading the horse with me. *Only a messenger. Not a soldier.*

I wondered if the farmer had heard the bitterness in my voice. Seeing the boy there in the farmyard had stirred more painful memories. First the hostler's remark about the breeding of a horse, and now the boy. Too much for one day.

But I couldn't keep the child out of my mind. There weren't very many children like him on this captive isle. *Mongrel seed,* the warlock of my father's garrison had called them. Most of the men in the garrisons had, at one time or another, Celae women — or Saesnesi women in the Summer Run — in their beds, whether the women willed it or not. But very few children came of these unions. Birthroot and ergot were not difficult to find. And while it was true that too much of either herb very often took the woman, too, when it cleansed the womb of the unwanted child, most women stood the risk rather than bear a half-Maedun child. As with anything, there were, of course, occasional exceptions — women who had the children and raised them and loved them. The woman back at the farmstead was obviously one.

My own mother had been another.

I realized suddenly that I had walked the good part of half a league down the track, leading the horse. The steady rhythm of the horse's gait showed no sign of lameness now. I gathered the reins, vaulted into the saddle, and put my heels to the horse's flank. Rested and eager now, the horse leapt into an easy canter. I tried to concentrate on the track ahead and banish the thoughts of small halfling boys from my mind. But it wasn't so easy. Despite my determination not to, I remembered only too well.

The time before Faghen, lieutenant to the commander of the garrison, had taken me from my mother was blurred in my mind. But the memory of that tall, dark man on the huge horse was as vivid and bright as if it had happened only yesterday. I had been Cynric then. Not Jonvar. I had not become Jonvar until much later.

I was not more than seven years old and had been playing in the dust at the edge of the garden when a shadow fell across me, blotting out the sun as if a cloud had rolled across the sky. I looked up to see the man on the horse staring down at me with an odd expression on his face. Fearfully, my belly cramping, I edged back, drawing away from the dark-clad stranger who watched me so intently.

"Cynric!"

I tore my gaze away from the Somber Rider and turned. My mother appeared in the doorway of the cottage behind me. Anxiety quivered in her sharp tone, but I could not help myself as I looked back up at the Rider. My mother ran across the beaten earth of the small yard, her white-blonde hair streaming behind her, and snatched me to her. I clung to her, hiding my face against her legs. But even as she pressed me against her, one hand protectively drawing my head tightly to the coarse fabric of her skirts, I looked up again at the Somber Rider.

The Rider glanced at my mother, then back to me.

"You remember me," he said, still looking at me but speaking to her. His accent was strange, thick and clumsy. I could hardly understand him, but something about the man's tone sent chills of fear deep into my belly. My mother had no difficulty comprehending the man's meaning.

"Aye, I remember you," she whispered.

The Somber Rider didn't look away from my face. Silver insignia glinted against the black of his uniform. "Mine," he said. A flat statement, not a question.

A tremor quivered through my mother's body, and she clutched me more tightly against her.

"Yes," she said hoarsely. Even then, I knew no one lied—no one *could* lie—to the grim, unsmiling men who dressed in black and rode tall horses.

"I'll have him, then." The man bent down in the saddle, grasped my arm, and snatched me away from my mother. Too frightened to cry out, I whimpered and tried to reach out to her.

She shrieked in rage and grief and took one step toward the Somber Rider before the spell took her. She fell to her knees, her arms wrapped around her belly. Her screams turned to cries of pain. I couldn't help her. All I could do was watch in horror. The Rider slung me across his saddle, as if I were nothing more than a sack of flour, and rode away from the cottage, leaving my mother sobbing as she knelt in the dirt.

I knew I would never see her again.

I found my voice. "Mama!" I howled. "Mama!" I struggled frantically, trying to squirm out of the Rider's grip, back down to the ground, back to my weeping mother.

The Rider's hand came down hard against my cheek, nearly stunning me. No one had ever struck me in anger before in my life. But the Rider wasn't angry. He slapped me the same way my grandfather swatted an animal's nose to discipline it. Shocked silent, I stopped crying.

"Silence, boy," the Rider said harshly. "The Somber Riders of Maedun do not scream and cry for their mothers."

I choked back my sobs, knowing that more crying would bring nothing but another stinging blow from the Rider's hand. Shuddering, I looked up at the man's face. It was drawn into stern lines of implacable disapproval. But there was something else there—something I was too young then to interpret or understand. It was only when I grew older that I began to realize that what I saw was the shadow of a gnawing hunger and need finally fulfilled.

13

For the best part of a season, I did not return to the mountains. My duties kept me busy riding between Clendonan, where Hakkar had his headquarters, and the western regions of Celi. Several times, I rode to garrisons in the Summer Run. But if I ever passed through the small village where I had been born, I was not aware of it. I could not remember even the name of the village. But now I found myself watching for familiar landmarks. I could not help thinking of the small halfling boy I had seen in the mountains and how the woman had sheltered the child against herself. And I found myself wondering if my own mother was still alive. She had held me to her as protectively as the Celae woman had held the boy, but she had not been able to prevent the man who called himself my father from peremptorily taking me from her.

The tall Somber Rider had not taken me directly to the garrison, but to a house in a city. I now knew the city was Clendonan, on the Tiderace. But the child Cynric knew only that he had never seen so many people before in one place. Frightened and confused, I had shrunk back against the tall Rider. Nor had I ever seen anything like the house the Rider took me to. The main room was larger than the cottage where I had lived with my mother. There were servants whose expressions never changed. It wasn't until I was much older that I realized the servants were kept deeply bespelled, and therefore harmless to the man they served.

The Rider carried me into a small room that contained a child-sized bed, a large wardrobe cupboard, and two chests of drawers. A woman waited there to take me. Still dazed and almost too frightened to speak, I went to her when she beckoned me. She took me by the wrist and led me not ungently from the room. I was bathed, combed, dressed in finer clothes than I had ever before worn, and taken back to the main room, where the Rider awaited me by a blazing hearth.

He made a dismissive sign, and the woman left the room. I stood with my back to the fire in the hearth, holding my hands clasped behind me, peering up at the Rider through the fringe of hair on my forehead. That odd expression was on the man's face again.

He said something I could not understand. I shrank back, shaking my head. The man made an impatient noise and spoke again, this time in thickly accented Saesnesi.

"What is your name?"

"Cynric," I whispered.

Without anger, without emotion of any sort, the Rider took one step toward me and slapped my cheek with an open hand, knocking me down. I was too stunned to cry. Twice the man had struck me for no reason that I could discern. I didn't know what was happening. I stared up at the Rider, who beckoned me back to my feet. Unsteadily, I rose, waiting for the next blow.

"Your name is Jonvar," the Rider said flatly. He stepped back again. "What is your name?"

"Cynric—"

Again, the open-handed slap. I stumbled back, but managed to keep to my feet this time. I raised my hand to my cheek, my lip trembling on the verge of a sob.

"Your name is Jonvar," the Rider said. "Your name is Jonvar, and I am your father, Faghen."

I blinked away tears.

"What is your name?"

"J-Jonvar."

The Rider smiled bleakly. "Yes. You are my son. Your name is Jonvar. Remember that."

As time passed, I learned to respond only to the name Jonvar, and to call the Somber Rider Father. And, as children do, I learned the Maedun tongue quickly and easily. I learned very quickly that I must never under any circumstances mention my mother or the fact that she was not a Maedun woman. Faghen returned to his duty in the garrison and left me alone in the big house in the city for long periods at a time, with only the half-alive servants and a Maedun tutor for company. By the time I was turning ten, I thought of myself as Jonvar and had almost forgotten that I had ever been Cynric.

Eventually I learned, too, about the curious expression on Faghen's face whenever he looked at me. No one ever told me the story—at least not intentionally. But from bits and pieces of conversation that children overhear without adults realizing it, I learned that three years earlier, Faghen's wife and son had died when a storm at sea destroyed the ship they had been aboard, on their way from the Isgardian port of Honandun to Celi to join Faghen. Faghen had been completely distraught at the loss of his son, whose name had been Jonvar. The boy had just turned five when he died. In bringing me, his bastard son, from the small Saesnesi village, Faghen had replaced the child.

When I was eleven Faghen took me with him to the garrison, where I began training with the sons of other Somber Riders. And while I had never learned to love Faghen as a son should perhaps love a father, I had learned to respect and honor him. By the time I was twelve I had learned to be contemptuous of the half-alive Saesnesi who listlessly worked the fields surrounding the garrison fortress. And at thirteen I vehemently denied even to myself that I had ever had any kinship with them.

At age fourteen I went, with the half dozen other boys being raised at the garrison, to the training fields to learn the arts of swordsmanship, archery, and horsemanship. Fortunately I proved to be quick and intelligent, and my body manifested a certain amount of gracefulness and deftness. I did well among boys who were older and larger than I. At fifteen I was consistently winning in competitions against the sixteen- and seventeen-year-old boys with both sword and bow, mounted or afoot. My father was well pleased with me.

When I was seventeen, less than a year before I would be declared a man and allowed to join the Somber Riders, the specter of my mother's blood rose to haunt me. I was on the practice field when a messenger came to fetch me to the quarters of the garrison commander. The messenger refused to answer any questions, and I thought I detected a sneer on the man's face.

There were three men in the chamber when I entered—the garrison commander, the warlock who maintained Hakkar's spell to keep the Saesnesi under control, and my father, who was now the garrison captain.

The commander sat in an ornate chair near the hearth. Unsmiling and stern, he looked first at me where I stood just inside the chamber door, then at Faghen.

"Is this the boy?" he asked expressionlessly.

Faghen nodded. "Yes, sir. This is my son, Jonvar."

I shot a quick glance at my father. He held his mouth in a thin, grim line, the rest of his face as immobile as river ice. He didn't look at me, keeping his eyes fixed unwaveringly on some point beyond the commander's shoulder.

The commander beckoned. "Come here, boy," he said.

I advanced slowly and went to one knee before the commander's chair.

"Tell me your name, boy."

"Jonvar, sir. Jonvar son of Faghen."

"Who was your mother?"

I hesitated. "Trecesca, sir," I said. "Wife to Captain Faghen."

The commander raised an eyebrow. "So you say," he said.

The warlock spoke for the first time. "Look at me, boy," he said, his voice soft but brooking no refusal.

I looked up, met the eyes that were darker than my own. Suddenly, I thought my head had burst asunder, that my wits had fled my shattered brain. The room whirled around me, ceiling and floor arbitrarily changing places alarmingly. I managed to catch my balance before I fell and knelt there, gasping for breath. I could no longer think clearly. My mouth fell open, and I swayed on my knees before the warlock. As abruptly as it began, the blurred, shredded sensation went away.

The warlock turned to the garrison commander. "He has a substantial amount of resistance to the spell, my lord," he said. "And he thinks of himself as a man of Maedun. A Somber Rider. But . . ." His voice trailed off, and he glanced at Faghen. The momentary malicious gleam in his eye was completely unmistakable. I thought I saw my father flinch, but the movement was hardly detectable.

"But?" the garrison commander asked.

The warlock shrugged. "His mother was Saesnesi. There is no doubt of it in my mind."

"None at all?"

The warlock shook his head. "None," he said implacably. "His blood is tainted."

The commander rubbed his bearded cheek. "I see." He turned to Faghen. "You knew this when you sent him to the training field, Captain Faghen."

Faghen stiffened and stared straight ahead. "The boy is my son," he insisted doggedly. "He trained with the sons of other officers and men."

"I have no doubt that he is your son," the commander said softly. "He favors you. But there is the small matter of his mother being Saesnesi."

Faghen said nothing.

"Mongrel seed," the warlock said, his lip curling in a sneer.

"He is one of the best on the training field," Faghen said quietly. "I find him to be a son worthy of my blood and my seed."

The commander drew in a deep breath. The skin around his nose and mouth tightened, went pale. It might have been anger. I couldn't tell. "I cannot accept this boy as a member of this garrison," he said. "Half his makeup is Saesnesi. He would be untrustworthy."

I must have made a poor job of keeping the shock and dismay from my face. The warlock glared at me. I had to make a conscious effort to close my mouth. Too many years had passed since I had even thought about my mother, or my Saesnesi blood. The appalling reminder returned to crash down over me like a shocking wave of cold water on a hot day.

I stared blankly up at the commander. But I *was* Maedun! How could he think I might fail in my duty and prove unworthy of the black uniform and cloak of a Somber Rider? How could he believe I might disgrace my father?

"Sir—" I began.

The commander frowned, and the words froze in my throat.

"I gave you no permission to speak, boy."

I shuddered and dropped my gaze to the flagstones in front of the commander's chair.

The commander looked at Faghen with a measuring glance. "As for you, Captain," he said, "you're dismissed. Confine yourself to your quarters until further notice."

Faghen's face became a stiff, unreadable mask. "Yes, sir," he said. He turned smartly and marched out of the chamber, not even glancing at me as he passed.

"And you, boy," the commander said. "Look at me."

I raised my eyes slowly, biting down hard on my lip to prevent it from trembling, but whether it was out of anger or fear, I didn't know.

"There may yet be some capacity in which you may serve," the commander said. "I will think on it. You're dismissed."

Stunned and knowing myself to be mortally wounded by the commander's words, I backed out of the chamber, then stumbled out into the courtyard. Beyond the commander's quarters, on the training field, the training master put the young men and boys through their paces with swords. His voice carried on the still air, sharp and harsh. But I could not force myself to return to the field. My disgrace would be common knowledge before the evening meal, and I could face neither the training master nor the trainees. Instead, I went to the stables and hid myself in the loft among the piles of hay. Too hurt and too angry to think clearly, I spent the day numbly watching the shadows wash across the pale mounds of hay, making then discarding fanciful plans for redemption. When evening fell, I returned to the quarters I shared with Faghen. He did not come out of his own bedchamber, and I went straight to mine. I fell exhausted into my bed, wondering whatever would become of me.

In the morning, early, before the trainees went to the training field, the commander called me again to his quarters. When I entered the spacious chamber, he was seated at his table, breaking his fast. He didn't look up as I approached and went to my knee on the polished flagstone floor. The commander kept me waiting while he unhurriedly finished his meal. When he finally looked up indifferently, I felt another strong surge of anger. It pushed back the hurt a little, and straightened my back. I was still the son of Faghen, captain of the garrison, second-in-command under the commander. I deserved better treatment from the man my father had served so faithfully for so long.

The commander leaned back in his chair, holding a mug of steaming kafe tea in his hand. The scent of it came to me, and I realized for the first time how hungry I was. I had not eaten since the midday meal the day before. But I steeled myself to let nothing show on my face. I would not disgrace myself or my father by showing any weakness whatsoever to the implacable commander.

"They tell me you have done very well on the training field," the commander said.

"I have had the privilege of good training," I murmured.

The commander raised one eyebrow, then nodded. "I see," he said. He cleared his throat and took a sip of the kafe. "I have decided how you may serve, boy."

I held my tongue, biting back angry words. I discovered how easy it would be to hate his condescending tone.

"They tell me you also have great skill as a rider," he said. "I believe you would make an excellent courier."

I looked at the floor, not trusting myself to speak.

A courier, when my father had been the commander's trusted captain. A *courier*! Allowed to carry a sword but to use it only in my own defense, never in Hakkar's service, or in service of Maedun. It was a mockery. An insulting sham. What Saesnesi or Celae would dare to attack a Somber Rider, courier, or soldier? The spell would tear their guts out before they might touch him.

Another surge of anger tore through me. My hand clenched into a tight, furious fist, but I was careful to keep it hidden from the commander. How stupid, I thought in blank amazement. How completely and utterly stupid. They would trust me with messages, some of which were of great and overwhelming importance, but they would not trust me to wield a sword in the service of Hakkar, or for Maedun's greater glory. If I was unworthy of the one, how could I qualify for the other?

It was the anger, not the shame and the hurt, that caused me to speak so rashly. "But I am a good swordsman and archer, sir —" I looked up at the commander, hiding for the first time my anger. I would become more adept and expert at it with practice.

"You will be a courier," he said flatly. "Mayhaps you will prove yourself reliable enough to serve someday as a trooper. But for now you will be a courier." He dismissed me with a wave of his hand and turned to the day's work piled on the table before him. I had no doubt that he had completely forgotten me before I was so much as out of the chamber.

When I returned to the quarters I shared with my father, Faghen was gone. The guard posted at the door informed me brusquely that my effects had been moved to the stable loft. I would sleep there until a place could be found for me in the barracks. Again, my anger flooded through me like a wave of molten lead.

If this was the way the Somber Riders of Maedun rewarded a lifetime of training and loyalty, I wanted no part of it.

I thought of the Saesnesi in the fields, laboring dully under the effects of the spell. I wanted no part of that, either.

The next day, I began my new assignment first thing in

the morning. The commander gave me a pouch containing the report he sent to the Lord Protector in Clendonan thrice a fortnight. Stoically, I took the satchel. I would be a courier. The only alternatives were death, or existing in abject slavery under the spell in the living death of the men who worked the fields and tended the flocks.

On that first long ride to Clendonan, I had time to think. At first, the pain and humiliation of being denied access to the training fields, of being barred from the quarters I had thought of as my own—my home—was a burden too great to bear. My shattered ambition to become first a lieutenant, then a captain like my father, lay like shards of broken glass in my belly. And I knew that, no matter how strong my determination to prove myself trustworthy, I would never be allowed to become so much as a simple soldier, let alone an officer, despite the commander's parting words. And all because of the portion of the blood in my body that came from my mother. Blood considered tainted.

I thought about my mother and hated her for what she had done to my life. Had she been there before me, I might have killed her. I hardly remembered her at all. What right had she to rise like a specter and kill my future? I hated her.

Entirely unbidden, a memory drifted into my mind. A fragment of melody. When I was very small, her singing had comforted me as I fell asleep. In spite of who my father was, in spite of what the Somber Riders had done to her people, she had loved her child.

The memory froze in my mind.

My mother had loved me.

Later, whenever I thought back on that first trip to Clendonan, I realized how close I had come to allowing my bitterness and anger and disappointment to turn me into a man with a rabid hatred for the Saesnesi, and by extension, the Celae. I could have allowed myself to hate my mother's blood, my mother's people, for my circumstances, and vented my rage upon them.

But I did not. Perhaps it was the memory of that sweet voice singing me to sleep as a child that prevented me from turning that way. Or perhaps it was the deep-seated practicality and pragmatism that Faghen had taught me over the years. It was useless to waste my energy in hating something that could not be changed. There was no sense in raging against a fate that was set.

Instead of letting myself get caught up in a furious turmoil of hate and anger, I let myself sink into a morass of resigned and bitter acceptance of the inevitable.

But, seeing the halfling child in the mountains had set an idea to worrying at the corner of my mind. I wondered at the future before that small boy. What fate was waiting for him. And was my own fate so inevitable? Might I yet be able to change it?

The possibility intrigued me.

14

The royal palace in Clendonan stood on a promontory above the city, looking out over the brackish waters at the head of the Tiderace. From where I stood on the terraced walk beside the stables, I could barely make out the blurred green of the Summer Run to the north of the tossing white-caps of the inlet. Clouds like bruises hung low over the city. Farther east, long, dark streamers of rain curved down from the clouds and swept across the water and sodden green fields. It would reach the city before long. The coming night was going to be a wet and chilly one—a night best spent indoors.

I had just the place to spend the evening. A place full of treasure, and as far as I knew, I was the only one who knew it was there.

I turned away from the pewter-colored water and made my way across the courtyard to a small door near the kitchens. As a courier, I had access to the palace. I wore the raven flash of Hakkar's personal service on the sleeve of my tunic above the lightning flash of a courier. A courier was almost as invisible as a servant. No one ever paid any attention to me. I had discovered that if I walked purposefully as if I were on an errand, no guard or officer, nor even any trooper, ever challenged me. The only time I had ever been turned back was once when I accidentally came too close to the Lord Protector's personal quarters.

Hakkar had left most of the furnishings in the palace unchanged when he commandeered it for his headquarters after the invasion. The tapestry wall hangings, the thick carpets on the floors, the statuary and paintings lining the corridors may have been decadently opulent to Maedun eyes, but they fascinated me. I had never seen anything so rich as the palace furnishings. Nothing like carpets, upholstered benches, or tapestries and paintings had ever been placed in any garrison headquarters I'd been in. Some were exquisite and lovely enough to take my breath away.

The tapestries and paintings, so carefully and artistically worked, spoke of a people gone soft and sedentary with their leisure. But those same tapestries and paintings sometimes depicted scenes of battle. I had studied enough tactics and strategy while I was in training to recognize the military adroitness of the battle scenes. The men who directed those battles were by no means decadent and soft.

Other tapestries and paintings portrayed scenes containing beings who were obviously gods and goddesses. They gave me my first insight into the Celae and the role that their gods and goddesses played in their lives. They were a far cry from the austere and unforgiving All-Father of the Maedun, whose wrath my father had held as a threat over my head if my performance in practice was not up to his expectations.

I had been in Clendonan only a fortnight when I discovered the forgotten library. I had proved myself to be swift and reliable as a courier. The Lord Protector surprised me by noticing, and brought me into his personal courier service. For the first while, I had little to do, so I spent my time exploring these passageways. I had begun wandering more to dispel my boredom than to indulge my wonder and curiosity. I had opened a door in a lower corridor one dreary, wet afternoon about a year ago, and found it full of piles of books and stacked sheaves of parchment, all of them thick with dust and cobwebs. The air was filled with the smell of grit and mildew. The only light came from three window slits high up near the ceiling. Judging by the undisturbed dust on the floor, no one had been in the room for years. Perhaps not even since the invasion.

Books!

Stunned with delight, I stepped into the room and closed the door carefully behind me.

Books!

I reached out to touch one of the books, brushing away some of the dust and cobwebs. Spots of mildew discolored the cover. When I opened it, the edges of the pages were marked by damp stains but looked relatively undamaged.

Books.

I hadn't seen or touched books since shortly after I had begun training at the garrison all those years ago. And here were a hundred books—mayhaps a thousand of them—and obviously no one but me realized they were here.

I had found treasure indeed. Treasure more dear than all the richly embroidered tapestries or brilliantly painted portraits. Treasure all my own.

I laughed aloud in pleasure, delighted by the irony of the situation. Had the commander of my father's garrison known I could read, I never would have been assigned as a courier. Hakkar and his officers preferred illiterate couriers. That way, they could be reasonably certain their dispatches would be read only by the persons they were intended to reach. But my father had intended me to be an officer. I had been taught to read shortly after my father took me from my mother. Not until I entered training had the lessons stopped. By then, I had developed an insatiable appetite for the knowledge contained in books. Reading was the thing I missed most when my field training began.

I ran my fingers lovingly down the page. It was, of course, written in the Celae language, which I could neither read nor speak. But it was beautifully printed and illuminated, a joy to the eyes, even if I could not understand the words.

I could learn to speak Celae. And if I could speak it, I might learn to read it. Once one knew that the letters made certain sounds, ciphering the words wasn't as impossible as it appeared. I remembered the Saesnesi tongue. It had come back to me slowly as I listened carefully to the men of the Summer Run when they spoke to each other. I understood the language as well now as I had when I was a child. With practice, I had taught myself first to sort out the letters, then use the letters to make words. I didn't read it as well as I wished I could, but I would improve with practice.

I wandered about the room, unable to prevent myself from touching the books. So many of them. They must have come from a great library. The prince or duke who had occupied this palace before the coming of the Maedun must have been a learned man, fully appreciative of the wealth contained in books.

But why had they all been piled so carelessly into this forgotten room? Surely the Lord Protector could use the information contained in this musty chamber. Had he wanted the library for another purpose, mayhaps, and ordered the books moved, and then forgotten them?

But it didn't matter. Who had moved the books to this place, for whatever reason, it didn't matter. I had found them, and they were mine.

On my first visit, I had merely looked at the books. On my second, I tried to worry out what one of the books was about. I failed, but was too exhilarated by my discovery to be discouraged. I would sort it out eventually. On my third visit, to my surprise and delight, I found a whole stack of books written in the Saesnesi tongue.

Slowly, I figured out the words and read the history of the Saesnesi. I discovered their heroic sagas—stories and

poems and songs, that had come down from a time long
before the era of written language. The sonorous rhythm of
the poetry sang to me, reminding me of the songs my
mother sang to me when I was very small, igniting a fire in
my heart.

To my complete delight and surprise, I discovered ref-
erences to a Celwalda—High Saesnesi Prince in Celi—
who bore the same name as I. Cynric, the first Celwalda to
call himself by that title when the Saesnesi first came to this
isle. I read as much as I could get my hands on about him.
The books referred to him as a brave man, a fierce and
canny fighter, astute and resourceful, and a wise leader to
his people.

I spent many hours as I rode thinking about that first
Cynric and all the Celwaldae who had followed him.
Slowly I came to realize the truth behind my mother's people. It had taken sorcery to defeat them. Not lack of bravery—they had never wanted for courage. Only the black
sorcery wielded by the ancestor of this Hakkar of Maedun
who styled himself Lord Protector of Celi had defeated the
Saesnesi. Not even the bravest of men could stand against
sorcery.

Somewhere deep in my shattered heart, a tiny spark of
pride kindled to life.

On a wet and chilly night in early spring, I made my way
through the corridors to the lost library. The book I
selected from a teetering stack contained songs of the
Celae. I could make neither head nor tail of what had to be
musical notations, but after years of practice, I could read
most of the words, translating slowly. Though I still
couldn't speak the language well, I could make sense of the
written word.

After glancing through the book, I found it hardly surprising that these books lay forgotten and moldering in a nearly abandoned corridor. Either Hakkar had banished the books here because of their inflammatory content, or they had been hidden for safekeeping. The last song in the book, handwritten in a spidery hand, told the story of the king of the Celae, and how he had been defeated by the invading army. It also told of two swords crafted by one of their great smiths for a king and an enchanter who would defeat the enemy—the Maedun, obviously—and free Celi.

Even I knew the prophecy. From the line of the Prince of Skai will come an enchanter who will destroy Maedun. My father had used the prophecy as a reminder for eternal vigilance. He had seen that I heeded it, too.

The song was written in a different color ink from the rest of the songs in the book, obviously penned by someone after the Great Invasion, after the Lord Protector took the throne in Clendonan. Mayhaps by the man who had brought the books here, where I eventually found them.

The candle I had brought with me guttered, and I looked up, startled. I had been in the library far longer than I had intended to be. The palace would be sleeping, except for the guards walking the corridors in pairs.

I closed the book and slipped it back into its place. Then, on sudden impulse, I picked it up again. It was hardly bigger than my hand, and only a little thicker than a thumbbreadth. I tucked it into my belt pouch. It fit as if made for it. Carefully, I blew out the candle stub, then listened at the door to make sure the corridor was empty.

I heard nothing. Quickly, I stepped out into the corridor and closed the door firmly behind me. I had no sooner turned away from the door and started down the passageway than two guards rounded the corner and confronted me.

"What are you doing here?" demanded the taller of the two.

Painfully conscious of the book secreted in my pouch, I held out my sleeve so he could see the courier insignia. "A message," I said.

"There's no one down here to deliver a message to," he said, suspicion puckering his brow.

"I know," I said with some asperity. "I must have lost my way. I think I'm lost."

His suspicion didn't lessen. "Where's your message!"

My heart jumped in my chest. I had no written message with me. And these guards knew that a lowly courier would never be trusted with a verbal message. My mouth dry, I reached into my pouch and brought forth the little book. "This is it," I said.

He took it and opened it at random. I held my breath. I highly doubted he could read, but he might know enough to realize that the words were not in the Maedun language. He frowned at the book, trying to look intelligent. My relief nearly buckled my knees. He couldn't read, and he had no idea the book was written in the Celae tongue.

"Who's this for?" he demanded.

I thought quickly. The only man in the palace who might read a book was Hakkar himself. Or his seneschal.

"The lord Baerg," I said.

The guard looked at me, still distrustful and doubtful. "The lord Baerg, is it? And who'd send the lord Seneschal a book such as this?"

I hesitated. "A woman," I said at last.

"A woman?" He pounced on it. "Who?"

I hesitated again. The guard grinned widely. "Ah," he said. "A woman not his wife." He laughed aloud.

"Exactly," I said. "Neither of them would wish me to divulge her name."

He handed me back the book. I tucked it again into the pouch. "That way," he said. "Around the corner and up the stairs. You'll find the Great Hall to your left. Go right for the seneschal's quarters."

I thanked him and hurried away, cursing quietly under my breath. I could not now take the chance of returning to the lost library for a long time. Not until the guard rotation changed in two fortnights. If that guard caught me again in that corridor, I doubted a fanciful lie about the seneschal and an imaginary woman would extricate me from the predicament. He'd certainly be suspicious enough to report my presence there to his superior. His superior would not be nearly so gullible and ready to believe a lie. Nor would he be fooled by a small book.

I was lucky this time. I'd best not rely on only luck in the future.

The next day, I rode again from Clendonan, out to the mountains in the west for the first time since I had seen the small halfling boy. As I came through the Dead Lands and passed the turnoff that led to the farm, I hesitated, wondering if the child was still there. But my saddle pack bulged with dispatches Hakkar was in a hurry to deliver to his garrison commanders in the west. I prided myself on making the trip faster than any of Hakkar's other couriers. I had found several shortcuts through the mountains that worked very well. Some of them were steep and narrow and dangerous, but taken together, cut a full day's ride off the trip to the coastal garrison and back to Clendonan. I had no chance to prove to Hakkar that I was an expert swordsman, but he knew I was an excellent horseman. The rugged mountain tracks gave me no trouble.

Spring had come to the mountains. The air smelled clean and fresh, the fragrance of green, growing things rising thickly all around me. The leaves on the oaks and silverleaf maple were just barely open, lending a dappled gold shade to the track. Small, brilliant white flowers starred the grass along the verge, and the bracken was more than belly-high to the horse. The barely discernible path that turned off the main track was dry and hard, offering no danger to the horse's hooves, no mud or ice to slip on and wrench a muscle or break a leg. Last year's dead leaves were dry and lay crumbling without protest back into the soil. I turned the horse onto a track that led upward through the trees to a ridge that snaked its way high above the river valley.

As I rode at full gallop along the shortcut, I found myself thinking of the boy on the farm. What would that child grow up to be? He would think of himself as Celae, just as I had thought of myself as Maedun. I wondered if the Celae were more accepting of *mongrel seed* than the Maedun were. Somehow, I didn't think they were. It was something interesting to contemplate.

I rode along the ridge between the trees and the edge of a steep bank above the river. Below, the water purling through the rapids sent a fine mist swirling and skimming over the rippled surface and soaking the tumbled boulders along the rocky shore. I saw it without paying attention to it, controlling the horse beneath me by instinct and long practice, fully preoccupied with my thoughts. It was a stupid, foolish thing to do. These mountains demanded vigilance, not preoccupation, and I paid dearly for my lapse. When the mountain cat screamed and leapt out of the tree, missing the horse by mere inches, it caught me completely by surprise.

The horse, startled and terrified, reared and spun on its back feet. Trying to control the horse with one hand, I drew my sword with the other and thrust it blindly at the big cat. I missed, and the cat sailed across the track and into the trees behind the horse. Before I could regain my balance, the edge of the bank crumbled under the horse's feet, and it plunged headfirst down the gorge. I hurtled over the flailing horse's shoulder to tumble helplessly down the bank. The last thing I remember seeing was the jagged rocks along the watercourse growing rapidly before my eyes.

I do not know how long I was unconscious, but the sun had climbed to stand directly overhead, burning the skin of my face. I first became aware of a raging thirst, then the pain. Pain seethed throughout my whole body, but mostly concentrated in my left temple and my left side above the waist. Each breath felt like a sword blade thrusting through my side. Broken ribs, I thought foggily. I wondered if they had punctured a lung. If so, I would surely die, drowning eventually in my own blood.

A high price to pay for a few moments of inattention.

It hurt so much to breathe, I had to concentrate my whole attention on breathing as shallowly as possible so I didn't move my chest very much. I couldn't even curl up to ease the bruises where jagged rocks dug into my back. I thought the pain in my chest alone might kill me.

A shadow fell across my eyes. It took me several bleary seconds to realize that something had moved between me and the sun. Slowly, painfully, I dragged my eyes open and looked up against the dazzle of the light.

It was a woman. Young, lovely. Very fair, with eyes as gray as the tightly folded graybells that grew so thickly in these mountains. For a wild moment, I thought I had died and been taken by one of the Kyriae, the female warriors of the old Saesnesi legends.

The girl standing over me carried a knife. She moved forward slightly and looked down at me. Her young face held no sympathy, no pity, no hope of offering either help or a warrior's reward. She was no Celae. Not with hair and eyes like that. And she was no Kyriae. She was real, and she was alive, and she held a lethal dagger. She looked something like the mother I could only vaguely remember.

I moistened my dry, cracked lips. "Saesnesi?" I asked, concentrating carefully on the word to make my voice come clearly from my broken mouth.

The girl held the knife before her. "Yes."

I held no illusions about what the Somber Riders had done to the Celae hiding in these mountains. I had not realized there were Saesnesi here, too, but I knew they would have been treated no differently than the Celae, fared no better. I could expect nothing but a quick death from this girl. My eyes felt filled with grit, and I closed them against the pain in my head and chest.

"Do it quickly," I whispered. "It will be a mercy." I coughed, and the taste of fresh blood burst suddenly against my tongue. Mayhaps I *had* punctured a lung. I waited for the bright pain that would release me forever.

But it didn't come. Foggily, I realized I was still alive. How odd. I opened my eyes again. The girl still stood over me, the knife in her hand glinting in the sunlight. I read irresolution on her face, a hesitation.

"You cannot hurt me more than I am already hurt," I murmured. "Even without your blade, I will die soon."

The girl crouched beside me. I smelled the faint fragrance of flowers and herbs coming from her shining gold hair, and the scent of her made me dizzy.

"Why are you alone?" the girl demanded. "Where are all of the others?"

"I ride alone," I replied, closing my eyes and turning my head away. It hurt my throat to speak. "I am a courier." I coughed again, and the all-encompassing rush of pain shrouded me in a dark mist. "Please," I murmured. "Some water . . ."

The girl unfastened a bullock's horn from her belt and took it to the water's edge. She filled it and brought it to me, then supported my head as she held the horn to my lips. Her gentleness surprised me, and I nearly choked on the water. The taste of it was sweet and cold and clean in my bruised mouth. I drank deeply, gratefully, and thanked her.

"How is it you speak our language?" she asked.

I let a faint smile twist at the corner of my mouth. I hadn't realized we were speaking Saesnesi. "I am half Saesnesi," I told her. "They call me Jonvar." I hesitated, then continued, realizing I had made my decision a long time ago. "But my name is Cynric. Aye, my name is Cynric."

The girl looked down at me for a long moment, indecision in her face. Finally, she said, "Your mother was Saesnesi?"

"Yes. She named me for the first Celwalda."

"My twice-great-grandfather was also named Cynric." I saw her come to a decision, saw her face firm with it. She got to her feet. "I am going to fetch the Healer," she said. "There is nothing I can do for you. I'll bring Gordan. He might be able to help."

I tried to protest but coughed, and the pain sent me spinning off into the gray mists. When I looked up again, she was gone.

15

I awoke to the glow of a banked fire. In the muted, wavering light, I picked out unfamiliar dark shapes around me, and for many minutes, I lay in confusion, not knowing where I was or how I had come to be there. My head didn't feel firmly attached to my shoulders, and an enervating lassitude flooded through my whole body.

Gradually, I remembered brief flashes of what might have been a dream. The scream of a mountain cat. A horse plunging wildly and out of control beneath me. Slick, wet boulders glittering in the sun as they grew terrifyingly large before my eyes.

In small snatches, then more completely, memory returned. I remembered the fall. And there was a girl by the river. Young, pretty, and Saesnesi.

How odd. She certainly should have killed me as I lay there among the stones, hurt and helpless. But she had not. I'd lost consciousness again after she left me, and regained it much later to find the girl and an old man bending over me.

The old man was not Saesnesi. Most of his beard and hair had turned to silver, but the glossy blue-black of youth still streaked it liberally. Celae, then. More fitting for him to be here, I thought irrelevantly. This is wild Celae country. Not Saesnesi lands.

From within the fevered prison of my pain, my dazed mind played tricks on me. I thought the old man's eyes glowed with a strange, soft light from his lined, sun-darkened face. Very gently, he had put a hand to my forehead and smiled at me. Not since Faghen tore me away from my mother had anyone touched me that tenderly.

"Lose the pain in sleep, lad," the silver-haired Celae man said quietly.

Miraculously, the pain ebbed away like water flowing into parched earth. A blessed peace stole through me, and I breathed for the first time without the knives of agony tearing through my chest. I had no time to thank him, to voice my inexpressible gratitude before the lassitude claimed me, and I closed my eyes and slept.

No pain invaded the soft, firelit shadows where I lay now. What manner of magic had been worked on me by the old man? I had never heard of anyone being cured of injuries so quickly. I was aware of only a dull ache in my head and chest, but the lances of pain were gone, and my breathing was easy and natural.

A Healer. The woman had called the old man a Healer. Gratefully, I came to the realization that the old man had worked his arts on me. If this were the loathsome Celi magic Hakkar spoke of, I was more than happy to be under its power. I would cough up no more blood. I would not die of my injuries. I might still die by a Saesnesi blade, but the thought could not arouse the worry or apprehension it should. It was enough at that moment to be free of the torment and able to breathe without pain.

Through the open window, faint in the night, I heard the thin cry of an infant. A moment later, a woman's voice began to sing very softly. I could not hear the words, but wonderingly, I recognized the tune. My own mother had sung it to me, before Faghen had taken me from her. More than fifteen years had passed since I had last heard it, but I knew it. It reassured me, made me feel secure in the unfamiliar bed. Come morning, I would have to deal with being a captive of the Saesnesi. But not yet. In the darkness, I smiled and drifted back to sleep.

•   •   •

I awoke again to find the girl bent over me. She was younger than I had at first thought. Mayhaps twelve or thirteen. Still a child in that coltish stage between childhood and womanhood, but showing the promise of beauty. She looked gravely down at me, gray eyes wide, as I struggled out of the clinging depths of sleep.

"Are you awake?" she asked.

"Almost," I said. I found I could sit up, but it felt as if I were unfolding myself a section at a time. My head and chest didn't hurt, but my muscles were stiff and aching as if I had spent all of the day before running up and down mountains. But once I was up, I had no difficulty staying up.

"Gordan said I should feed you and then help you outside," she said.

I thought about it for a moment. "Mayhaps you should help me outside, first," I said.

She read the embarrassment in my face and smiled. "Let's see if we can get you on your feet."

Again, I had the odd sensation of unfolding like an old hinged shutter. And like an old hinged shutter, I think I creaked. But with the girl's help, I made it outside to the latrine shed, then back into the house. I was weak and giddy and light-headed, but remarkably well considering the damage I had done to myself in the fall the day before.

I had to concentrate on not falling, trying not to lean too heavily on the girl's delicate young shoulder. I had no time to get a good look around. I had only an impression of a good-sized stone-built house amid a cluster of smaller houses. Beyond lay an orchard, and three stone cairns rose beneath the outstretched branches of the fruit trees.

The girl helped me back to my bed. It was in the main room. The room served the same function as a Great Hall, but it was far smaller. She pulled the blankets up over my legs and left me sitting propped up against a pile of fleece-stuffed pillows while she disappeared down a short corridor. She returned a moment later carrying a tray laden with fresh bread, cheese, and a bowl of broth.

"Gordan said you needed good food," she said.

"Gordan," I repeated. "He's the old man with the silver hair and beard?"

"Yes. Our Healer. He's Celae."

The bread and cheese were delicious, but I tired before I could finish them. The broth was easier to manage. I handed the bowl back to the girl, and she took it solemnly. "Who are you?" I asked.

"Denia," she said. "My brother is Wykan. He's leader here. He and our cousin Kier are out hunting right now. He'll be back this evening, though."

And be completely horrified to find a Maedun courier in his bed, I thought. In spite of the help Denia had given, in spite of the aid of the Celae Healer, I was not out of danger yet. I doubted that Wykan, who was "leader here," would be as hospitable and accepting as his young sister.

And I was right. Wykan and Kier arrived together as the sun fell below the crests of the western mountains, bearing between them the carcass of a deer. They were both fair-haired, their hair nearly the same color as a wheat field under the sun in autumn, neither of them not more than a few years older than I, somewhere in their late twenties, mayhaps. I had no difficulty sorting out which one was Wykan. He had a definite air of command about him. Somewhat akin to the aura a good garrison captain wore like a cloak. His hair and beard were neatly trimmed, and his gray eyes were very like his sister's eyes, but infinitely more cold, more knowing and unforgiving.

Kier was like him in features, but bigger, stronger. He looked as if he could break the neck of a deer with one blow of his huge fists.

I feigned sleep as they entered, trying to watch through slitted eyelids. I wanted to learn as much as I could before I had to face them. It occurred to me, too, that they might not kill a sleeping man out of hand. Buying all the time I could seemed like an excellent and intelligent idea.

"Who's that?" Wykan asked sharply. "What happened? Is someone hurt? Ill?"

Denia had been carding wool near the far window. She jumped to her feet and came to meet him.

"Who is that?" he asked, looking past her.

"A Somber Rider . . ." Denia began.

Wykan gave his sister a look of incredulous consternation and pushed past her to look down at me. He turned to her. "Are you mad?" he said, obviously appalled—as well he might be. "Bringing a Somber Rider here? What in the name of the Deity possessed you to do such a thing?"

Kier brushed past them, a stiletto in his hand winking in the light of the fire. "Kill him now," he said, his voice harsh. "Kill him and have done with it."

Denia caught his arm. "No!" she cried. "No, Kier. Leave him. Let me explain."

"You're defending him?" Kier asked, his face puckered in astonishment. "You're defending a Somber Rider, Denia? You? I can't believe it!"

Gordan came into the room. "I, too, defend him, Kier," he said quietly. "For good reason . . ."

"What good reason can there be for keeping a Somber Rider alive?" Kier demanded. "They've killed our people as if we were nothing more than dogs . . ."

Denia did not let go of her grip on Kier's arm. "Kier, his name is Cynric. He was born in the Summer Run . . ."

"He's a courier," Gordan said, placing himself between Kier and the bed. I held my eyes shut tight.

Wykan stepped around Gordan and looked down at me again. His mouth twisted into a sardonic smile. "You say he was born in the Summer Run?" he asked.

"Yes," Denia said. "He's part Saesnesi."

Bitterness I could almost taste welled up and overflowed in Wykan's eyes. "The Summer Run," he muttered. "This man, this enemy—born in the land I've never been allowed to see—" He looked angry enough to kill me with no further thought. But his face changed, and he looked up at Denia, an odd expression in his eyes. "Did you say his name is Cynric?"

"His mother was Saesnesi," she said.

"He was badly hurt," Gordan said. "His horse threw him, and he tumbled down onto rocks near the river. If Denia hadn't found him, I believe his injuries would have proved mortal. I gave him sleep before Denia and I brought him here. I used my art on his hurts. The healing process is well started now, but he lay for a long time before Denia found him. He has little strength. In the morning, he should be strong enough to tell you his story."

Denia still had not relaxed her grip on Kier's arm. "If you still want to kill him after you've heard his story," she said, "then I will not stop you."

Wykan watched Gordan. The old Healer stood straight and firm between Kier and me. He came visibly to a decision. "You believe him to be of importance to us, Gordan?" he asked.

"I do, my lord," Gordan said formally. "Important in the events we spoke of before. In the morning, you will hear and make your own decision."

We faced each other warily in the early-morning sunshine. Hostility and suspicion showed plainly in Wykan's face, in every nuance of his stance and posture. I might have been more adept at hiding my feelings. I hoped my taut nerves were not so apparent. My life hung more precariously in the balance than it had even when I lay injured among the river stones. What I did and said in the next few minutes would decide whether I lived or died.

I had a much better look at both Wykan and Kier in the morning sunlight. Wykan was about the same age as I, perhaps a year or two older. But those gray eyes had seen much, I thought. There was little enough of youth left to soften their steady, guarded appraisal. He was obviously the leader of this small band, even though there were several men older and more experienced in the tight little group. The old man, the Healer they called Gordan, had referred to him as "my lord" several times. More important, Wykan acted like a leader, a man who expected to be respected and obeyed.

I studied him, watching for the telling details that might give me an indication of what he might be thinking. But the closed expression gave away nothing he didn't want given away. He had enough self-control for two garrison commanders.

He was tall, with a nimble, well-muscled slenderness that was deceiving. There was far more physical strength and endurance there than expected, I decided. He gave the impression of remarkable competence and ability. Every man in the small band deferred to him without question. Even the commander of my father's garrison had not had that kind of imposing presence. In Wykan, the ability must have been instinctive, inbred, natural. There were certainly no high-ranking officers here to teach it to him.

The other one, the man called Kier, who never left Wykan's side, reminded me of a leather whip, or a tautly drawn bowstring. Above the gaunt hollows of his cheeks, blue eyes burned fiercely. His hand never strayed far from the dagger at his hip, and his hatred was a palpable thing when he glanced at me. That one wanted me dead and made no pretense about it. In my still-weakened state, I was powerless to defend myself. I had to rely on Wykan's cooler head.

I had managed to totter out of the house to the privy by myself with no help from Denia. She had not taken me back inside, but helped me to find a place to sit in the sun outside the door. She had given me another plate of bread and cheese, and a cup of cold springwater, then left me to my own devices while she went about her chores.

I had just finished eating when Wykan and Kier approached me from the village beyond the big house. A few moments later, Gordan the Healer joined us, finding a comfortable place to sit not far from me. Wykan sat on his heels in front of me with the supple, finely balanced ease of long practice. Behind him, Kier remained standing, his mouth drawn into a grim and level line, hostility surrounding him like a visible aura.

"I am Wykan," Wykan said. "I'm leader here. Gordan assures me there are good reasons for keeping you alive. I would hear your story, so I can decide for myself what to do with you."

"Where would you have me start?" I asked. My almost accentless Saesnesi clearly startled Wykan. The gray eyes widened slightly, then narrowed again.

He allowed a humorless smile to quirk at the corner of his mouth. Deliberate, I thought. This man was not the sort to let anything show if he didn't want it to.

"The beginning is usually a good place," he said. "You were born in the Summer Run?"

"Yes, I was. My mother was Saesnesi. My father took her to bed against her will—or what will she had left under the spell." I told the story as briefly and simply as I could.

Wykan interrupted me a few times to ask for clarification; otherwise, he listened with all his attention, his eyes never leaving my face. When I finished, he was quiet for a long time, digesting the tale.

When he finally spoke, he said, "So the Summer Run is not burned and bleak like the country just east of the mountains?"

I shook my head. "No. It's green as these mountains. There's a band of desolate country along the eastern slopes of the Spine and south of the wall—"

Wykan frowned. "The wall?" he asked sharply.

"Not really a wall," I said. "The foothills south of the northern mountains. They rise steeply, and someone said they looked like a wall."

"I see. Continue, then."

"The Dead Lands are not very wide," I said. "Not more than two or three leagues at the widest. Otherwise, the country is green. Hakkar's soldiers see that the Celae and the Saesnesi work the land well. It's a fertile land. But most of the production goes back to Maedun."

"What about the land from here west to the sea?" Wykan asked.

"Green, as well. Each garrison along the coast has a warlock with it. They keep Hakkar's spell strengthened to make sure the Celae are well under it. There are bands of people in these mountains not under the spell. Bands like yours, but of Celae. By staying more than two leagues away from the garrisons, they aren't affected by the spell. Its range is limited, but overwhelming within its limits, you understand."

Wykan glanced over at Gordan. "That's good news," he said thoughtfully. "We need not worry about the spell while we search for Celae to the west."

"If we can trust him," Kier muttered. "Remember. He's

one of them. He's a Somber Rider."

I knew there was no sense telling Kier that I wasn't a Somber Rider, and never had been. Kier would make no distinction between a courier and a soldier. I looked away from the burning blue of Kier's glare, back to Wykan.

"Where are the garrisons?" Wykan asked.

"I don't know where all of them are," I said. "I'm based in Clendonan, on the Tiderace. I know there's a garrison that lies near an inlet about ten leagues south of where the River Eidon flows into the sea, and there's another two leagues north of the inlet. I believe there may be three more scattered along the coast, but I'm not sure where they are. All told, there are perhaps twelve to fifteen garrisons in the west. Each garrison consists of two hundred men and officers. Sometimes there are officers' wives and children there, too."

"Celae or Saesnesi wives?" Kier asked, his eyes cold with rage and hatred.

I dropped his gaze. "No. They don't consider Celae or Saesnesi women worth the marrying. As I told you, the offspring are considered tainted and untrustworthy, not fit to serve the Black Sorcerer."

"But you serve him."

"As a courier only," I said. "I am one of more than twenty couriers Hakkar keeps at Clendonan. I am barred from the army, and from being an officer as my father was."

"A courier is not a bad job."

I allowed myself a bitter smile. "It is to a Maedun Somber Rider. Only those judged not fit to be Somber Riders become couriers. I was relegated to being a courier because the commander of my father's garrison knew it would be more galling than becoming a slave and working the fields like the other Saesnesi around the garrison. If he suspected I knew how to read, I'd probably still be in the

Summer Run, under the spell, or most likely dead because the warlock said I have a high resistance to the spell."

Wykan looked at me thoughtfully, his eyes cold and appraising. "Is that the only reason you wish to join us?" he asked. "Because they rejected you?"

I met the penetrating stare. "I had not thought of it until your sister found me by the river," I said truthfully. "Over the last several years, I've discovered a lot about the Saesnesi, my mother's people. I learned it was a blood I should be proud of. It took sorcery to defeat them. There were writings in the library in Clendonan that referred to Aellegh, the last Celwalda. He was a duke any man would have been proud to serve under. He fought bravely, and he was undefeated when they killed him."

"He didn't die out there," Wykan said. "He came here, to the safely of the mountains after the invasion, and he brought his son, who was also named Cynric, and kin-daughter here with him. He was my grandfather."

I stared at him. The blood drained from my head, leaving me dizzy and weak. "You are Celwalda?" I asked.

"I am," Wykan said. "The Cynric you are named for was my ancestor."

I took a deep breath. I straightened up, then struggled to my feet, supporting myself against the rough stone wall behind me. Wykan rose as I did, and we stood facing each other in the blazing sunlight.

"My lord—" I said softly.

The wariness and suspicion did not ease in Wykan's face. But it was Kier who spoke.

"You can't be taken in by him, Wykan," he cried harshly. "He's a Somber Rider—"

I looked at Kier, read the fury and hatred in those smoldering blue eyes. There might be one way to prove where my loyalties lay—a dangerous way. Something I had read in the old writings in the dusty books in the lost library. And I found myself wanting to do it. I had to declare myself one way or the other, and I wanted to be Saesnesi. Not Maedun. I reached out a hand to Kier.

"Lend me your dagger," I said.

Kier glanced at Wykan. Wykan hesitated, frowning, then nodded. Kier drew his dagger and placed the haft in my outstretched hand. I met Wykan's gaze, saw there the sudden flash of understanding as he realized what I was about to do—a gesture that had not been performed for generations. I smiled grimly as his breath caught in his throat, and he made a quickly aborted move toward the dagger, then dropped his hand and merely waited calmly as befitted a Celwalda of the Summer Run.

The dagger held firmly in my right hand, I raised my other hand. I bent back my left hand, my heart hand, stretching the skin of my wrist taut across the bones so that the veins showed clearly, faint blue lines against the skin. Then, slowly and deliberately, still looking at Wykan, our gazes locked, I used the point of the dagger to open the veins. Bright blood welled up in a flood and splashed to the ground at Wykan's feet.

16

Wykan stood in the bright sunlight, watching me with narrowed eyes. Behind him, even Kier stared speechless as my blood flowed in a narrow, scarlet river from the gash in my wrist.

The symbolism was ancient and specific. I offered my life's blood to nourish the soil Wykan ruled. He could accept me as an ally and vassal and stanch the flow of blood, or he could deny the offer and let me bleed to death. The choice was his. I watched his eyes, trying to keep my gaze level, steady, and outwardly calm despite the thundering rhythm of my heart. Surely all three of them, Wykan, Kier, and Gordan should have heard that fearful pounding. I thought I saw the flash of reluctant admiration glint in Wykan's eyes. Quick relief washed over me, and I knew I had won. He nodded slowly.

"Bind your wound," he said quietly. "I will accept your service." Gordan threw him a scarf woven of linen, and he handed it to me.

I wrapped the scarf tightly around my wrist, stopping the flow of blood. Then I went slowly to one knee and bowed my head. "My lord," I said clearly above the thumping of my heart. "My sword, my bow, and my life I pledge to your service, from now until the last days."

"Wykan, don't believe him," Kier cried. "He's still a Somber Rider, no matter what he calls himself. You can't trust him . . ."

Wykan looked up. "He's offered me both blood and loyalty . . ."

"I'll offer him death as the Somber Riders gave my mother death," Kier said, his voice low and savage. "I offer him what his people offer us . . ."

"Kier, have done!" Wykan's voice cracked like a whip. "I cannot kill a man on his knee before me."

"I can—"

Wykan caught Kier's wrist as the other man lunged forward, reaching for the dagger I still held loosely in my right hand. "No," he commanded hoarsely. "Have done, I say. Kier, you are my kinsman and my friend, as I am yours. Do not make me remind you that I am also your Celwalda."

I looked up at Kier. "I cannot change what the Somber Riders have done to you and your people," I said. "I can but say that they are now my people, too. I can help you. I can enter their garrisons, find out what they plan. I can even come and go to Clendonan unobstructed." Provided I didn't run into the guards who had seen me near the secret library.

"You go out to hunt again tomorrow," Gordan said, speaking for the first time. "Take him with you. It will make a fair test, I think."

"No!" Kier cried.

Wykan only glanced at him, then looked back to Gordan. "Is this something you've seen in the fire?" he asked.

Gordan shrugged. "I've seen shadows in the fire, my lord," he said. "But I believe this man will be useful to you. You will need him."

Wykan nodded. He looked at Kier. "You will *not* harm him, Kier," he said.

"If he betrays us . . ."

Wykan looked down at me. "If he betrays us," he said softly, "it will be my arrow that takes his life. That is my right."

We had been traveling since dawn, mostly in rigid silence, walking single file first across the shoulder of the mountains that rose behind the valley to the west, then down

along the edge of the gorge carved by the River Ovyn. Kier
walked in front, his heavy pack and his bow slung easily
across his back, I followed behind him, and Wykan
brought up the rear. Kier kept the pace fast. I had no doubt
that he hoped I was still weakened by my injuries, despite
Gordan's arts, and would rid him of the problem by simply
dropping from exhaustion. It was just as clear that Wykan,
too, knew what Kier was doing. But I hadn't made a
protest. Nor had I slackened my determination to keep up.

I carried a pack that was as heavy as Kier's and my
bow. Gordan had retrieved my sword from the riverbank
where I'd fallen, but I'd left it back at the village. Neither
Wykan nor Kier wore a sword. They left me little doubt
about the lethal accuracy of the Saesnesi longbows they
carried, though. The sagas recorded in the books secreted
in the lost library attested to the awe-inspiring power of the
longbow, as well as to the formidable force of the war ax.
But the Saesnesi had never been known for their skill with
a sword.

Wykan handled his bow with an ease that spoke of
long hours of familiarity with it, and years of practice.
Should he decide I was untrustworthy, I sincerely doubted
I could outrun or dodge his arrow.

I no longer wore the black shirt, tunic, and breeks of a
courier. The fall into the river had left them in ruined and
bloody tatters. Denia had found clothing to fit me among
the band—a shirt of pale cream-colored linen, tunic and
trews in a dark forest green. They made me far less con-
spicuous, but I still wore my black boots and cloak. I would
never pass for a Saesnesi—my hair and eyes were far too
dark—but from a distance, I might look like a Celae. At
least I no longer looked too much like a Maedun.

I had been expecting another protest from Kier when
we made ready to leave on the hunt. But Kier said nothing.

He had been grim, almost sullen, as we broke our fast with some of Denia's bread and cheese. But he had held his peace, which surprised me. And Wykan, too, I think.

When Wykan motioned him to take the lead as we prepared to leave the valley, the skin around Kier's mouth whitened in anger as he pressed his lips firmly together. When he spoke, his voice was almost a snarl, quivering with anger, tight and raw.

"Don't you trust me at the back of your pet beast?"

"You are best in the mountains," Wykan said mildly. "If you'd rather, I'll take the lead."

Kier said nothing. He merely straightened his shoulders and began walking. Silently, Wykan and I fell in behind him.

The mountains rose steeply around us once we were out of the valley. Great stands of cedar and fir spilled down the slopes toward the river. Farther down the mountain, deeper in the river valley, oaks, silver-leaf maple, ash, and alder crowded close to the watercourse, their leaves glimmering brilliant green in the sunshine. Occasionally, the startling, creamy white of dogwood blossoms flashed amid the variegated green. The early-morning air smelled of damp earth and green, growing things.

The sun crossed the sky slowly above us, hot on my back in the morning. The heat helped dissipate the last of the lingering stiffness and soreness in my muscles. I don't know how Gordan worked his magic arts, but I was humbly grateful to him. Three days ago, I had given myself over to death by drowning in my own blood. Today, I hiked easily enough along a mountain track, with the nearly euphoric exhilaration of surviving singing in my veins. Kier's glowering face could not sour my mood.

At midday, Wykan called a halt. We made a sheltered camp among a copse of silver-leaf maple by a wide pool

made by a small burn curving widely about a rocky outcropping. I helped Wykan build a fire while Kier went out
with his bow. Twenty minutes later, a fat hare sizzled on a
spit above the flames.

When we finished eating, I sat with my back to the
broad trunk of a maple and closed my eyes. The sun felt
good against my skin.

I heard Kier get to his feet suddenly and stride down to
the bank of the little stream. After a moment, Wykan followed. I opened my eyes to watch. He stood quietly by
Kier's side as Kier tossed small pebbles into the still, brown
water.

"What would you have me do, Kier?" Wykan's voice
came to me only faintly. "Kill him and let him die along with
all that knowledge that might be invaluable to us?"

"I don't trust him," Kier said. "I can't help thinking this
is a trick, that he means us harm."

Wykan picked up a small stone and lobbed it out into
the middle of the stream. "I trust him," he said. "Or, I trust
Gordan's assessment of him. And I trust what he's told us,
at any rate."

"And what hasn't he told us?"

"I don't know. Time will show us that. But Gordan
wouldn't have saved him if he had no purpose to serve for us."

Kier glanced at him, exasperation and annoyance
drawing the heavy blond eyebrows together over his nose.
"What possible purpose could a Somber Rider serve?"

"I don't know. Not yet." Wykan tossed another stone.
The sound of the splash blurred his next words. ". . . intend
to find out. And I'll decide then if it's worth it to us."

Kier made a disgusted noise with teeth and tongue.
"Don't expect me to slacken my vigilance," he said grimly.
"You're far too willing to accept a stranger at the value he
places upon himself. It's dangerous, Wyk, and you know it."

"I'm more willing to accept a stranger at the value Gordan places on him," Wykan said. He bent to pick up another smooth, round stone. Without looking at Kier, he said, "Would you have opened your veins for me, Kier?"

"Of course. Had you asked. Any Saesnesi would."

Wykan picked up another stone, but he didn't throw it. "Any Saesnesi would," he repeated. He glanced up at Kier. "I didn't ask him, Kier."

We found fresh tracks of a deer shortly after we set out again after the meal. We followed the tracks along a high ridge above the river. The deer appeared to be in no hurry, moving leisurely between the trees where the young growth thrust up through the carpet of old leaves. Less than an hour later, Kier brought it down with one well-placed arrow. I helped them butcher it. I probably got in the way more than I helped. I had never done it before. This was a quick education in living without the civilized trappings of a Maedun garrison around me.

We left the stag's entrails for the wolves and foxes. Wykan and Kier placed the head and the heart on a small cairn. "In tribute," Wykan said by way of explanation as he saw my puzzlement. "To Cernos of the Forest and Gerieg of the Crags. We always thank the gods for their aid in providing the deer."

Another insight into how the people of this island felt about their gods. I could not imagine a Maedun offering thanks to the All-Father for providing game.

The first long shadows of afternoon lay across the crags when we were ready to return to the valley. Bent nearly double under the weight of the meat and the hide, we began the long trek back. If we were lucky, we'd be back in the hidden little valley by dark.

As we walked just below the crest of the ridge, Kier

suddenly stopped and stood very still, staring intently down into the valley. He touched Wykan's arm and pointed down to the valley far below. I peered over Wykan's shoulders. For a moment, I saw nothing but the green expanse of valley and rock and river. Then I saw what Kier did. A handful of men rode through a clearing beside the river, made tiny as ants by the distance. They showed only as dark, moving specks against the trampled, sandy brown of the track.

"Five of them," Kier murmured, watching carefully. "It's early for them to be out. Not much past Beltane yet."

"They were thick as flies on a bloated carcass last summer and autumn," Wykan said. "We were lucky they're always so clumsy in the forest, and we heard them long before they could see us." He frowned and bit his lip thoughtfully as the five Somber Riders moved unhurriedly along the riverbank. "I don't like this. Something is going on. It's as if they mean to eradicate every Saesnesi and Celae hiding in these mountains."

"There's magic here," I said. "Hakkar wants to rid himself of it. It's a threat to him."

Wykan regarded me, one eyebrow raised in speculation. "Why do it now? Our people have been here for more than fifty years. It seems a strange time to start trying to wipe us out. Why now and not earlier, when we were less used to these mountains?" He looked back down the valley at the Somber Riders. They had disappeared into the trees. "We can't even kill them," he said bitterly. "My father and grandfather learned that to their detriment. If a Saesnesi tried to kill a Somber Rider, the spell, or the warlocks who wove them, turned any weapon — no matter if it was a sword, an arrow, or a throwing dagger — back on the man who wielded it." He made a bitter, disgusted sound with teeth and tongue. "Not many Saesnesi had died by their own weapons before my grandfather forbade trying to kill them."

"But they can be killed," I said. "The spell—"

"You'd like us to try, wouldn't you?" Kier said, glaring at me. "You'd like to see us dead by our own weapons."

I shut my mouth. I'd never convince him of the truth without the concrete proof of a dead body. Even Wykan looked skeptical. Well, proof could wait until I needed it.

Wykan shifted the weight on his back to a more comfortable position and turned away. Kier followed him. I glanced down, but no trace remained of the Somber Riders in the valley.

The sun had dipped below the western mountains, and late afternoon turned the distant hills deep blue and purple when we returned to the hidden valley. Gordan met us in a breathless rush as we approached the big house.

"Wykan, it's Denia," he said hoarsely. "Denia's missing. We can't find her anywhere."

17

Wykan dropped his pack heedlessly to the ground. "What happened?" he demanded, raw fear in his voice.

"She went out this morning to gather some mushrooms she'd seen near the bottom of the valley. They looked good—"

"Never mind that. Where did she go?"

Gordan shook his head. "We don't know. She never came back. Erden and Loig have been out looking for her all day and found no trace. They've gone out again—"

Kier clenched his teeth so tightly the muscles bunched and bulged at the hinges of his jaw. "We saw five Somber Riders in the Ovyn Valley," he said bleakly.

Gordan put his hand to his forehead, wearily rubbing his eyes. "Oh no. You don't think—"

Neither Wykan nor Kier answered him. They had forgotten me. I stood by the abandoned packs of venison and merely watched. All I could do. When I spoke, it startled them.

"Could she have lost her way?"

Wykan looked at me, bleak despair in his eyes. "There's only one reason people don't come home here," he said. "Somber Riders. Somber Riders hunt us as if we were little more than sport animals."

I think if I'd still been wearing the black uniform so similar to a Rider's neither he nor Kier would have hesitated to kill me where I stood. I couldn't repress a shudder as I thought of Denia in the hands of some of the Somber Riders I'd known at my father's garrison. Saesnesi women had disappeared there, too, but nobody ever made much of a fuss about it. At least not in the garrison. I had never thought much about how the Saesnesi reacted. And, right up to that minute, it had never occurred to me that I should care.

Wykan's hand went to the quiver of arrows at his hip, his fingers counting them over silently. He closed his eyes briefly, then stepped forward and touched Kier's arm.

"Come on," he said. "We'll go and look for her. Which way did she go, Gordan?"

Gordan pointed to the entrance to the valley. "That way," he said. "But Erden said they looked all around there and found no trace of her."

"Erden's a good hunter," Wykan said grimly, "but he's not the tracker Kier is. We'll find her."

I stepped forward again. "I want to come, too," I said.

Wykan glanced at me in quick appraisal. Then he nodded. "Three pairs of eyes are better than two," he said.

The tracks of the men who had gone out in search of her had all but obliterated Denia's. Kier searched through the maze of footprints and turned to follow the little stream, away from the faint path that had once led to the track. The path was seldom used now. A long-ago landslip had closed both the path and the main track through the mountains. The Somber Riders had eventually cleared the track, but never found a trace of the path. I knew the old landslip. I had ridden past it myself countless times and never seen the path.

We found the place where she had stopped to pick the mushrooms she had mentioned to Gordan. She had left a few of them in the damp shade by a fallen tree trunk. Instead of turning back toward the safety of the valley, she had wandered farther down the river, mayhaps looking for more mushrooms. She seemed to be following the little burn the Saesnesi called the Clearbrook to where it flowed into a larger stream that eventually became the River Ovyn. There she had begun walking on the bare stones along the watercourse where the other men had lost her trail, not knowing if she had crossed the Clearbrook and gone upstream or downstream along the Ovyn. She could not have crossed the wide and turbulent Ovyn. The shallower Clearbrook tumbled over stones that lifted their tops above the water, easy stepping-stones. She might have crossed the stream and gone upriver along the Ovyn. But the stony bank took no footprints, and we could not know for sure.

Kier stood on the rocks, looking bleakly first one way, then the other, as he carefully considered the terrain. Finally, he turned downstream.

"The going is easier here," he told Wykan. "She might have chosen this way."

Kier did most of the work tracking. Wykan and I merely followed him. I wondered if Wykan felt as helpless and useless as I did.

We followed the Ovyn for more than a league downstream, finding no trace of Denia, nothing to indicate she had left the rivercourse and gone up the bank. A league and a half was a long way to go to search for mushrooms. I think Wykan was just about to give up and suggest we try the area upstream of the Clearbrook when I spotted the clear print of a shod horse in the softened dirt between two stones at the edge of the water. Only inches away was a small heelprint.

"There," I said, pointing.

Kier went to one knee and traced the outline of the track with one finger. Small clods of dirt and a pebble had rolled into the heelprint when the horse had disturbed the ground.

"They came by very shortly after she did," he said. "Probably less than an hour." He looked up at Wykan, his eyes cold and stony as they shared the knowledge of what it might mean. Wykan's hand strayed again to the arrows at his hip, and he nodded. Kier rose and led the way across the rocks.

Only a little farther downstream, a scatter of mushrooms lay spilled in a heap of pale, creamy white against the gray of the rocks. Beside them a small, crumpled square of green cloth fluttered gently in the soft breeze. Wykan stooped to pick it up, spreading it across the palm of one hand. Tears made his eyes very bright as he looked up to the bank to his left.

"The main track is just up there," Kier said, glancing up the steep bank above the river. "She wandered too close."

We found her a few moments later at the top of the bank. I followed them more slowly, sudden pain twisting under my heart, as Wykan ran forward and flung himself to his knees beside his sister. She lay sprawled near a pile of dead bracken, her gray eyes wide in final terror, her face twisted in pain. Her torn and ruined gown, once a pale willow green, was rusty brown and stiff with dried blood.

When I saw what had been done to her, my heart turned over, and my stomach rebelled. The blood left my head in a rush. Giddily, I had to turn away, clutching at the slim bole of a birch for support as my belly expelled all I had eaten that day. Behind me, Wykan's strangled cry of grief grated harshly against my ears. No human throat could make a sound that anguished. Not without tearing loose the heart below it.

I didn't know. By all the gods of this island, I swear I didn't know.

But I had known. How could I not know? For most of

my life it had been right there before me. Every day,
Somber Riders took Saesnesi and Celae women to their
beds, against the spell-fuddled will of the women. And
every day, parties of Somber Riders set out lightheartedly
to hunt the wild Celae in these mountains the same way
men hunted game animals. For sport. For the joy of the
hunt.

This was not an "enemy." This was not a dangerous
rebel. This was a young girl just entering the threshold of
womanhood. A girl who had shown me kindness when I
had given up expecting kindness. This was Denia—

Gods pity me, at last I understood the difference
between knowing something intellectually, with my head,
and knowing something gut deep in my spirit and my heart.
The absolute horror of Denia's death, the appalling realization of what had been done to her . . .

My belly cramped again. Tears I couldn't stop stung
my eyes, streamed down my cheeks. Behind me, Wykan
drew in an audible long, shuddering breath. I wiped the
bitter, bitter bile from my lips with the back of my hand and
turned to look at him. He stood above the body of his sister,
his hair blowing in the slight breeze and face turned to
stone.

"No more," he said softly. He straightened slowly and
turned back to Kier. "I say this is enough."

Steeling myself, I went to stand by Kier. I looked down
at the girl's body, forced myself to catalog every wound,
each outrage that had been committed, each indignity she
had endured. Rage filled me, cold and hard, hate and fury
settling next to my heart like the solid ice along the river. I
had never felt like that before. Not since Faghen had taken
me from my mother had I allowed any emotion to seize control of my body or my mind or my spirit. I welcomed the
hate, the anger. Intensely and fiercely, I welcomed it.

Mayhaps it meant I was worthy to call myself a man.

"No more," Wykan said again. "It is enough. From this day forth, we fight back. Tomorrow, Kier . . . Tomorrow, we hunt Somber Riders."

"The spell—" Kier began.

"I can help," I said swiftly, interrupting him. "Let me help. I can show you how to kill them."

Wykan glanced at me. In his eyes I saw burning a ruthless and powerful disregard for the legend of invincibility the Somber Riders had carefully constructed in these mountains. He was past counting what the cost of revenge might be to him. Or to Kier. Or me. Finally, he nodded.

"You can accompany us," he said. "If you're wrong, you can die with us." He removed his cloak and wrapped it gently around his sister. Carefully and tenderly, he picked her up, holding her against him as if she were only a child. He refused Kier's offer of help and carried her alone back down the steep bank to the river's course.

Helplessly, still mired in the wash of my own stunning grief, I followed.

We hunted them down like vermin. As ruthlessly and mercilessly as they had stalked Denia. Kier tracked them as efficiently as he tracked the mountain stag, and we caught up with them shortly before sunset on the second day.

Kier stopped in mid-step, coming to point like a hunting dog sensing the quarry. "Smoke," he said softly. He unslung his bow quickly and slid the loosened bowstring up the shaft to hook it into the notch. "Can you smell it?"

I raised my head. The faint tang of woodsmoke and roasting meat drifted on the mild breeze. I nodded and unlimbered my bow. As I restrung it, I scanned the area ahead. A barely detectable stain of blue-gray rose against the green of the mountainside just beyond the next ridge.

The air above the trees shimmered slightly with the rising heat of the cooking fire.

"There, I think," Wykan said.

"I see it," I said quietly. "It's close."

Kier nodded. "Aye. Our quarry."

I glanced around. The track we followed lay in a narrow valley, bounded on one side by the river and the other by a thin band of trees below steeply rising cliffs. There must have been a wider area on the other side of the next rise to accommodate the Riders' campsite.

I smiled bleakly. "The first arrow will be mine, if you will permit, my lord Celwalda," I said softly.

Wykan's smile was grim. "You'll need to shoot very quickly to beat Kier or me," he said. "Let's go."

Kier stepped off the track and vanished into the trees. Wykan and I followed quickly. Moving noiselessly through the rough stands of cedar and maple, we crept to the top of the rise. The smell of roasting meat became stronger.

Kier dropped to a crouch behind a scramble of blaeberry bushes. He pointed. I sank to my belly, and Wykan noiselessly went to his knees beside me.

Below, the camp lay just off the track, hard against the base of the cliff behind. Two Somber Riders squatted before the fire, tending to a haunch of venison cooking slowly above the flames and coals. The rest of the deer lay half butchered a little distance away. Three more Riders sat under the trees, laughing and talking among themselves, paying no attention to the men cooking.

I had already drawn my bow. "Watch," I whispered softly. "They can be killed." I loosed the arrow. No sorcerous power tried to turn my arrow back against me. It flew straight and true, fletching whispering quietly, and pierced the chest of one of the men tending the haunch of venison. He stiffened, then fell forward into the fire.

Wykan was faster than I thought he might be. He had already nocked and loosed his arrow at one of the men sitting by the fire as I was in the act of nocking my second arrow.

Just as Kier loosed his second arrow, something crashed through the bushes beside us. I spun around in time to see a sixth Rider, his breeks only half laced, leaping toward Kier, sword raised to strike. Before Kier could do more than begin to reach for an arrow, I drew my dagger and lunged at the Somber Rider. The blade took him in the throat. He fell in an inert heap at Kier's feet.

Kier looked at me. For the space of four heartbeats, we simply stared at each other, taking each other's measure. I don't know why it seemed to be so important to me to have Kier's good opinion. It was Wykan I had sworn to serve.

"You saved my life," Kier said.

I shrugged and tried to make light of it. "You seem to have some value to my lord Wykan," I said, keeping my voice deliberately casual and indifferent. "And since he was busy, and I was closer, I took it upon myself to take care of the problem."

Kier stiffened, then inclined his head. "I thank you," he said, his voice taut and cold. His thanks might not have been given generously, but at least they were given. I was more than satisfied.

Wykan had not been idle while Kier and I sparred. There was only one Somber Rider still moving by the fire. He tried to scramble to his feet, face pale, frantically trying to see into the darkness beyond the firelight. Wykan stepped out into the light of the fire, arrow nocked, bowstring drawn back, as the Rider scrabbled toward the pile of weapons.

"So you'll know who killed you," he said, obviously not caring if the Rider understood him or not. He would understand the deadly aim of the arrow. Wykan loosed his last arrow, and the Rider fell.

Kier leapt the low tumble of rock and calmly slung his bow across his shoulder again. He looked around, studying each of the five bodies. Suddenly, he turned to Wykan and laughed breathlessly.

"They can be killed after all," he cried exultantly.

"Aye," Wykan said in grim satisfaction. "Aye, they can."

Kier threw back his head and cried out a savage howl of triumph. Wykan shivered and held up his hand.

"Quiet," he said sharply. "We don't know if there are any more of them around."

"The spell won't reach this high into the mountains," I said. "I think if they're going to turn your weapons back on you, they have to have a powerful warlock with them."

Wykan stared at me. "You *think*?" he repeated. "You're not sure?"

"Not until now," I said a little shakily.

Wykan looked at me in exasperation. "You and Kier make a good pair," he said, shaking his head. "Both of you are too impetuous by half."

Kier glanced at me, and for the first time, smiled. A tight, half-grudging smile, but a smile nonetheless. Then he looked at the corpses, understanding dawning. "This high, they become only men."

"Yes," I said. "They never meant you to know. In my dispatch pouch are letters to the western garrison commanders telling them to send out warlocks again with the patrols. It seems others have learned that the Riders aren't invincible."

"They never meant us to know," Wykan said. "We let them convince us they were invincible. Invulnerable." He nudged the corpse of the man I had killed with the toe of his boot. "These men had no warlock with them. Mayhaps they've grown too confident."

"I certainly hope so." Kier laughed, a harsh, cold sound in the flickering dark. "I believe there will be a lot fewer of these vermin in the mountains here from now on." He spit on the ground as if ridding his mouth of a foul taste.

"Aye, I think so," Wykan said. "We'll bury this carrion so the others won't know what happened to them. Free the horses. We have no need of them. And collect the arrows," he said. "They'll come in handy. And throw the swords into the river. Let them rust in silence." He turned to me. "Do you know any of these men?"

I barely glanced at the sprawled bodies. "None of them," I said, and shook my head. "I don't think they're from any garrison I carried messages to."

Kier gathered up the black-fletched arrows in their quivers. He hesitated only a moment, then handed me two of them. "You'll need them, I think," he said somewhat gruffly. "You've got a good aim. It's helpful."

18

We had strayed far from the village while we followed the murder-
ous vermin who had slain Denia. Just before the sun set
the next evening, we found a sheltered place between the
rock wall of a soaring cliff and a thick stand of mixed pine
and silver-leaf. Only a bowshot away, water bubbled up
out of a cleft in the rocks to form a clear, cold spring. I
fetched water while Wykan built a small fire and Kier
took his bow to hunt a rabbit for our evening meal.

Kier, as usual, was successful. Soon, two fat rabbits spit
and sizzled on sticks over the fire. Wykan sat watching the sun
slip behind the mountains, his face solemn and introspective.
Kier fed twigs and sticks into the fire, immersed in his own
thoughts. I sat down beside Wykan. He turned to look at me.

"It's not enough," he said quietly. "Revenge isn't
enough. It will never bring Denia back."

"No," I said. "But what else can we do?"

"I don't know." He drew in a long breath, let it out
slowly. "I don't know."

"I'm sorry."

He nearly smiled. "I know." He plucked a blade of the
short feather grass, then looked up again, past the deep blue
and purple of the hills in the west. "Gordan says a king will
come out of the west to free this poor blighted land." The head
of the grass stem blurred like an aurora around his fingers as
he twirled it. "I wish he had come in time to save Denia."

"A king out of the west?" I asked.

"Gordan has a Gift for fire Seeing," he said. "A king, he
told us. A king to rid us of the Somber Riders."

His words struck a chord in my memory. I put my hand

to the leather pouch on my belt, felt the solid, square edges within. Yes. I still had the little book. I brought it out and showed it to him.

"It speaks of a king in here," I said.

He glanced at it. "I can't read it," he said. "What is it?"

"Do you know the 'Song of the Swords'?"

He smiled. "Oh yes. I doubt there's any Celae or Saesnesi in Skai who doesn't."

"It's in here. And others."

He turned a page or two of the book and ran his finger across the words. "You read Celae?"

I half-shrugged ruefully. "In a way. I can translate it. Painfully slowly, mind you. But reading the words is one thing. Pronouncing them right is quite another."

He laughed. "I'll wager it is." He turned back to the last page and the "Song of the Swords." Again, he touched the words, almost as if caressing them.

"Gordan says this king's time is soon," he said. "He's Seen it in the fire. Two strangers come to Skai, and two swords gleaming in the night." He shook his head. "I hardly understand, but he says the strangers are important, and I must ally my people with them."

"Soon?" I repeated. "How soon?"

He laughed and shook his head. "Who knows? To a Fire Seer, soon could be any time within the next two or three generations."

Kier swore suddenly. Wykan and I looked up in time to see a billow of fragrant steam rising around him.

"I spilled the kettle," Kier said disgustedly. "The tea's all in the fire."

I laughed. "I'll fetch more water," I said. I left the book with Wykan and picked up the kettle. I lost sight of the camp in the thick undergrowth between the trees long before I reached the spring.

Behind me, someone shouted. The metallic rattle of bridle metal and the heavy thunder of running horses echoed off the side of the cliff. More shouting.

I dropped the kettle and ran. I sprinted back to camp, ignoring the branches whipping across my face, the thorns tearing at my clothing and skin. My foot tangled in a hidden root. I stumbled, nearly fell, but caught my balance and kept running. I came out of the trees at the edge of the small clearing just in time to see a troop of eight mounted men riding away. The sound of their laughter came clearly to me even above the clatter of the horses.

The camp was in shambles, churned by the hooves of the horses. Kier lay sprawled near the edge of the clearing, bleeding from a wound in his head. Wykan lay by the fire, my little book still clutched in one hand, the other hand in the flames. But he made no sound.

"No," I whispered. "Oh no."

I ran to Wykan, dragged him back. I turned him over. His open eyes stared up at me. Past me. He watched his gods, not this world.

Behind me, Kier groaned and climbed to his feet. I looked up as he dropped to his knees beside me.

"Wykan?" he asked, his voice thick.

I shook my head.

Kier sank back on his heels, cursing in a low, vicious monotone. I reached out and took the book from Wykan's fierce grip. It was still open to the "Song of the Swords."

"They caught us unaware," Kier said, his voice heavy with tears. "They didn't look like Maedun. They were dressed in tunics and trews like us. We thought they were Celae." He looked at me, pleading for me to understand how he had let them kill his Celwalda. "We thought they were Celae. Until it was too late . . ."

I looked down into the face of the man I'd sworn my

loyalty to. The man who had offered friendship. My Celwalda. My friend.

All my life I'd lived on this island. All my life I had known that there was no peace between the occupying army of Somber Riders and the men who lived in subjugation to them. Not until now had any of the dead been people I knew. People I liked and admired. Not until now.

I held Wykan's body in my arms, something akin to rage building in my chest, my belly. It clogged my throat, squeezed the breath from my lungs. I looked up at Kier.

"We killed the Riders who slaughtered Denia," I said. "We can kill these, too."

Together, Kier and I took Wykan home to his people. To his wife Brigeda and son Devlyn and daughter Liana. We stayed only long enough for the burial ceremony. When they had placed my Celwalda beneath a cairn at the edge of the orchard, I spent the rest of the day sharpening my sword and counting over my arrows.

Kier found me in front of the big house, near the edge of the steep embankment down to the river. He dropped into a crouch beside me and took out his dagger. The sharply honed edge glittered in the sun.

"I shall go with you when you leave," he said.

I looked at him. "You're welcome to come."

He met my gaze. "Wykan was my Celwalda and my kinsman. I will not let his death go unavenged."

I had to swallow before I could speak. "He was my Celwalda and my friend."

He got to his feet. "In the morning, then."

"Yes. At first light."

Just before the sun set, we came across the tracks of a troop of mounted men by the edge of a little burn. Water had not yet filled the deep print one horse had left only inches from the stream itself. Kier dropped to one knee to take a closer look. I nocked an arrow into my bow and scanned the trees on the other side of the stream. Nothing moved there.

"Fresh," Kier said. He touched the soft mud with the tip of one finger. "Not more than a few minutes, I'd say."

"Is it the same troop of men?" I asked.

"I can't tell. Mayhaps. But they're Somber Riders. Until we prove them otherwise, they're Somber Riders." Kier got to his feet and prowled upstream, then downstream. "I'd say not more than six or seven of them, I think," he said. "They crossed here, but I can't see where they came from. Too rocky here, and those dead leaves won't take a clear print."

I relaxed my grip on the bowstring and eased off the tension. "Let's go see what they're up to," I said. I looked around. We were deep in the tangled maze of rocks and seamed valleys. "This is an odd place for them."

Kier looked up quickly, a flash of suspicion crossing his face. "What do you mean, odd?"

I gestured around us. The densely packed trees turned the late afternoon into twilight. "Look at it. That track isn't a main track. In places, it's difficult to tell it's a track at all. Patrols don't usually wander far from a main track. They heartily dislike the mountains and the forest."

Kier nodded slowly. "You're right. It's strange to find them here. Just as it was strange to find them where we had camped when they caught us." He glanced across the stream. The faint track led up the steep bank, following the curve of the streambed, but out of sight behind the trees.

It occurred to me that Wykan would wonder why the Somber Riders were this deep in the mountains when they had no protection, no warlock with them. I tried to think as he might, as a leader rather than a follower bent merely on vengeance. This band of Riders might be part of something bigger, something more important.

"I wouldn't mind taking a close look at this troop," I said. "I wonder what they're up to?"

The Riders made no attempt to hide their trail. We caught up to them shortly after dark.

Kier and I lay belly down, hidden behind a low outcropping of rocks on the top of a rise.

Sunset was a little over an hour gone. The moon would not rise for an hour or so, and the darkness was almost complete. The faint glow of a campfire had led us to this sheltered ridge overlooking the streambed.

Four men sat around the fire in the shelter of a wide bend in the little burn, their backs to the steep embankment. There were more men that I couldn't see outside the circle of light cast by the small fire—perhaps three or four, judging from the tracks Kier had followed. The low murmur of their voices barely carried to the ridge above the whisper of water over the stones in the stream. None of the words came to me.

The troop was camped in a hollow formed by the wide bend of the stream. Low bushes of willow, alder, and silverleaf grew thickly against the rocky outcropping behind them. The air was thick with the smell of water and the sharp, resinous scent of burning pine. The mouthwatering aroma of roasting meat—venison or rabbit—carried gently on the breeze as the camped men prepared their evening meal.

I thought the troop of men had not picked the best place to settle for the night. Although the steep embankment offered shelter from the winds that swept down from the mountains around them, it turned the camp into a trap in the event of an attack.

It wasn't until one of the men got up to throw another log on the fire that I realized they weren't wearing the uniform of Somber Riders. Under the dark cloaks I had mistaken for black, they wore trews and tunics of green or brown or dark rust, and shirts of paler colors. I stared at them for a moment, then abruptly understood why they were so far off the main track. Beside me, Kier stirred uneasily.

"They look like Celae?" he whispered.

"So did the men who killed Wykan," I replied softly.

"They might be the same men." He began to rise to his feet, but I reached out and grasped his arm.

"Stay down," I said sharply. "Wait—" I stared down at the men around the campfire, concentrating. I listened intently, then heard it again. "They're not Celae. Not unless the Celae in these mountains have taken to speaking to each other in Maedun."

Kier said nothing, but he grinned, his teeth flashing white in the gloom. He fingered the hilt of his stiletto, an eloquent gesture that needed no words in explanation. I reached out to stay his hand.

"Wykan would want us to find out why they're in disguise," I said. "What do you think?"

For a moment, he said nothing, staring down into the Maedun camp. Finally, he gave me a wolfish grin. "It doesn't matter to me whether we kill them now, or kill them later. I have no woman waiting for me at the camp. It would be interesting to follow them and see what they do."

"And who sent them and why," I said.

19

I woke with a start as Kier touched my shoulder. The pale, wan light of dawn was barely bright enough to show me the trees surrounding the deadfall where we had taken shelter the night before. I had been asleep only a few hours. Kier and I had spent the night taking watches in turn to keep an eye on the Maedun masquerading as Celae, who were camped a safe distance away, beyond the ridge. It said something for Kier's growing, if reluctant, trust of me that he actually slept while I took the first watch.

"They're getting ready to break camp," Kier whispered. "Shall we follow them?"

"I'd like to know what they're up to," I said. "What are they doing?"

Kier indicated the ridge with a nod. "Just breaking their fast now, I think. We should break ours and be ready when they go."

The soldiers made little effort to be quiet or to keep their presence secret. If we had once any cause to believe they were what they pretended to be, any doubts vanished as the troop of mounted men moved off down the narrow little track. Free Celae—even arrogant free Celae—would certainly take care to remain as inconspicuous as possible. It was not unknown for patrols of Somber Riders to be as far from the main track as this little hollow by the stream. Real Celae would have no wish to tangle with a troop of Somber Riders.

Kier and I kept to the trees above the track. Below us, the troop of mounted men moved leisurely along the track. At midday, they built a fire in a clearing and roasted a small haunch of venison, laughing as they ate it. We watched from the trees on the flank of the mountain high above them, and ate a cold meal of dry biscuits, cheese, and dried meat. When the troop of false Celae set out again, we followed, keeping high enough on the slope above them so that the mounted men appeared small and insignificant.

Well before sunset, they made camp for the night not far from a fork in the track. In the morning, they breakfasted, but made no move to leave.

"I'd wager they're waiting for someone," Kier said softly as we watched from our perch on the mountainside.

"I'd wager you're right," I agreed.

He touched my arm. "There," he said.

Another troop of men approached along the fork in the narrow track. Perhaps a dozen men, all mounted on dark horses, all of them wearing Celae tunic and trews. Kier caught my arm and pointed.

"Look there," he said. "More of them, do you suppose?"

As we watched, the leader of the second troop dismounted and walked to the widening in the path where the two tracks met. He waited there for the leader of the men we had been following. The two men conferred for several minutes, but they were too far away for their words to carry up the slope of the surrounding mountains to where we lay.

"Twenty men in all," Kier said. "A full troop of them. I wonder if they have a warlock with them, even if they're supposed to be Celae and not Maedun."

I studied the mounted men. None of them wore warlock's gray, as far as I could tell. But if he were in disguise, mayhaps he wouldn't anyway. "It's hard to tell," I said. I smiled grimly and without humor. "Mayhaps we'd best not loose any arrows at them until we're sure." I indicated the leader of the second troop. "That man, though. I'd wager anything he's an officer." He had the swagger. And he held himself as if he were used to being obeyed. Even the way he wore his cloak slung back over one shoulder spoke of arrogance. A disciplinarian, that one. I'd stake my boots on it. I'd seen that posture in a dozen officers. My father among them.

Kier glanced at me curiously, then back to the two men. "How can you tell?"

"Look how he stands," I said. "As if he's on parade, even in those ragged clothes. He's used to being obeyed, that one. It's a common trait among all officers."

The officer finished speaking, then turned abruptly and went back to his waiting men. He vaulted gracefully into his saddle and raised his hand. The troop wheeled their horses as one man and followed him back down the track the way they had come at a quick canter.

"Well now," I said aloud thoughtfully. "I wonder what that was all about."

The first troop waited until the others were well out of sight, then continued along the other fork of the track. They were no longer as carefree as they had been. Nor did they make as much noise. They gave a good appearance of trying to hide their presence now. They'd received a severe dressing down from the officer, and they didn't like it even a little. The thought amused me.

The troop of Maedun masquerading as Celae appeared to be in no hurry as they guided their horses along the well-traveled track that followed the Eidon. They held their horses to a brisk walk, but Kier and I had little trouble staying with the troop. We kept to the trees above the track, jogging along on game trails that followed the ridges or the lip of the steep canyon the Eidon had cut through the rock. As midmorning approached, I glanced over my shoulder at

the sun and wondered how soon the troop would stop for a
meal. I was tiring more than I wanted to admit, but Kier
seemed unaffected by the arduous pace. His face, set in
lines of grim concentration, betrayed no weariness, no
trace of exhaustion. But then, if I listened to the tales Kier
told, he had always been able to run tirelessly all day if need
be, and still be ready to sit up late into the evening, drink-
ing ale, telling tales, and laughing with the young men of
the Saesnesi band. If so, I envied him his strength and
resilience.

We topped a ridge overlooking the main track along
the river. In the lead, Kier made a soft exclamation and
quickly dodged into the shelter of a thatch of willow.
"Down there," he said, pointing.

A panoramic view of the valley spread out below us as
I crouched beside Kier. Just visible through the canopy of
new leaves, a small trail joined the main track at the point
where a little burn flowed into the Eidon. The band of
Maedun had stopped by the ford where the track crossed
the little stream, and were watering their horses and
stretching their legs.

"I count seven of them," Kier said. "There are two
missing."

"Scouting ahead, I think," I said. "That's what I'd have
them doing, were I the troop commander."

Kier nodded. "Aye, probably," he said.

Farther up the trail, a flash of movement caught my
eye. I had to stare hard to make out two figures making
their way toward the intersection.

I touched Kier's shoulder and pointed. Kier followed
the direction of my pointing finger. His eyes narrowed as he
caught sight of the two figures. "I see them," he said softly.
"They're going to run right into those impostors in a
moment or two."

The two moved stealthily, obviously trying to make no noise, keeping to the shelter of the shrubbery at the edge of the grassy track. One of them looked to be little more than a boy, shorter by half a head than the man in the lead, and much more slender. I noted with interest the boy wore a sword sheathed in a harness across his back rather than on a belt and hanging by his hip. The man in the lead wore a weapon at his hip. It looked very much like a Saesnesi long dagger, even though the man was clearly not Saesnesi. Neither of them carried a bow, nor any quiver or arrows.

"Four to one," I said. "Not the best of odds."

Kier turned to me, a fierce, wolfish grin skinning his lips back from his teeth. "I say we rearrange the odds a tad," he murmured. "Surely two to one is fairer than four to one."

I didn't take my eyes off the tableau on the track below. But I grinned, too. Mine might have been a twin to Kier's.

"Even fairer," I said, "when both of us have bows. I rather like those odds."

One of the Maedun spotted the two approaching strangers. He shouted, alerting the rest of the troop. I rose to my feet and began to slither my way quickly and quietly down the slope. At the same time, suddenly and shockingly, the smaller of the two men on the trail drew his sword and charged forward. The sound of his high, ululating war cry resounded in the still air, echoing off the granite face of the mountain. That was the one thing I had not expected, and the audacity of the move stunned me. But even as I gasped in surprise, I realized the two had very little choice. They could not outrun a troop of mounted men.

Kier and I were still out of bowshot range when the Maedun overwhelmed the taller stranger. The boy shouted something, and took up a defensive position above the man's body, still swinging his sword with unflagging skill

and energy. Somewhere behind me, Kier swore vehemently. He flung himself forward, dragging an arrow from
the quiver on his hip and trying to nock it on the run. I fum-
bled for an arrow. Only a few more yards. Just a few more
yards, and I could be reasonably certain of hitting what I
shot at.

I tripped over a creeper and dropped my arrow.
Stumbling and swearing, I caught my balance. No time to
retrieve the arrow. Later, mayhaps, but not then.

On the track below, the fallen man scrambled to his
feet, then turned and ran. For an instant, I thought he was
deserting his companion, then I realized he was trying for
the horses. A good move. If he could capture two horses, he
and the boy stood a chance of escaping.

No time for the bow. I hurtled past Kier, my sword
drawn. I could feel the wild grin skinning my lips back
from teeth. I plunged into the midst of the fray, battling my
way to the side of the boy, who still fought savagely on his
own. I shouted at Kier to pick off the men behind us, and
swung myself around to guard the boy's back, while the
other stranger seized the reins of one of the horses.

I heard the approaching horse before I saw it. I
shouted a warning to Kier, who knelt at the edge of the
track. Even as Kier turned, arrow nocked and ready, the
Maedun horseman was upon him. I shouted again, but had
no time to do more.

But I had forgotten the taller stranger. Ahorse now, he
spurred the horse at the mounted Maedun bearing down
on Kier. Even as his long dagger sliced into the disguised
Maedun's throat, the Maedun's sword caught Kier across
the ribs. Kier sprawled into the track, bleeding.

"Kier!" I shouted. But I couldn't disengage from my
own battle. I couldn't leave the young swordsman alone. I
turned back in time to see the young stranger swing his

sword and nearly slice the last remaining Maedun in half.

I jumped back, ready to run to Kier. But the stranger spun and raised his sword to swing it at me. How stupid of me. I understood instantly. To the stranger, I was only one more disguised Maedun. I leapt back, holding my sword point down at my side.

"No," I shouted. "Hold."

The stranger hardly hesitated. I swore and scrambled back out of reach. I knew very few words of Celae, but I tried again. "No! I'm a friend! Stop!

Interlude

Horbad

20

The walls and ceiling of the cave pressed down on him. Beneath his feet, the sand was damp, stinking of salt and mildew. Horbad clutched the torch tightly and forced himself to move forward, rounding a slight curve. The darkness became more oppressive as the cave entrance vanished behind him.

A whole mountain loomed above his head. And standing on the promontory, the vitrified rock fortress Rock Greghrach. All that weight — he shuddered, tried to take a deep breath, but the clinging, stifling atmosphere inside the cave clutched his chest like an icy hand.

Just a few more steps. The small alcove opened off the main corridor only a little more than a hundred and fifty paces from the entrance. It seemed like more — it seemed like several furlongs. Several *leagues*!

There were tales of nomadic Laringorn sheepherders who made their winter homes in caves along the western edge of the great Ghadi Desert. Horbad shuddered again. How could any man live in a cave? Actually sleep with all that immense mass of rock weighing on him?

He held his torch higher. His shadow leapt and danced on the wet rock ahead near his feet. At high tide, the sea lapped at the entrance to the cave. Sometimes the extreme high tides of late spring brought the water flooding into the cave itself, almost to the alcove where the stones grew.

Beyond the alcove, the cave opened into a vast, echoing cavern. He didn't know what was in that cavern. He had only once been able to force himself to glance into it. The feeble light of the torch picked out strange formations of white rock, as if the rock itself had melted and run down from the ceiling of the cavern like candle wax, then frozen.

Melted rock. By the All-Father, what if it melted again while he was in the cave, and flowed over him, trapping him?

He put out a hand to steady himself against the damp rock wall and took a deep breath. Only a little farther now. He put one foot resolutely in front of the other and took the few paces that brought him to the alcove.

The light from the torch nearly masked the faint green glow of a stone half buried in the sand. He went to one knee and scrabbled with his fingers. The stone was covered with grit, and the light it gave off was feeble. But with the right spell, and the spilling of the right blood, it would shine brightly enough to be seen in daylight. And when it sensed the magic of a Celae Rune Blade, it would spark and glitter and fizz in the hand of a man imbued with the magic to react with it.

Horbad glanced around quickly, but saw no other stone that was "ripe" for the plucking. But one would do. For now. He dropped the stone into his pocket, turned, and made his way out of the cave as quickly as he could without running.

Hakkar reached out a finger and touched the stone. Except for the mild green glow and the faint suggestion of carved swirls, it looked like an ordinary water-smoothed river stone. Not exactly like the Tell-Tales his father had used. Those had to be keyed to a specific user of magic. These for some reason resonated with the curious magic in the swords the Celae called Rune Blades. And since Rune Blades were carried only by those close to the rebel who called himself Prince of Skai, the stones had proved an excellent way of tracking down the line from which the enchanter of the prophecy was to come.

"Have you found a suitable Celae?" he asked.

"I believe so," Horbad said. "But we'll need to find a man to lead the attack party."

"Your pardon, my lord Hakkar," a new voice said. "I believe I can be of service to you there."

Hakkar turned quickly. One of the soldiers who had been standing guard outside his door stepped into the room and went to one knee, head bowed so deeply that his forehead nearly touched his other knee. Horbad couldn't have been more surprised if one of the figures in the tapestries on the walls had stepped out and spoken.

"Who in Hella's name are you?" Horbad demanded, outraged.

Hakkar reached out and put a restraining hand on his son's arm. "Hold," he said. He watched the man closely for a moment, but the guard didn't flinch. Nor did he rise from his position. Hakkar detected no servility in the posture. Just respect. As it should be from an officer or a ranking official. But it was hardly what he expected from a lowly guard. The man piqued his curiosity.

"Speak, then," he said. "Just how do you think you can help me. And who are you?"

The guard raised his head. He was not a young man. Gray laced thickly through the black of his hair and beard, and deep lines ran from the sides of his nose to bracket his mouth. "Once, I was a captain of your Somber Riders, lord," he said. "Once I was second-in-command of a garrison near the eastern shore of this island."

Hakkar raised one eyebrow. "You have fallen into disgrace if you are now nothing but a guardsman," he said.

"Yes, sir," he said. "I failed to put my duty before my desire for a son. I was wrong, and I have been properly punished for it."

Hakkar shot a quick glance at Horbad, who stood by

the window, frowning at the guardsman. "I see," he said softly. "Continue. How can you be of service to me?"

"Before I transferred to the eastern shore, I spent four years in these western mountains, lord. And now I've spent another five years here. I believe I came to know how the Celae there think and react. What you're looking for, would it be the so-called Prince of Skai?"

"It might," Hakkar said cautiously.

"Then I believe I know how I can find him and eliminate him for you."

"Do you, now?"

"Yes, lord. First, I believe that sending a patrol of Somber Riders into the hills would be a waste of time. The wild Celae would spot them easily and avoid them. They do, after all, know those accursed hills better than we do."

"And how would you track down this self-proclaimed prince?"

The guard allowed himself a small smile. "Send a troop of Celae to catch him, lord."

Startled, Hakkar stared at him. "Celae?"

"Yes, lord." Again the half smile. "Celae have black hair, as we do. I'm sure there would be Celae clothing to fit a troop of Somber Riders."

Hakkar raised one eyebrow. "We've sent small companies of men out in disguise. None of them has returned."

The guard nodded. "I know, sire. But I think I know what happened."

"You do?" Hakkar lounged back in his chair, a thoughtful expression on his face. "Suppose you tell me, then."

"My lord, I mean no disrespect. But I believe you sent men who did not know the Celae. They would not know how to act, and would give themselves away."

"And you know how the Celae act?"

"I have made a study of them, my lord."

"It might work, Father," Horbad said. "If we give this man a Tell-Tale and teach him how to use it, I think it might work rather well."

Hakkar nodded. "It might," he said. He turned back to the guardsman. "You'll get your chance to redeem yourself," he said. "Bring me this man who calls himself Prince of Skai, and not only will I reinstate you, I'll raise you to commander and give you a garrison. What is your name?"

"Faghen, my lord," the guardsman said. "My name is Faghen."

Light came only from two guttering torches standing to either side of a brazier. A man lay bound and gagged on the floor between the torches, curled on his side. A man in warlock's gray knelt behind him, his back to the door.

Faghen nearly stumbled as he followed Hakkar into the room. Fear clogged his throat, but he took a deep breath and told himself that regaining his honor was worth any ordeal.

"Over here," Hakkar said as matter-of-factly as if he were ushering a guest into his private study. "Kneel right here." He gestured toward the feet of the bound man, to the left of the warlock.

Faghen dropped to his knees and looked down. The bound man was Celae. Dark blond hair. Brown-gold eyes. Mayhaps even Tyadda. Faghen glanced at him again. No, mayhaps he was too strongly built to be Tyadda. They tended to be more slender. More supple.

"He has some magic," Hakkar said. "He'll serve the purpose quite nicely, I think." He went to his knees on a cushion which had been behind the prisoner, and made himself comfortable. "Have you got the stone?"

Faghen pulled the smooth, oval stone from his pocket and held it out. "Right here."

"Good. Be ready when I tell you."

"Yes, sire."

Hakkar drew a wickedly curved dagger from his belt. He tested the blade with his thumb, then glanced at the warlock. He said something, and the warlock nodded. The prisoner's eyes went wide in terror. His throat muscles worked, but the gag prevented him from crying out.

Faghen leaned back to keep well out of the way of the dagger. Hakkar stooped and stabbed the dagger into the prisoner's abdomen, ripping the blade viciously upward. As the steaming, glistening entrails tumbled and spilled out onto the floor, Hakkar dropped the dagger and thrust his hands into the man's belly. The prisoner threw his head back in agony. The cords of his neck stood out like steel bands against his pale skin, then vanished as he went limp. His bound limbs twitched, then stilled as the strength drained from his body with his blood.

A pale, golden mist rose from the tangle of guts around Hakkar's hands. Slowly, it circled his wrists, climbing inexorably along his blood-splashed arms. It began to shimmer, softly at first, with faint, iridescent color barely visible in the gold mist. As it reached his elbows, the colors became brighter, flashing and flaring, blues and greens and bright saffron.

"Now," Hakkar cried.

Faghen nearly gagged. But he clutched the small stone tightly in his hand and thrust it into the bloody abdominal cavity between Hakkar's two hands. The brilliant, coruscating colors exploded. Threads of black laced through the billow of light and color. Faghen wanted to cry out, but he couldn't breathe. The stone in his hand turned his blood and bone to ice, then burned until he knew his palm and fingers were little more than charred meat clinging to dry and brittle bones. He couldn't pull his hand back, couldn't move.

Then, as quickly as it began, it was over. The light was gone. The man on the floor was simply a dead man, disemboweled. Hakkar pulled his hand out of the corpse's belly and sat back on his heels. He dismissed the warlock with a nod, then looked at Faghen.

Slowly, in wonder, Faghen held out his hand. The flesh was unharmed, whole. The stone flashed a bright, poisonous green. It was warm and comforting, nestling into the palm of his hand.

Hakkar smiled. "Ah, good," he said. "Sometimes it doesn't work. But this time it did." He got swiftly and gracefully to his feet. "The commander here will give you men," he said. "Good luck in your hunt." He paused on his way to the door. "If you succeed, I'll see you're richly rewarded."

Faghen clenched his fists, his lips pressed together tightly over gritted teeth. His anger burned in his chest and belly with a grim, cold fury, but he held it back by force of will. The ten men he had hand-picked at Rock Greghrach sat their horses quietly behind him, beyond the fork in the trail where he stood facing the leader of the second, smaller troop. These men had been provided him by the commander of Rock Greghrach; their leader was the commander's son. Brash, overconfident and arrogant, the young man had also proved he was an inveterate idiot.

"We heard you long before we saw you," Faghen said, his voice calm and quiet despite the rage burning in his guts. "While I realize you speak nothing of the barbaric Celae tongue, I might remind you that shouting back and forth to each other in our own language is not exactly likely to convince any Celae hiding in the mountains here that you are one of them."

The young man had not even the grace to look chagrined. "There are none around here to overhear us," he said, his voice bored. "We've already cleaned this area out long since. We found a nest of them—three or four— just beyond that ridge not more than three or four days ago."

"I see," Faghen said pleasantly. "And you doubt that any more might be around? Hunting or even traveling from one hidden enclave to another?"

The cadet gave him a blank look. "Why would they come here? They know we'd know they were here."

Faghen took a deep breath, let it out slowly through his nose. "Cadet, I suggest you return post-haste to Rock Greghrach and report your findings to your father. Tell him I will be there within the fortnight to make out my personal report to Lord Hakkar."

"Yes, sir. We'll take the main track, sir." The cadet offered him a sloppy salute, and turned back to his own small troop of men.

Faghen took note of the swagger in his step, unclenched his fists and took another deep breath. The inept fool thought this assignment merely a lark, an excuse to gallop madly through the forests and mountains in sport to hunt Celae. Faghen wished he could simply drop the cadet over a high, steep precipice somewhere and forget he had ever seen him. Unfortunately, there was the distinct possibility the comman- der might miss his son and ask inconvenient questions. However, there was also the faint possibility that the young fool in his Celae disguise might encounter a troop of Somber Riders along the main track who would shoot first and con- firm identity later. Faghen sighed again. It was, unfortu- nately, a very faint hope. He spun about briskly and returned to the men awaiting him beyond the fork in the road.

His second-in-command stepped forward and handed him the reins to his horse. "Do you think it did any good?" he asked, watching the small troop by the crossroad.

Faghen swung himself into his saddle. "I highly doubt it," he said. "But I suppose we can hope."

The Second glanced at the cadet, who was leaning against his horse, one arm flung casually across the saddle as he spoke with his men. He shook his head. "Bumptious fool," he said.

Faghen allowed himself a half smile. "Exactly. But perhaps his father has hopes for him on this assignment." His smile turned down at the corners. "Especially as the Lord Horbad should still be at the fortress. The commander might look upon it as a chance to let his son shine in the presence of Hakkar's son."

The Second let all his teeth show in a cynical grin that mirrored Faghen's. "He's made a mistake," he said.

Faghen nodded. "Indeed," he said. He raised his hand to his troop and waved them forward as he set his heels to the flank of his horse.

The commander of Rock Greghrach was also a fool, Faghen reflected. But the man was a fool in the same way he, himself, had been one. Far better to make sure one's own career was secure rather than risk everything for a son who, for whatever reason, was not worthy of the gamble. And who would know that better than he?

The stone Tell-Tale in his pocket was his guarantee of fortune. Even more, the commission he carried in his saddle pack, signed by the lord Hakkar's own hand, and sealed with his personal seal, was Faghen's key to regaining all that he had lost. He would not fail in this assignment; he would not waste this chance. If he had to ride rough-shod over stupid and short-sighted men like the commander and his imbecilic son, then he would do so, and with no qualms whatsoever.

He hoped the witless cadet would not frighten off their quarry. He had a secondary strategy ready to put into effect if that happened. And a plan for revenge against the man or men who crossed his purpose. The thought of the high, rocky precipice gave him a flicker of grim satisfaction.

Part 3

The Seekers

21

Cynric sprang back as the stranger spun about, sword raised to strike. He held his own sword point down, harmlessly out of the way, away from his body and behind him. The stranger must surely see he was no threat. To the boy, he would appear to be no more than another disguised Maedun.

The boy?

Staring at the stranger, he took another step back, nearly stumbled in shock and surprise.

The stranger's face resembled a beardless boy's face only in that it had never needed a razor. Nor would it ever need one. The dark gold hair, worn hanging across the shoulder in a plait as thick as a man's wrist, burnished like polished metal, was far too long for a man's hair. And it was certainly no man's spirit that glared out through those gloriously golden brown eyes.

A woman. By all the gods of this place, it was a woman!

He had never heard of such a thing. No Maedun woman ever touched a man's weapon on pain of death. Yet, incredibly, this woman not only carried a sword, she used it with the skill and dexterity that came only with long, hard hours of practice.

"I'm a friend," he said again. She didn't understand. His accent must be too heavy. Too thick. "A friend!" He leapt back to the verge of the track.

The woman finally realized that he was not fighting. She stopped her swing with an effort that left her gasping and stared at Cynric. The other stranger dismounted and ran to her side. He said something in a low, urgent tone. Without a word, she thrust the sword back into its scabbard and ran back to the bend in the trail where the Maedun had first seen them.

Cynric sheathed his own sword and sprinted down the track. Kier lay crumpled on the hard-packed dirt, his face pale as milk. Blood turned his tunic into a sodden mess and stained his hands to the wrist as he tried to press his wadded-up tunic into the wound. He had managed to stanch the worst of the blood flow. Cynric dropped to his knees beside Kier.

"Is it bad?" he asked quickly.

"Bad enough, I think," Kier replied, his voice grating and harsh. "I'm alive. How long I'll stay that way may be debatable." He grimaced, then coughed. No bright blood bubbled around his nose and mouth. So the chest wound probably didn't go through to a lung. A mercy, Cynric thought. Kier tried to look down at the wound, but fell back, panting. "I think the blade caught on a rib," he said.

Cynric looked up as the strange man dropped to his knees beside Kier. He said something in the Celae tongue. Cynric shook his head to indicate he didn't understand. The man nodded, then held out a thick pad of folded linen. His meaning was unmistakable. Blood still oozed sluggishly from the wound in Kier's side. Cynric pulled up Kier's shirt and tunic. The stranger leaned forward and pressed the pad to the wound, then bound it tightly against Kier's ribs with another wide strip of linen the woman handed to him.

Like the woman, he had dark gold hair and golden brown eyes. He was tall—nearly as tall as Cynric—with the slender, supple grace of a willow and the resilient strength of the tree. A bruise the size of a duck egg, the center split and bloody, matted the hair above his right ear. The woman stood close at his left shoulder, her eyes narrowed as she glanced down, first at Cynric, then at Kier.

"Saesnesi?" she asked. She indicated Kier. "This man,

he's Saesnesi?" Her Saesnesi was as good as Cynric's, but with a light accent he couldn't quite identify.

Cynric nodded. "Yes. Saesnesi," he said. "I, too. My father was Maedun, but I am Saesnesi."

The woman nodded. "The bandage—" She put her hand on Kier's chest. "It's been steeped in yarrow decoction. It will help to stop the bleeding."

"Thank you," Cynric said.

The man glanced at him, one eyebrow raised in speculation. "Saesnesi?" he said skeptically. "Surely an odd Saesnesi." He spoke with a curious, lilting accent, unlike the woman's.

"I'm a friend," Cynric said. "Not like those." He gestured with his chin toward the bodies lying sprawled in the track by the little stream. "I was born in the Summer Run. My mother was Saesnesi."

Kier laughed softly, then coughed again. Relieved, Cynric still could see no crimson bright blood bubbling around his nose and mouth. "I thought he was a strange Saesnesi, too," Kier muttered. "He's proved to be a friend."

The stranger nodded in acceptance. "You need help, my friend," he said to Kier. He glanced up at Cynric. "And quickly if he's going to live," he said in a softer voice.

"There's a Healer in his valley," Cynric said. "A man who heals by magic. If we could get him back there—"

"How far?" the woman asked.

"Two days' travel."

"He won't make it," the man said flatly. "But we're not more than a few hours' travel from my steading. There's help for him there with my people. We'll take him there."

"Your people?" Cynric asked.

"The Tyadda," the man said. "I am Davigan Harper." He made a formal gesture toward the woman. "This is my . . ." He hesitated for an instant, then smiled. "Iowen al Gareth, who is my wife."

Cynric looked at the woman again and wondered that a man might have a woman who was also a warrior as wife. And more, accept it as easily as this man Davigan Harper seemed to.

"Stay here with him for a moment," said the man who called himself Davigan Harper. "We'll need a litter for him. My people are not far, but he's a big man. I think it will take two of us to carry him. He should not be jolted around overly much."

"We'll want the horses, too," the woman said. She turned abruptly and began to cross the track.

Cynric turned his attention back to Kier. He appeared to be unconscious, his face pale and pinched with pain, his bloodless mouth drawn down at the corners. But the padding of yarrow-soaked bandage had done its work. As far as Cynric could tell, the bleeding had stopped. Kier's face twitched with a spasm of pain, and he muttered something. Cynric reached down and touched his shoulder.

"Be easy, my friend," he said softly. "We'll get you to help as soon as we can."

It took only a few minutes to rig a litter and load Kier upon it gently. Cynric took the head and Davigan the foot, and they set out following Iowen, who led the horses.

By midafternoon, Cynric wasn't sure how many more wonders he could absorb. Surely meeting a warrior woman who carried a wondrous sword was sufficient shock for one day. Now, they faced what certainly appeared to be a solid wall of rock, but he had watched numbly as Iowen and two of the horses melted right into the granite and disappeared.

He glanced at Davigan, knowing his own face registered blank disbelief. Why he hadn't dropped his end of Kier's litter from sheer astonishment, he didn't know. His heart quailed at the thought of walking right up to that wall and pushing through it.

"It's only an illusion," Davigan explained. "A Tyadda masking spell."

Cynric shook his head, then looked at the cliff wall again. But if the only way he could get help for Kier was to follow Iowen through that rock, then he would take it on faith that he *could* walk through the wall.

Davigan laughed. "Go ahead," he said. "I promise you it's only an illusion."

"So you say," Cynric said. He took a deep breath, shrugged, then stepped forward. He closed his eyes just before his body met the rock. Instead of harsh, sharp, unyielding stone, he met only a momentary resistance, as if he pushed against a rain-softened parchment stretched across a window opening. An odd, whirling sense of dizziness and disorientation swept over him. He nearly stumbled. But then he was through. He glanced back over his shoulder and got a shocking glimpse of Kier's head and shoulders on the stretcher, his hips and legs disappearing into nothingness. Behind him lay the narrow gorge that had led them to the cliff face. It shimmered and wavered as if he were looking at it through a sheet of running water. Davigan appeared through the shimmer, carrying the other end of the stretcher. Cynric repressed a shiver, shook his head again, and followed after Iowen and the horses.

Before him lay a long, narrow valley. A stream wound through the valley floor, and trees freshly green with spring growth crowded the sloping walls. A cluster of small cottages lay near the stream, their neatly thatched roofs gleaming bright gold in the sun streaming through a break in the clouds. Four people left the shelter of the village and hurried out to meet the new arrivals. Cynric found himself relieved of his burden and gently but firmly hustled into the village, where he was led first to a hot bath, then a good meal.

He wasn't sure who these people were, but they obviously knew Davigan and welcomed him. And, because he had come with Davigan, they made him welcome without reservation, despite his Maedun black hair and eyes. It startled him, and he realized it was the first time in his life, he had ever met with unconditional acceptance. It gave him something to ponder.

The bodies of the troop lay scattered carelessly on the crossroads like abandoned and broken toys. The clear skies of day had become cloudy as the sun sank toward setting. The thick gloom of twilight turned the bodies to dark, anonymous lumps, stripped of identity. Faghen crossed his wrists on the bow of his saddle while two men made their way from bundle to bundle, looking for signs of life. The Second stood in the track, arms folded on his chest, watching silently.

Faghen could find no pity in him for the ill-fated cadet. If ever the truth of this slaughter came to light, it would not surprise him to discover that the arrogance and stupidity of the cadet had been at fault. The young fool was certainly no loss, although Faghen felt a slight twinge of sympathy for the father. But again, a man needed to look first to his own career. Foolishness about furthering the career of an unworthy son led to disaster.

One of the troopers rose from where he had been crouched on one knee beside a body, and spoke to the Second. The Second nodded, turned to Faghen.

"One of them is still alive, sir," the Second said. "He might be able to tell us something."

"I'll come to speak with him." Faghen dismounted and followed the Second. The trooper pointed to one of the fallen men. Without emotion, Faghen recognized the cadet. He lay faceup with one leg nearly severed, the ground around him soaked and slimy with his blood. The shaft of an arrow protruded from the soft tissue in the hollow above his collarbone, but it was the leg wound that was obviously the fatal one. The cadet's face already looked withered as he hovered close to death.

Faghen dropped to a crouch beside the cadet. "Can you hear me?" he asked.

The cadet moved his head slowly and painfully. "Celae," he whispered. His voice sounded like the wind in dry rushes. "Caught us unaware."

"How many?" Faghen asked.

"Don't know."

"Which way did they go?"

The cadet tried to shake his head. "Don't know." His tongue, pale as a grub under a log, moved to moisten his cracked lips. "Took our horses."

"But you don't know which way they went."

"Didn't see them." He tried again to moisten his lips. "Had a traitor with them," he whispered.

"I see," Faghen said.

The cadet blinked, a slow, painful movement. "And a woman," he said. "A warrior-maid. She carried a sword."

Faghen drew back, startled. "A what?" he demanded.

"A woman." The cadet's voice was fading. "Dressed as a man, but a woman." He made a feeble gesture toward his leg. "She did this to me. That sword . . ."

"You're sure?"

"Sure." The cadet looked up at him, eyes wide with pain and shock. "Help me."

"Of course." Faghen reached for the shaft of the arrow thrusting up from the cadet's throat. "I'll help you die, you fool." He twisted the shaft violently, severing the large vessel in the throat. It took only a few seconds for the cadet's heart to pump out what was left of the blood in his body.

The Second cleared his throat. "Sir, he seems to have succumbed to his wounds. How unfortunate."

Faghen straightened and wiped his hand on the thigh of his trews. "So it would appear," he said mildly. "What a tragedy for his father back at Rock Greghrach. It seems that the cadet will not, after all, be covered in glory in the presence of the lord Horbad. What a pity." He glanced up at the swiftly darkening sky. "We'll have to camp for the night soon. Detail a party of men to bury this carrion, and have the rest see if they can find any tracks the Celae might have left."

"Sir?" The Second hesitated.

"Yes?"

"The traitor the cadet mentioned." He cleared his throat diffidently. "What do you make of that?"

Faghen looked up at the mountains rising all around. They made him uneasy, and he wished he were well away from them. He ran his fingers through his hair to hide the shiver that rippled down his back. "I don't know," he said at last. "But if the occupation army can produce an idiot like that cadet, surely it can produce a turncoat."

The Second frowned. "I don't like it."

"No," Faghen agreed. "Neither do I. I think we must find this party. I want to see that woman who uses a sword."

"A *woman*, sir?"

"That's what he said." Faghen looked down at the dead cadet, and shrugged. "Does that sound familiar to you, Second?"

"I—I don't think so, sir."

"Think," Faghen said. "Hakkar is looking for the man who calls himself the Prince of Skai. And the Prince of Skai is served by a warrior-maid." He allowed himself a grim smile. "It would appear that we have run across the trail of the man we seek." He nudged the dead cadet with the toe of his boot. "How clever of this idiot to find him for us, wouldn't you say?"

"Very clever," the Second agreed, and gave Faghen a frightened glance.

Faghen waited until the Second had gone back to the troop. A woman with a sword, who defended a man. It could mean only one thing. He glanced over his shoulder to make sure that neither the Second nor the troop were paying attention to him, then pulled the Tell-Tale stone from his pocket. He had not thought he would have need of it so soon.

The stone pulsed with faint green light. It sensed the presence of one of the swords Hakkar coveted. The woman's sword? It seemed likely. And if she was what he thought she was, Hakkar and Horbad would reward him richly for capturing the man she guarded.

The stone burned against his palm. He turned, holding the Tell-Tale like a lodestone Wayfinder. And, like a Wayfinder seeking the Nail Star, the Tell-Tale shivered in his hand, then drew him slowly about until he faced northwest.

She had gone deeper into the mountains. And taken his quarry with her. The pull of the Tell-Tale wasn't strong and sure, so the woman and the sword weren't nearby. But he now knew where to start looking.

Iowen sat in a comfortable chair and watched the interplay of glowing red and deep black shimmer through the fire on the hearth. The first few drops of rain spattered against the window. She held a cup of willow bark tea, sweetened with mint and honey. The soothing dance of light and shadow seemed to help her headache as much as the willow bark tea.

Outside the window, the small village of the Tyadda steading lay silent in the deep shadow of a cloudy night.

Davigan's mother, still stately and regal at over eighty, had seen to it that they were given a small cottage, which they shared with the two Saesnesi. Even now, the one named Kier lay comfortably in bed, tended by two of the priestesses from the shrine. The steading had only one Healer like Brynda. Competent and capable, she had already used her arts on Kier. The priestesses watched over him now to make sure he rested as he must to regain his strength. The other one, the strange Maedun-Saesnesi halfling who called himself Cynric, had not left his side.

Thinking of Cynric made her smile to herself. She had shocked him, she thought. But why would a man brought up by Maedun know about bheancorans?

Across the small room, Davigan sat with an old man. Anarawd ap Dallwyr sat on an upholstered bench, leaning comfortably against the cushions of the back. His fingers absently played with the strings of the small knee harp he held, sending trills and showers of notes into the room like sparks of light as he spoke with Davigan. Davigan sat on a low stool before the bard, leaning forward intensely. If Iowen concentrated, she could hear what they were saying. But concentrating made her head hurt. She was content to let herself drift in the warmth and tranquillity of the room.

A pulse of pain shot through her head. She closed her eyes dizzily and a knot of nausea tightened in her belly. The cup of willow bark tea fell from her nerveless fingers and shattered on the hearth. She clenched her teeth, but didn't quite suppress the gasp of agony that rose to her lips. When she opened her eyes again, Davigan knelt in front of her, his face drawn taut with concern and anxiety. Behind him, Anarawd stood, eyebrows pulled together above his thin, hawklike nose, watching her thoughtfully.

"I'm sorry," Iowen said. Her voice quivered, but she couldn't stop it. "I didn't mean to disturb you."

Davigan reached up and touched her cheek. "You're ill," he said. "Let me fetch one of the priestesses to help you."

Iowen began to protest, but Anarawd stepped forward and bent over her. He put his hand to her forehead and peered into her eyes. She stared back. His eyes, even in the dim firelight, were clear and golden, and held her gaze in thrall. The touch of his hand on her temples seemed to draw the pain from her. He nodded, then leaned back and took her hands.

"Close your eyes, child, and tell me what you see."

Iowen obeyed, then cried out. *Assassins. Glaring green stones pulsing insanely in the night. Glowing blades, runes spilling down the finely forged metal. Blood and darkness. Men dead and mutilated and crying for revenge. Green fire and golden glow.* She twisted away from Anarawd, pain lancing through her skull and churning in her belly. Anarawd let go of her hands and put his hand again to her forehead. The appalling visions faded.

"I see," he said softly. "There's only one way you can rid yourself of that pain, child."

Davigan looked up at him, pale in the firelight. "How?" he asked quickly. "We'll do anything."

The bard cupped Iowen's cheek for a moment, then dropped his hand. "Take her to the Dance of Nemeara," he said, speaking to Davigan but watching Iowen. "Take her to the Dance, and she'll be cured of this malady forever."

Iowen could not tear her eyes from his gaze. She might drown in those golden depths. Her throat and mouth felt suddenly too dry. "But I have a Gift for dreaming true," she murmured. "I don't want another. I don't want to go to the Dance."

"Mayhaps not, lass," Anarawd said. "Mayhaps not, but in any event, you must."

"I'll take her," Davigan said.

"You must leave with first light on the morrow," Anarawd said. "First light, and get there before nightfall the next night."

"Before nightfall?"

Anarawd nodded. "Else it might be too late," he said. "Every moment she delays, the pain will be worse. Poor lass. It's her Gift, you see. It's been overlong in coming."

"What Gift?" she asked. She brushed her hand across her eyes, as if she could brush away the burning pain.

"I don't know, lass," he said. "Mayhaps clearer Vision."

"I would come with you when you go." Cynric had come into the room without Iowen noticing him. "If you'll have me." He stood in the doorway leading to the small bedroom. Behind him, like a dark shadow, stood Kier.

"And I," Kier said. "I promised my lord Wykan that where Cynric goes, I, too, go. If you'll have me, also."

Davigan smiled. "You are more than welcome," he said. "I believe you'll be needed."

Kier frowned. "There may be a problem in that I have no resistance to Hakkar's spell if we have to go within a league or two of one of their strongholds."

Anarawd the bard turned slowly and studied first Kier, then Cynric. "Tomorrow, both of you will have what you need," he said. "Both of you."

Cynric's eyebrows rose in surprise. "I have resistance to the spell," he said.

"Aye, lad, you do," Anarawd said. "But you have not the protection of the gods of this island."

"Do I need it?"

Anarawd nodded wearily. "Yes. You will all need it, and soon."

22

A gentle touch on his temple woke Cynric. Startled, he sat up to see the younger of the two Tyadda priestesses bending over him. Tayora, her name was, he remembered. She carried a small, shielded lantern in one hand, a goblet in the other.

"It is time," she said softly. She held out the goblet to him. "Please drink this, my lord Cynric, then come with me."

He took the goblet and glanced around the room. Kier's bed was already empty.

"Please drink the wine now," Tayora said. "We must not be late."

He lifted the goblet and drank. The wine was pleasantly sweet, but left an odd aftertaste in his mouth. Tayora took the empty goblet and placed it on a chest while Cynric got up and pulled on the light tunic she handed him. She beckoned to him, and he followed her, belting the tunic about him as he left the room.

She led him out of the tiny village, out beyond the shrine, and into the woods, moving swiftly and certainly through the trees, her lantern like a will-'o-the-wisp before him in the dark. The trees were old and tall, thickly leaved. The branches closed above them, forming a verdant tunnel among the massive boles. He caught only occasional glimpses of the stars as he hurried through the forest behind Tayora.

The trees opened quite suddenly, and Cynric found himself standing at the edge of a small glade. Tall oak trees surrounded the open space. Ivy wound its way up the ancient boles and fell from the lower branches in a living curtain. He stood between the slender trunks of two ash trees, which grew like a gate into the glade. On the opposite side of the clearing, two holly trees grew close together. The holly trees and the ash trees made him think of two pairs of sentinels.

The moon silvered the whole glade in pale light and deep, black shadow. In the center of the glade stood a small circle of standing stones—seven of them, each half again as tall as a man. Kier sat cross-legged in the center of the circle. He did not look around as Cynric entered the glade, but sat quietly, gaze lifted to the stars, as if entranced.

"Please go and sit beside him," Tayora said softly. "It is almost time to begin."

He took a step forward, then stumbled and nearly fell as a wave of not-quite-dizziness swept over him. He glanced questioningly back at Tayora, who smiled at him in reassurance and encouragement. He began to walk to the stone circle, feeling decidedly odd, as if he were no longer firmly anchored to the earth. He found he had to be very careful of his balance. He was certain he could feel each individual muscle and tendon in his body moving in a precise and ordered flow in response to the commands of his mind. He was uncannily conscious of each pebble, each small twig, each blade of grass or fallen leaf beneath the soles of his feet.

At the same time, something strange seemed to be happening to his vision. As he sat down beside Kier, he began to see things he had never noticed before, small details that had escaped him, and he wondered how he could have missed them. He saw the delicate and intricate way each leaf on the trees fit into the complex pattern, the graceful curve of a grass blade bending to interact with its neighbor. When he looked at Kier, he saw the same wealth of previously unnoticed details. He saw the clever, powerful articulation of shoulder, elbow, and wrist; of hip, knee, and ankle. He noticed the finely molded lips, the ingenious fashioning of eyelid, and the shaping of the eye itself. He began to marvel at the wonder of how a man had been put together with such beauty of function.

He looked down at his own hands, saw the same wealth of detail there. How very odd. Why was it he had never before seen how clever and functional was the design of a man's hand? It was truly a marvel.

He looked up at the standing stones around him. The moonlight washed softly over them, and he saw that they were not smooth as he had first thought, but carved with intricate designs that gave the impression of human figures embedded into the stone. As he looked closer, he realized they were *not* stones after all, but men and women. He recognized them slowly from their images in the tapestries and paintings along the corridors of the palace in Clendonan. The woman there in front was Adriel of the Waters, who had always been the special patron of the seafaring Saesnesi in their longboats. Beside her stood the powerful figure of Gerieg of the Crags. A magnificent rack of antlers rose proudly from the forehead of Cernos of the Forest. Rhianna of the Air was there, as was Sandor of the Plains, and Beodun of the Fires. The last was one Cynric did not recognize at first, one who radiated warmth and compassion and love. He knew finally that she represented Celi itself, that she was the *ðarlai*, the Spirit of the Land, the Mother of All. He felt their eyes on him, sensed first their silent appraisal of him, then at last their acceptance.

Someone moved behind him. Cynric did not turn as the man behind him knelt. Strong hands gently descended on his shoulders. Another robed figure stepped into the circle to stand in front of him. A quiet sensation of peace descended over him, and he closed his eyes.

"We come to you in supplication, Protectors of this isle."

The rich, mellow voice seemed to come from all directions at once around Cynric. It was more than a voice; it was a chorus, softly and intricately blended to sound like one all-voice. In his heightened awareness, he heard music in the tones. Then, although he heard nothing, he sensed the consent of the circle of gods and goddesses for the Speaker to continue.

"We are your children. We honor you as our guides and our protectors and our sovereigns."

Again, the unspoken approval flowed out from the circle around Cynric.

"This man Cynric Faghenson of the Saesnesi is not of our blood, but he is also one of your children, a man born on this soil, born beneath this sky. We wish to make him one with us that he may have the protection from the dark which you grant to us."

This time, Cynric heard the response. "It shall be so."

From behind him, he heard a man speak. "From me to you, Cynric Faghenson, man of the Summer Run, man of the Saesnesi, man of Celi. My blood to yours. My spirit to yours. My soul to yours. Flesh to flesh, blood to blood, bone to bone. Be born of my seed."

The woman who had been standing quietly in front of Cynric stepped forward, then knelt before him. She reached out and cupped his face between her palms. "From me to you, Cynric Faghenson, man of the Summer Run, man of the Saesnesi, man of Celi. My blood to yours. My spirit to yours. My soul to yours. Flesh to flesh, blood to blood, bone to bone. Be born of my body."

Energy pulsed and flowed into Cynric's body through the hands on his shoulders. It coursed through his veins, along his nerve fibers like music thrumming on a harp string.

The singing energy filled him, seeped into every muscle, every sinew, every tissue of his body. It surged up, then sparked from him to the woman. He felt himself being drawn into her, becoming a part of her, sharing her body and her spirit and her soul in the special and unique way a child shares with his mother. The energy became infused with a deep and abiding love, a soaring joy, sensations more pure, more clear, more sharply defined and distinct than anything he had ever dreamed possible. It grew in him, quickening as beautifully and surely as a child quickens beneath its mother's heart, suffusing him in its warm glow. It grew with him, into him, fusing with him, becoming part of him, stretching itself to enfold him completely in its generous warmth.

Then, even as a child must leave its womb, be parted from its mother, he felt himself parting from the woman. The sense of loss was devastating, and he cried out in despair. The sensation of being one with the beauty which was the woman diminished and faded. The woman dropped her hands from his face, stood up, and stepped away. The interplay of energy between them ceased, and he became aware that his soul had reentered his own adult body—that he was no longer the infant of the woman's womb. The man's hands no longer touched his shoulders, but the strange energy still pulsed and flowed within him, throbbing like wild music through his blood, along the fibers of his nerves, while the voices of the seven gods and goddesses sang around him.

Like a newborn babe, forced against its will into the harsh, unfriendly world, he bent his head, covered his face with his hands, and wept.

He heard the all-voice again, softly this time, filled with compassion and understanding and love. "Awaken, Cynric Faghenson, child of Anarawd and Ysande, son of Nemeara . . ."

•   •   •

Cynric awoke early through habit. In the next room, someone already moved around, and the aroma of freshly
brewed kafe tea permeated the air of the small room.
Immediately aware of where he was and why, he flung
back the blankets and crossed the room in three strides to
Kier's bed.

Kier's bed was empty, the covers smoothed neatly, and
Cynric didn't know how long he'd been up. He glanced
around as one of the priestesses entered. She smiled at him.

"Your friend has recovered well," she said. "There's no
sign of fever. He's with the others, out there." She nodded
toward the main room.

"Thank you," Cynric said.

Outside, the morning had only just dawned cloudy and
cool. A gusty wind rattled the ivy trailing around the window, and, to the north, random streamers of rain arced
down from the black clouds, but had not yet reached the
hidden valley.

Cynric went to the bedroom door. It opened directly
into the small common room. Kier sat at a table, a cup of
kafe tea and a plate of bread and cheese before him. He
watched as Davigan Harper and the warrior-maid Iowen al
Gareth readied themselves to continue their journey.

"Are you leaving now?" Cynric asked. "Am I late?"

Davigan paused, looking up from the travelpack he
was fastening. "We're all a little late," he said. "We wanted
to be gone by first light. But Anarawd told us to let you
sleep." He smiled. "Last night must have been tiring for
you."

Cynric had difficulty remembering the night before
clearly. It might have been a pleasant dream. He could not
express his gratitude to Anarawd and Ysande. He glanced
down at his hands. Truly a work of art, a man's hands.

Wykan had been convinced that these two were important in the future of the country. For a man who called himself a bard, Davigan was not at all unhandy with the long dagger he carried, but it was obvious he was not a trained warrior. Cynric glanced at Iowen, who was busy placing items carefully into her travelpack. Just as obviously, the woman was a trained and thoroughly competent warrior. But one woman was hardly enough protection in a country where every turn threatened danger. And while Kier could not wield a sword as the woman and he did himself, Kier himself was more than adequately competent with his bow. Three people protecting one man's back were better than one.

"I've never felt better," Cynric said truthfully.

Kier smiled. "Nor I," he said.

Davigan nodded. "Then gather your things," he said. "We leave as soon as we can."

Davigan led them to the stable, where four horses were saddled and ready. Cynric had to smile a little at Kier's obvious discomfort. He'd had little opportunity to learn to ride in his life.

"What if I fall off?" he asked Cynric.

"Imagine yourself to be a cocklebur," Cynric said.

"A cocklebur," Kier repeated, looking at his horse askance. "Well, if it means going with you, I shall learn to be a cocklebur."

A spate of rain met them as they left the Tyadda village and the sheltered hanging valley. Cynric led the way down the gorge, with Kier following perched precariously on the horse's back. Behind him, Davigan and Iowen made sure they left no telltale tracks to lead any enemy to the entrance of the valley. When they were well clear of it, Davigan took the lead, Iowen riding at his left side, and turned westward toward the towering peak of Cloudbearer in the distance.

•   •   •

All morning, through spatters of rain and gusty winds, the
Second followed the tracks of the Celae. Three men walking, leading four horses. Faghen wondered at that. Why
walk when horses were available? Something was happening that he didn't quite understand yet.

The three had been careful. Only occasionally did the
Second's keen eyes find a hoofprint or a bootprint in the
soil. The sightings were far enough apart to force the troop
to travel very slowly while the Second ranged back and
forth at any of the myriad places where the Celae might
have turned off the game trail.

Just after midday, the Second lost the tracks completely where a narrow ravine joined the wider river valley,
disgorging a leaping, tumbling stream into the river. He
found one heelprint in the soft soil between the stones
along the streambed. It seemed to be heading up into the
ravine. But the floor of the gorge was rocky and took no
prints. Less than a furlong up the stream, they located a
place that would have made a good shelter for the night,
but no indication that anyone had used it recently.

Beyond the overhanging cliff, the rocky ground gave
way to grass and young bracken. But the Second found no
trace of footprints in the springy growth. The troop followed as he made his way nearly a league up the burn with
no results. Ahead, the ravine ended in a soaring granite
cliff. The stream shot out of a narrow cleft, the white, purling water arcing outward to tumble into a pool surrounded
by bracken-covered rocks and thickly crowding trees.

"They must have gone back out, sir," the Second said.
He wiped the sweat from his brow with his hand. "They
couldn't have gone farther up this ravine. I must have
missed the tracks."

Faghen suppressed a surge of annoyance. He, himself,

was not the tracker the Second was. The man was doing his best. Faghen could only wish his best were better.

"Then we'd best go back to the river and see if we can find their trail there," he said mildly.

"Yes, sir," the Second said.

An hour later, he found half a hoofprint beside the game trail. He dismounted and knelt to look at it more closely.

"Is it one of the horses we've been following?" Faghen asked without dismounting.

The Second traced the track with his index finger. "I think so, sir," he said. "See this? A small nick in the shoe near the frog? Yes, I'm sure it's one of the horses the Celae took from the other troop." He straightened and rubbed at the small of his back. "I'd say they're riding the horses now, sir, too. The tracks seem to be deeper, as if the horses were heavier."

Faghen nodded. "When might we expect to catch up with them?"

The Second shook his head. "I'm not sure, sir. The rain isn't helping things at all. I can't really tell how far behind them we are. It might be only a few hours. It might be a full day." He shrugged. "But they appear to be heading west. That might help us."

"West, is it?" Faghen asked. He looked up, but could see nothing but trees and mountains. Slipping his hand into his pocket, he pulled out the Tell-Tale. It pulsed and shimmered, but gave him no indication of direction. The magic he sought was close by, but something thwarted the stone's sorcery. Some greater magic blanketing it?

He looked up at the solid cliff and the bleak and cloudy sky above it.

Greater magic, mayhaps. But where?

•   •   •

Iowen's headache grew worse as the day wore on. She sat her horse only by effort of will, nausea bubbling through her body, her head pounding with every pulsebeat. By the time they stopped for the night in the shelter of a shallow cave above the trail, she could hardly speak. She found the thought of food intolerable. While the others ate, she wrapped herself in her blanket and cloak and huddled down on the sandy floor of the cave and tried to sleep.

She wasn't sure if she could ride in the morning if the pain didn't abate during the night. She didn't notice when it began to rain, and the water poured over the lip of the little cave like a waterfall over a precipice.

Just before twilight on the second day, they came down out of the mountains and out onto a green coastal plain. Wind whipped the water of the bay into a white frenzy, and rain streamed down out of the sky in a solid curtain. Cynric helped an exhausted Kier slide gratefully to the sodden ground when Davigan called a halt. Just to their left lay a small fold in the ground, thick with hazel trees and willow. The small overhang might provide a little shelter from the driving rain, but Cynric doubted they could persuade a fire to light, even if they could find any wood dry enough to burn.

"Do we camp here tonight?" he asked.

Davigan shook his head. "We've arrived," he said. He pointed. "The Dance is just over there."

Cynric wiped the rain from his eyes and followed the direction of Davigan's pointing finger. He drew in a sharp, astonished breath as he stared. Even shrouded by mist, its outline blurred by poor light and rain, the Dance of Nemeara was a striking and impressive sight. Dark against the gray of the sky and rain, the triple ring of standing stones sat in the center of the flat plain. The imposing menhirs of the outer ring stood starkly black against the silver rain, crowned in pairs by massive lintels to form trilithons. The middle ring of stones bulked slightly smaller, gracefully joined all around by capstones, polished like jet to reflect the wan pewter of the sky. The inner ring, standing alone without lintels, was not really a ring at all, but a horseshoe of seven menhirs enclosing a low altar stone that reflected the unsettled sky like a mirror. Cynric had the incongruous but distinct impression of a jewel cradled safe in cupped and loving hands.

"Power . . ." His voice was not much more than a whisper, but harsh and startling in the silence. "There's so much power in there . . ."

"A place of immense power, they tell me," Davigan said. "Not an easy place to stop beside."

He turned to Iowen to help her from her horse. She nearly fell from the saddle into his arms. Cynric leapt to help him. Her face, washed by the rain, was as pale as chalk, and her eyes looked like bruises against her skin. She had been getting worse and worse as the day wore on, and now that they had reached their destination, Cynric worried that she might not survive the night. Davigan smoothed the sodden hair out of her eyes and looked toward the Dance.

"She'll be all right once I take her to the Dance," Davigan said, but he sounded uncertain.

Something about the way he stood, the way he stared at the Dance, his eyes narrowed and steady, struck Cynric with an odd sense that he had seen this before. Mayhaps it was the latent power of the Dance reaching out to strum a familiar chord along his skin, but he suddenly knew the truth. He turned to Davigan.

"I had thought you were the Prince of Skai," he said quietly. "You have a bheancoran." He took the small book from his pouch and held it up. "I've read this until I know it by heart. It contains tales of Prince Keylan and his bheacoran Letessa. Stories, too, of King Tiernyn and his bheancoran Ylana, and Prince Tiegan and his bheancoran Brynda." He shook his head in wonder. "You're not the Prince of Skai, are you, Davigan?"

Davigan smiled. "No. I'm not."

"Yes," Cynric said. "You're king of all Celi. Uncrowned, but still the king."

"I am."

Cynric went to one knee. "Then I am doubly pleased to serve you, my lord," he said. He glanced toward the Dance. "Will you go in there with her?"

Davigan looked at the looming circle of standing stones, almost invisible in the gloom of twilight. "No," he said remotely. "She carries my soul in her heart and my unborn sons in her womb. But, no. I won't go with her. I will stand watch with you out here while she is in there. It's not my place tonight. But hers."

23

Rain plastered Davigan's hair to his forehead. Water streamed down his face and drenched his tunic and shirt. His boots were sodden, making unpleasant squelching sounds as he walked. Iowen seemed to weigh little more than a child of twelve in his arms. Her head rested on his shoulder, her eyes closed, a small frown drawing her eyebrows together. If she felt the rain, she gave no sign of it. Her face was as pale as the underside of the clouds overhead. A small blue vein in her forehead pulsed with the same rhythm as the beating of her heart he could feel against his chest through both their tunics.

Twilight was just turning to dark as he slipped through the entry trilithon of the Dance. The rain slackened instantly, and when he passed into the inner circle, it stopped completely. He hesitated, holding Iowen closer to him.

If he thought about it, he supposed he should be surprised and frightened, but his worry for Iowen wiped all other concerns from his mind. Legend said the Dance of Nemeara was a place of magic, a place where the gods and goddesses walked as easily as people walked their village square.

And who knew what the gods and goddesses might or might not do? Mayhaps they disliked getting wet as much as mortal men did, and simply did not allow the rain to fall within the Dance unless they specifically wished it to fall.

Iowen made a soft sound of protest as he went to his knees beside the polished altar and put her down on the grass. The stone of the altar was warm against his body, as if the sun had been beating down on it all day. Around the altar, the open horseshoe of seven megaliths stood silent and tall.

"I don't want to stay here," she murmured.

He put his hand to her forehead and gently brushed back her wet hair. "I know," he said. "But you must. Otherwise, you won't ever rid yourself of that headache, and it might be the end of you. I couldn't live in a world where you weren't."

She roused herself and got painfully to her knees. She said nothing, but misery and pain carved deep lines into her face, bracketing her mouth and nose, outlining her eyes. The skin around her mouth was pinched white. Cradling her head in her hands, she closed her eyes and leaned against the altar stone.

"For me," he murmured, tracing the line of the crown of her head with his fingers. "If you won't do it for yourself or the child, then do it for me. Please, Iowen. For me."

She looked up at him, then looked away. Her nod of acquiescence was barely visible in the deepening gloom of night. He touched her soft hair again, then got to his feet.

"I'll be waiting outside for you," he said. "I promise you I won't leave here without you. One way or the other."

"Davigan, my head hurts so much . . ."

"I know, love. But it won't for much longer."

She closed her eyes and rested her head on the altar stone, pale as her own ghost. He got to his feet, hesitated for a moment, wanting desperately to hold her and stay with her through the night, knowing that he couldn't. Finally, he turned his back resolutely and strode out of the Dance.

Iowen knelt in the soft grass, bent forward, her forehead against the smooth, polished surface of the altar stone.

Nausea curdled in her belly; her head pounded with pain. If she hadn't known it was ridiculous, she would have sworn it felt as if a small, burrowing animal was fighting to get out of her head, and that her head was in very real danger of exploding.

But the cool surface of the stone felt comforting beneath her cheek, soothing the thundering pain. She opened her eyes, but saw nothing. Far in the distance, a tiny point of light danced against the velvet darkness. Then, as she watched it, the light wavered, expanded, took shape.

Two men . . .

Held within the darkling shimmer of the light, two men faced each other across a wide circle of grass starred with white, luminescent flowers. The air between them crackled, as charged with tension as the air just before lightning strikes. The sky above them glowed with a strange light that was neither dawn nor dusk, and cast no shadows. Behind the first man stood the looming presence of the Dance of Nemeara. Behind the second spread a bleak, sere vista of gray drifts of ash and cinder.

Iowen nearly forgot about the pain in her head. Disbelief and shock chilled her as she realized she was watching Donaugh the Enchanter and Hakkar of Maedun—grandfather to the present Hakkar who called himself Lord Protector of Celi. The sword in Donaugh's hand, runes glittering furiously in the fey light, was none other than Heartfire. It vibrated with urgency in his hands, and the smooth, translucent horn of the hilt fit his grip perfectly. Flaring light twisted around the blade, reflecting on Donaugh's face. The air around Iowen shivered with the sword's fierce, sweet song. It chimed around her until its soaring sense of power stripped the last vestige of pain from her.

Hakkar of Maedun was dressed in unrelieved black,

his black hair and eyes blending with the shadows around and behind him. He held his sword raised before him, its obsidian blade spilling darkness around it as a broken ewer spills water. It reminded Iowen of a hole torn in the fabric of the world, trapping and swallowing all light.

"I misjudged you, hedge wizard," Hakkar said softly. "I had not thought you powerful enough to draw me here."

Donaugh flexed his hands around the hilt of Heartfire. "I think you'll find me as formidable a foe as your father found my father."

"I rather doubt that. But I shall not underestimate you again. You may be sure of that."

"You do me honor," Donaugh said.

"You and I will settle our quarrel here," Hakkar said.

"Then come and meet with Celae magic, sorcerer."

Even though Iowen had heard the tale so often that she knew it by heart, her breath caught in her throat. Instinctively, she looked to the shadows of the looming trilithons of the Dance. Transfixed, she watched as a slender figure stepped out into the glow beyond the megaliths, her silver-gilt hair flowing across her shoulders. The air above her left shoulder shimmered, but Iowen saw no shape within the brightness.

Donaugh's lost love — Eliade, daughter of Elesan. And mother to Aellegh, who was Wykan's grandfather.

Hakkar plunged forward, body tense, the black sword in his hands describing a vicious and deadly arc through the fey light. Donaugh leapt back, bringing Heartfire up to meet the obsidian blade. The two swords met with the crash of cymbals, and bright sparks shot up into the air around them.

The two men moved with the grace of dancers, sweeping back and forth and around the circle. Sparks flew as the blades met in thrust and parry, slash, and riposte, first high, then low. Tirelessly the men fought, first one attacking, then the other. The air rang with the fierce music of their weapons meeting.

The blades struck more sparks as they met, then parted. Blue and green and amber from Donaugh's sword twisting and braiding around sullen red and orange from Hakkar's blade, all rising into the uncanny glow of the sky. Flashes of color matching the sparks glinted off the silent megaliths, spilled brilliant runnels of color along the bleak, gray dunes of ash and cinder beyond the circle. Between the shadowy woman and Donaugh stretched a faint silver web. It might have been woven of spider silk, so fragile and delicate it looked. Power vibrated along the web, ebbing and flowing with the rhythm of Donaugh's battle with Hakkar, but the woman didn't move.

Slowly, slowly, Donaugh beat Hakkar back, pressing him inexorably toward the desiccated wasteland called forth by Maedun blood magic. Hakkar gave ground reluctantly, his face twisted into lines of strain as he struggled to stop Donaugh. Every inch Donaugh gained cost him more strength than he could replace, his determination reflected in the agony squeezing his eyes to narrowed slits, his mouth to a grim, bloodless line. Grace and fluid dexterity gave way to sheer, dogged, labored effort.

Donaugh slipped in the sodden grass, lost his footing. He went to one knee. Hakkar leapt forward, shouting in triumph. His caliginous blade swept forward and down, spewing darkness as it moved. Off-balance, Donaugh tried to raise Heartfire. Hakkar's sword flashed beneath Donaugh's sword. The edge bit into Donaugh's arm, just above the wrist. The glowing sword spun off into the darkness, Donaugh's severed hand still clinging to it. Its shadow, cast by its own light, whirled across the grass, as sharp and distinct as the sword itself. Hakkar reversed the swing of his sword and the tip of it sliced cleanly into the soft tissues below Donaugh's ribs.

Iowen cried out in terror as Donaugh fell back, blood pouring from the stump of his wrist and the wound in his side. Hakkar raised his sword for the killing blow.

The woman in the shadows made no sound. She plunged forward. Stooping low in a quick, graceful movement, she snatched up the shadow of the sword even as it spun past her. In her hand, it took on substance and weight, glowing with its own ghostly light. Without pausing, she thrust the shadow sword deep into Hakkar's side.

Hakkar's eyes widened in shock. He stumbled, groping with his left hand for the wound in his side. Donaugh's lost love drew back Soulshadow for another blow, but Hakkar's outline shimmered, grew transparent. As he vanished, so did the sword in her hands.

The swords glimmered in the darkness, then faded. Iowen saw them, quiescent and waiting, lying in the cave of her dream. And all around them, the obscene, poison green glare of Tell-Tale stones. The stones flared rapaciously, as if they sought to swallow the swords whole.

Iowen moaned as the pain in her head came back like waves crashing onto a shore. She closed her eyes and lowered her head back to the altar stone.

"I'm sorry this is so difficult for you, child."

Startled, Iowen fell back and stared up as a woman stepped from one of the megaliths. She carried a golden ewer cradled in the crook of her arm. Her hair, as gold as her ewer, hung down across her shoulder in a plait as thick as Iowen's arm. Behind her stood another woman, whose moon silver hair floated around her like a mantle. Iowen's breath caught in her throat. She recognized them both. Adriel of the Water and Rhianna of the Air.

Behind them, the others stood in their places by their standing stones. Cernos of the Forest, with the tall, stately rack of antlers rising from his brow, who had provided a tine from those antlers to fashion the hilt of Heartfire and Soulshadow. Gerieg of the Crags, with his hammer that smote the mountains and brought down thundering landslips, who had touched Cloudbearer itself and drawn forth the molten metal Wyfydd Smith used to forge the blades. Beodun of the Fires, carrying the lamp of benevolent fire and the lightning bolts of wild fire or needfire, who had provided the fire to heat the blades. Sandor of the Plains, with his hair like wild prairie grass blowing about his head, who had provided the baldric and scabbard, woven of grass and reeds as strong and tough as tooled leather. And the *darlai*, the Mother of All, who had engraved the runes into the blade.

Iowen turned slowly back to Adriel and Rhianna. Adriel's enchanted ewer had quenched the swords, and Rhianna's magic had woven the silver threads of music and magic through the hilts. Speechless, Iowen could only sit back on her heels and stare.

"We have a Gift for you, daughter," Adriel said softly.

Iowen shook her head. "Not magic," she said. "I have not the wisdom to use it properly."

Adriel smiled. "Magic, yet not magic," she said. She put a silver goblet down on the altar, filled it with water from her ewer. "Here, daughter, drink this. It will ease the pain, and you will feel better. I promise."

Iowen reached for the goblet, hesitated in fear. "What will it do?" she asked.

"Bring forth your Gift," Adriel said. "Yours is Vision, daughter. You have seen Heartfire and Soulshadow vanish. Now you must seek the place where they were forged if you wish to find the swords."

Iowen wrapped her hands about the goblet, but didn't raise it. "Have I any choice in this?" she asked.

Adriel smiled and shook her head. "No, daughter. Heartfire and Soulshadow are Rune Blades. They seek their proper owners. You are their tool, as Donaugh was their tool. As were his father Kian before him and your father before you."

Iowen looked down at the goblet in her hand. The water in it swirled and glimmered. "No choice," she whispered.

"You may choose not to drink," Adriel said. "If you do, your pain will remain with you, growing worse."

Iowen took a deep breath, then raised the goblet to her lips. The water flowed sweetly into her mouth, and she closed her eyes as the last of the pain in her head dissolved as if the water itself had taken it.

24

Iowen left the Dance at dawn. She felt lighter than a bubble in a wine goblet, rinsed as clean as the forest after the rain, wrapped in calm serenity. To the east the sky glowed in soft shades of gold, turquoise, and pink. The rain had stopped sometime during the night, and to her eyes, the whole world looked fresh and clean and new. On her back, Whisperer murmured quietly, its music blending with the rhythmic beat of the sea and the sweet, pure notes of birdsong.

Cynric sat before a small fire, half hidden in the shelter of a fold in the land. The kettle steaming gently on the fire sent vapor redolent of kafe tea into the air. He looked up, startled, as she dropped lightly into hollow. Behind him both Davigan and Kier lay wrapped in their blankets, sleeping soundly.

He followed the direction of her glance. "He just fell asleep," he said. "He was awake until nearly dawn, watching the stone circle. He was worried about you."

"Yes, I know," she said. "Let him sleep. He needs it."

"You look much better." He plucked the kettle off the fire and poured a cup of tea. Without a word, he handed it to her, then poured a cup for himself.

She smiled and accepted the tea. "Thank you." She had eaten nothing the day before. The tea tasted delicious, wondrously restoring. She warmed her hands around the cup and savored the rich aroma.

Out of the corner of her eye, she caught him studying her when he thought she couldn't see him. His eyes flicked often to Whisperer in its scabbard across her back. The frank curiosity on his face amused her.

She turned to him and set her cup down on the grass by her foot. "Does it bother you?" she asked.

He started guiltily. "Does what bother me?"

"This." She put her hand on Whisperer's hilt. "That I'm a woman, and I carry a sword."

He met her gaze levelly. "I find it a little disconcerting, I think," he said, and she found she liked his honesty. "I was brought up with the law that no woman touched a man's weapon on pain of death." He smiled apologetically. "That entirely precludes a woman carrying a sword and knowing how to use it better than most men."

"You say you served Wykan, yet you've never heard stories of the Celae bheancoran?"

"I've read of them. In this." He showed her the small, leather-bound book, the pages yellow and brittle with age. She leafed through it carefully. It contained page after page of bard lore—the sagas and songs, the legends and myths, all meticulously set out in a neat, precise hand. On the last two pages, in different handwriting, someone had inscribed the "Song of the Swords," carrying it over onto the flyleaf.

"Reading about bheancoran and actually meeting one are two different things," he said, smiling.

She traced the words on the page with a careful finger, hardly listening. "I suppose they are," she said absently. Swords and stones. What was it about swords and stones she had to remember?

"I've heard of the Prince of Skai, of course. Hakkar has placed a handsome price on his head."

She shook off the strange preoccupation and tried to concentrate on what he was saying. But something cold ran icy fingers down her spine. *Swords. Stones.* "My father," she said. "He came to Skai more than twenty-five years ago to retrieve his father's sword. But he didn't kill Horbad.

Davigan's brother Daefyd did." She laughed softly, without humor. "My family and Hakkar's have been tangled together for nearly a hundred years." She put her hand to her belly. Only a faint pulse of life beat there gently beneath her heart, but it was certain and definite. What part would this child, or these children, have to play in that great tangle?

"You use that sword very well," he said.

She smiled and poured herself more tea. "I began learning swordwork when I was still a knee-child," she said. "I knew I had a calling. Bheancoran know they're to be bheancoran even when they're small."

"Bheancoran is warrior-maid?"

"Partly," she said. "And partly soul companion and confidante. All the princes of Skai have bheancoran. Because he was of Skai lineage, our king, Tiernyn, had a bheancoran, too, and so did his son Tiegan."

Cynric glanced over to the shelter where Davigan still slept. "Davigan is Tiegan's son?" he asked.

She smiled. "Yes. His son by his Tyadda wife."

"The Tyadda," he said thoughtfully. "An ancient race here, or so they told me at the steading."

She nodded. "Yes. They were here when the Celae came. But the Celae didn't conquer them." She laughed. "They married them." She reached up and took hold of her braid and played with it for a moment. "This is typical of the Celae who intermarried with the Tyadda. Dark gold hair, brown eyes. But sturdier than the Tyadda." She let the braid drop. "How long have you been with Kier?"

He shrugged. "Less than a season," he said. "Before I pledged my service and my loyalty to Wykan, I was a courier for the Lord Protector of Celi, based in Clendonan."

Startled, she stared at him. "You were a Somber Rider?"

Dusky color crept into his cheeks. She couldn't tell if it

was anger or embarrassment. "No, not a Somber Rider," he said. "A courier. The only thing lower than a courier is a kitchen servant." He grinned suddenly. It changed his whole face from brooding introspection to delighted mirth. "The difference is the kitchen servants stay warmer in winter next to the hearthfires."

"How did you end up a courier?" she asked. "And how did you come to be with Kier?"

He told her his story. She listened carefully. He had not led an easy life, growing up trying to please a perfectionist father. Her own life in exile on Skerry was luxuriously comfortable in comparison. She watched his face as he spoke. Pain, bitterness, and anger washed in waves across his features when he spoke of the day the garrison commander had relegated him to being a courier. Then pride and a certain essence of peace followed as he spoke of Wykan and Kier.

"What about your father, Cynric?" she asked. "Do you know what became of him?"

The corners of his mouth turned down momentarily in a quick grimace. "I've neither seen him nor heard from him since the garrison commander dismissed him," he said. "He never returned to our quarters, as far as I know, and I was barred from them the next day."

"I'm sorry," she said softly. "I think you cared for him."

He looked down at his hands. "I don't know," he said, his voice so low she had to strain to hear it. "I believe I respected him. But cared for him? I don't know. He wasn't a man who wanted anything more than to be respected and honored. I tried to give him that. Mayhaps I failed miserably, and that's why everything came apart." He paused for a moment, then shrugged diffidently. "But I believe I've found my place," he said at last, giving her a smile both rueful and shy, one at the same time that she found utterly charming. "And I have friends for the first time." He looked at her, and one eyebrow quirked in what might have been amusement. "It seems I've also found my king and my queen."

"Your queen?"

He gave her a solemn, half-formal bow. "You, of course, my lady. You're Davigan's wife. That makes you queen, does it not?"

Startled, Iowen stared at him. That she might be queen had never before occurred to her. She had been quite content to be bheancoran to the uncrowned king. But queen? It was a truly astonishing idea.

"Why, I suppose it does," she said in confusion. "How very odd that seems."

Davigan woke and flung off his blanket. A smile broke across his face, and he came quickly to her side. "You're well again," he said.

She put her hand to his cheek. "Yes," she said. "And I believe I know now how to find the swords. But we've need to hurry."

Hurry. Yes. Hurry. Memory came flooding back, and she nearly stumbled. Davigan caught her arm.

"What is it? Are you all right? What's wrong?"

She turned to him, shivering, but could not speak . . .

Small, oval stones. Glowing swords. Green fire consuming everything. No swords of power. No king. No enchanter. No freedom for Celi. The island bound in chains forever.

The Second stared in awe at the massive stone circle. He shuddered visibly and turned to Faghen. "What is it?" he asked. "It gives me the colly-wobbles."

Faghen was not about to admit to the Second that he, too, found the standing stones disquieting and disturbing.

In the strong, midmorning sunlight, the megaliths glowed silvery gray and cast an odd pattern of barred shadow across the grass. Something about the stones made his Tell-Tale stone go mad. He couldn't prevent himself from touching it often. It shivered against his thigh through the fabric of his trews, first colder than winter rain, then hot enough he was certain he'd find its imprint branded into his skin. This was not something that Hakkar or Horbad had warned him about. Then he wondered if they knew about the strange phenomenon.

"I'm not asking that you walk into the middle of it," he said testily, unable to keep the irritation out of his voice. "Tell the men to search carefully. See if they can find any sign of them around it. This must be where they were heading."

The Second hung back. "It's obvious they aren't here now, sir," he said somewhat sulkily.

Faghen turned in his saddle to look at the Second. "I can see that, Second," he said bitingly. "However, if we want to know where they've gone, we're going to have to locate where they were so we can follow their tracks. Do you agree with the logic of that?"

The Second's cheeks turned an unpleasant shade of mottled red. "Yes, sir," he said. Reluctantly, he gathered his men and directed them to begin searching for sign.

The men spread out around the stone circle. They moved gingerly, reminding Faghen of skittish horses, ready to shy at the first flitting shadow. He noted with cynical amusement that all of them—including the Second—seemed to be able to judge within inches how far away they could remain from the standing stones in the search without earning his scathing anger. When the Second found the campsite to the south of the circle, the men gathered as far from the standing stones as they could, all of them looking relieved.

The Second was on one knee beside the remains of a campfire when Faghen dismounted. He put his hand down onto the dead ashes, then looked up, his expression once again controlled.

"Still warm, sir," he said. "But barely. They left here hours ago. Probably just after dawn. And look here, sir—" He got up and led Faghen to a tangle of willow thatch. Carefully, he stooped down and pushed a clump of young growth aside. The clear print of a bootheel showed plainly in the soft, moist dirt. He traced it with his finger, around the half-moon shape of the back of the heel, the deep notch in the front. "This is a standard-issue riding boot. The cadet was right. There's a traitor riding with them."

Faghen bent to study the print. The heel print could definitely have been made by any Somber Rider. He nodded, then straightened up. "So it would seem," he said. "Or one of the Celae has stolen a pair of boots. But I think it more likely that the cadet was right about the turncoat." He allowed himself a cold smile. "Even an imbecile can be right on occasion."

"There are tracks of four horses over there," the Second said, waving toward another clump of trees. "They left here going south. Shall we follow them?"

Faghen raised one eyebrow. "Of course," he said. "I believe the Lord Protector is anxious to speak with the rebel who calls himself Prince of Skai. And I—" He pulled on his riding gloves and meticulously fitted them to his fingers. "I am anxious to speak with a Somber Rider who keeps company with Celae."

25

The ridge overlooked the mouth of the River Eidon where it flowed into the deep blue waters of the Ceg. Among the trees below, Cynric could just make out the ruins of a wooden building. Beyond, close to the rugged shore of the inlet, two towers still stood tall above the tumble of broken stones that had once been a palace. Weed-choked and covered with young saplings, the crumbling outlines of the courtyard were barely discernible. New growth blurred the crisp lines of the tower. More than fifty years of abandonment had nearly completed the process of giving the land back to the forest.

"Dun Eidon," Davigan said softly beside him. "They say it was a beautiful place once. Even more beautiful than Dun Camas, Tiernyn's palace near Clendonan."

Iowen turned in her saddle to look back at Davigan. He sat his horse, unnaturally still, looking down at the ruins of the palace. He pointed. "Just down there. That's where the village was. You can see nothing of it now. The Maedun burned it shortly after Brennen took what was left of the people to Skerry."

"Let's hope there aren't any Maedun around here now," Kier said grimly as he scanned the valley.

"The ghosts of the slain Celae might still walk here," Iowen said. "They say the carnage was terrible." She leaned forward. "My father was born here. His mother is buried near the old wall."

Cynric shivered. As he thought of those slaughtered men, women, and children, the sun seemed to dim and the air to grow perceptibly colder.

"The shades of Celae shouldn't bother us much," Davigan said. "We've come to help, after all." He studied the area carefully. "The forge might be difficult to locate in all that."

"It would be down there by the river," Iowen said. "Near a ford. Over there, I think." She pointed to an opening in the trees, choked by new growth but still discernible. "That might have been the road there. We'll have to follow it down to the valley."

Davigan gave her a crooked smile. "Standing up here isn't going to find it for us," he said. "Follow me carefully."

He urged his horse down the slope toward the ruined palace. Iowen followed. Cynric let Kier go ahead, then fell in behind. As they came closer, Cynric could see that nothing other than wild animals had been that way for a long time, mayhaps years.

They passed close to the crumbled walls of the courtyard. A huge mound of stones stood piled next to the moss-grown wall—a massive cairn raised by the strength of grief. The new green of bracken, graybells, and foxgrass softened its outline. Cynric glanced at Iowen. Beneath that cairn lay her people. She rode with her face averted, tears glittering on her lashes.

The silence was heavily oppressive. No birds sang as they road past the young trees growing in what had been the courtyard. Nothing moved except them. Ahead of him, Davigan shivered and turned his head away, and Cynric tried to repress his own shiver.

The air hung heavy over the ruined palace and felt cold on his back despite the bright spring sun lowering to late afternoon in the west. Faghen had brought him up to pay at least lip service to the gods, but he had never considered himself particularly open to the otherworldly *presences* the priests claimed to experience, to expound as the ideal. And while he wasn't sure if the souls of the slain went to the everlasting joy of Annwn, he did not believe that they hovered above battle sites. But there was something about this devastated palace, something about the stark cairn rising beside the tumbled wall, that chilled his blood and troubled his spirit. He felt much more comfortable when they were well past the broken ruins and riding out along the vestigial track leading upriver.

Less than a furlong upstream, they came to a small burn flowing into the Eidon. Iowen reined in and dismounted. She led her horse to a dead chestnut tree that stood alone. Another cairn, but smaller, stood beneath it, all but reclaimed by the forest. Without a word, she pushed through the tangled undergrowth. Davigan and Kier dismounted and followed close behind her, none of them speaking. Cynric hesitated for a moment. He wasn't sure if his presence would be welcome. Then Davigan glanced back over his shoulder and beckoned. Cynric took a deep breath and followed.

The ruin of the forge stood well off the road, not far from the ford, close enough to the small burn so that the cold, clear water to quench the hot iron would be close at hand. Another chill rippled down Cynric's back. Iowen had come straight to this place, not deviating in the slightest. As if she knew it would be here, even though she had never seen it before. As if led by the urgency and fear she brought with her from the Dance. Magic. Perhaps not the soul-freezing sorcery practiced by warlocks, but magic nonetheless. He hunched his shoulders uneasily.

The building was unmistakably a forge. The thatch of the roof had fallen and turned to dust. In places, the rotted shreds and tatters still remained. Cynric thought they would crumble at a touch, so fragile they looked. Some of the timbers of the wall had splintered like matchwood and lay blurred and lost under a thick blanket of new bracken, and moss furred the two walls that still stood upright. The front wall was gone but, incongruously, the doorframe still stood, leaning to the left, solid enough but no longer guarding anything of value. The wooden door stood drunkenly open on half-rusted hinges. Faint ghosts of old brands still showed on the wood, faded from charred black to pale gold against the weathered soft silver sheen of the door.

Iowen stood for a moment before the ravaged building, her arms straight down by her sides, her eyes wide and unblinking. Cynric detected no sense of reluctance or hesitation in her stance. The vertical line traced between her eyebrows by the fear and tension were gone, erased by the sudden easing of her mood. Almost expectancy. Or even contemplation. An odd expression stole across her features, transforming it into the face of someone he didn't know. He thought that she watched something none of the rest of them could see. Then she took a deep breath and stepped inside the derelict smithy.

Inside, the stone of the furnace still stood. Nearby, the Smith's hammer lay across the iron anvil, both disintegrating with rust. On the one remaining wall hung implements of several different types. A grain scythe without a handle, a half-finished sword, a shovel blade. On the adjoining wall hung the Smith's tools for shoeing horses and mules, alongside an assortment of shoes, now rusted red. The leather of the bellows had rotted, hanging in shreds across the wooden frame and smoothly worn handles.

Davigan remained by the door, Kier beside him. Cynric was quite content to watch from a distance as Iowen walked slowly to the bellows. Her hands moved across the skeleton of the frame as if they caressed the leather that had once sheathed it.

Kier took a step forward, as if to enter the smithy. Davigan made a quick, imperious warning sign with his hand, signaling Kier to stay back.

"What is it?" Kier asked sharply. "What's wrong with her?"

"She's Seeing," Davigan murmured. "We must not disturb her."

"The swords?" Cynric asked.

Davigan raised one shoulder in a slight shrug. "If this is truly where they were created, it might be," he said. "In any event, she'll tell us when it's time."

"I hadn't expected to find it so quickly," Kier said. "But it makes sense to start here where they were forged."

Iowen fell to her knees before the furnace. Even from his place behind Davigan and Kier, Cynric could see that her pupils had widened until her eyes looked like black pools in her pale face. His back was becoming accustomed to the cold chills as he watched her. Hers was a face behind which the soul had fled to somewhere else.

Iowen knelt before the furnace, one hand resting lightly on the cold stone. Her head ached with a fury to bring tears to her eyes and blur her vision, but she couldn't close her eyes to clear them. Slowly, the scene built around her, nebulous at first, transparently overlaid on the ruin of the long-abandoned smithy, then with more solidity until she no longer saw anything but the vision. Davigan was gone, Kier and Cynric with him. The door where he had stood was flung open to the coolness of a late-autumn afternoon.

The Smith stood beside the forge, watching, waiting. Around him, seven shadowy figures stood half hidden in the gloom behind the forge, their attention on the Smith. Without surprise, Iowen recognized the seven gods and goddesses. They never so much as glanced at her, but she knew they accepted her presence. She turned her gaze to the Smith. He wore a leather apron covering his chest and belly. His powerful arms, thick as a normal man's thigh, were bare and gleaming in the eerie light. Broad-shouldered and heavyset, he stood easily half an armlength taller than Iowen. In one hand, he carried a square hammer, its handle polished by years of use to the smooth sheen of silk. Startled, Iowen recognized Wyfydd Smith, and the song echoed in her head.

Armorer to gods and kings
Wyfydd's magic hammer rings.

On the walls of the smithy hung the tools of the Smith's trade, bright and shiny with constant use and care. A wooden vat of water stood next to the anvil, spare hammers in varying sizes on a block of wood that served as a table. The beaten-earth floor had been swept clean and water sprinkled to settle the dust. The thatching of the roof looked fresh, and the smithy smelled pleasantly of clean, fresh straw, the earthy scent of the freshly dampened floor, and the fading tang of hot, molten iron.

Everything lay in readiness, waiting . . .

The Kingstar blazed across the western sky, leaving a fiery trail of incandescent haze behind it. It plunged down through the lesser stars, and its seething tail brushed across the upthrusting head of Cloudbearer. As the Kingstar passed, smoke and flame poured out of the top of the mountain, sending gouts of brilliant embers soaring into the black sky.

Straight as the flight of an arrow, the Kingstar slanted down through the sky, blinding in its brilliance, searing Iowen's eyes as it flew past her. The air hissed and crackled to its passing. Behind it came a molten stream of gleaming metal, pouring from the smoking summit of Cloudbearer.

The forge exploded into flame. Light flared around the interior of the smithy, sending black shadows writhing and dancing along the silvered walls until the forge ran with brilliant color, red and gold and orange. Wyfydd reached high and pulled a bar of the sparking metal from the sky, whirling it above his head and then down into the molten heart of the forge fire.

Iowen watched unsurprised. It was right and fitting. The fire of the forge came from Beodun of the Fires himself; the metal was the gift of Gerieg of the Crags.

The face of the boy pumping the bellows was red, as much with exertion as from the heat that radiated from the white-hot coals. He was very young, Iowen thought. Not more than nine or ten, but already the work had given a solid definition to the muscles of his arms and chest. He worked tirelessly, almost effortlessly, raising and lowering the handles on bellows that were larger than he, but no sound of the rush of air moving to fan the flames in the forge came to Iowen.

The bar of metal from Cloudbearer lay in the fire, glowing brilliant white-orange with a life of its own. Using a pair of bright tongs, the Smith pulled the metal from the Kingstar fire and laid it upon the anvil. The heat oiled the skin of the Smith's bare shoulders and arms with a film of sweat. The muscles beneath the bronzed skin rippled and flowed as the hammer beat down on the glowing metal.

Slowly, slowly, the metal on the anvil began to take shape as the Smith's hammer drew it out. When it lost its malleability as it cooled, the Smith thrust it back into the fire. Time after time, the bar of metal flattened to a thin sheet beneath the hammer. The Smith folded the sheet, pleating it into layers, and let the rhythmic beating of the hammer draw it out again in an endlessly repeated cycle. Behind him, against the wall of the smithy, a shadow smith built a shadow sword in vivid counterpoint.

Iowen was aware of the shadows moving across the beaten earth of the floor, but time had no meaning here. Before her eyes, the swords began to take shape. Long after the cutting edges would have been sufficient for use, the Smith continued to fold and draw out, fold and draw out. Strong and flexible, these blades would take and keep an edge no matter what they were asked to cleave through.

The last part to be shaped was the tang, the point that would fit into the hilt. When it was done, the Smith lifted the blade and held it above the oaken vat lined with bright metal. Adriel of the Waters stepped forward and tilted her enchanted ewer. Water flowed over the golden lip and into the vat, bright and sparkling, clean and cold and sweet. When the vat was full, she stepped back. The Smith plunged the glowing blade into the water. A cloud of steam rose, thick and fragrant, as the blade sizzled, then cooled. Behind him, in echo against the wall, a shadow smith quenched a shadow sword.

One by one, the gods and goddesses brought their gifts for the sword to add to the gifts of Beodun, Adriel, and Gerieg. Cernos stepped forward, one of the tines from his antlers in his hand. Wyfydd took it and bent it around the naked tang for a hilt, long enough to be used two-handed, light enough to be wielded with one hand. Rhianna wove her air magic into an intricate web of silver to embellish the glowing, translucent horn of the hilt. And last, Sandor of the Plains held forth a baldric and scabbard braided of tough prairie grasses, as lustrous and strong as gilded leather.

Wyfydd lifted the sword and presented it to the *darlai*. She stepped forward and ran her finger down the gleaming blade. On the wall behind her, the shadow of the sword leapt stark and clear, appearing as real as the sword itself. Sparks flew from beneath her finger and fire ran down the metal, etching runes into the blade. The music of magic swelled to a lilting crescendo.

> *Music to the hilts he gave*
> *With magic did the blade engrave . . .*

When the *darlai* stepped back, the runes blazed up, brilliant as the cut facets of a gem, and the words flared in the smoky light. Iowen could almost see the words. They were tantalizingly close to making sense. Words of power. Words of magic.

The words in Davigan's voice echoed in Iowen's mind as she watched. She could not read the runes on the sword. But there was no reason why she should. The sword was not hers.

Finally, Iowen saw the sword, fully completed, lit from within with the light of the faceted runes, rise from the workbench and move eastward, becoming transparent as it receded. The shadow sword faded with it, until it was gone, both of them swallowed up by the blue haze of distance.

The swords came to rest in a deep cavern, safe between the mountains and the sea. Then something happened. Maedun blood sorcery, thick as pitch in the air, reacted with the gentle magic of the blades. In hidden corners of the cavern, faintly glowing points of light came to life, looking like nothing more than marshfire on a moonless night. But points grew until they became nearly as big as hen's eggs.

The malevolent green glare reached for the swords' magic, greedily sucking life from it. The glow of the swords dimmed imperceptibly at first, then more quickly.

Iowen found herself on her knees in the ruins of the old forge, the cool light of dawn staining the sky outside the gaping door. She climbed unsteadily to her feet and walked out into the open air, blinking at the brightness of the day after the dim illumination of the vision. She stumbled, and Davigan put his arm around her.

"North," she said. "North and west. Follow the swords . . . Oh, hurry. Hurry before it's too late." She closed her eyes, the refrain coming to her lips without conscious volition. "No swords of power for the king. No king. No enchanter. Chained forever lies Celi . . ."

26

For two days, they followed Iowen, who followed a vision. It led her north and west, sometimes along a well-defined track, sometimes along the bed of a stream, sometimes through the trackless wilderness of the thickly forested flanks of a mountain. They met nobody on the track, neither friend nor foe.

Iowen ate little and slept less, her eyes fixed glassily on something only she could see. A febrile flush stained the pallor of her cheeks as she rode leaning forward over the bow of her saddle. At night, she tossed in her sleep, wrapped in her cloak, twisting like a woman caught in a fever dream. And always, her lips formed words silently. "Hurry. Hurry. Hurry."

Cynric tried to make her eat a larger portion of the meal when they stopped for the night on the second day. She brushed him aside without speaking. Distracted, jittery, fidgety, nervous. She worried him, but he finally gave up in frustration and went to sit beside Davigan on the other side of the fire.

"I worry about her, my lord," he said quietly, frowning and watching Iowen across the fire. "She begins to look ill again."

Davigan tried to give the appearance that his attention was on the small wooden flute he was carving, but his gaze flicked to Iowen too often. The glimmering light of the fire caught on the blade of his knife as he pared sliver after sliver from the barrel of the flute. Cynric had never before seen a man making any sort of musical instrument, and the process captivated him. But if Davigan wasn't careful,

Cynric thought in fascinated bemusement, he was going to shave the bell of the flute to transparency. Davigan looked down at the flute, made a rueful face. He dropped it into his lap and put his knife away.

"She has a lot to worry about," he said. "I don't know much about those Tell-Tale stones she speaks of, but I do know that if they really can destroy the magic in Heartfire and Soulshadow, there's little hope for Celi." He rubbed the flute on the sleeve of his shirt and shook his head. "There's little you can do for her, I think." He made a help-less gesture. "I know even less of the Sight than I do of Tell-Tales. I'm told it's not a comfortable Gift at times, though."

"Iowen has told me that, too," Cynric said, glancing at her.

"It pains me to see her like this," Davigan said. "But I trust her. And I trust the goddess who gave her this Gift." The fragile barrel of the flute snapped in his fingers. He looked at it ruefully, and tucked it inside his tunic. "And I trust both of them enough to hope we'll find the swords in time to be of use."

"Mayhaps it's best to leave her be," Kier said from across the fire. "Gordan becomes all strange and fey like that when he's Seeing, but as soon as the vision is gone, he's better." He got to his feet and stretched. "I'll take first watch tonight. We'll want to get an early start again tomorrow."

On the morning of the third day, Cynric awoke to find Iowen already up. She stood beneath an oak tree, one hand resting against the massive trunk, staring up at the high ranges of mountains that rose, tier on tier, to the northwest. For the first time since they had discovered the old forge, there was natural color in her face, and her eyes had lost their hollow, burning glaze.

"Good morning," she said in her normal voice, still

watching the mountains as the sky behind them brightened from gold to turquoise.

"You're back," he said.

She turned to him. "I'm back," she said. The pallor had gone from her cheeks. Her color looked more normal to him. More like herself again.

"And the swords?"

"I can't see them any longer. They're gone now. Somewhere up there." She waved a hand to indicate the ridge of mountain that descended in massive steps from the flanks of Cloudbearer to the sea. The sharply serrated peaks made a natural lookout to the west, north, and south. Before the Maedun invasion, a watchtower and a small stronghold for the Companions of King Tiernyn had stood on the promontory overlooking the sea.

Kier came yawning and stretching out of his blankets. He crossed the small clearing to join them. "Still north and west, then?" he asked.

"Yes," Iowen answered. "But carefully. There are enemies ahead."

"Somber Riders?" Kier asked.

Cynric looked at the folded ridge of peak and crest. "What else around here?" he said. "If I'm right about where I think we are, there's a garrison stronghold near there. Rock Greghrach they call it. There are bound to be patrols of Somber Riders all around it."

Iowen laughed without humor. "Adriel didn't promise this would be easy," she said. "The swords may be guarded even better than we thought. Have you been there?"

Cynric nodded. "Yes. Several times, carrying dispatches from Clendonan." The corners of his mouth turned down in residual bitterness. "But I'd highly doubt anyone there would recognize me. Couriers, servants . . ." He shrugged. "Who looks at either?"

Davigan came silently from the campfire to join them where they stood beneath the oak. Iowen turned to him immediately, warmth and quick pleasure lighting her face, reflecting his own.

A unit, Cynric thought suddenly. *They're a unit just as surely as hilt and blade combine to form one sword.* He wasn't sure he understood why the insight caused a pang of regret to pluck at his heart.

"Are you all right?" Davigan asked, all his attention focused intensely on her, a frown of concern drawing his eyebrows together above the bridge of his nose. "You've looked so ill since we left Dun Eidon. I was worried again."

"This Gift isn't a comfortable one," she said. "And worrying about the swords being destroyed doesn't help. But it won't kill me." She managed a smile. "It's finished with me for a while, though." She shot a quick, amused glance at Cynric, suddenly more like herself. "Cynric can stop fussing over me and acting like a goose with one gosling."

Cynric felt the heat rise in his cheeks, and he looked away as Kier laughed. "Gander, surely," he said, managing to keep his voice light enough.

In the space between one step and the next, a cold, black fist of panic closed around Cynric's heart, squeezing the breath from his lungs. Dark shadows swirled in front of his eyes, and he gasped aloud. He pulled his horse to a stop, looking around nervously for the source of his uneasiness. He recognized the sensation only a moment later. The same cold dread had seized him when the warlock had frozen him with the full force of the spell in the commander's workroom. The same fear constricted his chest, made his heart pound frantically and his skin creep in horror. He saw the same fear and repugnance reflected on Kier's face.

"The spell . . ." Kier muttered, his face pale as chalk.

Davigan immediately came to his side, leaning across
the space between the two horses. He reached out to touch
Kier's arm.

"It can't harm you," Davigan said gently. "You're protected now. Remember the ritual at the steading? You're
under the same protection that Iowen and I are. You're
aware of the spell, but it can't drown you."

Kier took a deep breath. Cynric glanced at him in concern. The panic etching Kier's face receded. In the circle of
standing stones, Anarawd the bard and Ysande, wife to
Anarawd, had adopted him, passed on to him their own resistance to the spell of the Black Sorcerer. He began to relax.

"I'm all right," he said at last. "I wasn't expecting to feel
it like that."

"Tyadda magic can't prevent Hakkar's spell from making itself felt," Davigan said. "It can only help you resist
succumbing to it."

Cynric looked up at the ridge rising ahead of them.
"Down here, we're within a league or so of the fortress," he
said. "I don't like getting so close. There could be a troop of
Somber Riders coming down this way at any time. It might
be best if we could go around it to the east."

"We can't." Iowen's voice sounded flat and inanimate.

Cynric glanced at her. She sat her horse quietly, wrists
crossed on the bow of her saddle, looking up at the top of
the ridge where it dipped sharply toward the sea. Her eyes
were wide, drowned and glazed again, as they had been
while she was following the sword. No expression moved
in her face.

Davigan understood before Cynric. "The swords?" he
asked.

Cynric shot a puzzled glance at him, then realized what
he meant. Iowen's Gift again possessed her.

"The swords," she replied, not looking at them, only at

the crest of the promontory. She pointed. "They're just there. Under that promontory. In a cave. Where the sea meets the stone."

Cynric followed the direction of her pointing finger. He bit his lip and looked first at Davigan, then at Kier. "I think I know the place," he said. "The promontory thrusts out into the sea something like the prow of a ship. The garrison fortress is built near the top of the prow. There are several caves in the north wall of the ridge. Not quite right under the fortress, but near enough. Within half a league of it, at any rate."

"Can they be seen from the fortress?" Davigan asked.

Cynric frowned. "I don't think so," he said. "At least, not from anyplace in the fortress I've been in. But everyone's bound to know the caves are there. I don't know if anyone's ever explored them, though." He made a face. "The Maedun don't like mountains, and they especially don't like caves. Our . . . Their country is as flat as the surface of the sea, for the most part. No caves. To a Maedun, a cave is . . . unnatural, I suppose. A man might go into one out of curiosity, but not much beyond where the light from outside reached. But if the warlock or the commander forced some troopers to check out the caves, they'd go, of course. Reluctantly, but they'd certainly go in."

"And find the swords?" Kier asked.

Davigan turned slowly to look at him. "The swords are well hidden," he said. "The song says so."

"*Hidden long by Myrddin's spell, Enchanted now 'til blood will tell.*'" Iowen whispered the words, still looking at the distant promontory.

Kier glanced up at the ridge, then looked at Cynric. "How do we get to those caves without walking right through a nest of Maedun?" he asked. "We can't go by way of the shore."

"No," Cynric said. "We can't. At high tide, the water washes right up against the foot of the cliff. But I think we can go around the fortress. They've cut a lot of the trees down on the approach, but I think we can get past farther east. It will take us more than half a day out of our way, but it should be safe enough." He glanced up at the sun. It hung low over the crest of the promontory, staining the snow-covered eastern peaks with brilliant gold. "With luck, we'll get there shortly after first light tomorrow."

"No," Iowen said sharply. "No. We can't wait. We have to go now. We can't go around. We have to get there as soon as possible."

"We can't go right past the fortress," Cynric protested.

"We must."

"Iowen, be reasonable," Davigan said. "There are Somber Riders as thick as berries on a rowan tree all through here."

"If you won't come with me, I'll go myself." Iowen's voice rose. "We have to go now!"

"Iowen—"

She reached across and seized Davigan's sleeve. "If we don't go now, the swords will be destroyed. And us with them!"

The stone in Faghen's pocket scorched his flesh right through the fabric of his trews. His heartbeat pounded with the rhythm of the stone's pulsations. They were close now. Very close. The Tell-Tale drew him forward.

"Sir, here!" The Second waved an arm like an excited boy. "Do you see it, sir?" He pointed to a nick in the shoe. "It's the same as the other one we found."

Faghen thrust him aside, intent only on the guidance of the stone. He urged his horse forward, thrusting ahead through the trees. Rock Greghrach lay ahead, standing on the promontory above the sea. He could think of no reason why the quarry would be heading toward the fortress, but the stone could not be wrong.

The sword—and the woman—were not far ahead. That meant the rebel prince was well within his grasp.

"You're wasting time," he said harshly. Barely contained urgency hammered at his belly. "Let's go. Now. Hurry. Now!"

The Second's face flushed a painful red, but he didn't drop his gaze. "Yes, sir," he said. He grabbed the reins of his horse and swung into the saddle.

Faghen spurred his horse into a gallop. The Second and the troop followed, but it hardly mattered. All that mattered was the stone, and the quarry.

Close now. Very close.

27

Cynric led them in a wide circle, first northeast, then north, and finally northwest. The prickly chill of Hakkar's spell against Cynric's skin abated until he was only peripherally aware of it, so he assumed that they followed the outside perimeter of area where the bespellment was strongest. He was quite happy to maintain that distance. The memory of the chill emptiness trapped within the Dead Lands was still too fresh in his mind, too immediate.

The spell was heavier, more intense, than he remembered it being the last time he was here. But it worked differently here than it did in the Dead Lands. Although it could certainly smother his spirit and his will despite his natural resistance—had he not the protection of being adopted by the Tyadda—it didn't affect the vegetation. Here were no vast areas of sere and burned grass, shriveled and withered trees, or lifeless bracken. Mayhaps not as bad as the Dead Lands, but bad enough.

The track leading from the gate of the fortress followed the crest of the promontory for a little less than half a league before curving down the flank of the ridge to join the main track through the mountains. They could not reach the other side of the crest without crossing it.

They halted for a long moment, listening intently, before crossing the track. Cynric had just decided it might be safe when he heard the staccato rhythm of hooves against the beaten earth of the track and the musical jingle of bridle metal.

"Down," he whispered harshly. "Get down!"

He slid from his saddle and went to his mount's head,

muffling the horse's nose and mouth against his tunic. Instantly, both Davigan and Iowen were on the ground, pressing themselves against their horses' heads, murmuring soft words of reassurance to them. Cynric frantically motioned Kier to dismount. For a stunned second, Kier didn't move. He didn't realize the horse would call to the other horses on the track unless prevented.

There was no time. Cynric lunged, seized Kier, and pulled him awkwardly out of the saddle. He wanted to pull the horses and himself farther back into the undergrowth at the side of the track. But the Somber Riders would surely hear the noise as the horse moved through the bushes. They should be well enough out of sight.

Kier stepped closer, took the head of his own horse. Cynric relinquished it in relief as Kier pressed his cheek to the scratchy hide between the horse's eyes and stroked the horse's neck. He gave Cynric a quick grin, and Cynric nodded in acknowledgment.

The thunder of hooves grew louder until it seemed to surround him, and lasted for what felt like two lifetimes. Gradually, the sounds faded in the distance, and he lifted his head to look around.

Cynric handed the reins of his horse to Davigan and ventured out onto the track, looking both ways. Finally, he beckoned quickly, motioning them across the track and into the trees on the other side. Iowen led her horse across, then Davigan went, leading both his horse and Cynric's. A moment later, Kier followed.

"Wait here a moment," Cynric whispered. "There's something I must do." He slipped back into the trees and used his sword to lop off a branch from a clump of willow. He ran back across the track, then used the branch as a broom to obliterate any tracks they might have left. He brushed away the tracks of the troop of Somber Riders with their own, but that couldn't be helped. There was nothing he could do about it now.

He mounted his horse, still holding on to the willow branch, and pointed with it. "That way. There's no path, but I can find the north face of the promontory."

Behind him, Iowen rode leaning forward intensely, her face white and pinched, her eyes wide. The skin seemed stretched too tautly over her cheekbones, and the bones themselves looked too sharp, as if they would slice right through to the surface. Her fear was a palpable thing in the air, causing her horse to dance nervously beneath her.

Cynric found himself praying to gods he didn't know that they would be in time.

The combers crashed thunderously against the rocks at the foot of the cliff where it thrust out into the sea like the prow of a ship. Columns and clouds of flung spume and spray drifted in the air, falling like rain against the splintered rock. Above, drifts of gulls circled in the clear dawn light, their soft, mewling cries sounding faintly on the wind.

Iowen dismounted and dropped the reins of her horse. She walked quickly to the edge of the cliff and looked down. Below, a wide strip of wet sand glistened between the rock and the bubbling foam as the breaking waves receded back out to sea. Such a long distance down. Davigan followed her.

"The tide's coming in," he said. "In less than three hours, it will be up against the foot of the cliff."

"The cave is just down there," Iowen said, pointing to a tumble of broken rock at the foot of the cliff. Only a spill of shadow showed against the wet rock of the cliff face. Nothing that looked as if it might be the mouth of a cave. But she knew it was there as surely as she knew the sun rose in the east every morning.

"I'm going down there," she said.

"No," Cynric cried. "Anyone on the northwest wall of the fortress can see you. You can't—" He reached out to pull her back, but she wrenched herself away.

Davigan seized her arm. "Not yet, Iowen," he said firmly. "We have to wait until dark."

She yanked her arm out of his grasp. "No." She was nearly sobbing. "No, I have to go now. Or it will be too late."

They didn't understand. They just didn't understand. They couldn't see the malevolent green glare creeping toward the hidden swords. They couldn't feel the swords' agony as their own magic weakened.

The strength of Hakkar's spell beat against her skin and her mind like a strong gale. On her back, Whisperer muttered uneasily in a minor key. Even with the protection of her Tyadda blood, she thought the spell might too easily overwhelm her.

Overwhelm her while it fed the green stones.

She flung herself toward the cliff edge. Davigan cried out, but she eluded his grasp and plunged over the cliff edge. It was steep, but not impossibly so. She scrambled down, clutching at clumps of sea pink and thistle for balance. Small stones and clumps of earth slithered with her down the slope.

Then the firm, level sand of the beach was beneath her feet. She gathered herself and sprinted across the hard-packed sand.

A huge slab of leaning rock the size of a fortress gate lay angled across the entrance to the cave. Dark shadow hid the narrow opening. Iowen stood panting before the rock, trying to catch her breath.

She turned as Davigan, Cynric, and Kier stumbled to a stop behind her.

"There," she said. "Behind the rock. It's not a wide entrance, but it's there." She drew Whisperer, then took a deep breath and dived through the opening.

Darkness closed about her. But it was the familiar darkness of her dream, and she knew every twist and turn of the corridor. She put out her hand to where she knew the torch would be and found it waiting, then handed it to the man behind her.

It was Kier. The flint of his tinderbox sparked bright in the darkness, then the thin, guttering flare of the torch threw long, wavering shadows across the cave floor. She turned to make her way farther into the cave, knowing they would follow, the soft sound of their footfalls behind her as the cave closed around her.

The torch guttered and smoldered, giving off more smoke than light. The walls of the narrow corridor gleamed damply in the uneven light. Cynric shuddered and hunched his shoulders, trying to fight off the conviction that the weight of the mountain pressed down on his head, ready to crush and smother him. As they penetrated deeper into the cave, the smell of mold and damp became stronger, over-powering the scent of burning pine pitch coming from the torch. Here and there, patches of greenish phosphores-cence glowed faintly on the slimy walls, and he could see Iowen's silhouette moving against the glimmer.

More than once both he and Kier had to duck their heads to avoid braining themselves on low projections of rock thrusting down from the ceiling. But if Iowen and Davigan ahead of him noticed the dip and sway of the torchlight, they gave no indication. Their shadows raced ahead of them, shrinking and leaping with each movement of the torch Cynric carried. They moved on smoothly, apparently not bothered by the uneven floor or by the potentially lethal projections of rocks.

No sound penetrated the darkness except the hushed, cushioned padding of their footsteps against the damp sand of the floor. Once, Kier swore softly as he put a foot wrong and trod on Cynric's heel, but the faint breeze coming from the interior of the cave carried the sound away with it.

The breeze blowing in Cynric's face carried a deep chill. He shivered again as the torch guttered. The smoky shadows leapt at him, and he fought against the feeling that the walls were creeping toward him. He turned sideways as the corridor narrowed, quelling a brief stab of fear that the passageway would not open again. Behind him, Kier breathed an audible sigh of relief as the corridor again became wide enough to accommodate their shoulders.

A few steps later, as suddenly and breathtakingly as a bolt of lightning, they walked out of the narrow corridor and into a vast chamber. The feeble light of the torch picked out massive columns of limestone joining ceiling to floor, creating row on row of high, vaulted recesses that reminded Cynric of nothing more than the interior of a huge shrine.

Iowen made a soft sound. "Just as it was in my dream," she murmured, and the echoes of her voice hissed and whispered through the chamber until they became a chorus of voices, all hushed in awe.

28

Faghen looked up at the towering crag of broken rock that loomed above the strip of sand. He glanced back down at the footprints in the sand. They seemed to disappear right into the bulk of a massive slab of rock. A cave. A hollow beneath the soaring crest of the promontory.

Behind him, the men of his troop stood uneasily in a semicircle as far from the cave mouth as they could without stepping into the rising tide. Even the Second hung back, obviously reluctant to come closer to the cave.

Faghen thought about the four people who had entered the cave. A cold chill ran down his spine, and he repressed a shudder. How could anyone deliberately and voluntarily walk under the earth? It would be too like being buried alive. The reward he would collect from Hakkar for capturing the Prince of Skai didn't seem worth the horrors of walking into that cave. Not even the strident urgency of the stone could force him through that narrow crevice.

The Second nervously adjusted the buckle of his sword belt. He was pale, his mouth drawn into a thin, tense line. Most of the rest of the troop, less adept at hiding their feelings, looked apprehensive, even mutinous.

Faghen couldn't fault them. If he ordered them into the cave, they would revolt. If they defied him and disobeyed his orders, he would be forced to execute them, and that would defeat his purpose.

The Celae had gone into the cave. And the turncoat Somber Rider, too, by the tracks in the sand. But they would have to come out again . . .

The Second cleared his throat. "Might this be the place they were heading for?" he asked.

Faghen turned to look at him. The Second was mayhaps overly ambitious and sometimes too sly, but he was no fool. He could think, and he drew some surprisingly accurate conclusions.

"It's likely," Faghen said. "And if this is the place they were heading for, they might come out with a treasure or two." Which wouldn't hurt his case with Hakkar, he thought, if he presented it to him.

The Second managed a weak grin that was almost a smirk. "We needn't go in after them, sir, I should think," he said diffidently enough. "After all, they *do* have to come out again."

Faghen would not allow himself to smile. "They do, of course," he said.

"And we'll be out here to meet them when they come out," the Second said with more confidence.

"There might be one problem with that," Faghen said. "Look around. Do you see any cover we can use to lay our ambush?"

The Second's face fell, then became thoughtful. "The cliff itself, sir," he said. "The tide is almost at flood." He pointed to the ridge of crisped, ragged seaweed on a ledge about man-high above the sand. "I'd say that was the high-tide mark. We might find places just above it and wait. They won't come out until after the tide turns. We can capture them as they come out of the cave."

Faghen nodded. "You've thought it out very well," he said. "That's what I'd do. Deploy your men, then."

The cave opened into a vast chamber. Cynric stumbled to a halt. Kier bumped against him and dropped the torch. Cynric snatched it up before it could hit the ground and go out. A deep throbbing, felt more than heard, beat through the cavern. For one fearful moment, he thought the mountain might be moving, ready to collapse. Then he realized he heard the rhythm of the sea beating with the cadence of a great heart. The heartbeat of Skai itself.

Davigan made a small exclamation of surprise, and the echoes hissed and rustled until they filled the cavern and came back sounding like a dozen voices in chorus. Limestone pillars growing up from the floor met columns melting down from the ceiling, white as bone in the flickering torchlight.

"I dreamed this," Iowen said softly. The cave made music of her voice. "The swords should be just ahead of us there." She stepped out of the narrow corridor to stand beside Davigan.

Cynric jumped, startled, as the torch flashed and flared brightly in his hands. The light streaked from one column to the next, glittering, leaping, growing, running like liquid fire around the chamber, striking sparks of green and red and blue and violet from the columns as if each pillar were made of crystal gems. One after the other, they caught the torchlight and erupted into evanescent fire, sending sparks of shimmering rainbows of color and light to all corners of the immense gallery.

A flat, tablelike slab of stone stood alone beside a massive pillar, its shadow looming tall and dark against the glistening white of the limestone. On its flat surface, two swords lay glimmering in the coruscating light. The steel of the blades shone brightly, and the translucent material of the hilts pulsed with living fire in amber, gold, and warm brown. Lines of deeply cut runes flashed and glittered in a long spill down each blade, sparking like facets of a gem.

"You'll have to get the swords, Davigan," Iowen said, her voice hushed.

Davigan looked at her, one eyebrow raised in question. "Me?" he said. "Are you sure?"

"In my dream, I thought the man who picked up the sword was our son, but it might have been you. In any event, it was not I."

Davigan squared his shoulders. His shadow leapt and swayed before him as he stepped into chamber. Cynric took a half step to follow him, then thought better of it. He didn't need to see Iowen's hand shoot out in an arresting gesture to know that the cavern was not his place. Not now. Not ever. He could only watch.

Davigan advanced steadily, the uneven footing hardly hindering him. When he finally reached the table Cynric thought of as an altar, he hesitated and glanced back over his shoulder at Iowen. The torchlight glittered in his hair, giving bright sparks of copper and red to the dark gold. His eyes, shadowed beneath his eyebrows, were wide and alert.

"Pick them up, Davigan," Iowen said again. "You are king of Celi, and the swords were made to defend and protect Celi."

Davigan turned back to face the altar. As he put out his hands to take the swords, Cynric forgot to breathe for a moment. Something in the air fizzed and effervesced gently as Davigan's right hand closed over the hilt of the first sword. But when he tried to grasp the second, Cynric could have sworn Davigan's hand passed right through the translucent horn of the hilt. The outline of the second sword shimmered and wavered. It disappeared to Cynric's eyes. When he looked at Davigan's shadow, it seemed alive in the pulsating light. Cynric shivered. The shadow of the second sword, the sword he could not see, was as sharp and distinct against the uneven floor as if it had been painted on creamy parchment in thick, black ink.

Magic. The air was saturated with it. He felt it against

his skin as distinctly as if it had been falling rain.

A scabbard Cynric hadn't noticed before lay on the altar. Davigan picked it up and carefully sheathed the sword. The runes glittering along the blade flashed once before disappearing into the scabbard. On the cavern floor, the shadow sword slid home into its shadow scabbard in perfect harmony with the sword Davigan held.

The blaze of light reflecting from the pillars quenched

"The other sword—" Kier's voice sounded hoarse, as if his throat were nearly too dry to speak. Cynric turned and met his astonished and bewildered gaze. "It's gone. There were two . . ." He blinked at Cynric. "Weren't there?"

"I saw two, then only one," he said. He shook his head, half in awe, half in disbelief. "Magic. This place is thick with it."

Davigan made no attempt to wear the sword. He turned away from the altar table, carrying it as if it were a child—or fragile as finest crystal—cradled gently in his arms. When he reached Iowen, she raised one hand tentatively as if to reach out and touch the sword. Then she bit her lip and dropped her hand.

"Not for me," she whispered. "The song says, *'Only seed of kings may lift Wyfydd's sword, take Myrddin's gift . . .'*"

The torch flickered dimly. Cynric glanced at it, startled. It was nearly out. With luck, it might last until they regained the entrance of the cave, and daylight.

Whisperer trembled against Iowen's back. Softly within her head, the sword's song whispered in a curious mix of joyful greeting and breathy warning. Whisperer recognized the presence of Heartfire and Soulshadow. Like called to like. But Whisperer also recognized the surrounding danger. Iowen found the combination both elating and disturbing.

As she stepped out of the cavern, back into the narrow corridor, something flickered wanly green by her left foot. Whisperer shrieked. Iowen reacted by instinct alone. She brought Whisperer up, slammed it down onto the sickly green glow. The stone exploded into a blinding sheet of green-white, enveloping her in a smothering, soundless mist. She choked, staggered, nearly fell.

Then it was gone. Whisperer's voice subsided again to a soft, uneasy murmur. Iowen blinked the grit from her eyes. She could breathe again.

Davigan grabbed her arm, swung her around against him. "Are you all right?" he demanded.

"Yes," she said, and realized in surprise she was. No more squirming, nervous agitation gripped her heart. The queasiness and nausea no longer churned in her belly. At her feet, the last of the green glow had disappeared. Hakkar's spell might still hang heavy in the air like misty drizzle on an autumn day, but Heartfire and Soulshadow would no longer be here to react with it, to form any more of those ghastly Tell-Tales. "I'm fine, Davigan. Yes. Just fine. Let's hurry out of here."

Ahead around a bend in the narrow corridor, a faint gleam of light hazed the darkness. Not until she knew the end of the cave was in sight did she realize how disquieting she found the darkness. She quickened her steps to stay close behind Davigan. Something flickered briefly against the murky light ahead, then was gone.

Cynric swore softly. The guttering light thrown by the torch vanished abruptly as he thrust the torch head into the wet sand underfoot. Darkness closed about them like a fist that the faint glow of cloudy light ahead only made deeper and blacker. The hissing susurration of a sword being drawn whispered through the darkness.

"Someone's out there," he muttered as he brushed past her, running. "Take care. Be quiet."

Iowen reacted automatically, without conscious thought. Whisperer's hilt seemed to leap into her hand as she followed Cynric. An odd, blurred snap behind her resolved itself into the sound of Kier's bowstring sliding into place.

She rounded the last corner. Bright sunlight slanted into the mouth of the cave through the triangular gap between the leaning slab of rock and the living rock of the mountain itself. The light starkly silhouetted Cynric, sword drawn and ready, as he leapt toward the narrow opening. Blinded and dazzled by the westering sun, she hesitated. She heard rather than saw Cynric hurl himself out of the cave shouting in Maedun about danger and rock falls.

Still blinking the glare from her eyes, she sprang through the gap behind Cynric and into the midst of at least a dozen men still confounded by Cynric's abrupt, shouting arrival among them. The instincts instilled by long years spent sparring with the Swordmaster took over. She whirled to meet a sword swung by a startled but determined Maedun. She ducked under the deadly arc of his blade, then used her momentum to sweep Whisperer in a flat curve. The edge caught the Maedun near the notch of shoulder and throat.

Something whistled past her ear like an angry hornet. Out of the corner of her eye, she saw another Maedun go down, the shaft of an arrow protruding from his chest. In the next heartbeat, another Maedun collapsed at her feet, felled by a second arrow, and she nearly stumbled over him.

Davigan surged out of the cave, carrying only his short sword. Iowen spun around, instinctively placed herself to guard his left. Two Maedun had backed Cynric against the stone slab that guarded the cave entrance. Davigan stabbed one of the Maedun; Kier's arrow took the other. A wild, fierce grin stretching his lips back from his teeth, Cynric grimly turned to meet another foe, placing himself to Davigan's right.

One of the Maedun sheathed his sword and ducked away, slipping out of the confusion. He turned and ran down the narrow strip of sand, casting a glance back over his shoulder. Iowen saw the movement out of the corner of her eye, then dismissed the running man as no danger to her or to Davigan.

Someone shouted. She spun around in time to see the leader of the Maedun, the officer, leap at Davigan, sword slicing the air in a deadly arc. She threw herself forward desperately. The hilt of the sword, cushioned by the officer's hand, smashed into her temple. She went to her knees in the sand, the foam of the retreating tide bubbling around her legs.

The officer kicked her aside as if she were no more than an annoying small dog, and lunged at Davigan. Cynric turned, desperately driving forward to place himself between Davigan and the officer. Davigan ducked the first savage slice and leapt back. Cynric spun around, sweeping his sword in a backhand arc toward the officer.

Then, as Iowen watched helplessly, the color bleached from Cynric's face. His eyes went wide and stunned, and he hesitated. His swing faltered, stopped. For the space of half a heartbeat, the officer seemed to be as startled as Cynric. Then he shouted and thrust forward. Davigan leapt back, but too late. The blade of the officer's sword sliced into the small of his back.

Davigan dropped his short sword, stumbled two steps toward Iowen, then went to his knees. An odd, listening expression grew on his face, his eyes wide in astonishment. Then the light faded from his eyes, and he toppled gently to his side.

Iowen's heart surged painfully. For a moment, she thought it would tear itself loose in her chest. Screaming incoherently, she came to her knees. Using Whisperer like a lance, she plunged the blade deep into the officer's belly. The officer grunted, then fell at Davigan's feet.

29

Too numb even for grief, or pain, or fear, Iowen crawled on hands and knees to Davigan. He lay on his back, open eyes staring up at the endless blue of the sky. No breath stirred in him, the throbbing pulse in his throat gone. He lay completely still, in absolute silence, and somehow diminished, as if Skai itself had already begun to take him back into its womb. The breeze gently riffled the hair that lay in a spill of dark gold across his forehead, bright against the pallor of his skin.

She knelt beside him and reached out to brush the stray lock of hair away from his eye. Her hand trembled uncontrollably, and she had to concentrate to touch the hair. It felt like silk against her fingers, but lifeless and lank, all its resilience gone, as if it had drained with his life into the ground.

"No," she whispered in a hopeless, keening litany. "Oh no, no, no, no . . ." She put her hand up to cover her mouth to stop the appalling sobbing. Great, shuddering waves of horror flooded through her body. Her limbs trembled as if with palsy. She thought her heart and guts had been torn physically from her body, leaving a huge, yawning void, black and empty as the pits of Hellas. For a moment, she was sure she would die just from the intensity of the pain itself.

Oh, gods, how could this happen? How could he be taken from her like this? Why did she still live while he lay dead? How could she go on living without him, and without the bond that had become so integral a part of her?

She bent forward, sobbing, knowing she couldn't live now. She had nothing to live for. Her soul lay dead on the ground before her, and she could not live without him. She pressed her forehead to her knees and clenched her teeth, trying to stop the crushing wave of pain washing through her.

The need for revenge swelled in her chest. She still held Whisperer clutched tightly in her hand. The sword's song murmured softly in the back of her mind—a low, keening wail in a mournful minor key. *Vengeance,* the song cried. *Vengeance.*

But there were no Maedun left alive. She looked up and saw Cynric kneeling by the side of the man she had killed—the man who had slain Davigan. Blinded by the pain and the fury, she turned on him, her face contorted in rage.

"You," she cried. "You let him die! Murderer! Assassin! You let him die!"

He flinched back from her, still kneeling at the dead man's side. The tortured anguish that twisted his face hardly registered with her in her own distress and torment.

"Why didn't you kill him?" Iowen cried, sobbing. "You were right beside him. Why didn't you kill him?"

Kier bent down to touch her shoulder. She slapped his hand away, her attention intent on Cynric.

"Why? Why?"

The pupils of Cynric's eyes spread until they appeared to fill the black-brown of the irises, bleak and lost and grief-stricken. He might have been looking into the deepest pit of Hellas. Guilt and shame and desolation painted his face, and he looked away from her.

Her belly cramped. She cried out in fear and wrapped her arms about herself, as if by sheer force of will and effort, she could hold Davigan's unborn sons within her womb.

"No," she murmured. "Oh no." Not the babes, too. Not the father and the children, too. She couldn't bear losing everything. She couldn't bear it.

Kier reached down again and put his hand to her shoulder. "My lady . . ."

She shook off his hand. "No!"

"We must go," Kier said, his voice harshly urgent. "We've great need of hurry. We mustn't be here when they return."

"I won't leave him," Iowen said. She brushed a lock of hair from Davigan's forehead. "I can't leave him."

Kier put both hands on her arms and dragged her away from Davigan's lifeless body and to her feet. He turned her to face him, still holding tightly to her upper arms.

"My lady, for the sake of the children you bear," he said, "for the sake of the swords Davigan died to find, we must go. It is imperative we go now. If we wait any longer, the Somber Riders will be back, and we will all die here. If that happens, Davigan will have died for nothing. His life will have been wasted. And so will Wykan's."

She looked up at him. The sense of his words gradually penetrated the fog of distress and suffering in her mind. She took a deep breath to steady herself, then nodded.

"Of course," she said quietly. "Then we must go."

Cynric knelt on the blood-sodden ground beside the Somber Rider, his hand still resting on the man's back in an almost tender gesture. The sight of him squeezed at her heart like an ironclad fist. How could he treat that man as if he were worthy of pity? How dare he show grief for the man who had killed Davigan? The man she had killed herself because he had not. Because he had lost his courage and faltered.

She pulled away from Davigan and walked with slow

and deliberate steps to Cynric. She stood over him for a moment, looking down at him coldly and dispassionately.

"Twice a traitor," she said, the bitterness in her voice like acid in her throat. "You betrayed your father's people, and you've betrayed mine. You let him be killed. You stood by and let him die. By your inaction and cowardice, you let your king die."

Cynric looked up at her, his face drawn bleak in grief and agony. "My lady, forgive me," he whispered. He looked down at the Somber Rider. "Forgive me, but I could not kill him. He is—he was my father."

Iowen stared blankly at him, unable to comprehend his words. But she had to look away from the expression in his eyes—from the reflection of the tragic immediacy of her own loss. Then Kier was there, and she turned into the shelter of his arm.

"You're not able to think about this yet, my lady," Kier said softly. "But would you have had him become a kin-slayer? Even for Davigan, would you ask a man to kill his own father?"

She looked up at him, lost in her own pain, not yet willing to admit another's grief might be as agonizing as her own. The deep, hollow ache within her spirit and soul threatened to drown her. He looked down at her. She saw only the sorrow in his eyes. Tears blurred her vision, and she could not see.

"We must go," he said. "Before they return with more men. We must go now."

Iowen glanced irresolutely at him, then at Davigan. So still. He lay so still. She found her voice. "I can't leave him," she said hoarsely. "I can't—"

"Would you have him die for nothing?" Kier repeated.

Mutely, she shook her head.

He gathered the swords and placed them in her arms.

For a moment, she stood cradling them against her breast as if they were infants, drawing an odd, remote comfort from the cold length of them. Finally, she nodded. She let Kier take her arm and lead her away. She neither noticed nor cared if Cynric followed them.

Horbad, son of Hakkar, looked down at the sprawled bodies at his feet. Twelve Maedun Somber Riders and one Celae man. Seven of the Somber Riders had died arrow-shot. Five of them succumbed to swords. And there had been only four Celae? It seemed an uncommonly uneven contest, considering the outcome. Faghen, despite his calm assurance in Rock Greghrach, had certainly not managed to fulfill his undertaking.

The waves lapped and swirled around the corpses, giving the illusion of life to flaccid limbs as the water retreated. The sea had nearly claimed one of them as the tide ebbed quickly. It had already taken one. Horbad could barely make out the bobbing corpse among the foam-streaked waves.

"I came for you immediately, Lord Horbad," the Second said righteously, eager for approval. "Just as you commanded me." Blood still oozed from a scrape over his cheekbone, but the sword cut in his arm had stopped bleeding. He held the arm close to his chest, the wrist clutched in his other hand. "I couldn't carry the man with this wound, but I knew you'd want to see for yourself."

Horbad stooped and brushed the dark gold hair back from the face of the Celae man. The wide eyes, a peculiar shade of golden brown, stared sightlessly up at him. No pulse throbbed in the marble-pale throat; no breath stirred in the strong chest. Horbad nodded thoughtfully. The man appeared to be the right age and, the Second assured him, had been served by a warrior-maid.

"You're sure of him?" he asked.

The Second nodded eagerly. "Oh yes, my lord," he said. "That's the one who styled himself Prince of Skai. The lieutenant was convinced of it." He wet his lips nervously with his tongue. "Please, Lord Horbad, I understand there's a reward . . ." His voice trailed off as Horbad stared coldly at him.

"What of the woman?"

The Second looked away. "Gone, my lord. Swept away to sea with the tide, most likely."

Horbad raised one eyebrow. "Dead?" he asked.

The Second drew himself up and straightened his shoulders. "I saw her fall," he said. "I thought the lieutenant had killed her."

Horbad nodded. "I see," he said. He looked down at the dead man by his feet again. "Then she'll bear him no posthumous children," he murmured. "Father will be most pleased to hear that."

"The line is ended, then?" the Second asked.

"So it would seem." Horbad turned and beckoned to two of the Somber Riders. "Gather him up," he said, gesturing to the Celae man's body. "Go gently with him. Don't damage him any more than he is already. We'll take him back to Clendonan with us as proof."

The Second reached out to touch Horbad's arm, then snatched back his hand as if he had been burned when Horbad shot an icy glance at him. "The reward, my lord?" he asked, half eagerly, half apprehensively. "I've delivered the renegade prince to you and your father. Surely the reward should be mine?"

"The reward?" Horbad repeated.

"Yes, my lord. The reward Faghen was to get? Should it not be mine? You can't deny the man is no more threat to you."

Horbad studied the Second thoughtfully for a moment or two. The color drained from the Second's face until he was as pale as the churning foam carried by the surf. But he stood his ground and didn't cringe away. Nor did he drop his gaze. His avid desire for the reward, for the commission, was as palpable as haze around his head. Finally, Horbad nodded.

"Consider yourself raised to lieutenant," he said. "I'll speak with the commander of the garrison when we return."

The newly made lieutenant inclined his head respectfully. "Thank you, my lord," he murmured.

Horbad turned away and began to walk back toward the cliff path. He beckoned one of his Somber Riders with a flick of his finger. "Kill him," he said dispassionately, without glancing back at the Second. "If he'd betray one commander, he'd betray the next."

Deep in the shadow of the cave mouth, Cynric put his hand to the hilt of his sword. But when he tried to draw it, pain like fire lanced up his arm, into his chest. He fell to his knees, arms wrapped around his chest, gasping for breath, tasting blood where he had bitten his lip to prevent himself from crying out with the agony. Tears of frustration stung the backs of his eyes.

So, even with the threads of Tyadda magic simmering in his veins, he could not raise a weapon against Horbad. The Tyadda adoption ceremony had not been enough to counteract and overcome his lifelong conditioning. He could not draw a weapon against the Lord Protector of Celi, nor against the Lord Protector's son. His Maedun blood carrying the *geas* was ingrained too deeply in his soul. Davigan's blood cried out in Cynric's soul for retribution, but Cynric found himself completely incapable of answering the demand.

He crouched, eyes closed, in the wet sand and rested his head against the rough rock of the cave wall. The slick, slippery fronds of seaweed felt cool and soothing against his temple. When he raised his hand to his face, he wasn't sure if his cheeks were wet with the flung salt-spume or tears.

Outside, the voices went on. Only two of them. Horbad and the man disguised as a Celae. Gradually, Cynric comprehended they had mistaken Davigan for the Prince of Skai. And they believed Iowen to be dead, too. Dead and swept out to sea. The realization of what it meant came to him in a shattering eruption of understanding.

If Hakkar and Horbad believed the Prince of Skai was dead, then Skerry was safe. They would send no army to scour the northern island for the prince or an enchanter arising from his line. Iowen would be safe in Skerry, as would the children she bore. They could grow up in safety until they were old enough and strong enough to claim the swords their father had died to secure for them.

If he could not kill Horbad for Iowen in revenge for Davigan's life, then he could at least bring her assurances that Davigan's children would not have to fear for their lives every waking moment. Mayhaps it would be some comfort for her, make up in some small way for his perfidy and inadequacy, his failure to save Davigan's life. If he could not ever offer her his love, he could pledge his service. And his life as forfeit for the safety of the children.

The imprint of the sword Davigan had dropped still marked the damp sand by Cynric's knees. He bent forward and placed the palm of his right hand on the indentation made by the hilt, as if he took the actual sword into his hand. Closing his eyes, he vowed by all the gods and goddesses of this island, promising Davigan that he would guard his sons as if they were his own children. If Iowen

would permit, he would be constantly at their sides, and
while he lived, for as long as he lived, no harm should come
to them that he could possibly prevent.

Gradually, the voices outside the cave faded as
Horbad's Somber Riders bore Davigan's body away.
Cynric remained still, waiting until he was sure they were
well away. When he finally emerged from the cave, the sun
lay low on the western horizon.

They had left his father's corpse on the shore to rot in
the sun or be swept into the sea. Carrion for carrion eaters.
He hardly paused to look down at him.

He turned north and made his way around the wide
bay. Seaweed made the going treacherously slippery.
Barnacles sharp as razors studded the rocks. By the time he
reached shelter where the forest spilled down to the shore,
the leather of his boots hung in shreds on his feet, and blood
flowed from dozens of wounds on his hands, arms, and
legs.

He knew where Kier was taking Iowen — where Iowen
must go. Even he had felt the power of those swords. But
they would not leave Skai. There was only one place where
they might be safe until Iowen's sons came to claim them.

The pale cone of Cloudbearer rose to the north, its
crown touched by the last rays of the sun. Blazing with brilliant golden fire, the mountain glowed like a beacon to
guide him to the Dance of Nemeara, which lay at its feet.

He caught up to them on the evening of the third day
on the edge of the coastal plain where the Dance of
Nemeara threw hard, black shadows across the rippling
carpet of grass. Iowen had dismounted from her horse and
stood quietly with the swords in her arms, watching the
Dance glow in the last rays of the setting sun. Cynric
crossed the dew-soaked grass and went to one knee before
her.

"My lady," he said.

She put out her hand, touched his head, but said nothing.

Cynric bent his head. "My lord Wykan's death released me from my vow to him, my lady," he whispered hoarsely. "I would pledge myself to your service. To guard you and your children until you and they have no more need of me."

Iowen raised him to his feet. For the space of nearly fifty heartbeats, she said nothing. His breath rasped at his throat, and he feared she would send him away.

Finally, she nodded. "I will accept your service," she murmured at last. "Your pain must be nearly as great as mine."

Cynric clasped her hand. "But between us, my lady, we will keep Davigan's sons safe until they can take up those swords."

"Aye, we will." She smiled. "Yes, Cynric. We will."

Epilogue

The stone Dance stood vast and silent on the green coastal plain.
Behind it, the bulk of Cloudbearer rose to the twilight sky
as if watching over it. The setting sun painted soft colors in
shades of rose and gold and blue and purple across the
megaliths. Circle within circle, the stones glowed softly in
the fading light.

Iowen stood between Kier and Cynric, watching the
Dance. Then, for a moment, she thought she saw something move within its shadowy depths. Her breath trembled in her chest, and pain wrapped tightly around her
heart. Heartfire in its plaited and gilded scabbard seemed
to quiver in her hands. She raised one hand slowly to push
the hair back from her eyes and frowned in concentration.
But nothing moved among the stones now. Mayhaps she
had seen only the grass rippling to a random breeze.

Cynric touched her arm gently. She turned stiffly to
look at him. Her own sorrow and grief reflected back at her
from deep within his eyes.

"I would accompany you inside, if you wish, my lady,"
he said quietly.

The magic of the Dance moved like the breeze across
her skin, raising the small hairs on her arms, the back of her
neck, along her spine. Cynric's eyes were wide and shadowed in the fey light, as if he, too, felt it as strongly as she.
Like her, he had no desire to enter the circle. As she
watched, he shivered visibly, then tried to hide it with a
smile. She smiled back gently.

"No, Cynric," she said. She turned to look at the Dance
again. "This task is mine alone, I think."

"I'm afraid for you," he said hoarsely. "If you go in there, I'm afraid you won't come out. I'm afraid you'll try to join Davigan in Annwn."

She closed her eyes to trap the tears behind her lids. She should have joined Davigan long ago, back at the cavern. No bheancoran should outlive her prince. The pain of the breaking of the bond tore at her heart, at her spirit. Too much to bear. Too much . . .

"I have to place the swords on the altar," she whispered.

"I can do that," Cynric said. "Or Kier can. Please, my lady. Let us serve you in this."

She looked down at the scabbard she held. Heartfire gleamed solid and firm in her hand. The nebulous shimmer of Soulshadow around it like an aura gave her the disconcerting and disorienting impression of double vision.

"Can you take both of them?" she asked, then smiled as a helpless expression filled his eyes. He could lift Heartfire, but not Soulshadow. The shadow sword vanished like smoke when anyone else took the scabbard. "You see, don't you? This is my task, Cynric. For Davigan and for the next king."

"Then remember the next king," Kier said. "You carry him, Iowen. Think of him. For his sake, if not your own, you must live."

She placed her hand on her belly. It was still flat and firm, but the small glow of the children there warmed the palm of her hand. The shadow of the Dance shivered in the grass as a breeze rippled the blades. She took a deep breath, then began walking.

Behind her, neither Cynric nor Kier said anything. They didn't understand. They thought she was reluctant to enter the Dance because she was afraid she might die there. But she wasn't afraid of dying. Death meant being reunited with Davigan. She was afraid because she didn't know how she would explain to the gods and goddesses of the Dance that she had failed to protect her king as a bheancoran should. She feared their recriminations.

But the swords had to be given into the protection of the Dance and its guardians. They could not leave Skai—not until they were in the hands born to wield them.

Only seed of kings may lift
Wyfydd's sword, take Myrddin's gift.

The hushing whisper of wings broke the stillness around the Dance as an owl swooped out of the glowing sky to brush across the grass. It lifted silently back into the air and vanished into the shadows cast by the looming megaliths. Dew-wet blades of grass clung to her boots as she walked, their perfume rising around her like smoke. A faint breath of wind touched her cheek and lifted the hair on her temple, cooling the fevered flush of her cheeks. She paused momentarily between the massive stones of the entry trilithon and took a deep breath, then stepped resolutely through and into the circle.

The sun was gone, and only pale streaks of color still lit the western sky. The polished surface of the altar stone shimmered faintly in muted tones of gold and turquoise, reflecting the twilight. She approached the altar slowly, but with firm, unwavering steps. Heartfire nestled into her arms like a child, wrapped in its plaited grass scabbard. In the fey light, she thought she could see Soulshadow clearly outlined beside it, Heartfire's dark twin.

She forced her steps to remain steady until she stood before the altar. Around her, the seven standing stones remained silent, barred with shadow. She hesitated, not knowing quite what to do next.

Something not quite audible broke the silence, some-

thing just under the threshold of hearing. A new shadow
spilled across the dew-wet grass. The tall figure of a man
stood framed by the gateway trilithon. Silent as a shadow,
he moved to stand between the capped menhirs of the second ring of standing stones. Iowen nearly stopped breathing as the man stepped between the stones and approached
the altar.

He wore a long robe, pale in the moonlight, girdled by
something that glinted like gold. His hair and beard, silver
as the moon itself, framed a face carved into austere planes
and hollows, the eyes shadowed by silver eyebrows. In his
hands, he carried something long and narrow, and the flash
and sparkle of stars blazed at one end.

Quietly, the man crossed the grass toward the altar, his
feet making no disturbance among the young, green blades.
He gave the impression of vast age and wisdom, but moved
with the lithe grace of a youth.

"You have the swords, my lady Iowen," he said, his
voice like the murmuring of wind in reeds.

"I—yes," Iowen said. "Who are you?"

He smiled. "You should know me," he said. "I have
known many of your line. Surely they have spoken of me."

"Myrrdin," she said, her mouth nearly too dry to form
the word. "The guardian."

"Yes. I am the guardian."

"I have Heartfire and Soulshadow." She held them out
to him. "I brought them to you for safekeeping."

"Then put them on the altar, child," he said. "They
belong there until their owners come to pick them up."

Iowen hesitated, then turned to the altar. She set
Heartfire carefully on the altar, making sure it lay precisely in the center. Soulshadow lay beside it, crisply outlined in the shadow cast by Heartfire's own glow.
Myrddin stepped forward and carefully placed the sword

he carried beside them. Runes spilled down the blade, sparking softly in the last of the twilight. On the pommel, a clear crystal, big as a plover's egg, gleamed gently.

"Do you know this sword, child?" he asked.

She looked at the sword, then at him. "Kingmaker," she whispered. "It's Kingmaker. Tiernyn's sword."

"The king's sword," he said. "And a king shall come to claim it soon. Its time will come again." He stretched out his hand and held it above the swords. His skin looked translucent as parchment.

Light flashed around the swords. Kingmaker vanished like a star fading at dawn. Brilliant flares of color leapt above the polished altar, wrapping around Heartfire and its shadow. The light stabbed into Iowen's eyes, and she looked away. When she could see again, all of the swords were gone.

"They're safe now," Myrddin said. "The swords used you cruelly, but you've done well, child."

She shook her head. "I have lost my king," she said. "I failed in my duty as his bheancoran."

He smiled and shook his head. Without a word, he raised his gaze and looked over her shoulder, at something behind her. She spun around so quickly, she nearly stumbled.

Davigan stood between two capped megaliths. "Failed in your duty?" he said, and laughed softly. "Oh, my very dearest, not at all."

She said his name and fell to her knees because her legs would no longer support her. He came to her, gave her his hand, raised her to her feet. The skin of his hand felt cool and strange, as if it were carved from warm wood.

"They let me come back to bid you farewell, beloved," he said. "And to tell you that you haven't failed at all. You guard all that's left of me now. My sons." He touched her cheek, and she shivered. "Our bond included them, you know."

"Davigan . . ."

"I've only a moment," he said. "Just this short time between twilight and dark."

"I can't bear to let you go . . ."

He raised her hand to his lips. "Don't you know I'll be waiting for you?" he said. "For as long as it takes, I'll wait. Nothing can separate us for long."

He stepped away from her. She put out her hand to him, but nothing stood before her but empty air. She dropped her hand, then pressed it to her belly. The spark of life there glowed warmly against her palm. She turned away from the altar and walked out of the Dance.

Just outside the entry trilithon, she looked back. The megaliths stood black and stark against the deep blue-black of the sky.

"Soon," she whispered.

Cynric came forward to meet her. He stretched out his hand, and she took it.

"Take me home," she said. "I'm ready to go home."